Impossible
The Original Trilogy

Books

Monster

Traitor

Avenger

Monster

Impossible #1

By Julia Sykes

© 2013

For my "vanilla" friends: Ashton, Eva, and Anna.
Thanks for understanding and never judging me. Love
y'all!

xxx

Chapter 1

My heart stopped as a strong hand clamped over my mouth, muffling my scream. Something cold and round was pressed against my cheek. I didn't have to see it to instinctively know what it was: a gun. To make up for its brief silence, my heart was suddenly pumping in double-time, my pulse racing in my veins as terror spiked through me.

"Are you a doctor?" A deep voice asked from the backseat of my car where the man had been hiding. His tone was rough, with a ragged edge of desperation.

His hand left my mouth so that I could answer. I considered screaming for help, but the gun that was pressed against my face stopped me. Instead, I swallowed hard against the lump in my throat.

"Y-yes," my voice was unusually high and shaky.

The muzzle of the gun shifted to my ribs, pressing hard into my flesh. "You're going to drive exactly where I say. If you don't, I won't hesitate to kill you. Understand, doc?"

My heart was in my throat now, cutting off my ability to speak. So I just nodded to communicate my understanding.

"Start the car and head for the City," the voice commanded. "We're going to Brooklyn."

My hands were trembling, so I gripped the steering wheel hard to ensure that I didn't swerve all over the road. I didn't dare betray the fact that there was something wrong; if I was stopped by the cops for reckless driving, god knows what this man would do to me before I could even yell for help.

I struggled to keep from hyperventilating, worried that even the tiniest movement would jar the gun against my ribs, sending a bullet searing through my lungs and up into my heart. My mind had been frozen in those first few minutes of shock, but it suddenly came whirring to life again as all of the gruesome possibilities of what might happen to me ran across it. Gathering up my courage, I forced the words out of my mouth.

"Where are we going? What do you want from me?" I struggled to keep my voice steady, desperate not to betray my terror to the man who held my life in his hands. It was obvious to me that he was unbalanced, and his evident desperation only made him that much more volatile.

It was a mistake to speak. The unyielding metal was only pressed harder into my ribs, making me wince as pain flared.

"I didn't say you could talk," the voice said sharply. "Just keep driving. Turn right here."

My mouth snapped closed, and I pursed my lips together to hold in my questions. I followed his directions, his voice the only sound breaking through the tense silence. Between the pain and my stark terror, my mind was threatening to succumb to hysteria. I ruthlessly held it at bay, focusing solely on following the man's clipped instructions. I reached for the cold void within me, that place where my heart had existed so many years ago. With long-practiced ease, I allowed cool logic to govern me rather than giving in to emotion. Emotions were volatile and sure to bring nothing but pain. They were useless and destructive, and I had never been more grateful of their absence within me than I was now. A clear head would be my only chance of getting out of this alive.

"Pull into the garage here," the man ordered after what seemed to be both the longest and shortest drive of my life. My stomach was in knots as I drove up the ramp into the dimly-lit parking garage. It was deserted; there was no hope for help here.

"Park here, and then get out of the car. Don't you dare make a sound," his voice was a threatening growl.

As soon as my hands left the steering wheel, they started shaking hard, making up for the forced stillness from their grip on the wheel. The pressure of the gun left my side, and I breathed a sigh of relief. But my reprieve from my fear didn't last long. I knew that I was still in easy range, and I didn't dare try anything stupid. Like running away as fast as I could, as my mind was screaming at me to do.

I shoved back my instinct to flee. Giving in to primal urges was a sure way to get myself killed.

I heard the car door slam, and then the muzzle of the gun was at my lower back.

"Walk." The man prodded me along with it, and I didn't hesitate to comply. I moved carefully, trying to walk at a slow, even pace, avoiding sudden movements that might make it look as though I was trying to run.

We arrived at a heavy door with a keypad set into the wall beside it. "Press nine-three-two-eight," he said in a clipped voice. His tone was strained again, and I couldn't help but wonder at it. Was he uneasy about what he was doing to me? His steady grip on the gun told me that that probably wasn't the case. He needed me for something. His desperation and determination told me that much. Once he had whatever it was that he wanted from me, I might be able to appeal to the humanitarian side of him that had been clouded by his intense need.

My mind flitted to what it might be that he needed from me. I fiercely hoped that it wasn't as horrific as what I was imagining.

I punched in the code, nearly pressing the wrong keys with my trembling fingers. Even though my logical side was in control, I wasn't impervious to the adrenaline that came along with extreme fear.

"You're going to have to have steadier hands than that, doc," my captor said cryptically. The door buzzed and there was a clicking sound as it unlocked. "Inside." He pressed the gun into my back for emphasis.

We walked down a short corridor to an elevator. With his free hand, the man reached around me and punched the call button. The doors pinged open, and I meekly walked into the small compartment that would take me god knew where. The walls of the elevator were mirrored, and I could see my captor for the first time.

He was young, maybe in his mid-twenties, with closely-cropped dark hair and a hard-edged jaw. His mouth was set in a grim line, but his brown eyes betrayed the same strain that I had detected in his voice. The man was tense, upset. And that scared me more than anything. A man on the edge could be more dangerous than a cold-blooded criminal.

I caught my own reflection as he punched the button for the ninth floor. My grey eyes were wide, the fear that was making my heart hammer in my chest evident in every strained line of my pale face. But other than that, I looked completely normal: light brown hair pulled back into a tight bun and my collared shirt and slacks perfectly straight and wrinkle-free. The contrast with my wild expression was jarring.

All too soon, the doors opened, and I was being ushered down another hallway. We stopped outside an apartment. The paint on the door was cracked from the pervasive damp that left the hallway smelling faintly of mildew. We clearly weren't in one of the nicer parts of town.

He fumbled with his keys, reaching around me to unlock the door. Once he had kicked it open, he gave me a particularly hard shove, and I stumbled across the threshold.

The door closed behind me with a sound of finality, and I couldn't help the fine tremor that rippled across my cool skin.

"Sean!" The man called out. There was no answer. "Sean!" Fear colored his tone this time. He pushed me forward, guiding me towards a bedroom. When I saw what was inside, I stopped in my tracks. But my captor wasn't having it, and he shoved me into the room.

There was a man lying on the bed. His face was pale, contrasting shockingly with his dark auburn hair. His eyes were closed, and, most alarming of all, there was a dark stain on the front of his shirt and a crimson pool soaked the white sheets beneath his left shoulder.

My instincts as a doctor kicked in, and I momentarily forgot my dire situation. I rushed toward the man who was lying prone on the bed, quickly taking inventory of the source of the bleeding. Strips of cloth had been tied around his upper arm. Only they had already soaked through, and they were wrapped far too tightly. That was a good way to lose a limb.

I rounded on the dark-haired man.

"What happened?" I demanded.

"He was shot," my captor answered simply.

I glared at him. "Then why isn't he at a hospital?"

The man glared back. "I can't take him to a hospital. You'll have to fix him."

"What?" I half-shrieked. "He needs medical attention. Urgent medical attention. What do you expect me to do? I'm a pediatrician, for god's sake!"

"Fuck!" He cursed, his brow furrowing as he ran a hand over his buzzed hair in agitation. Then his eyes narrowed, and he leveled the gun at me. "You went to med school, so you'll have to do. Besides, I don't have time to snatch another doc. Fix him."

I blanched as I was once again in the line of fire, but I plowed on. "I can't," I insisted. "You have to take him to a hospital, or he's going to die. He's lost too much blood."

The man's face twisted into a snarl, and he cocked the gun with an ominous click. "We're not going to a hospital. If you tell me you can't save him, I'll kill you now."

I swallowed hard. I knew that there wasn't anything that I could do. I was going to die. I looked at the bleeding man's pale face and felt a twinge of sadness. *He* was going to die.

"I'm sorry," I whispered. "I can't do anything for him. Not here. Not without any equipment."

My captor's expression was anguished. "What if you have this?" He asked desperately, reaching into his large jacket pocket. He pulled out my first aid kit that I kept stashed in my car.

My heart leapt. I had medical gloves in there, tools for sewing stitches, and gauze to wrap a wound. If I could save this man, even if there was a slim chance, I had to. This was about more than the gun that threatened me; this was about my deep-seated desire to preserve human life.

I held out my hand insistently. "Give it to me," I demanded. "How long ago was he shot?"

The man bristled at my domineering tone, but he was going to have to deal with it. His friend would likely bleed out without my help, and he knew it.

"About two hours ago. It didn't look that bad, but it won't stop fucking bleeding. He was conscious an hour ago."

I would have spared him a glare for being such a fucking idiot, but I was too focused on my task. My fear had taken a back seat to my concern for saving this man's life. Despite the circumstances, I wasn't about to watch him die. I couldn't live with myself if I allowed that. And my captor probably wouldn't allow me to live if I failed.

The man was lucky that I had more equipment stocked in that small box than would usually be found in a standard first aid kit. I sanitized my hands and pulled on my medical gloves. Even though I wanted to save the man, I wasn't keen to put myself at risk of communicable diseases. I pulled out my utility scissors so that I could cut away the makeshift bandaging.

Out of the corner of my eye, I noticed my captor stiffen. "If you hurt him, I'll shoot you where you stand," he threatened.

"Well, thank god he's unconscious, or this would hurt like a bitch," I snapped, irritated at the pointless interruption. "As it is, it'll hurt like hell when he wakes up."

I didn't spare my captor another glance, but instead focused on my patient. I hadn't been lying; I was a pediatrician.

But that didn't mean that I didn't have a good idea of what I needed to do. As soon as the bandages were removed, a fresh wave of blood seeped out of the open wound. My captor had been right: as bullet wounds went, it could have been much worse. There was a long furrow cut deep into his bicep. It wasn't a through-and-through, and, even better, the bullet wasn't lodged in his body.

But what seemed fairly superficial could quickly turn lethal. If his brachial artery had been hit, he would have bled out long before I had gotten here. As it was, if blood loss didn't kill him, an infection most likely would.

My fingers were steady as I cleaned the area with iodine. My residual terror had been completely overridden by reason and clear logic. Everything else fell away as I focused on my primary objectives: prevent infection, stop the bleeding. With practiced ease, I closed the torn skin with neat sutures. True, the cuts that I usually patched up weren't anything near this serious, but the principal was the same. When I was satisfied with my work, I re-wrapped the wound with proper bandages and gauze from my med kit. Finally, I grabbed the two extra pillows on the bed and placed them under his arm in order to elevate it.

Sighing, I sat back. He had lost a hell of a lot of blood before I had gotten to him, but he should make it through. His skin was still shockingly pale and cool to the touch, but his chest rose and fell in an even rhythm.

"He needs more blankets to prevent him from going into shock, and he'll need antibiotics to fight off an infection," I told my captor. I had almost forgotten that he was there, but now that I was no longer absorbed by my work, the reality of my situation came crashing back down on me. I suddenly felt utterly drained as the adrenaline that had been driving me seeped from my system. My voice was hollow when I addressed him again.

"I did what you wanted." I looked up at him. The slackened lines of his face betrayed relief, but there was still a hint of distress in the dark brown depths of his eyes. It gave me a spark of hope that he might not kill me after all. "Will you let me go now? I promise I won't tell anyone."

He frowned down at me, uncertain. His hand that was holding the gun twitched, as though he was tempted to go ahead and eliminate me. My sense of relief when he didn't was short-lived when he reached into his pocket and pulled out a syringe. I tried to jerk away as my panic spiked again, but he caught me easily, jamming the needle into my arm.

"I still need you in case something goes wrong," he explained dispassionately.

Warmth seeped into my veins as the sedative entered my system. The sensation might have been pleasant if I wasn't so terrified of losing consciousness. But the soporific fog rolled over me with insidious intent. Fear finally triumphed over logic, but the scream that resounded through my skull never left my lips. The world swirled around me, and the sweet drug pulled me mercilessly into the dark waters.

■■

My mind was strangely fuzzy as I stirred to wakefulness. I never had any difficulty awakening in the morning, but my eyelids were heavy with sleep. I was tempted to fall back under. My alarm clock wasn't beeping; I should have another few minutes to stay in bed.

But there was an insistent sense of *wrongness* that pricked at the corners of my mind, and the unease roused me. Sunlight seared my eyes when I forced them open, and I tried to shade them with my hand to give them a chance to adjust. Only, I was stopped short as my wrist jerked against something hard and unyielding. Dread churned to life in my gut, and I twisted my neck so that I could look back at my hand. My left wrist was handcuffed to a metal bedpost.

Everything came flooding back: the kidnapping, the dying man, the world spinning around me as blackness took me. I gasped as the terror that had claimed me in my last seconds of consciousness came roaring back to life. I jerked at my hand reflexively, desperate to free myself. My efforts were rewarded by nothing but bruising pain.

There was a low moan beside me, and I looked over to see that I was lying next to the man whose life I had saved the night before. Through my terror, I noticed that the white bandages were colored by crimson splotches.

Again, I harnessed the cold, clinical side of myself, embracing rationality rather than succumbing to panic. Attending to the injured man would grant me the focus that I needed to avoid my volatile emotions.

I rolled onto my side and propped myself on my elbow awkwardly, reaching out for him with my free hand. I needed to check on the wound, so I began to slowly unwrap the gauze from around his arm. He was completely still as I worked, likely still unconscious from the blood loss, but some color had returned to his cheeks.

I took a moment to more thoroughly examine the man whose life I had saved. Now that he no longer had the pallor of death upon him, his skin was lightly tanned. His jaw was strong and masculine, covered in rough stubble that gave him a rugged aura. His dark auburn hair glinted hints of gold in the morning light, which cast shadows beneath his angular cheekbones.

My fingertips inadvertently brushed against his bare skin as I unwound the bandages. Although the touch was light, his deep green eyes snapped open in response. He moved faster than I could comprehend, and I suddenly found myself on my back, his weight pressing me down into the mattress. He held my free hand above my head, pinning it there. His forearm was against my neck, applying pressure to my windpipe.

"Who are you?" He growled fiercely. "Where am I?"

My mind was two steps behind, still shocked by the sudden turn of events. My mouth opened and closed like a fish out of water as I struggled for an answer. But he wasn't pleased by my hesitation, and he pressed his arm down harder, nearly cutting off my breath entirely.

I jerked fruitlessly against his grip on my wrist. My cool calm had abandoned me entirely. As much as I might have told myself that logic would be the key to my survival in this situation, the primal part of my brain was much stronger than the rational one. My fear was a toxic thing, burning away my ability to form coherent thoughts.

"Who are you?" He asked again, half-shouting this time. His green eyes were ablaze with some inner fire, a furious inferno that threatened to swallow me up.

"Cl-Claudia," I gasped for breath. "Claudia Ellers."

"Sean! What the fuck?" My abductor's voice barely grazed the surface of my awareness; all of my senses were honed on the man who had me pinned. I felt so small beneath him. He could easily crush my windpipe, ending my life as effectively as the gun that had threatened me the night before.

A pair of hands suddenly closed around his shoulders, and his weight left me as he was jerked away. He cried out as the jarring movement pulled at his stitches. He fell back onto the bed, clutching a hand to his injury as he winced in pain. I greedily gasped in air as my racing heart beat painfully against my ribcage.

"What the hell is going on, Bradley?" The man – Sean - demanded through gritted teeth.

Bradley glared down at his friend angrily. "You were shot, asshole. What the fuck do you think you're doing moving around like that? You're going to hurt yourself."

Sean closed his eyes and groaned. "Shit," he mumbled under his breath. "I forgot that he shot me. That motherfucker." His brow furrowed, and he was suddenly glaring at Bradley. "I hope you gave the bastard what he deserved."

Bradley rolled his eyes. "I was a little busy saving your life. Sorry, you ungrateful douchebag." His words were harsh, but his relief was clear in his eyes.

Sean took a moment to get his bearings, taking in his surroundings. "How am I home? How am I not in a hospital?" He turned his hard gaze on me. "And who the fuck is she?"

Okay. That was it. I was tired of being assaulted, tired of being disrespected. Especially when I had saved the man's life. Anger was a far preferable emotion to fear; anger sharpened my mind, whereas fear was debilitating.

"Oh, I'm nobody," I snapped, my voice dripping with sarcastic venom. "Just the woman who brought you back from the brink of death. You're welcome, asshole." I tugged at the cuffs that tethered me to the bed, turning my glare on Bradley.

"And it wasn't enough that you kidnapped me at gunpoint and threatened my life? Now you have to go and chain me up like some animal?" I scoffed. "I should have just let him die."

Bradley's face tightened in fury, and his hands clenched into fists. "The only reason you're still alive is because he is. If you don't want that scenario to change, I suggest you shut the fuck up."

"What did you do, Bradley?" Sean demanded, his tone incredulous. "You *kidnapped* her? That goes way beyond anything… You know you can't come back from that, right? What are we supposed to do with her now?"

His friend looked at him levelly. "You know I couldn't take you to the hospital. Not without getting you arrested. I didn't have another choice. I wasn't going to let you die. The doc here patched you up. You'll be fine now."

Sean lifted his hand as though to run it through his hair in frustration, but he gave a small cry of pain and quickly dropped it back onto the bed beside him. "That hurts like a bitch," he hissed. He turned his eyes on me. They were no longer burning, but they were dark with pain. I felt a moment of sympathy for him, but then I reminded myself of how he had just assaulted me, and my heart hardened.

"Do you have anything for the pain?" He asked me.

"No," I said flatly, feeling a surge of vindictive pleasure. But I immediately felt guilty about it. It was my calling as a doctor to fix people, to alleviate their pain. I dropped my eyes, a bit ashamed of myself. "I'm sorry," I said softly.

"I'll get you some pain killers from Jerry," Bradley said, cutting a glance at me. "But first…" He trailed off, studying me intently as he wrestled with something internally. Finally, he blinked, his mind made up. "Is he going to be okay, doc?"

"Y-yes," I forced out, uncertain of what answer would keep me alive. If he no longer had a use for me, then he might decide to dispose of me. But if he believed I had failed him, then I was definitely dead. "So long as he gets some antibiotics and the bandages are changed regularly, he should be fine."

Bradley regarded me appraisingly. "I think I can handle that," he said finally, nodding. My heart dropped when he pulled his gun from his waistband.

I had answered wrong.

"Please," my voice hitched. "Don't do this. I won't tell anyone. I swear-"

"Bradley!" Sean's hard voice cut across me. "What the fuck do you think you're doing? You're going to add murder to kidnapping now? What are you thinking, man? This isn't you."

"I'm doing this for you, Sean," he told his friend, never taking his eyes off me. "There's no other way."

There was a terrifying click as he cocked the gun, and my heart stopped.

Chapter 2

"Stop, Bradley!" Sean shouted. With a grunt of effort, he struggled upright, his fists clenched threateningly. "I won't let you do this."

Bradley glared at his friend. "What other choice do we have? Let her go? She'll go running to the cops as soon as she leaves." His voice was strained, and his hand shook slightly. "I'm not going to let anything happen to you, Sean." With that fervent promise, his hand steadied, the uncertainty in his eyes giving way to hard determination.

The gun remained trained on my heart, which was now fluttering wildly in my chest. I hardly breathed for fear that any sudden movement would make the gun go off, ending my life in the space of a second. Despite Bradley's deranged determination to keep his friend safe no matter what it took, the way his fingers had trembled let me know that he had some reservations about killing me.

"I won't say anything," I forced out, my voice strangled. "I swear. Please..." That was all I could manage; traitorous fear had risen up in me, squeezing my throat like a boa constrictor until I couldn't draw breath.

"Put the gun away, Bradley," Sean's voice was hard and unyielding. "I'll never forgive you if you do this. She saved my life. We can't kill her."

I stared up at Bradley, my eyes wide and pleading, praying that he would listen to his friend. He glanced over at Sean.

"And what are we supposed to do with her?" He shouted, his frustration getting the best of him. "You know we can't let her leave."

Sean jerked a hand through his hair. "Fuck!" He barked out. "I don't know. Keep her here for now. Then we can figure out what to do."

Bradley stared at me for a moment, his mouth set in a grim line. Finally, he lowered the gun, tucking it back into his waistband. His eyes were enigmatic, and I wasn't sure if it was a sense of morality or fear of his friend's displeasure that drove the action.

Once the immediate threat of death was removed, I collapsed back onto the bed, all of my muscles turning to jelly. The clinician in me rationally told me that I was going into shock, but the rest of my brain didn't give a shit about what she said. I was trembling all over, gasping for breath. But my lungs wouldn't seem to expand, and my skin went cold as my vision blurred. I wrapped my free arm around myself as I shook, my mind completely consumed by the residual fear of what had almost happened to me.

"Hey, doc," came a gentle voice from beside me. There was a reassuring hand gripping my shoulder. It was hot, its warmth seeming to spread throughout my body, pushing back the ice in my veins.

"Claudia. Take a deep breath," the voice ordered.

I complied, raggedly sucking in air. Once; twice. The third time, my breathing came easier, the deep, regular rhythm soothing me. I blinked several times, my vision clearing. The first thing that came into focus was a pair of gorgeous green eyes, their depths filled with concern. Sean smiled down at me gently.

"That's better," he said softly.

I should have been repulsed by my captor's touch, but my mind was such a tangled mess that it couldn't process any more explosive emotions. I just laid there, staring up at him stupidly. He jerked when Bradley cleared his throat pointedly. His kind expression shifted suddenly to an unconcerned mask, and he backed away from me.

I was left reeling, trying desperately to gather the pieces of myself back together. I had to maintain my rationality. My situation was capricious enough as it was without me going into hysterics. And Bradley was so unstable that any sudden actions on my part could set him off. Although he was relieved that his friend was going to recover, he was still clearly on edge, wrestling with the fucked up situation that he had gotten himself into. It was obvious that he hadn't thought through the ramifications of abducting me, and although he was prepared to kill me, a part of him was still uncomfortable with the idea.

"There's just one problem with this plan," he said to Sean snappily. "People are going to be missing her. If they find out she was kidnapped, then they'll come looking for her. They might trace it back to us."

Sean's brow furrowed as he thought for a moment. "Then we call her family and her work to give some excuse," he said finally. "I'm not letting you kill her."

Bradley cocked his head at me, considering. "Well, that all depends on how cooperative she is." The way he kept referring to me in the third person, as though I wasn't even there, got my hackles up. It indicated that he was classifying me as less than human in his mind in order to rationalize what he was doing. I propped myself up on one elbow and glared up at him, silently demanding that he acknowledge me.

"Where's your cell phone?" His voice was harsh, but I didn't miss the way he shifted uncomfortably in response to my challenging stare.

I gritted my teeth, not wanting to answer. But defying him would be foolish. He was on edge, and my best shot at self-preservation was to make him believe that he was firmly in control. "In my purse. It's still in my car."

Some of the tension in his shoulders eased at my capitulation. "Alright, I'm going to get it. But if you try anything while I'm gone…" He left the threat open-ended, making it all the more frightening. I swallowed hard. Despite myself, disturbing thoughts of what he might do to me ran across my mind. Sean had convinced him not to kill me, but that didn't mean that he wouldn't do… other things to keep me in line.

He left the room, locking the door behind him. As though I could go anywhere when I was cuffed to the bed, I though derisively. And somewhat dejectedly. I could feel Sean's eyes on me, but I resolutely stared up at the ceiling. For the first time since the beginning of my ordeal, tears were pricking at the corners of my eyes. And I was determined not to betray my desperation to these men who had captured me. I had already shown enough weakness in front of them. I didn't have time to fall apart. Appeasing Bradley was only putting a Band-Aid on the situation, serving as a stopgap until I could devise an escape plan. And I would need all my wits about me to accomplish that.

Uh-huh, a voice in my head said snidely. *Good luck with that.*

"So," Sean said, breaking the tense silence. "This is awkward."

Awkward?! Was he honestly making a joke about my situation? Bradley was terrifying in his instability, but Sean posed a much more serious threat if he could be so nonchalant. Sure, he had convinced Bradley not to kill me, and he had been kind to me when I was having a panic attack. It occurred to me that perhaps it wasn't Bradley who I needed to fear when it came to physical threats other than death. If Sean wanted to keep me around, that couldn't be a good thing. I remembered how he had held me down, his hand around my wrist and his arm at my throat. If he could overpower me so easily in his weakened condition, he could do far worse once he had regained his health.

It was imperative that I not show any further weakness. I summoned up a glare to prove to him that I could be just as cool as he appeared to be.

"I think you're confusing the word 'awkward' with the term 'completely fucked up,'" I snapped. "'Awkward' is when you accidentally text the wrong person. 'Awkward' is when you trip over nothing and fall on your face. 'Completely fucked up' is when you kidnap a woman, threaten her with a gun, chain her to a bed, and tell her that life as she knows it is over. Can you see the difference there?"

His eyes darkened, and I hoped that I wasn't imagining the shame in his expression. "Okay, doc," he said lightly. "You're not up for chitchat. I get it."

Anger bubbled up within me, burning away my fear. How dare he make light of what he was doing to me? I opened my mouth to hurl venomous words at him, but I stopped abruptly.

Bradley's approaching footsteps registered just before the door unlocked. I tried to suppress a shudder as he entered again. Sean was injured, weakened. And he wanted to keep me alive. I decided to ignore the darker possibilities behind that motivation. Survival was the primary imperative for the moment. Avoiding abuse was secondary.

Bradley fished my cell out of my purse. "Alright," he said. "You only have one missed call: Work." He raised a quizzical eyebrow at me. "So, it seems I don't have to be too concerned about anyone missing you. I'm assuming that you don't have a husband or a boyfriend? No one who would panic when you didn't come home?"

My cheeks flamed. I hadn't been in a relationship since before I started med school. What might have otherwise been a mildly embarrassing fact about my life now proved to be a major problem. If I hadn't kept myself so isolated, maybe there would be someone in my life who would worry about why I had gone missing.

I just haven't had the time to date, I lied to myself. But I knew that the reason went deeper than that; I hadn't trusted anyone enough to open up to them in years. I had never felt ashamed of that fact before, but now that Bradley questioned me about it, I felt pathetic. And utterly alone.

I considered lying. I wanted to tell him that someone would notice my absence. But that simply wasn't true. Who would I tell him to call? One of my work colleagues? They were the only people that I could even remotely consider to be my friends, and it wasn't exactly like we went out for cocktails after work.

Bradley was right: no one would miss me. And I hated him for making me admit it. Finally, I shook my head, confirming his assumption.

He glanced down at my phone again. "Well, it seems there's no one to contact but your work." His gaze turned inward, considering. "What excuse should we give? Illness? No, you could get over that quickly." He shot a hard look at Sean, as though he was angry at his friend for forcing him to keep me around. "And since I don't know how long you'll be with us, that won't be feasible." He snapped his fingers as an idea came to him. "Your mother died. You have to go home and will be off work indefinitely."

I glared at him, hating him even more fiercely for cutting to the core of me, for bringing my deeply-buried pain to the surface. "You're about fourteen years too late for that," I hissed. "My parents died when I was thirteen."

Out of the corner of my eye, I saw Sean's hand twitch, as though he wanted to reach out to me. But I didn't want his pity, and I certainly didn't want him touching me, so I shot him a forbidding look. His expression hardened to that blank mask again, and his hand clenched into a fist, held resolutely at his side.

But Bradley was eyeing me skeptically. "How?" He demanded, clearly testing me.

"Car crash," I said tersely.

Bradley studied me for a moment, assessing my story. I kept my face blank, not giving away my lie lest he think that I was lying about them being dead. That much was true, at least.

"Fine, then," he finally continued. "Your foster mother died. I assume you were in the system?"

More painful memories. I just nodded jerkily.

"Okay," he said. "I'm your foster-brother, and I'm calling to let them know that my mother has died. You're coming to comfort me in this difficult time."

I tried to suppress my derisive snort. As though I would ever comfort that jackass, and I certainly wouldn't waste one second mourning my foster mom. I had been nothing but a meal ticket for her, and she turned a blind eye when Marcus…

"What's his name?" Bradley asked, intercepting my dark thoughts. "Your foster brother. You had one right? What's his name?" He insisted.

I glared up at him, hating him as I said the disgusting name through gritted teeth. "Marcus," I ground out. "Marcus Ames." I knew that I was making a mistake in betraying more of my weaknesses by showing my long-harbored ire, but I couldn't hold it in. Not when I was forced to think of *him*.

I never allowed myself to think about him or my foster mom. Nor did I allow myself to think about my parents. They were all in my past, and dwelling on them was pointlessly painful. Now Bradley was stirring those dark memories when I most needed to avoid them. My reality was precarious enough without opening up old wounds.

Bradley was already dialing my work number, taking no particular interest in my show of emotion. "Don't make a sound," he said, a warning in his tone.

A few moments passed in heavy silence as I seethed and the phone rang.

"Hi, this is Marcus Ames, Dr. Ellers' brother," Bradley said into the receiver. His brow furrowed, and he shot a glare at me, clearly wondering if I had tricked him in some way. "I'm her foster brother," he explained.

I knew why there was some confusion. I had never told anyone at work that I had a brother. Or any sort of family for that matter. I kept things pretty close to the vest. That way, no one would ever give me those pitying looks that I hated so much, the ones that had followed me for years after my parents' deaths. They had only stopped when I had created a new life for myself in med school, throwing myself into my work so that there was no room in my world for anyone else, for anyone's pity.

"She hasn't mentioned me?" Bradley glowered at me, his hand twitching towards his gun. Sean tensed, ready to make a move against his friend if he threatened me. Again I wondered at his motivations for keeping me alive. Was it his conscience or something more sinister that made my life valuable in his estimation?

Noticing Sean's aggression, Bradley frowned and stopped himself short. "Well, she asked me to call," he plowed on. "My mother has passed away, and Claudia has come home to help make funeral arrangements. She wanted me to let you know that she won't be able to come in, and she's not sure when she might be ready to return to work. She's pretty torn up about it."

Another pause. Bradley's frown deepened.

"Alight," he said, his voice tight. "I'll put her on."

He pushed the phone to my ear, putting his hand on his gun at the same time. "Back me up, bitch," he hissed at me.

"Claudia?" The receptionist said my name questioningly.

I wanted to scream, to tell her I needed help. But one glance at Bradley told me that I wouldn't live long enough to get the words out. Sean's demands to keep me alive didn't matter; all that mattered to Bradley was his own safety, and he would gladly sacrifice me for that. I swallowed hard.

"Ava," I said, my voice ragged with suppressed emotion. Too bad she would interpret it as grief rather than fear for my life. "I'm sorry I didn't call sooner. I just found out that Darla... That my foster mom died." I had to force myself to call her "mom." The woman didn't even deserve to be classed as human, much less a mother.

"Oh, sweetie, I'm so sorry to hear that," the sympathy in Ava's voice was genuine. And I hated her a little for it. "Take as much time as you need. I'll get your appointments shuffled around."

"Thanks," I forced out the word. I most certainly was not grateful that Ava was buying this hook, line, and sinker.

Bradley took the phone from me and ended the call before I had time to say anything else. He was staring down at me, his eyes burning.

"Why didn't you tell me that they didn't know about your foster family?" He demanded.

"You didn't ask," I replied as coolly as I could, trying not to shrink back in the wake of his furious stare.

He let out a low growl, his muscles tensing as he took a threatening step towards me.

"Bradley!" Sean's voice cut in sharply. He sat up fully, his arms cording as he flexed threateningly. "Leave it." Bradley's glare rounded on his friend, but Sean held it, his deep green eyes steady, implacable. But he was going very pale, and the red stain on his bandages was blooming.

"Shit," Bradley said, all menace leaving him.

Seeing that his friend was no longer threatening me, Sean allowed himself to fall back on the pillows, and he was unable to suppress a small groan as the soft impact jarred his injury. Some of my harsher suspicions of his motives melted. Surely a man who only wanted to keep me around for his own use wouldn't cause himself pain just to spare me from his friend's abuse?

"What's wrong?" Bradley demanded of me. "I thought you said he would be fine."

"Well, he *would* be if he didn't have to keep straining himself because of your hot head," I snapped, reaching out to check the bandages. I was stopped short by the cuffs. I rounded on Bradley with a curse. "Can't you take these off? I kind of need my hands to do this."

His eyes flicked from me to Sean, unsure.

"For fuck's sake, Bradley," Sean said. "What could she possibly do to hurt me?" His irritation sharpened his tone, but it was the barely-concealed pain in his voice that swayed his friend.

Bradley pulled a small key out of his pocket and unlocked the handcuffs. I gratefully rubbed my sore wrist and flexed my fingers, working the blood flow back into my hand. The little flash of pain sharpened the anger that I felt towards Sean.

I saved the life of a man who wants to keep me locked away indefinitely. And now I was going to continue treating him. It seemed my desire to preserve human life was overriding my own sense of self-preservation.

He did *save your life,* another voice said. I suppressed the urge to snort at it derisively. Yeah, he saved my life from his deranged friend who had only abducted me in the first place to save his sorry hide. Sean might not have been holding the gun on me, but it was just as much his fault that I was here. What kind of man couldn't go to the hospital after being shot? Sean was obviously some sort of criminal, as was his friend. Bradley had said that he could get painkillers and antibiotics. Not to mention the sedative that he had handy to use on me the night before. Kidnapping and murder might not be these men's usual MO, but they were far from innocent.

Despite my anger, my hands were gentle as I began to unwrap the gauze around Sean's arm, revealing the angry red slash. Some of the stitches had ripped open from his sudden movements. I gathered up the first-aid kit and retrieved the needle and suture thread in order to close the wound once again.

Bradley was looking on anxiously. "You look like shit, buddy," he said to Sean, who had gone very pale.

Sean's lips curved up in a small smile. "I've had a rough day," he said, his voice low and roughened by pain. "What's your excuse?" His laugh sounded forced.

Bradley didn't look remotely amused. "You're hurting him," he snarled at me.

"He hurt himself," I snapped. "It's not my fault that I'm having to replace his stitches while he's conscious." I glared up at him for emphasis, but something I saw in his muddy brown eyes softened my heart a little. There was fear there, terror. No matter what else Bradley was, he was a fiercely loyal friend, and the man lying on the bed before me clearly meant the world to him. In his mind, Sean's life was worth more than that of an innocent woman. As twisted as it was, I recognized love in his eyes, the kind of love that comes from a deep-seated bond between people who are such a part of each other that one wouldn't know how to live without the other. It was that look that made me drop my snarkiness.

"Look," I said, more gently this time. "A bullet tore a chunk out of his arm. That's going to hurt. And so are stitches. I'm doing everything that I can with what I have."

Bradley stared at me, Sean's ragged breathing the only sound cutting through the tense silence. Finally, he nodded jerkily.

I finished my work quickly, stitching him up more easily this time now that the wound wasn't so obscured by his blood. Once my task was complete, Bradley reached for me, gripping my wrist hard. I winced as his fingers dug into the ringed bruised that had been left around it by the harsh bite of the handcuffs.

And now he was pulling them out again.

"You don't have to -" I began.

"Shut up," he barked as he fastened one cuff around my wrist and the other around the bedpost. His eyes bored into mine, and I detected no trace of compassion in their depths. For a moment, I thought that I had gotten through to him when his concern for his friend left him emotionally vulnerable. But now it was obvious that he was firmly shutting any notion of my humanity out of his mind. I could be dealt with more easily if I wasn't really a person in his eyes. He would think of me simply as *other,* an outsider, a potential threat that could be eliminated if necessary. I knew that the only reason I had been allowed to live this long was for Sean's sake. He had told Bradley that he wasn't a killer, but I wasn't so sure that was true.

I bit back the angry curses that I wanted to hurl at him. Sean was unconscious again, and who knew what Bradley might do to me if he wasn't awake to come to my rescue?

My rescue? I bit back a mad laugh. No one here was going to save me. That was for sure. Sean might not be a murderer, but he was still my jailor.

Still, I was surprised to find that some of the tightness in my chest loosened when Bradley left the room, the lock sliding home behind him. Although my rational mind told me that both men were equally responsible for snatching my life away from me, a deeper part of me recognized a humanity in Sean that was all but absent in Bradley. I was disconcerted by how lighthearted he had remained in the face of what was transpiring, but I was beginning to suspect that that had less to do with callousness and more to do with glossing over his own discomfort with the situation.

I looked over at his sleeping form, watching intently as the color slowly worked its way back into him. As I watched his breathing return to a deep, normal rhythm, I took inventory of his powerful body. His arms were corded, all of his muscles perfectly defined as though they had been carefully carved by a master sculptor. A part of me recognized that he was attractive in his perfection, beautiful even. But his strength was a weapon that could be used against me, not something to be admired.

But as the minutes ticked slowly by, I found it impossible to stop staring at him. If I had to be trapped in a room with a strange man, I guessed Sean wasn't my worst option. Especially so long as he remained unconscious. Besides, focusing on his physical beauty kept my mind from wildly speculating about what might happen to me.

Would Bradley kill me the next time he came to check on Sean? How long would I be trapped here? Would even Sean turn on me once he was healed?

No, memorizing every line of Sean's handsome face, every facet of color in his dark auburn hair, was far less terrifying than contemplating my future.

Chapter 3

I had no idea how much time had passed, but I was thoroughly bored; there was only so long I could stare at Sean without feeling distinctly uncomfortable with my appreciation for his physique. So when I heard his low groan, I was almost thrilled at the sound. The long silence was broken, at least.

His eyes were clouded over, confused for a moment. He was clearly disoriented after being unconscious for so long. His head turned, and his gaze focused as it landed on me. A lopsided, lazy smile broke out on his face.

"Hi, gorgeous," he said, a cocky note in his voice. Then his brow furrowed. "No offense, sweetie, but I don't really remember last night." His smile widened as his eyes roved up and down my body, coming to rest on my cuffed hand. "And I must say that I'm very sorry for that. Looks like it was a good time."

I gasped, momentarily taken aback.

Gorgeous?

Some part of my brain noticed that there was a curious lilt to his deep voice that I couldn't quite identify. I liked the way it sounded as he stared at me appreciatively. No one had looked at me like that in years. I hadn't let them…

My moment of flattery quickly faded as I mentally slapped myself. Staring at Sean for so long obviously hadn't done wonders for my sanity. Anger rose up within me as the full horror of his implication occurred to me. His appreciative attention was most certainly *not* something that I should be excited about.

"Listen, jackass," I began, my voice hard. "I didn't *sleep* with you. I saved your life, in case you don't recall. That pain in your arm isn't a sex sprain. You were shot, idiot. Besides," I added with venom, "I don't really care to sleep with you after what you've done to me. You're holding me here against my will, remember?" I jerked at the cuff for emphasis.

Sean frowned as comprehension dawned in his eyes. Was that… shame in his expression? I sincerely hoped that it was.

"Oh. Yeah," he said simply.

"Yeah," I spat at him.

He sighed heavily and tried to stretch his cramped muscles, but he stopped quickly, wincing at the resultant pain. I wanted to feel a surge of vindictive pleasure, but it didn't come. Instead, the clinician in me softened towards him, unable to bear seeing a patient in pain.

"How are you feeling?" I asked gently.

"Fine," he said through gritted teeth.

I snorted derisively. "Uh-huh," I said, my voice dripping with sarcasm. "Because you look just fine. You were shot, you've been unconscious for hours, and you haven't had any pain killers." I pinned him with a hard look. "I'm a doctor. Don't think you can lie to me."

To my surprise, he let out a small chuckle and smiled at me roguishly. "I'm not going to get anything past you, am I, doc?" He asked, clearly amused, as though I was being cute.

I huffed indignantly, but inside I was momentarily struck dumb by his cocky smile. It was doing something funny to my insides.

"I have a name, you know," I snapped to cover the strange sensation. "It's Dr. Ellers."

The grin didn't disappear. "I thought you said your name was Claudia," he said.

"You can call me Dr. Ellers," I said more emphatically, trying to maintain some sense of dignity in this situation.

"I like Claudia," he insisted. "It's pretty. Unless you prefer 'doc'." His eyes were dancing.

"Fine," I snapped, throwing my hands up in exasperation. Only the cuff jerked at my wrist painfully as I did so, and I couldn't help the small yelp that escaped me as it dug into my already-bruised skin.

Sean's grin instantly melted into a frown. "I wouldn't do that if I were you," he stated the obvious.

"Oh, you wouldn't, would you?" I asked angrily. "Thanks for that sage advice."

There was that strange darkness in his eyes again, as though he was ashamed. "I'm sorry," he said quietly. His eyes locked on mine, sincerity flooding their deep green depths. "And thank you. For saving my life."

My own eyes widened, suddenly taken aback. Gratitude was the last thing I expected from him; I had just been convincing myself that he was a cocky asshole. Damn it, why did he have to keep making me soften towards him? It would be so much easier if he would just let me hate him.

"You're welcome," I said quietly. Then I shook myself, forcing my voice to harden. "But you do realize that as a doctor I was compelled to save your life by the Hippocratic Oath; don't think that I harbor any particular affection for you. In fact, it's just the opposite. I should have just let you die. Only, your douchebag friend didn't really give me an option."

Sean's frown grew deeper, the lines of his face twisting downward in anger. "Listen, *doc*," he placed emphasis on the disrespectful nickname, "I never want to hear you say a bad word about Bradley again. Understand?"

I fought the urge to move away from him, suddenly intimidated by the power that was rolling off of him like a palpable thing. But I summoned my resolve, lifting my chin and returning his glare silently. No way was I going to promise to be polite about the asshole who had kidnapped me.

Just then, I heard the lock click back, and the door banged open to reveal the bastard standing in the doorway.

"What the fuck is going on in here?" He demanded. "I heard raised voices." He shot a glare in my direction. "Are you upsetting him, doc?" He asked dangerously.

"It's Claudia," I snapped. "And he seems to be upsetting himself."

Bradley started to advance on me, seething with anger.

"Bradley!" Sean snapped. "It's fine, okay? The doc here was just being a bit snippy," he said disparagingly.

There was no trace of the kind, vulnerable man who had thanked me just moments before. Maybe it would be easier to hate him than I had thought.

Bradley stopped in his tracks, turning his glare on his friend. "I won't let the bitch upset you," he said roughly.

Sean laughed. "I think I can handle a few barbed comments from a hysterical woman," he said derisively.

Hysterical woman?! I opened my mouth, ready to hurl more "barbed comments" at him. But Bradley's hard growl stopped me.

"You had better keep your mouth shut if you know what's good for you," he warned.

While I felt comfortable enough exchanging angry words with Sean, Bradley was another matter. My insults seemed to roll off Sean like water. And while that irked me, it didn't scare me like Bradley's aggression did. So I pursed my lips against the furious words that I wanted to fling at him. Bradley held my glare for a moment, then shrugged, turning to Sean.

"I got some antibiotics and painkillers for you, buddy," he said, his voice suddenly gentle. He handed his friend a couple of pills and a glass of water.

"What kind of painkillers?" I demanded, the doctor in me wanting to make sure that the drugs wouldn't thin his blood.

"Oxycodone," Bradley snapped. "You have a problem with that?"

No, Oxycodone should be fine, but... "Where did you get that?" I asked, curious. Surely Bradley hadn't been able to get a prescription for it.

"None of your business," he said dismissively, not even glancing my way. My suspicions that Bradley obtained his drugs illegally were confirmed. As though I had needed any further proof that the men I was trapped with were criminals. The confirmation didn't bode well for my chances of getting out of this place alive.

Sean had already swallowed the pills, so I guess my consent didn't matter. But I supposed it didn't really matter where Bradley had gotten them, so long as they alleviated Sean's pain. Despite my anger at him for the situation that he had put me in, I would never feel pleasure at someone else's suffering.

"Thanks, man," Sean said gratefully.

Watching him drink the water made me suddenly, acutely aware of my own needs. No, I couldn't ask Bradley for that. It was far too embarrassing. But what was I going to do? Deny my needs indefinitely? As though that would work.

"Ummm…" I said quietly, blushing.

"What is it now?" Bradley asked shortly, his patience wearing thin.

"I need the bathroom." My cheeks burned with the admission.

Bradley blinked, as though this eventuality had never occurred to him. "Oh," he said. He cocked his head at me, considering. Sean cleared his throat pointedly, and I was surprised to find him staring Bradley down, an imperious eyebrow raised.

"Fine," Bradley snapped, realizing that he couldn't deny me. Pulling a key from his pocket, he unlocked the cuffs that had held me so cruelly. I couldn't suppress a small sigh of relief as the feeling of freedom washed over me.

But then Bradley patted at the bulge in his waistband where he stowed his gun. "Don't try anything stupid," he warned.

I scowled at him, wishing that the gun would go off and shoot off his dick. Okay, so maybe I wouldn't mind seeing *him* in pain.

It took effort to push myself up onto my feet, my cramped muscles protesting after being trapped in the same position for so long. Out of the corner of my eye, I could see that Sean's mouth was hardened into a grim line, but I didn't have time to contemplate what that meant; my needs were too insistent.

Bradley positioned himself behind me, giving me a push in the small of my back so that I stumbled forward. "This way," he instructed, his voice gruff.

I headed for the door, and I realized that I would be able to see the rest of the apartment for the first time since I had been captured. This could be my opportunity to search for escape routes.

We walked out into a small living room, which had a cramped kitchen connected to it. I caught a glimpse into a second bedroom, and I realized that Bradley must live here with Sean. There were three windows: one in the living room, one in the kitchen, and one in Bradley's bedroom. There was a fire escape outside of the living room window, but I made sure not to let my eyes linger lest Bradley realize what I was doing. He prodded me towards the door between the two bedrooms, and I opened it to enter the bathroom. I went to close the door behind me, but Bradley stopped me short with a strong arm against it.

"Uh-uh," he said. "The door stays open."

I glared at him. "No," I said staunchly. Bradley just gave me a hard, unyielding stare. I sighed in exasperation, gesturing to the one tiny window in the bathroom. "What am I going to do?" I demanded, somewhat disparagingly. "Crawl out of that?" I might be fairly skinny – a result of being a workaholic with no time to cook a proper meal – but there was no way I could wriggle through that small space. The realization made my stomach sink, but there wasn't anything I could do about it. And I was desperate for Bradley to leave me alone and let me get on with it.

"Fine," Bradley said. "But you have three minutes. Then I'm coming in."

I nodded curtly. It seemed that was the best I was going to get.

I heaved a sigh of relief as I shut the door sharply behind me, sliding the lock home. That might have been a dangerous choice, considering Bradley's short fuse, but I didn't care. I relished my moment of privacy, taking time to splash cold water on my face after I had finished my business. I looked at myself in the mirror. My usually meticulously styled hair was a mess, so I quickly pulled out the pins that held my bun in place. An idea coming to me, I pocketed them; they might come in use later.

My long dark hair fell around my face in waves, framing my high cheekbones and accentuating the paleness of my skin. My eyes looked tired, and there were dark circles beneath them. I could hardly believe that Sean had called me "gorgeous" when I was in such a state.

I was interrupted from my reverie by a pounding on the door. "Time's up," Bradley snapped.

Clenching my fists, I forced myself to unlock the door, to face the bastard again. I considered making a run for the front door as we walked through the apartment, but I knew that I wouldn't get two steps before Bradley ended my life. So I grudgingly re-entered the bedroom. Once I reached the bed, Bradley grabbed my wrist hard, yanking my hand back towards the metal rail where he would cuff me again.

I couldn't stifle a small cry as he pressed on the ringed bruise around my wrist, causing pain to shoot up my arm.

"Please," I said, ashamed at how desperate I sounded. "Don't do that. It hurts."

"I don't -" Bradley began coldly.

"Don't bother, Bradley," Sean cut him off. "There's no need to do that. You think I can't handle one clearly fragile woman?"

Fragile? I wanted to squawk indignantly. But Sean was arguing on my behalf, so I decided it was best not to say anything.

Bradley stood his ground for a moment, not letting go of my wrist. He only tightened his grip, and I couldn't hold in a sharp hiss as the pain increased.

"You're insulting me, buddy," Sean said, his tone light, almost joking. But there was a seriousness in his eyes that told his friend to back off.

Bradley was tense, but he released me. I rubbed my wrist tenderly, trying to alleviate some of the discomfort. I was again struck by the odd sensation of gratitude towards Sean. He had proven to be my savior several times.

But no. That was wrong. He might have stopped Bradley from killing me, but he still kept me captive here, refusing to release me. Just because he didn't want to see me in physical pain didn't mean that he was at all innocent. I again hardened the walls around my heart.

"I'll be right outside," Bradley said to me threateningly. "If you try anything stupid, I'll cuff you again."

I swallowed, nodding. I didn't want that to happen. So I settled for folding my arms across my chest in a small show of defiance, but otherwise I held my tongue. I maintained my hard stance as Bradley swung the door shut. I didn't allow myself to break eye contact with him until the lock clicked into place and he was hidden from view.

Coiled tight from my tense situation, I jumped slightly at the sound of Sean patting the bed beside me.

"Sit down, doc," he ordered lazily.

I glared at him. I had spent enough time on that bed beside the disturbingly handsome man already. "I'd rather not," I said drily. "And I thought I told you to call me Dr. Ellers."

His expression froze for a moment, as though taken aback by my gumption. Then his grin widened. "Sit down, Claudia," he re-phrased, addressing me slightly more respectfully. But it still wasn't a question; it wasn't enough for me. Fighting the temptation to be charmed by his heart-melting smile, I held my glare.

He blinked once, then chuckled, a deep, rumbling noise. "Suit yourself," he shrugged. But he stopped quickly, cut off by a wince as the movement jarred his injury.

"You should try to avoid sudden movements," I advised.

He grimaced at me, his dark eyes full of pain. "No shit, doc," he ground out through gritted teeth.

I frowned back at him, piercing him with a sharp glare.

After a moment, he rolled his eyes. "No shit, *Claudia*," he corrected. Then he yawned widely. "Your antagonism is wearing me out. That can't be good for my health," he accused, but there was a lightness in his tone that suggested that he still found me amusing.

"That's the oxycodone," I said, trying to suppress a small smile. Despite everything, his easy humor was catching; his levity in the face of intense pain seemed to infect me. "You should rest more," I said kindly.

"You're a lot bossier than most of the women I find handcuffed to my bed, you know," he said. He patted the bed beside him again. "Now sit down. Watching you stand there all tense is making me tired."

"You *should* be tired," I reiterated, but I found my knees folding as though of their own accord. Still, I was careful to position my body as far from Sean as possible, practically perching on the edge of the bed.

It didn't escape his notice, and his eyes were mocking as he spoke. "I won't bite you, you know." Then his grin turned wolfish. "Not unless you want me to, that is. I'd be quite happy -"

"Not in a million years," I said, cutting him off sharply. While his flirtatious insinuation didn't set off the internal alarm bells that it probably should have, I wasn't about to establish a precedent for letting sexual innuendos slide. The very thought was disgusting given my situation. "Now, before you go off into some drug-induced lucid fantasy, let's get something straight: You are not to touch me in any way. You may think that your eighth-grade flirting is cute, but it's pretty fucked up considering that the *only* reason I'm in your bedroom is that you won't allow me to leave. So whatever your perverted little mind is imagining, don't let your fantasy include me as a willing participant."

The predatory grin was gone from his face as though I had slapped it away. His expression darkened, the lines of his face drawing downwards. He suddenly couldn't seem to meet my eye. "Claudia, I...."

"You what, Sean?" I asked angrily, hurling his name out like a curse.

"I'm sorry," he said finally, looking up at me through his long, dark lashes. "I'm sorry I can't let you leave."

"But you can," I said, desperation coloring my tone. "I promise I won't tell -"

"You just can't, Claudia!" He said harshly, his eyes snapping up to burn into mine. They were ablaze with an anger so intense that I scooted away from him as far as I could without falling off the bed. The man before me was so different from the flirty, arrogant boy I had seen only moments earlier; this man gave off an aura of power that threatened to overwhelm me. It frightened me almost as much as Bradley's gun.

But I refused to show how intimidated I was. Summoning up all of my courage, I met his furious gaze. "You should get some rest," I said coldly.

His fierce expression melted into something almost contrite. "Claudia..." He trailed off, not finishing whatever it was that he was going to tell me. He looked frustrated and a little lost.

Most of my frostiness ebbed in the wake of that small show of vulnerability. Sean truly seemed to regret the fact that he was holding me prisoner. I broke from his gaze, suddenly uncomfortable with the emotional intensity of what was passing between us.

After a few minutes of silence, I peeked at him out of the corner of my eye and noticed that his eyes were closed, but his muscles were tense. A little furrow persisted between his brows, but after a while it eased, his breaths coming more evenly as his body relaxed. Despite the intensity of our altercation, the drugs had pulled him under as he had attempted to calm himself. And I was grateful for that.

What was wrong with me? I should feel nothing but hatred for this man who was holding me against me will; I certainly shouldn't be feeling… whatever that was that he had made me feel. As he lay there sleeping, Sean looked… well, not harmless, but certainly not evil. Unlike Bradley, he did seem to care if I was in pain, but he was also fiercely insistent that I not be allowed to leave.

What had I witnessed that made me so dangerous? Well, for one, I could report Bradley for kidnapping me. And I supposed that for all of my promises that I wouldn't tell anyone, I would probably turn on Bradley as soon as humanly possible. But what about Sean? Would I turn him over to the police? After he had saved me from Bradley?

Of course I should turn him in. Sean was a criminal. Potentially a dangerous one.

Something about the idea didn't sit right with me. It was easy to envision Bradley leading a life of crime; he had proven his indifference for my life time and again. But Sean seemed... well, I wouldn't say sweet, but at least humane. And passionately so. I thought of the intensity in his eyes when he had stared Bradley down, refusing to let him murder me.

And then there was the Sean who was a boyish flirt. I should have been disturbed by any sort of sexual insinuations on his part. But I hadn't felt more at ease since my abduction than I did when I was exchanging banter with him.

I shook myself quickly. Why was I reacting this way to my jailor? It was twisted and wrong; everything within me was telling me that I was only becoming attached to Sean because he had proven to be my protector from Bradley.

Besides, I thought darkly as my eyes roved over him again, *it doesn't hurt that he's easily the hottest man I've ever seen.*

To be honest, I hadn't been this close to any man since before med school. I was probably only so strongly affected by him because I had gone without sex for seven years. Of course lying on a bed for hours next to a beautiful man was going to mess with my head.

Seven years. God, it sounded so pathetic when I thought about it in concrete terms.

I just haven't had time for that, I assured myself, only making me sound even more pathetic.

I tore my eyes from him, forcing my gaze to fall somewhere – anywhere – else. Now that Sean was unconscious again and I was no longer restrained, I had the opportunity to explore my prison. The first thing I focused on was the window. Could I escape through it? Peering out of it, my heart sank as I realized that I was far too high up to leave that way, and there was no fire escape to climb down. It seemed that my only hope would be the living room window, and that would be guarded by Bradley.

Shit.

I sighed heavily. I guessed I would have to find something to occupy my time until I could devise a way to get around Bradley and get to that window.

I eyed the chest of drawers. I suddenly felt very unkempt, decidedly uncomfortable in the clothes that I had slept in. Maybe Sean had some sweats or at least a t-shirt I could borrow.

What, you want to wear his clothes now? I thought disparagingly at myself. But I'm a bit of a neat freak, and I was uncomfortable in my rumpled shirt and slacks. I opened the middle drawer and found a stack of t-shirts; I didn't dare open the top one in case I found his boxer shorts.

I shot a glance at Sean, not wanting him to see me changing, but he was clearly out. Still, I changed as fast as I could, covering myself quickly. The shirt nearly swallowed me whole, falling almost halfway down my thighs. Sean's musculature evidently filled out a shirt. I inhaled deeply, sampling his musky, masculine scent that clung to the clothing. It was intoxicating.

I shook myself and turned my mind to finding some sweatpants. I reached for the bottom drawer, where I would have kept my own slacks. Only when I went to pull it open, it seemed to be stuck. I jerked at the handle hard, but it didn't budge. It was then that I noticed the small keyhole set into the dark wood; the drawer was clearly locked. My curiosity was piqued.

I wonder what he keeps in there…

No. I didn't care. I jerked open another drawer, perhaps a bit harder than was strictly necessary. There: sweatpants. I pulled them on hastily and tightened the drawstring, shoving the locked drawer from my mind.

My eyes flitted to the bookshelf that sat flush with the wall beside the bed. In fact, it was the only piece of furniture in the room other than the bed and the chest of drawers. Now that I really noticed it, I was struck by how large it was. Even when I stood, the top shelf still sat higher than the top of my head, and I'm not a short woman.

On the top shelf, there were maybe a dozen books on carpentry. Some of them were how-to manuals, but it seemed that several of them were coffee table books, volumes that celebrated woodworking as an art form.

I found myself glancing over at Sean. *I wonder if he knows how to…*

I cut off that line of thinking, turning my attention back to the bookshelf. The rest of the shelves were filled by Fantasy novels. There were your classics like *The Lord of the Rings*, but I was surprised to find *Harry Potter* tucked in next to *The Wheel of Time* series.

Why, Sean, I thought with a small smile, *it seems you're a bit of a nerd.*

My eyes were drawn to him again, more appraising this time. He had struck me as a cocky playboy, had intimidated me as a dangerous criminal, but it seemed that there was another layer to this enigma of a man. I had thought that looking over the bookshelf would distract me from him, but it had only intrigued me more.

I absently ran my fingers along the spines, feeling the cracks in the bindings where Sean must have folded the books back on themselves while he read. I stopped at a particularly worn novel, squinting curiously at the title. The spine was so destroyed that the words were completely obscured. It seemed Sean had read this one over and over again. Giving in to my curiosity, I pulled it down from the shelf. *A Game of Thrones* by George R. R. Martin.

The title seemed vaguely familiar; I was fairly sure that this had been made into a TV series. But I didn't allow myself time for TV, so I couldn't be sure. In fact, I hadn't had time to read a book for pleasure in years. Every time I picked up a book these days, it was to study.

But it seemed that now I had nothing but free time, and there weren't any medical books on the shelf. So I carefully settled myself down on the bed, putting as much space between myself and Sean as I could manage, and I began to read.

A few hours later, my eyes were glued to the book, roving over the pages as quickly as I could consume the words.

"Don't," Sean groaned softly beside me.

I was immediately torn from the pseudo-Medieval world in which I had been immersed and slammed back into the present.

Sean was trembling, all of his muscles taut from some unseen strain.

"Stop," there was a pleading edge to his tone.

Shit. This could happen with oxycodone. Patients sometimes experienced vivid dreams, and right now it seemed like Sean was trapped in a nightmare.

I was immediately drawn to him, overwhelmed by the need to comfort him. I reached out for him, tentatively touching his hand. Little sparks seemed to dance over my skin at the contact. Despite the discomfiting sensation, I grasped his hand firmly, tracing my fingers over the rough callouses on his palm.

"Shhh," I said gently. "You're okay, Sean. It's okay."

I settled myself down beside him, stretching out on my side. I watched as the tension left him, the lines of his face relaxing as I comforted him. The rhythm of his breathing was hypnotic. The steadiness of it relaxed me, and I found myself growing sleepy. I had been through so much, and my body was giving in to exhaustion. Without even noticing what was happening, I drifted off to sleep beside him, still holding his hand in mine.

Chapter 4

I awoke feeling contented, my body pressed up against something warm. Someone nuzzled my hair affectionately, and I sighed happily.

My eyes snapped open in shock. My body seemed to have shaped itself around Sean's hard one, my head on his shoulder and my chest pressed up against his side. I was still holding his large hand with my small one. I jolted upright, scooting away from him quickly. That's when I saw it: the bulge in Sean's jeans. His erection was obvious, straining against the thick material. And it was undeniably large. I couldn't help but stare, wide-eyed.

"Didn't anyone ever tell you it's rude to stare?"

I jumped, startled out of my rapt state. My eyes snapped to Sean's, and my cheeks burned ret hot as I registered the amusement in his gaze. That cocky grin was back in place. The man knew how good he looked, his effect on women, and he was clearly conceited as hell.

"But I don't mind, you know," he continued on as though not affected by my embarrassment one iota. To the contrary, he seemed to be relishing it. A dark flame flickered in his eyes as they flicked down to my torso, a twisted, satisfied smile breaking out on his face as he saw that I was wearing his clothes. His eyes roved upward to my red cheeks and then back up to my eyes, capturing me in his smoky gaze.

Snap out of it! I ordered myself harshly. I quickly brought my walls back up, schooling my expression to a disdainful scowl. Awakening beside him had caught me off guard, and my reaction to the sight of his arousal had been even

more confounding. I should have been terrified, not…
entranced.

"Well I *do* mind," I snapped. "What have I told you
about your sordid little fantasies? They're totally fucked up." I
drew back from him further, resolutely not looking at his crotch.

He reached for me quickly, grabbing my wrist. "Claudia
-" He began, his tone contrite. But I wasn't having it.

"Don't touch me," I hissed, yanking my hand out of his
grip. Or I would have, if he hadn't been infinitely stronger than
me. As it was, it was like pulling against the unyielding metal
cuffs again. So I settled for spearing him with a pointed glare.

Finally, he released me, something akin to regret in his
eyes. He ran a hand through his hair in frustration, mussing it in
a way that impossibly made him look even more appealing, as
though he had just enjoyed a good fuck…

I needed to get out of here, to get away from this god-like
man who was quickly driving me to madness.

I stood abruptly and began pacing back and forth beside
the bed, suddenly feeling claustrophobic, as though the room was
far too small. Sean's aura seemed to fill the small space, his
masculine scent pervading the air, choking off my ability to
reason as it invaded my mind.

"Claudia?" He asked, concern lacing his tone. I didn't
answer. "Claudia," he said my name more insistently this time.
"What's wrong?"

I rounded on him, stopping my pacing abruptly. "What's
wrong?!" I shrieked at him. I was close to the edge of panic, so
I focused on my anger instead, fighting to keep myself grounded.
"I've been kidnapped by a horny jackass, that's what's wrong.

One who doesn't seem to have any plans to let me go. Ever. So what, am I supposed to just be fine with it when you make a pass at me when I can't get away? Am I supposed to be fine with it when you get wood and then leer at me like that?"

His expression had gone from guilty to furious in the space of a few seconds as he listened to my short tirade.

"Listen, doc," he snapped. "Your options are either Bradley insists on killing you, or you stay here indefinitely. I went with option B. Sorry if that gets your panties in a bunch, but the way I see it, I saved your life. And I'm going to get morning wood. I'm a red-blooded man; of course I'm going to get a hard-on if I wake up with a beautiful woman pressed against me." His brows drew together. "And I don't recall forcing you to *cuddle* with me."

I gasped, blanching at his words. How dare he act like this was *my* fault?

"*I'm* the one who saved *your* life, in case you don't recall," I said acidly. "All you did was take my life away from me. Sure, I'm still breathing, but what am I supposed to do? Stay locked in this room forever? What kind of life is that?"

"What do you want from me?" Sean half-growled, the ferocity of his expression making me take an involuntary step back. "I can't let you go, but I won't let you die. That's the best I can offer you."

"How magnanimous," I spat. "If you really weren't some kind of twisted monster, you would let me go." I couldn't help the pleading edge that bled into my tone as I said it.

"This isn't up for debate, doc," he shouted, incensed by my words. "You're not leaving."

Tears filled my eyes, and I quickly turned away from him to hide them. I never cried in front of anyone. Never.

I blinked hard, willing the stinging at the corners of my eyes to dissipate.

"Claudia?" His voice was suddenly gentle, soothing. And that curious lilt as he said my name so sweetly made something quiver inside me.

But I didn't answer; I knew that if I spoke the quaver in my voice would give me away.

"Shit," he cursed softly. "Claudia, I -"

The sound of the lock clicking back cut him off, and Bradley burst into the room. He advanced on me.

"I thought I warned you not to upset him," he said angrily. His strong hands were on my shoulders, shoving me harshly. My back hit the wall, my head cracking against it. The world spun as pain spiked through my skull, the shock of impact reverberating through my brain. Bradley's furious visage filled my vision, and I tried to shrink away from him. But the wall at my back prevented me from doing so, and I found myself trapped against it, pinned there by his strong hands on my shoulders and his menacing stare.

"Bradley!" Sean's voice was sharp, jabbing at the tension between us but not quite penetrating it.

When Bradley spoke, his voice was low and dangerous. "Apologize," he said, a threat in his tone.

I hesitated, still disoriented by the pain. But he shook me ruthlessly, doubling my discomfort as the sudden movement made the fast-growing lump at the back of my head throb.

"Apologize!" He said again, more harshly this time.

"I..." I gasped for air, struggling against the sudden tightness in my chest. "I'm sorry."

"Bradley, that's enough," this time it was Sean's voice that held a dangerous edge. I tore my gaze from my tormenter, and I was shocked to find the same furious expression that had been focused on me only moments before now turned against his best friend.

Although Bradley's back was to Sean, he still seemed to sense his ire. With a scowl, he released me and rounded on him. I had to focus to keep my footing.

Sean was still glaring at Bradley. "What is wrong with you? Stop fucking doing that. She's not hurting me. We just had a little disagreement, that's all. I can fight my own battles. And I won't allow you to abuse her. Not after she saved my life."

Bradley's mouth was hardened into a grim line, but after a moment he nodded jerkily. "Fine," he said curtly. "She's your responsibility then. You're the one who wants to keep her here, so you're going to have to keep her in line."

"I'm pretty sure I can handle her," Sean said coldly.

They stared at one another for a minute, neither backing down. Then the tense moment was broken suddenly when Sean's stomach growled loudly. Bradley's hard expression melted instantly. "You should eat something. I'll get you some food."

Sean's face was still twisted down in a frown. "Get something for Claudia too," he demanded.

Bradley's glare returned. "I thought I just said she was your responsibility."

"Well," Sean began, his tone tight with suppressed irritation, "I can't exactly take care of myself right now, so I'd appreciate it if you could help me out."

Bradley's scowl deepened, but he gave another short nod before turning on his heel and leaving the room. For the first time, he left the door open. I breathed a sigh of relief. Maybe he truly had given up on "being responsible" for me. I knew that I would face much better treatment at Sean's hands. And maybe this meant that I might be able to explore the apartment on my own, perhaps get to the fire escape?

I knew that I would have to bide my time, earn Sean's trust. And make sure that Bradley was out of the apartment.

I could hear the clatter of dishes in the kitchen, and my own stomach growled as I suddenly realized how hungry I was. I had been running on adrenaline, but now that I was slightly more relaxed with my situation I became acutely aware of my physical needs again. And right now I could really use some food and water.

So I waited for my jailor to bring me a meal, like I was in prison. I grimaced at the thought that I was now completely dependent on these two men to survive. How long would I be at their mercy? How long until I could escape?

A few minutes later, Bradley appeared in the doorway, carrying two sandwiches and two glasses of water on a tray. Sean sat up in bed, wincing at the movement but otherwise making no sound of discomfort.

"You should take some more pain killers after you eat," I told him.

He rolled his eyes at me. "Yes, doc," he said, but his voice was mocking rather than meekly compliant. His disrespectful tone and insistence on using the diminutive nickname when Bradley was around pissed me off to no end. But I bit my tongue.

Be nice. Build trust.

Still, I couldn't bring myself to thank Bradley as he handed me my sandwich. I noticed that Sean's looked much more appetizing than mine. His was piled high with ham, while mine had one slice of cheese between two cold slices of bread.

Prison food is probably better, I thought darkly. But it turned out that it tasted fairly good; I was that hungry. I gulped down the water, thirstier than I had ever been in my life.

We ate in silence, the tension between Sean and his friend still lingering in the air as Bradley leaned back against the wall, arms folded over his chest as he watched the two of us carefully. I pretended not to notice, schooling my face to nonchalance as I forced myself not to wolf down my food. Even so, I was finished in all of three minutes.

Once my hunger and thirst were sated, I again became aware of how uncomfortable I was physically; I hadn't had a shower since the day I had been taken.

"Ummm..." I began, worried about making another request of Bradley. So instead I turned my gaze on Sean as I spoke. "Can I take a shower?" I hated myself a little bit for asking permission. Like a child.

Sean's face softened as he met my eye. "Of course. Sorry, I should have thought of that." He looked me up and down, again taking in the fact that I wore his clothes. The corner of his mouth quirked upward, as though he couldn't help it. I felt myself blush under his scrutiny. "I guess you'll be needing new clothes, too," he said after a moment.

Sure, I wanted to say snidely. *I would love an orange jumpsuit. Or maybe some old-school black and white stripes. Orange isn't really my color.*

But I held it back. I really did want some fresh clothes, and the way that Sean looked at me while I was wearing his made me distinctly uncomfortable.

"Yeah," I replied instead, "that would be nice." But it didn't feel nice. My stomach twisted as I realized that getting a new wardrobe meant that I was definitely staying here for a while. I felt like Belle in *Beauty and the Beast.* I wouldn't be surprised if the chest of drawers turned anthropomorphic, bursting into song as it proffered me eighteenth-century French dresses, telling me, "You'll look ravishing in this one!"

I couldn't suppress a small sigh, although I knew I should try to look grateful in order to ingratiate myself with Sean, my own personal Beast. Only he was far, far sexier. I frowned at myself, disconcerted by my wayward thought.

Sean was studying me quizzically, clearly trying to read my thoughts through my expression. I shot him a small, sweet smile. His brow only furrowed deeper, as though he could tell that it was a deception. But I held the expression firmly in place, and after a moment he gave a little shrug, turning his attention back to Bradley.

"You think you could do me another favor, buddy?" Sean asked. Bradley glowered, knowing what was coming.

"I am *not* going shopping for her," he said staunchly.

Something in Sean's eyes darkened slightly, but his voice was light and joking when he spoke. "I know that your sense of style is equivalent to a blind old schoolteacher's who shops at the Family Dollar, but it's not like I'm asking you to go on a reality show to be America's Next Top Stylist."

Bradley didn't seem to find his words remotely funny. Sean rolled his eyes. "I'll pay for it. And I'll owe you one."

There was a moment's pause, and then an evil smile spread over Bradley's face as a thought came to him. "If I do this, you're coming to Jolly Lolly's with me as soon as you get better."

Sean groaned. "Aw, man, you know I hate that place. The only thing more disease-ridden than the girls in there is the carpeting. And the only thing more desperate is the décor's serious need of an overhaul. I feel like I need a shower just thinking about it." He gave a dramatic shudder.

Bradley was still grinning. "I know you hate it. So that's why it's part of the deal. You torture me, I get to torture you."

Sean looked at him levelly. "Going to pick up a few women's clothes is not torture," he said flatly.

"No," Bradley agreed easily, "But it's my own personal version of hell."

"I would say that Jolly Lolly's is hell, but even the Devil wouldn't dare venture in there." Sean looked as though he had a bad taste in his mouth, but a slight curling of his lips and his dancing eyes gave away the fact that he was enjoying bantering with his friend. Seeing them like this, I could understand why Sean cared about Bradley. Up until now, I had only seen the man as my captor and would-be murderer, but he seemed almost human as he joked with his friend.

"Fine," Sean assented with a long-suffering look. "I'll go once. One night only. You got that?"

"Well," Bradley said lightly, "that all depends on how many more favors you ask me to do."

"I'll do everything I can to avoid it," Sean promised. Then he flicked his fingers at Bradley, dismissing him imperiously. "Now run along, errand boy, the lady needs something to wear."

Bradley gave a derisive snort, but he turned with a little wave. "I'll be back as soon as humanly possible," he said over his shoulder before shutting the bedroom door behind him.

"There's no need to rush," Sean replied loudly.

"Oh, believe me, there is," he called back as he slid the lock home. "I'm getting this over with as quickly as possible."

With that, he was gone. I had thought that the tightness I held in my chest would disappear with him, but if anything my lungs only contracted further now that I was utterly alone with Sean. Awkward silence stretched between us as I wracked my brain for something to say, anything to ease the odd tension that was building between us. Unlike the furious, taut tension that had filled the room as Sean and Bradley faced off, this one had a different quality to it, as though the air around us was electrically charged, little sparks of it pinging across my skin.

"Soooo," Sean drew out the word pointedly, only drawing further attention to whatever it was that had sprung up between us. My eyes snapped to his. There was a mocking laughter in their green depths, as though he knew something that I didn't. "It's going to be a long-ass day if we sit here in silence. Care to try having a civil conversation? You know, one where you don't snap at me every second sentence. It's a cute habit, but it does make talking a bit difficult." He gave a dramatic sigh. "And I honestly don't know if I could handle your onslaught in my fragile condition. You might just be the first woman to break me." A cocky, lopsided grin that said I would do nothing of the sort spread across his face.

A cute *habit?!* The man was infuriating, and I had half a mind to snap at him again. But looking into his dancing eyes, I decided not to rise to his bait. *If only I* could *break him,* I thought resentfully. But I knew full well by now that Sean wasn't a man to even bend, much less break. He had demonstrated that through his harsh refusal to release me. And through his imperviousness to my barbed comments. It was my turn to sigh, resignedly.

"Fine," I said shortly. "The weather really is lovely today. Not that I can really tell while cooped up in here, but the view through the window is nice."

"Hey," Sean said easily, likewise refusing to rise to my bait, "beats solitary confinement. You get a room with a view and an excellent conversationalist as a cell mate. What more could you ask for?"

I rolled my eyes at him. "That has yet to be determined. So far all I see is a cocky, horny asshole. I wouldn't exactly call our verbal volleys 'great conversation.'"

Sean gave a low, rumbling chuckle. "You're just full of fire, aren't you? Well, I don't mind. Keeps things interesting." His expression suddenly turned deadly serious. "Enough about the weather. I have a very important question for you. Consider carefully, as your response will determine whether you're cool or not. Claudia," he said my name solemnly. "What is your favorite TV show?"

I flushed. Great. Seemed like I was about to be deemed "uncool." And that idea bothered me more than it should.

"Ummm… I don't really watch TV," I admitted after a moment.

Sean's eyes went wide, astounded. "Okay," he said after a moment. "How about your favorite book?"

My cheeks only flamed hotter. "I don't really read for pleasure either."

He was looking at me as though I were an alien.

I made an exasperated noise, feeling defensive. "Maybe *Grey's Anatomy,* then."

He looked even more thunderstruck. "That's not exactly a 'fun' book," he said. "What are you, a robot?"

"I'm a doctor," I snapped. "I don't exactly have time for things like TV and books that don't pertain to my work. Funnily enough, I value being good at what I do over allowing insipid dramas to take up space in my brain."

His expression shifted, considering me. "Definitely not a robot," he nodded after a moment. "You're far too easy to get a rise out of for that. But not entirely human either. Do you have any life outside of your job?"

Okay, that hit a nerve. Some part of me knew that he was joking, that he didn't mean anything by it, but it was too close to the truth. It was a truth that had been made painfully clear to me since my abduction: no one cared that I was missing.

"I was right," I said with venom. "Turns out you are a shit conversationalist." I folded my arms across my chest and turned my back on him, unwilling to let him see the hurt in my eyes.

"Claudia," he said my name gently. "Look, I'm sorry. I didn't mean -"

"You never do seem to say what you mean," I snapped. "We're done talking."

I knew that this was a dangerous move; it went against my plan to ingratiate myself with Sean. But I would just have to behave myself to earn his trust. Being compliant didn't mean that I had to pretend to be his friend.

I seethed in silence, the time passing interminably slowly as that strangely charged tension grew between us again. But this time there was an uncomfortable edge to it, like the unpleasant tang of sulfur burning. Whatever there had been between us earlier was tainted now. And it was almost easier this way. It was certainly far less disconcerting.

As much as I didn't ever want to see Bradley's face again, it was almost a relief when he unlocked the bedroom door.

"Here," he said, not even looking at me as he tossed a bag of clothes in my general direction. I peeked inside: some dresses from a charity shop and a pack of underwear that looked like they actually had come from the dollar store. I wasn't sure if he was just being an ass or if he really did have a "sense of style equivalent to a blind old schoolteacher's who shops at the Family Dollar."

What got my hackles up more than anything was the complete absence of slacks or jeans. I never wore dresses; they feminized me too much, would make people take me less seriously at work. But I wasn't at work, might never go again. Was I doomed to a future of being cast in the role of "fragile woman"? Okay, I might not be the strongest person physically, but I had worked hard to build an image as a tough-minded, competent modern woman. Even so, I pursed my lips, worried that Bradley would take the clothes away if I complained. But I wasn't about to say "thank you." So I settled for a glare.

"Can I have that shower now?" I asked Bradley coldly.

My only response was a grunt and a jerk of his head. I took it as a yes. Gathering up the bag, I marched past him to the bathroom, refusing to let him prod me along now that I knew the way. I closed the door firmly behind me, although he still stationed himself outside. What did he think I was going to do, escape by melting down through the drain like Alex Mack?

Okay, so maybe I had watched some TV when I was younger. Still, I got the feeling that my sadly outdated pop-culture references would only make Sean mock me more.

I shook myself, angrily shoving his hurtful words from my mind. *I am* not *letting him get to me,* I thought determinedly.

I let out a little relieved sigh as I peeled off my dirty clothes and started the water running. My nose wrinkled as I took in the state of the shower, which looked like it could use a good bleaching. This was clearly a "boy apartment." The neat freak in me felt the urge to clean it, but damn it if I was going to play housekeeper for them. I was their captive, not their mother.

I stepped tentatively into the tub, but I soon forgot my discomfort with the men's dubious cleaning habits as the warm spray hit my body. I reveled in it, letting the heat of it bleed into my tense muscles until they fully relaxed for the first time in days.

Reaching for the shampoo, I found myself frowning again. It was a generic supermarket-brand man-product that had a salty tang to it. No more Herbal Essences for me, it seemed.

Unless I ask like a good girl, I thought, my mouth twisting down in distaste.

Nope, I wasn't going to ask for anything else that made my situation seem more permanent.

So I rubbed some equally man-scented shower gel between my hands and began furiously scrubbing at every inch of my skin, as though I could wash away the memories of what had happened to me. But there was no point in trying to forget; it wouldn't change my situation. I could only move forward, bide my time, and formulate a plan to get to that fire escape.

There was a pounding at the door, jerking me out of my dark thoughts.

"Time's up," Bradley called harshly. "I'm not going to let you run up the water bill, princess."

Princess?! God, how could the man possibly make me hate him any more than I already did?

Reluctantly, I sluiced off the last of the soap and shut off the water. The towel that Bradley had left out for me was thin and ratty. Of course. Still, I wasn't about to give him the satisfaction of complaining about it. I wasn't going to let him know that he was getting to me.

There wasn't a hair dryer in sight. No hope of taming my wavy hair to its usual orderly appearance, then. Whatever. Who was I trying to impress? And no makeup either. But that didn't really bother me; I never wasted time on it anyway.

Grimacing, I blindly pulled one of the dresses out of the bag of clothes and jerked it down over my head. I gazed at myself in the mirror, shocked to find that I looked so much like myself and yet unlike myself. There were my same grey eyes, the same little dimple in my cheek that I secretly liked. But my alabaster skin seemed impossibly paler than usual, and my usually carefully-styled hair fell around my face in a damp, untamed mass of dark waves.

I wanted to linger in the bathroom, to extend my moment of privacy. But looking at myself was making me feel slightly queasy, so I elected to get away from my reflection. When I exited the bathroom, I walked meekly back to the bedroom that was my prison cell without Bradley directing me.

Bide your time. Be compliant. Build trust. Repeating my new mantra in my head made the idea of behaving myself easier to swallow.

Sean's eyes were immediately drawn to me, roving over my body in a way that I told myself I did *not* appreciate. I didn't. But my slight blush told me otherwise. Had seven years of celibacy really made me so desperate that I would react to a man who I should hate?

His eyes met mine as he shot me a slow, lazy smile, and something strange stirred in my belly.

Yes, apparently it had. Damn it, why hadn't I made time for even a casual fuck in that time? Because I didn't do casual, that's why.

No, it's because you don't do intimacy, a nasty, truthful voice said in the back of my mind.

Shut up! I snapped at it, funneling my anger at myself into a scowl at Sean.

He seemed unaffected by my show of ire, his grin only widening as though he found me *cute* again. I gritted my teeth and forced back the angry words that threatened to bubble forth.

Be civil, I ordered myself.

"It's a shame I missed shower time," he said, still captivating me with that cocky look. Unbidden and unwanted images of Sean's wet body against mine flitted through my mind, his hard muscles sliding against my flesh as we stood entwined, naked under the hot spray…

What the fuck, Claudia? How was I going to survive being with this man? What power did he hold over me to make me react to him in this way? I mentally shook myself.

"We really should clean that wound," I said clinically, trying to win some authority back in this situation.

"Ah," he said, almost leering now. "So it seems shower time is back on the table, after all."

I folded my arms across my chest. "Not in a million years," I said coldly. I turned to Bradley, who was still hovering in the doorway. "I need a soft, wet cloth and some mild soap," I said imperiously, taking control.

But Sean immediately took me back down a few pegs. "Why, Nurse Claudia, are you going to give me a sponge bath?"

"It's Doctor Ellers," I snapped. "And this is purely a clinical procedure, not some kinky fantasy you're cooking up based on a sordid porno. Do you want to die from an infection? Because believe me, there is nothing sexy about that."

He held up his hands, placating. "Alright, alright," he said, but his eyes were still dancing with mirth. "Sexy is kind of my thing, so I wouldn't want to go ruining it."

I glowered at him, but it had no effect. After a moment, I threw up my hands in exasperation, turning away from his disconcertingly perfect face and reaching for my first aid kit. I wiped my hands down with antiseptic and then pulled on a pair of medical gloves. Taking a deep breath, I approached Sean.

I pierced him with a sharp look. "If I hear one more disgusting word out of you, I'll stop. Then it'll be up to Nurse Bradley to take care of you."

Sean gave a dramatic shudder. "No, thank you." Still, he couldn't seem to help but smirk at me. "I promise I'll be good."

While Bradley went to fetch what I had asked for, I began to unwrap the gauze covering Sean's arm. I could feel his eyes on me as I worked, but I resolutely kept my focus on what I was doing. Now that I was so close to him again, I found myself being caught up in that alluring aura that pulsated around him. I tried to shove it from me as though I could mentally force it away, but it kissed at my skin, little tendrils twining around my arms as though trying to bind me to him.

It became even more impossible to ignore once Bradley silently handed me the soapy cloth. When the wound was revealed, I gently began running it over Sean's flesh, wiping away the dried blood that had caked on his skin. But as I did so, my fingers brushed against him, and the electricity that seemed to crackle around us spiked up my arm even at the light touch, leaving my skin tingling. I heard Sean hiss in a breath, and I wasn't sure if it was from the pain of the wound or if he felt the same thing I did.

Unable to help myself, I glanced up into his eyes. That dark flame flickered within them, burning deepest green. I had to suppress a shudder at the intensity of it, and I forced myself to sever the connection between us, turning my attention back to what I was supposed to be doing.

True to his word, he allowed me to work in silence, and I redoubled my pace, anxious to get away from him. Still, I worked carefully, unwilling to cause him pain as I carried out my task. I had to suppress a small sigh of relief when I finished, forcing myself not to draw away from him too quickly.

"Ummm…." Sean began, uncharacteristically hesitant. I looked up to find a curious expression on his face that I couldn't decipher. "Would it be alright if I took a shower?"

I blinked, taken aback by this sudden shift in attitude. Was he really asking my permission? "Sure," I said after a moment. "That should be fine. Just be careful not to touch the wound. Can you stand on your own?"

He rolled his eyes at me, the cocky man returning. "I'll be fine, doc." He pushed himself up on one elbow, swinging his legs over the edge of the bed. But he winced as the movement jarred his injury, and Bradley was instantly at his side. Placing an arm around Sean, he helped him onto his feet.

"I can walk on my own," Sean said defiantly.

Bradley eyed him skeptically. "Are you sure? At least let me help you -"

"Uh-uh," Sean said staunchly, cutting him off. "You and I are *not* having shower time together. Not to break your heart or anything, but I'm just not that into you."

Bradley scoffed at him but released him reluctantly. Sean swayed for a moment, but he quickly found his footing. He moved very carefully as he walked slowly towards the bathroom, Bradley following anxiously in his wake. Still, Bradley wasn't too distracted to lock the door behind him, confining me in my cell.

So it seemed I wasn't trusted yet. I pursed my lips and repeated my mantra.

Bide your time. Be compliant. Build trust.

Chapter 5

I awoke the next morning and cursed silently at myself. I was pressed up against Sean again, my hand gripping his forearm. My swift movement away from him caused the bed to shift, and his eyes fluttered open. He gave me that slow, lopsided smile that did funny things to my insides. I dropped my gaze, trying to shake off its effect. But that was a mistake. My eyes instantly fell on the huge bulge in his sweatpants. The size of it was even more apparent now that it wasn't constrained by his jeans.

"You're staring again," he said pointedly as he noticed my shameful behavior.

I jerked my eyes away as my cheeks burned. I elected not to say anything. I knew that if I did open my mouth, I would hurl venomous words at him. And that would definitely not be a point in my favor in the whole building trust thing.

But other than that one comment, he didn't pressure me to talk to him, instead allowing me to read in peace for the day. I was grateful for that. Really I was. Not talking meant that he couldn't hurt me again with his careless words. And he couldn't mess with my thought processes with his heated looks.

But not talking also meant that time passed very slowly. So I immersed myself in *A Game of Thrones,* devouring the first book in the space of two days.

We worked out a little rhythm to our days: Bradley would bring us our meals, he would escort me to the bathroom when I needed it, and I would relish the moments of privacy that I stole when I was allowed to take a shower. But there was a decidedly disconcerting part to every day. Every morning, I would find myself curled up against Sean, as though my sleeping self couldn't help but succumb to his hold over me. And then the first thing I would see would be the bulge in his pants, followed by that knowing smile on his face that made something quiver inside me despite my best efforts.

I chose to ignore the feeling, unwilling to dwell on what it meant. Instead, I threw myself into Sean's books. I hadn't been lying to him; I hadn't read for pleasure in years. I couldn't deny that it was kind of nice to not have to think of anything, to just lose myself in a good book. I had forgotten what a release the escapism could be

Three more days passed, and I was doing a good job of sticking to my plan: be civil, but don't be too friendly with Sean. Being perpetually alone with him in a confined space was hard enough. If I pretended to be charmed by his infuriatingly cocky demeanor, I knew that I would only be inviting more lewd innuendos and distinctly unsettling smoldering looks. Even with minimal talking, I still felt that strange connection between us pulsing in the air as we sprawled out on his bed for most of the day, a silent companionship growing between us.

I might not have been very experienced sexually, but I wasn't an idiot. I knew that the connection I felt to him was lust. And it was flagrantly apparent that the feeling was mutual. It didn't help that Sean was nothing but kind to me, and he was careful not to encroach on my personal space. The fact that he was behaving honorably when it would have been so easy for him to sate himself only endeared me to him further. Of course, I still hated him for holding me captive. I did. But that was difficult to remember sometimes when he acted sweet and looked so goddamn sexy.

Driven by my determination to ignore my body's traitorous reactions to Sean, I devoured the epic sequel to *A*

Game of Thrones before throwing myself into the third book, *A Storm of Swords*. The fictional world held between those pages was my only means of escape from Sean, and I cleaved to it desperately. But allowing myself to become so absorbed in something that he loved dearly was a mistake.

On the third day, my audible gasp broke the silence between us.

"I know what part of the book you're on," Sean said sagely from beside me. It was as though he had been waiting for me to crack.

"Oh my god," I said in a rush, unable to hold myself back. "Did that seriously just happen?"

"Yep. The series is pretty amazing, right?" He was grinning, obviously pleased that I was enjoying something that meant so much to him. His perfect, purely joyous smile – almost boyishly innocent – momentarily stunned me.

I just nodded dumbly, not managing to formulate any words.

"See?" He said with satisfaction. "I knew you weren't a robot. We just needed to expose you to some quality literature." His expression turned smug. "Spending some time with me will be good for you. You can join the human race again."

My heart twisted as I realized the irony of his words. "Can I?" I asked softly, almost beseechingly.

His face darkened immediately, anger tinged with sadness. "You know I can't let you go, Claudia," he said. He spoke quietly, but his voice had a hard edge to it that told me this wasn't up for debate.

I swallowed back my disappointment, not daring to contradict him. Getting into an argument would only undo all of my efforts at civility.

"You should read *Harry Potter* next," he said lightly. "They're supposed to be kids' books, but they're really addicting. Besides, we need to catch you up on your pop culture knowledge."

I went along with the abrupt change of subject, and I plastered on a teasing smile.

"How did you become such a nerd?" I asked, part of me genuinely curious. "It doesn't really go with the rest of your tough-guy, ladies' man persona."

He gave me a mock-offended look. "I'll have you know that nerdy is the new sexy," he said, his tone laced with false hurt. But something flickered in his eyes. Was that real pain that I saw in their emerald depths? But it was gone as soon as it had appeared, so quickly that I couldn't be sure that I had actually seen anything there at all.

"Besides," he continued on, "I also do some work-related reading. You're not the only one who's committed to their job."

I glanced over at the books on the top shelf. "You're a carpenter?" I asked, surprised to find myself actually interested.

"Yep," he said, grinning. "A damn good one, too." Then he frowned. "Unless getting shot fucks all that up." He looked at me questioningly, true concern etched in the lines of his face. It seemed that for all his cockiness, he was deeply passionate about his work. I was shocked to realize that we actually had something in common, and I found myself developing a grudging respect for him.

"You should be fine," I said reassuringly. "It'll take a while for your muscles to fully heal, so you should take it easy for a while, but you should be back to yourself in a few months."

He let out a small sigh of relief, his expression turning curiously serious. "Thank you," he said, his voice level and sincere. "For everything you've done for me."

"You're welcome," I replied softly, taken aback by the gratitude in his eyes.

"So," he said abruptly, puncturing the intimate moment. "Tell me more about you. What's your story?"

What's my story? I thought grimly. *My parents died when I was thirteen, I lived in the hell that was the Ames household for the next four years, and then I spent the next seven years throwing myself into my studies and shutting everyone out of my life and my heart.*

I wasn't about to admit any of that. Especially not to Sean. He made me feel vulnerable enough as it was without me ripping open deep wounds and exposing my heartache. So he would get the cheery, cliffs-notes version that I gave everyone who asked me the same question.

"Well, in a nutshell: I graduated high school with honors, went pre-med at Columbia, then got my MD at NYU." I paused, unwilling to divulge more. "So, where did you go to college?" I asked, diverting the conversation back to him.

I immediately regretted the question as his expression tightened ever so slightly. But his voice was casual when he spoke. "I didn't," he said. "Carpentry is kind of the family business, so I did an apprenticeship under my dad. I've pretty much been working at it my whole life."

"Oh. I'm kind of the same way, you know," I chattered to cover the slight awkwardness that had arisen between us. "My dad was a surgeon, and I always wanted to be like him. There was never a doubt in my mind that I wanted to go to med school."

"So you're a surgeon too?" Sean asked, rolling with the new conversational direction.

"No," I admitted. "I decided to become a pediatrician. I wanted to work with kids."

To care for them in a way that the Ames never cared for me.

Sean distracted me from the dark thought with a roguish smile. "Do I get a lollipop then, Dr. Ellers?" He asked, his eyes dancing.

His playful mood was undeniably infectious. "Only if you're a good boy," I stipulated, mildly surprised to find myself smiling.

His grin widened, more a predatory baring of the teeth now. "That's not really my style," he replied, his voice low and rough.

My breath hitched in my throat as I suddenly found myself trapped in his dark, smoky gaze, and I was unable to summon up the will to break the connection. I suddenly longed for that delicious electric jolt that I received every time I touched his skin. I wanted that contact, wanted to run my fingers over the contours of his perfectly sculpted muscles...

"Sorry," I said, trying to hold my ground. But my tone was low and breathy, a voice that I hardly recognized as my own. "I'm fresh out of lollipops anyway."

"Tease," he accused huskily. He reached out for me, and I didn't flinch away. A part of my brain knew that there was some reason that this was a very bad idea, but all I could focus on was the way that my heated blood pulsed through my veins, thrumming through them until it reached a deeper part of my body. His fingers traced my jawline, leaving a burning trail from my ear down to my chin. He gripped it firmly between his thumb and forefinger. I shivered, enthralled by the way his touch made my skin come alive, relishing the way that he held me in place for him as he slowly moved in to take me, his full lips twisted upward at the corners, his eyes burning into mine.

No! The rational part of my mind screamed at me.

But my body was ordering me otherwise. Heat pooled in my belly, and there was an unfamiliar tingling between my legs.

God damn it, Claudia! Stop being an idiot! Are you so desperate for your freedom that you're willing to whore yourself out for it?

That thought was enough to snap me out it. What the fuck was I thinking? What had happened to my cool rationality? I had certainly never done anything as reckless as this. Long days of confinement with Sean and torturous, confusing sexual impulses had robbed me of my usual iron control over my actions and emotions.

"Don't," I said softly, my voice slightly pleading. I wanted to get away from him, but I couldn't seem to bring myself to pull away. I needed him to release me from whatever spell he had me under.

He paused, his lips inches from mine. "Claudia." His hot breath fanned across my face as his voice caressed my name, and I almost broke.

"Please," I forced out, desperate.

His eyes clouded over for a moment, and then he blinked hard. His lazy, cocky expression instantly slid back into place as he pulled away from me, relinquishing me from his touch. I let out the breath that I didn't realize I had been holding, awash with relief.

But also disappointment. I bit my lip hard. My emotions were a roiling, tangled mess. I forced them back, straining to match Sean's nonchalance.

"I may not have any lollipops," I continued on smoothly as though our conversation hadn't been interrupted, "but I can cook dinner for you to make up for it."

A plan was forming in my mind. It seemed I might get out of here sooner than I had hoped. And then I could get away from Sean, escape from the invisible chains that he seemed to be using to bind me to him. Yes, I was getting out of here tonight. I had to.

■■■

I smiled slyly to myself as I pulled on one of the dresses from the bag of clothes after my shower. It was a bit low-cut for my taste, but my chest is fairly small – barely a B cup – so I told myself it wasn't too slutty. I briefly wished for my slacks again, but quickly pushed them from my mind. That wouldn't matter in a few hours; I would be back at my house with my own wardrobe.

I used my bobby-pins to pull my hair half-back, using a few more than was strictly necessary. I would need them later. Then I opened the medicine cabinet, pleased to find that the boys had a large bottle of Benadryl tucked in next to their shaving cream. I counted out ten pills and then paused. Where the hell was I going to conceal these? Looking down at my light cleavage, I sighed. There was nothing else for it: I tucked the pills into my bra, distributing them carefully so that I didn't look too lumpy.

Looking in the mirror, I practiced a sweet, innocent smile. When I deemed myself prepared, I squared my shoulders as I left the bathroom, ready to execute my plan.

Okay, so maybe I'm not the best cook in the world, I admitted to myself as I headed for the kitchen, Bradley silently in tow. It wasn't like I ever took the time to cook for myself, but I was sure that I could handle pasta. And I knew that I could make a mean chocolate cake, a leftover skill from a high school Home Ec class that I was counting on.

When I got to the kitchen, I turned to Bradley. "Did you get everything on the list?" I asked, trying not to sound too bossy.

He nodded, frowning. He clearly didn't appreciate being my errand boy.

"Thanks," I said with forced politeness. He just stared at me. "Ummm..." I began hesitantly. "Would you mind not watching me while I cook? It makes me really uncomfortable."

And if you don't agree, I'm seriously considering knocking you out with a frying pan and making a run for it.

But my other plan was much more elegant and far less risky, so I plastered on a genial expression.

Bradley said nothing for a moment, considering me.

"For god's sake, Bradley," Sean's voice drifted through the open bedroom door. "Leave the woman in peace."

Bradley's brows drew together forbiddingly. "Fine," he said shortly. "But I'll be sitting right here, so don't think you can try anything." His hand moved to the bulge in his waistband where he kept his gun. I got the message loud and clear.

"Okay," I replied, trying to keep my voice from shaking. This was going to make my plan far more dangerous than I had anticipated.

But thankfully, Bradley sat down on the couch and flicked on the TV, facing away from me. So long as his eyes stayed glued to the screen and Sean remained in his bedroom, I would be fine.

You can do this, Claudia, I steeled my resolve.

An hour later, the cake was in the oven, and my marinara sauce was coming along nicely. Water, sugar, corn syrup, and cocoa powder were boiling away in a separate pan. I shot a furtive glance in Bradley's direction, making sure that he wasn't looking my way.

Now for the tricky part.

I angled my body away from the living room and reached into my bra for the Benadryl. Thank god Bradley had actually bought a mortar and pestle for me. Wasting no time, I quickly ground up the pills to a fine white powder. On its own, it would taste horribly bitter. But the chocolate should mask that.

I poured the powder into the boiling, sugary mixture and then whisked in chunks of semisweet chocolate. When it was dark and smooth, I spooned out a tiny amount and touched it to the tip of my tongue. Perfect. I tried not to look too pleased with myself.

When the cake was ready, I sliced out a piece for myself and set it aside before liberally pouring the sauce over the rest of it.

"Okay," I called. "It's ready!"

Sean stirred from his bed as I plated everything up and set it on the small dining table in the corner of the living room. I tried my best to avoid shooting longing, anticipatory looks at the front door.

To my surprise, Sean chose to sit beside me rather than Bradley. I couldn't hide a small flush of pleasure.

Stop that! I ordered myself. Thank god I was getting away soon.

Dinner was awkwardly silent. Things were strange between Sean and me after our almost-kiss this afternoon, and Bradley had nothing to say to me, of course. The only sounds were the scraping of forks, and the occasional appreciative noise from Sean.

When it was time for desert, I couldn't help licking my lips in anticipation as I served up the chocolate cake.

"The sauce is too sweet for me," I answered the unspoken question in Sean's eyes. "But I hope you like it." I smiled at him sweetly.

"I'm sure I will," he said with an answering smile. Then he took a huge bite, and I felt a surge of vindictive triumph.

He closed his eyes blissfully as he swallowed. "Oh my god, Claudia, this is amazing. I haven't had anything this good since my mother last cooked for me."

"Oh?" I asked, making conversation. "How long has that been?"

The lines of Sean's face went taut, and he no longer met my eyes. "Two years," he said quietly. "She died two years ago."

My heart sank. I had had no idea. I knew the pain of losing a parent, and I hated to see that Sean knew it too. Ignoring Bradley's furious glare, I spoke to Sean softly. "I'm sorry," I said sincerely.

Seemingly of its own accord, my hand reached out, finding his beneath the table. I squeezed it gently, reassuringly. His head jerked up, his wide eyes meeting mine. His hand clenched to a fist, his muscles tensing at the contact. But he didn't pull away. After a moment, he relaxed, and his fingers tentatively closed around mine.

He turned his attention back to the cake, tearing into it with gusto. Guilt washed over me again, but I shoved it back.

I didn't care about Sean. I didn't. Or at least, I didn't care about him as much as I cared about my freedom.

A thought suddenly occurred to me: Would I go to the police when I escaped? I fiercely wanted Bradley to go to jail for what he had done to me, but could I betray Sean? Yes, he had ensured my captivity, but he had saved my life and protected me from Bradley's volatility. And in the days that I had lain beside him on his bed as he recovered, I had grown to realize that he wasn't a bad person, even if he was a criminal. I wasn't sure what crimes he was guilty of committing, but they couldn't be anything too heinous. Bradley had been the one to abduct me, and I was sure that Sean would have prevented him from doing so if he had known what his friend had planned. Surely Sean didn't deserve to go to jail for anything as serious as kidnapping.

No. I couldn't think about that. I would cross that bridge when I came to it. For now, I needed to stay focused on my immediate goal.

Although he didn't say anything complimentary – predictably – I was pleased when Bradley polished off two large slices of cake. Unfortunately, Sean stopped at one, seeming to have lost his appetite. I prayed that one slice would be enough.

I volunteered to do the dishes like a good little woman and then meekly returned to Sean's room. Bradley was sure to lock the door behind me.

I relished the thought that I would never hear the sound of that lock clicking closed again.

I sat as far from Sean as humanly possible as we read silently, determined not to be affected by his allure again. I couldn't help glancing over at him furtively every few minutes, looking for signs of drowsiness. After a while, he began blinking more slowly, yawning more often. Eventually, he rested his open book on his chest as his eyes slid closed.

Hardly breathing, I watched him for a few minutes. "Sean?" I whispered his name softly. No response. "Sean?" I said more loudly. Still, he didn't stir.

Thank god.

If Sean was this deeply asleep, then Bradley must be out too. Moving carefully so as not to make any noise, I tiptoed to the door. I knelt before it, eyeing the keyhole as I took two pins from my hair. For the first time, I was glad of growing up with the Ames family. I had learned to pick locks so that I could come and go from the house as I pleased, could escape from them just as I was escaping from Sean now.

The click as the lock sprang free seemed to reverberate throughout the room. I winced and looked back at Sean, but mercifully he hadn't woken at the sound. I stood and grasped the doorknob, turning it achingly slowly. All of my muscles were taut as I eased the door open, slipping out through the smallest crack I could manage. I didn't dare risk the sound of closing it. Besides, it would be pretty clear to Sean that I was gone when he woke up. Which hopefully wouldn't be till morning.

I forced myself to walk slowly across the living room. It seemed I wouldn't need to use the fire escape, after all; I was going to walk right out the front door. I would have given myself a mental pat on the back for so brilliantly executing my plan if it weren't for the fact that I was scared shitless.

When I was out in the hall, I broke into a run, unable to restrain myself any longer. I punched the button to call the elevator, bouncing on the balls of my feet as I waited for it to arrive. Once inside, it seemed to move achingly slowly as it descended to the parking garage. Unfortunately, Bradley had hidden my purse from me, so I wasn't going to be able to take my car. I would just have to make it on foot. Hopefully I could hail a cab once I got to the street.

As soon as the doors pinged open, I flung myself from the elevator and ran for the door, throwing it wide as I burst out into the night. I breathed in deeply. The scent of asphalt and gasoline had never smelled so sweet.

I ran through the parking garage, but when I reached the street, I stopped in my tracks as I took in my surroundings. I was in a bad neighborhood. A really bad neighborhood. One where it was definitely not a good idea to go on an evening stroll by oneself, especially not when wearing a low-cut dress.

But there was nothing for it. Steeling my resolve, I stepped out onto the street, walking quickly. I was desperate for a cab, but there wasn't one in sight. And I didn't dare stop a random car; I didn't want to draw attention to myself. I would just have to get out of here as fast as possible. Staring straight ahead, I focused on my goal in order to keep my fears at bay.

But that was a mistake. That's why I didn't see him until it was too late.

A large hand closed around my wrist, jerking me hard to my left. I gasped as I lost my footing, stumbling into the alley. A strong arm was around my waist, pinning my arms to my sides. I opened my mouth to scream, but his hand closed over my mouth, muffling the sound. Panic shot through me as I writhed in his grip, but my struggles were futile.

"I'll let you scream for me later, whore," said a low, husky voice in my ear. I was engulfed in the stench of whisky and stale sweat. "No one around here will give a shit. But I want you to be quiet for now. You see, this is my favorite part. The part where you fight. You fight until you realize that there is no way you can win. That's when I get to see the light leave your eyes."

He released me suddenly, shoving me forward harshly. I caught myself against the wall, the bricks scraping my hands. I used the momentum to push myself back, turning to run. But he was too close, too strong. He grabbed my shoulder, spinning me around and shoving my back up against the unyielding wall. I tried to scream again, but his hand was back over my mouth.

"Not yet, sweetheart," he practically cooed. He pressed his body up against mine, and I could feel his growing hardness against my hip. My stomach churned. I was going to be sick.

I shoved at his chest, clawed at his arms, but he just gave me a twisted leer, reveling in my frantic efforts. The shadows obscured his face, but I could see a maniacal gleam in his pale blue eyes. A look that chilled me to the core.

That's when the cold, horrible realization dawned on me: I was going to have to stop fighting. If he wanted me to fight, then I wouldn't give him the satisfaction. Dropping my arms and forcing my limbs to stillness, I glared at him defiantly.

His leer twisted into a furious snarl. "What do you think you're playing at, bitch?" He growled, dropping his hand from my mouth.

"Refusing to play your twisted game," I spat at him.

Pain exploded across my cheek as his hand cracked across my face. I cried out, shocked and suddenly disoriented as my head spun. I blinked hard to clear my vision, only to find myself staring into his eyes. If I had thought Bradley's eyes cold and inhuman, he was practically warm and friendly compared to this monster. Despite my resolve to show no fear, I felt myself trembling.

"Oh, you'll play," he said smugly. "They all do, in the end."

His wet tongue traced a slimy line up my cheek, and I gagged as bile rose in my throat. His hands were pawing at me, leaving a toxic taint everywhere that they touched. Then they were on my thighs, easing slowly up my dress.

I couldn't help it; I started fighting again, my nails shooting out like claws to gouge his eyes out. He just smiled as he caught my wrists easily, pinning them to the wall on either side of my head.

"See," he whispered. "I told you that you would play."

A scream was ripped from my throat, crying out my fury, frustration, and terror into the uncaring night.

Chapter 6

Hot tears were forming in my eyes as my body instinctively struggled against my attacker. He held my arms above my head, one of his hands easily encircling my small wrists. His other hand was touching me again, trailing slowly down my throat before tracing a line down my sternum, stopping at the top of my cleavage.

He smiled down at me, his eyes devoid of any shred of humanity. I knew what he was going to do, and there was nothing I could do to stop it. I jerked desperately against his grip.

"Please," I begged, my voice ragged as I forced it through the tightness in my throat. "Don't."

His smile twisted into a horrible, rictus grin as he gripped my breast hard, squeezing painfully.

The tears spilled down my cheeks and I let out a despairing sob. I hated myself in that moment, hated myself for giving in, for showing weakness to this man who wanted nothing but to break me. But he was right: I couldn't help but play his game. And I hated myself all the more for proving him right even as I tried to kick at his shins. But he was too close for me to get any momentum, and my efforts were fruitless.

A furious roar echoed through the alleyway, filling the cramped space. My attacker was torn away from me as something hit him hard from the side, knocking him to the ground. Someone was atop him immediately, driving his fist downward. There was a sickening crunch as it made contact with the man's face. He gave a pitiful cry, but the man assaulting him didn't stop. He pummeled him once, twice more, until my attacker was making sick, gurgling sounds as he gasped for breath.

The man pushed himself up off of him, pulling out a gun as he did so. He aimed it directly at my attacker's heart. There was a loud click as he cocked the gun, and for a moment, I hoped that he would fire it.

"Get out of here," he growled, his voice low and dangerous. "If I ever see you in this neighborhood again, I won't hesitate to kill you. Understand?"

The bloody man nodded jerkily as he forced himself upright, clinging to the wall for support as he pulled himself out of the alleyway, desperate to get away. He shot one last look at me, pure hatred filling his eyes. I shuddered and dropped my gaze, unable to look at him any longer. Instead, I turned my eyes on my savior.

Sean's expression was furious, and I trembled in the wake of his glare. Or maybe that was just the residual shock of what had happened to me. Whatever it was, it was too much for me to handle. My shaking knees gave way beneath me, and I could see the ground rushing up at me.

But I never felt the impact. Instead, a pair of strong arms caught me, lifting me up to cradle me against a hard chest. Panic spiked through me at the feeling of being restrained, and a small, strangled cry escaped me as I writhed in his grip.

His large hand stroked my arm soothingly. "Shhh, Claudia. It's just me," he said, his tone low and reassuring. "You're safe now."

Safe.

I buried my head in his chest, breathing in his now-familiar scent. I didn't even realize that my hands fisted in his t-shirt, clinging to him like a lifeline as my tears soaked it through. Blindly, I allowed him to carry me. I didn't care where we were going, so long as it was away from that alleyway.

Sean murmured reassuringly at me in a soft, soothing tone as I cried silently in his arms. Although his words were sweet, his muscles were corded around me, his whole body tense. Was it from the effort of carrying me, or was it something else?

I peeked up at him through my lashes. He wasn't looking at me. Instead, he stared straight ahead. The lines around his eyes and mouth were taut, as though he was under some sort of strain. Was he angry with me?

He shifted me in his grip, and a door swung open. My stomach dropped as I realized that we were going back into his apartment building.

I stared up at him pleadingly. "Please, Sean," I begged raggedly. "I just want to go home."

The lines of his face only deepened, and still he refused to look at me. When he spoke, his voice was tight with suppressed anger. "I can't take you home, Claudia." Then he added, more softly. "I'm sorry."

Tears continued to slide down my face as I closed my eyes, unwilling to look at him any longer. It wasn't inconceivable that he had awoken so quickly; he hadn't eaten very much of my spiked cake, after all. I would have been devastated that my plan had failed if I weren't so grateful that he had been there to save me from being raped. How was it that I could feel such gratitude towards him and such hatred at the same time?

After a few minutes, a bright light filtered through my closed eyelids, and I instinctively blinked. Sean's face swam into view, an odd expression etched across it. There was concern, compassion, relief, and... fear? And anger. Definitely anger.

I dropped my eyes so that I no longer had to face his burning gaze. That's when I noticed the red spray dotted across his white t-shirt: my attacker's blood. My stomach twisted at the memory of Sean's violence even as I couldn't help but feel gratitude.

But there was a bigger red splotch on his arm, one that was slowly growing larger.

"Sean, you're hurt," I said, distracted from my thoughts by the sight of his injury. His gunshot wound must have broken open. "Put me down," I insisted, sounding more like myself.

He looked at me skeptically. "Can you stand on your own?" He asked, leveling me with a hard look that dared me to lie to him.

I rolled my eyes at him. "Of course I can," I said. "I'm not the one who's hurt."

His face darkened, the anger overriding all other emotions. His movements were carefully controlled as he set me down on my feet, his muscles straining again. I recognized it now for what it was: repressed rage.

"You're not hurt?" He demanded harshly. He grabbed my shoulders and spun me around so that my back was to him. I was staring at my reflection in the mirror; he had brought me into the bathroom.

My eyes were wide, a wild light in them; my hair was a tangled mess; and there was the shadow of a bruise appearing on my right cheekbone where my assailant had backhanded me.

"Oh," I said softly.

"*Oh?*" He said incredulously. "Is that all you have to say? What were you thinking? Do you have any idea…?"

He trailed off, his eyes clouding over.

I rounded on him, my anger rising to match his. "What other choice did you give me?" I hissed. "Did you just expect me to stay here like a good girl? To allow you to keep me as your *pet* forever?"

His hand clenched to a fist, and a muscle in his jaw ticked as he gritted his teeth together. "I don't have a choice here, Claudia," he ground out.

"Yes, you do!" I insisted, my voice accusatory. "And you're making the wrong one!"

The tears were back, hot and angry this time. I swiped them away, then winced as my knuckles ran across my injured cheek. His fingers encircled my wrist, pulling my hand away from my face. I looked up at him, startled by the shock of his touch. The feeling of him holding me, his long fingers trapping my wrist as effectively as a manacle, made something quiver inside of me. His expression had softened, and the furious blaze in his eyes had given way to that darker flame again. It seemed to burn into me, the heat of it cutting to my core, awakening an answering warmth within my chest. And between my thighs.

"Here," he said softly, reaching for my face with his free hand. "Let me."

His thumb lightly traced the line of my cheekbone, wiping away the wetness on my face with a tenderness that shocked me. It stood in such jarring contrast to the way he held me so firmly. The sensation of his rough, calloused skin against mine made my flesh tingle. He was such an enigma: unbearably cocky, somewhat terrifying, and shockingly tender by turns.

And I couldn't seem to resist him.

His hand shifted to cup the side of my face. His touch was feather-light, but I found that I couldn't move; I was locked in place as though he were holding me in an iron grip. My gaze involuntarily flicked from his eyes to his full lips, and I unconsciously licked my own.

The corners of his mouth twisted upward, a knowing smile. He inclined his head forward, inching towards me at an agonizingly slow pace. His eyes were studying mine as he neared me, gauging my reaction. And there was a playful light there as well, as though he was enjoying making me wait.

Well, I wasn't standing for that. I wasn't going to let him toy with me. But instead of pulling away, I acted on an insane impulse: I wrapped my free hand around the back of his neck and pulled him down into me, crushing my lips to his.

For a moment, his mouth was still against mine. My only warning was a low, rumbling growl. His hand left my face to tangle itself in my long hair, fisting at the nape of my neck. He pulled sharply, and I drew in a shocked breath at the slight pain as my head dropped back in response. Only when my lips were offered up to him in the way that he wanted did he finally take my mouth.

His lips were hard and demanding, forcing mine to shape to his with almost bruising force. The delicious sparks that had danced across my skin from his lightest touch were finally ignited as though they had met with an accelerant. Flames bloomed within me, racing through my veins until my whole body was ablaze, utterly consumed by the erotic heat that Sean had awoken within me. And I gave in, reveling in it. I had never felt anything like this before, and I wanted more, craved it. All thoughts of where I was and what was happening to me were gone from my mind. All I knew was that Sean was touching me, and I never wanted him to stop.

He obliged me as his tongue delved between my lips, tangling with my own as I fought to match his intensity.

But I never stood a chance. He pressed his body into mine. I would have stumbled if he hadn't steadied me with his grip on my hair. He didn't release my mouth as he pushed me backwards. I gasped in shock as my back came into contact with the wall. I barely had time to register the fact that he had released my hair before he grasped my wrist firmly. Never having let go of the other, he drew my hands up sharply, pinning them against the wall on either side of my head. The coolness of the tiles contrasted deliciously with the heat of my skin, and I shuddered in pleasure at the sensation.

The part of me that would usually be screaming at me to struggle was oddly silent. Instead, I went completely still, compliant. His tongue took possession of my mouth, stroking my own tongue firmly as he explored every inch of me. The feeling of him inside of me, claiming me, made me suddenly, acutely aware of another area that I desperately wanted Sean to fill. There was something warm and wet on my thighs, and my core pulsed in need. I pressed myself up against his hard thigh, a strange whimpering sound escaping me. I could feel his lips curve up into a satisfied smile as he continued his relentless assault on my senses.

He shifted his grip on me, his fingers reaching to entwine with mine. But when he pressed his palms to mine, I couldn't hold back a small cry as pain seared across them.

Sean drew back from me immediately, breaking the connection between us. He grasped my hands gently this time, holding them carefully as he inspected the scrapes on my palms where I had torn them against the brick wall in that alley...

The flames within me were doused instantly as reality hit me like the shock of ice cold water to the face. How could I have possibly enjoyed what Sean was doing to me after almost being raped minutes earlier? How could I possibly want any man to touch me after that? This was so fucked up. *I* was so fucked up. And it was all Sean's fault.

I quickly extricated my hands from his grip, and I was disgusted to realize that a part of me was reluctant to do so.

Unable to meet his eye, my gaze fell on the red stain that marred his bandages. "I should check your stitches," I said, forcing myself to sound clinical.

He ran a hand through his hair, mussing it in that sexy way. "Shit," he said under his breath. "Claudia, I -"

I shot him a frosty look, a silent warning.

He dropped his hand, his shoulders slumping slightly. "Alright," he said. There was a flicker of distress in his eyes, but his face was quickly schooled to an unconcerned mask. He stripped his shirt off compliantly, and I forced myself not to admire his perfect body.

I was hesitant to touch him, worried that I would be caught up in his power again. "You should go to the bedroom," I said, my tone detached. "I'll have to clean out the cuts in my hands and then I'll come patch you up."

He reached out for me. "Do you want me to help -?" He began kindly.

I jerked my hands away as though his touch would scald me. "Just go," I said coldly, lifting my chin to stare at him defiantly.

His brows drew together, and the hand that he had extended turned to a fist. He held my gaze for a moment, challenging me. But I wasn't backing down, wasn't going to turn to putty in his hands again. Seeming to recognize that I wasn't going to yield, he turned and walked away stiffly, his muscles once again taut with repressed anger.

I didn't allow myself to breathe out a sigh of relief until I had locked the bathroom door behind him. I wanted to fall to pieces, to slide down onto the cold tile floor and cry until all of my tears were dried up. I couldn't understand what was wrong with me. Sure, Sean had shown me some compassion, and it was possible that I had allowed myself to be charmed by his cocky, self-assured side. I had certainly allowed myself to be pulled in by his physical beauty. But there had to be more to it than that.

He saved you, a voice whispered inside of me. *So many times.*

Was that it? Was I coming to view him as my savior rather than my captor? Was that how I had been able to fool myself into thinking that I wanted him even after he had returned me to my prison? I had been so close to freedom…

And what kind of freedom would that have been? I went cold at the thought of the pale-eyed man who had attacked me.

How long do you think that man would have allowed you to live when he was finished with you?

I shuddered, forcing my thoughts away from him. So my first escape attempt had failed. I was alive to keep fighting, and that was what mattered; I wasn't about to give up. I hadn't been lying to Sean: I refused to remain here as his pet doctor for the rest of my life, my existence reliant on the whims of the men who held me captive.

I wasn't going to allow myself to fall apart. I squared my shoulders and turned on the sink faucet, adjusting the water so that it was lukewarm. With a hiss of pain, I forced myself to gently work soap into the long, thin abrasions that marred my palms. They weren't too deep, but cleaning them stung like a bitch. When I was finished, I inspected myself carefully. I didn't think I would even need Band-Aids.

I couldn't help but linger in the bathroom. I wanted to stay in there, to savor my privacy. But Sean was bleeding in the next room, and despite my anger with him, I couldn't bear the thought of him in pain. Taking a deep breath, I unlocked the door and navigated through the darkened living room until I reached the warm glow of Sean's bedroom. Tentatively, I stepped inside, calling myself a coward for not meeting his eyes as I approached the bed.

As I unwound the gauze from around his arm, I was grateful for the thin barrier that the medical gloves provided, lessening the electric effect of Sean's skin touching mine. I worked quickly and quietly, making four new sutures to replace the ones that he had broken open while saving my life. He endured silently, not even tensing as the needle pierced his skin. The air around us was heavy with suppressed emotion, suffocating me as it pressed tightly against my lungs. It was a relief when I finished bandaging the wound; I could finally put some much-needed distance between us again.

"I'm going to take a shower," I said quietly, still not looking at him. I didn't wait for any sort of acknowledgement or permission. Now that I thought about it, I felt horribly dirty, as though trails of grime were encrusted on my skin where the pale-eyed man had touched me. My hands, so steady moments before as I had stitched up Sean's wound, were now trembling as I fumbled to turn on the shower. I turned the temperature as hot as it would go before stripping off my slutty dress and stepping under the scalding spray, letting the uncomfortable heat of it scour the filth from my skin. I longed for a loofa to scrub it away, but as it was, my fingernails would have to do. After a few minutes, the rational part of my mind realized that I was causing myself too much pain; I was rubbing my skin raw.

I forced myself to draw in a deep breath. *Calm down,* I ordered myself. *Think of something else.*

My mind turned to Sean of its own accord, the memory of his furious roar, the strength of his arms as he held me, carrying me away from my assailant.

"You're safe now."

And it had been true. Despite everything, I knew deep down that all he wanted was for me to be safe, whether that meant standing up to his best friend or fighting off a rapist in the street. He had put himself in danger for my sake tonight when he could have easily solved all of his problems by letting me die.

But what about protecting you from himself?

It was obvious that Sean wanted me. And – I forced myself to admit – I wanted him too. Why couldn't he respect my wishes and keep his distance? Was it possible that he found himself just as drawn to me as I did to him? Did he also feel that nearly preternatural connection that seemed to tether me to him despite my best efforts?

The memory of his kiss flitted across my mind, and my body began to burn from more than just the heat of the water that pounded down on me. The way that he had handled my body, demanding complete control as he took my mouth…

That unfamiliar pulsing between my legs was back. I had never experienced this, this… wanting. Sean had awoken something within me that no man ever had before, that I had never allowed any man to awaken before. How could I be disgusted by the taint on my body one minute and allow Sean to light it on fire the next? My stomach was churning, half-disgusted by myself and half-thrilled at the memory of Sean's domineering touch as he had kissed me.

Well, perhaps one good thing would come of this: the tortuous sexual tension between Sean and me might have been mercifully siphoned off by that kiss.

But I was just fooling myself.

Chapter 7

As soon as I entered the bedroom, my eyes were drawn to him like a magnet. He was staring at me, a curious light in his eyes as his gaze flicked up and down my body. My cheeks warmed as I realized that my nipples were still hard from his kiss, the little peaks of them clearly visible though the thin nightshirt I wore.

I did my best to pretend not to notice as I positioned myself on the bed as far from him as physically possible, praying that I wouldn't cuddle up to him in the night. I was tempted to sleep on the floor to ensure that it wouldn't happen. But that would just prove to him that he had some effect on me, some hold over me. And I wasn't about to betray my uncharacteristic vulnerability when it came to him.

I stared resolutely up at the ceiling, my muscles drawn tight as I tried to ignore the pulsing tension between us. How I hated it.

"Do I have to lock the door?" Sean asked quietly, his voice tinged with shame.

"No," I said shortly. I wasn't going to try to escape again. Not tonight.

He paused for a beat. "How did you get out earlier?" He asked.

"Bradley forgot to lock the door," I lied. I hoped he would buy it; I didn't want him to take away my hairpins. I might need them again.

"Alright," he said after a moment. But his tone was skeptical. I held back the sigh of relief that I wanted to release.

It seemed he had been affected enough by the drugs that his memory was hazy.

"You should get some sleep," he said after a moment.

I huffed out a breath, saying nothing. Right. Like I was going to be able to sleep with my mind in overdrive. But to my surprise, my exhaustion got the better of me. After everything I had been through, my body insistently pulled me under. I was out in minutes.

■■■

His hot, putrid breath blew across my lips as he panted against me in gleeful anticipation. Rough, dirty hands were groping me, ripping at my dress. My fingers clawed at him, but they seemed to pass through him as though he was an apparition, and he leered at me as my desperate efforts to fight him off had no effect. I tried to scream for help, but I couldn't seem to make a sound. He gripped my shoulders, shaking me.

"Claudia," he said my name insistently. But it wasn't the soft, inhuman voice that I remembered. "Claudia. Wake up," the deep, familiar voice ordered.

His comforting, musky scent surrounded me, enfolding me like a warm blanket.

"Sean," I breathed his name like a prayer as I looked up into his gorgeous green eyes. His browns were drawn together, betraying anxiety. His arm snaked around me, pulling me into him. I clung to it, the strength of his hold reassuring me. I felt safe, protected.

He brushed my sweat-dampened hair back from my forehead, stroking it tenderly. I closed my eyes and leaned into his touch.

ust a dream," he said gently. "You're safe now."

"Don't leave me," I mumbled, sleep pulling me back under.

"Never," I thought I heard him say softly.

But when I woke the next morning, I was sure that I had imagined it.

■ ■

"Why is this door unlocked?" Bradley's voice jerked me from my slumber. "And what the fuck happened to her?" I opened my eyes to find him standing in the doorway, studying me. His eyes were focused on my cheek, taking in the bruise that had formed there overnight. The slight throbbing let me know that it must look bad.

Bradley's attention shifted to Sean, who was sitting upright with a book resting on his chest. "I thought you were all for treating her humanely. What did she do to make you snap?" He began to advance on me. "If you hurt him, bitch…" he began menacingly. I scooted back from him, intimidated, but I was stopped short when my back hit the headboard.

Sean was on his feet in an instant, positioning himself between his friend and me. His expression was taut, the lines of his face etched with anger. "I didn't do that," he growled.

Bradley glared at him. "Well I sure as hell didn't. What did she do, slam her face against the wall?"

"No," Sean said quietly. "She was attacked in the street last night. After she escaped," he added reluctantly.

"What?!" Bradley demanded, his face a thunderhead. He tried to sidestep his friend to get to me, but Sean blocked him again.

"Calm down, Bradley," Sean ordered levelly. "I got her back, and everything's fine now. Besides," he added, his tone hard. "*You* forgot to lock the door. Did you expect her to just stay here when she knew she had a way out?"

Bradley's eyes clouded over in confusion. "I'm sure I did…" Then he shook his head. "Fuck. I was so tired last night. I guess I screwed up." He eyed my injury again. "At least someone taught you a lesson," he said with grim satisfaction.

Sean growled, his fingers curling into fists. "Get out, Bradley," he said, the warning in his tone clear.

Bradley took an involuntary step back, his eyes wide with shock. "What the fuck, Sean?" He demanded. "Are you really going to fight me? Because of *her?* What has she done to you? I brought her here to save your life. I risked my fucking neck for you. And now you're siding with her over me?" His eyes narrowed at me. "I don't think she should stay in here with you anymore. I'm moving her to my room." He reached into his pocket and pulled out the handcuffs. I couldn't suppress a shudder as they glinted cruelly in the morning light.

"No," Sean said, fury bleeding into his tone. "Get out, Bradley," he ordered again. "Now." That aura of power surrounded him again, rolling off of him in forbidding waves.

Bradley paused, glaring at his friend. "Fuck you, Sean," he spat. But mercifully he shoved the cuffs back into his pocket and stalked out of the room, slamming the door behind him before locking it with a sound of finality.

I let out the breath that I didn't realize I had been holding. "Thank you," I said, my voice small.

Sean didn't answer me. "Ass," he muttered under his breath. He closed his eyes, pinching the bridge of his nose and drawing in a deep breath. When he opened them again, they were clear of that furious light that had blazed in them moments before. His cocky mask was back in place, and he shot me that sexy, roguish smile.

I felt an odd twinge of pity for him; my presence here was clearly destroying his relationship with his best friend. Part of me hated the thought of having caused him pain. But on the other hand, it was his own fault. If he would just let me go, he and Bradley wouldn't be fighting all the time.

But his grin remained firmly in place as he made a visible effort to shove back his consternation. He did a good job of hiding it, but I could see the turmoil in his eyes.

Nevertheless, he moved nonchalantly as he reached out for the bookshelf, taking down *A Storm of Swords* and handing it to me.

"We'll make a nerd of you yet," he grinned. I couldn't hold back an answering smile.

"Don't count on it," I retorted lightly.

As I took the book from him, my fingers brushed against his. A little jolt shot up my arm, my fingertips tingling like I had just received a shock of static electricity. Our eyes met, and the darkness that I saw in his let me know that he had felt it too.

I drew away from him quickly. "Thanks," I said, trying to keep my voice level.

Recognizing the dismissal, he pulled away as well, allowing me my personal space. Still, as he settled down beside me with his copy of *Kushiel's Dart*, I couldn't help but long for more of that delicious contact. After our steamy kiss last night, I knew just how good his touch could feel. That kiss hadn't lessened the tension between us; it had ratcheted it up ten notches.

I stared at the pages of my book, but none of the words were sinking in. Instead, I was driven to distraction by thoughts of our brief moment of passion in the bathroom, flashes of decidedly discomfiting memories flitting across my mind. I found myself shifting my position often, crossing and uncrossing my legs as I fought to ignore the insistent tingling between my thighs.

I could sense Sean watching me occasionally, could practically feel his lopsided smirk as his eyes flitted over me. But I ignored him resolutely; I didn't want to invite more flirtatious behavior. I knew that I wouldn't be able to handle it. With a few words and the lightest of touches, he would pull me back under his spell, exerting that power over me that I couldn't seem to resist.

Unbearably long, uncomfortable hours passed as I mechanically turned the pages of my book. When the late afternoon sunlight began slanting through the window, I finally broke. I couldn't handle the tense silence any longer.

With a heavy sigh, I allowed my eyes to focus on Sean, as they had been longing to do all day. He met my gaze immediately, his smile holding an edge of triumph at my capitulation, as though he had just won some small battle between us. And damn it if he hadn't.

"So," he began. "What do you want to talk about?"

Not last night, that's for sure.

"Not the weather," I said instead, allowing a small smile to play around my lips.

"Okay," he said easily. "How about you tell me more about you." It was a statement, not a question. My stomach dropped slightly. I wasn't really one for sharing. He had let me get away with the abbreviated version of my life when we had spoken before. I didn't know how much I was ready to reveal to him now.

"Okay," I assented, somewhat reluctantly.

"How is it that you don't have a husband or boyfriend?" He asked bluntly. "You're intelligent, successful, beautiful; How come some dashing, wealthy businessman hasn't snapped you up by now?"

I fought back a frown. We were already treading into painful territory. But a part of my mind was amazed at his assessment of me. *"Intelligent, successful, beautiful"?* He didn't think me a cold fish who was basically man repellent?

"I just haven't had the time to date," I hedged.

"Ah," he said. "The classic workaholic excuse." He speared me with a look that penetrated more than skin-deep. "What's the real reason, Claudia?" He asked softly.

I glared at him, not ready to divulge the real reason: my carefully-guarded pain that had hardened my heart in the years since my parents had died. If I didn't allow myself to care about anyone, then no one could hurt me.

His expression softened. "Okay," he moved on, allowing me my secret. "When was the last time you *did* go on a date?"

Great. We had gone from painful to embarrassing. But the silence between us was driving me crazy, so I was desperate for a distracting conversation. That was what made me crack.

I sighed, capitulating. "Seven years," I admitted, unable to meet his eye as I said it.

He let out a low whistle. "Damn," he said, a touch of incredulity coloring his tone. "So that was what, during college?"

"Yeah," I said. Well, now that I had started, I guess it wouldn't hurt to give him this whole story. It wasn't like there was much to tell anyway. "He was a junior, I was a sophomore. He said he loved me, and I believed him. But it wasn't much more than a fling. It was over before the end of Spring semester."

"Ouch," Sean said. "Sounds like a real douchebag."

"Pretty much," I agreed. After my trust had been betrayed by the first man I had ever been with, I had given up on the whole idea of dating. I had told myself that my career was more important. But ever since I had been abducted by Bradley, I had been forced to realize how unfulfilled my life truly was. I didn't have any significant relationships, and I didn't know what to do with my day if I didn't have my job to go to. Sean had been right; I might as well have been a robot, devoid of human emotion.

But now he was getting under my skin, slowly chipping away at my walls. And I couldn't decide if I was grateful or resentful.

"Have you had sex since then?"

I gasped. Wow. Had he actually just asked me that? I glared at him again. That was far too personal. And definitely not something that I wanted to admit to him, not when he so obviously had *a lot* of experience under his belt.

He chuckled at my forbidding expression. "Alright, alright," he said, placating. "A lady doesn't kiss and tell." But his dancing eyes told me he knew my answer full well.

"New topic," he continued on. "Why did you choose to become a pediatrician instead of a surgeon like your dad?"

God, was a there a single question he could ask me that didn't hit a nerve?

"I told you," I said. "I like helping kids."

"Why?" He pressed.

I was quiet for a moment. But something in me wanted to share this part of me, craved the release of talking about it, as though it would draw the pain out of my soul like poison from a wound.

"Because they need someone watching out for them." I took a deep breath. "Like no one ever watched out for me." My voice was barely audible.

His hand covered mine, the warmth of it seeping into me, comforting me in a way that I hadn't known since my parents had died. I looked up at him through suddenly damp lashes, dreading to see the pity that would fill his eyes. But there was nothing there but compassion, empathy even.

He knew; he understood. I remembered the way that his expression had tightened when he had admitted that his mother was dead, how he had reluctantly accepted my silent comfort as I held his hand under the dinner table. I realized in that moment that it was more than simply lust that pulled me to him. I had only seen flashes of his pain, but I could tell that deep down he was just as broken as I was.

My fingers entwined with his, trusting him to see my vulnerability. Without thinking, I found myself leaning into him. He held perfectly still, his breathing turning shallow as I slowly, tentatively pressed my lips to his.

There was a moment of hesitation, as though he didn't want to spook me. Then his hot mouth gently shaped itself around mine. His hand was around the nape of my neck, not tugging at my hair as he had done the night before, but firmly holding me in place for him nonetheless. I shuddered at the sensation of the dominance of even this light touch, and I felt myself melting for him, giving myself over to him.

His tongue traced the line of my lips, and I opened for him. He stroked into my mouth, shallow forays as his tongue teased the tip of mine. A low, husky moan that I hardly recognized as my own escaped me as my body voiced my craving for more. He responded instantly, no longer holding back.

His hand shifted to the front of my throat, applying pressure so that I was forced down onto the pillows. The act awoke something primal within me, the recognition of his utter dominance making me go limp beneath him as I demonstrated my submission to the alpha male. And all the while his tongue never left my mouth. It was now delving into me deeply, making me think of other places where he might penetrate me...

The thought made my nipples harden and my pussy contract.

Pussy. I had never thought of my sex in such lewd terms before. But the raw nature of the word felt right when Sean was taking me like this, claiming my body.

He suddenly tore his mouth from mine, but his lips were instantly on me again, brushing against the skin at the hollow beneath my ear. My flesh warmed as he kissed it, tracing little figure-of-eight patterns across the sensitive area with his hot tongue. Then he drew back, pursing his lips and blowing cool air across my enflamed skin. I shivered, all of my nerve endings jumping to life at the sharply contrasting temperatures.

His low, rumbling chuckle seemed to vibrate through me, letting me know that he knew exactly what he was doing to me. It was a sound of pure, masculine satisfaction. He was relishing toying with me, teasing me.

His hands suddenly fisted in the thin material of my nightshirt. He paused a beat, grinning down at me predatorily as I watched him with bated breath. With a sharp jerk of his powerful arms, the fabric parted for him easily.

The sudden cool air on my hyper-sensitive breasts, the pure eroticism of the act, made me arch up into him, silently begging for his touch. But his hand was on my sternum, shoving me back into the mattress roughly.

"I didn't say you could move," he growled.

I moaned, and I wasn't sure if it was from frustration or arousal at his words. My clit was pulsing madly, throbbing in need. And he was so close to my burning nipples. If only he would touch them…

He obliged me immediately, and I only remembered just in time to keep still beneath him. It took every ounce of my willpower to do so as his tongue flicked across the hardened peak, sending a jolt of electricity straight from my breast to my sex, making it clench around nothing. I whimpered beneath him, needing more. I could feel his smile against my flesh as he slowly kissed around my areola, teasing me, torturing me.

Then his teeth closed around my nipple, biting hard. I cried out at the shock of it, amazed to find that the spike of sharp pain only made my pussy burn hotter. I writhed beneath him as my fingers dug into his shoulders, no longer able to resist disobeying his order. His cock was hard against my hip, and I craved for him to fill me with it.

"Please," I groaned. "Sean, please." I pressed my hips up into him, grinding against him.

In a move faster than I could comprehend, his mouth left me. There was a loud *crack* as his hand came down on my soft flesh. A burning, stinging sensation bloomed on my breast. I gasped in shock at the pain.

"I told you to stay still."

I stared up at him, wide-eyed. His expression was hard, forbidding. I trembled beneath him, torn between fear and intense arousal at his treatment of my body. I relished his control. If he was in charge, then I wasn't really at fault for what was transpiring between us. I didn't have to worry that what I was doing was wrong; I didn't have to question everything that I was feeling. Losing myself in the wildness of our passion, I fully engaged in his game, giving myself over to him.

"I... I'm sorry," I forced out through heaving breaths.

His expression twisted upward into a satisfied smile, one with a slight edge of cruelty. He reached out for me, and I braced myself for further retribution. But he cupped my face in his large, calloused hand, tracing his thumb lightly across my lips. My tongue darted out, licking at him tentatively. He applied pressure, easing his thumb into my mouth. I swirled my tongue around it, sucking gently.

His green eyes filled with unmistakable lust. And a hint of wonder. "Fuck, Claudia," he breathed. His cock twitched against me as he hardened impossibly further. He pulled his thumb from my mouth and leaned into me. My lips parted for him, ready to accept his kiss.

But he stopped suddenly, his eyes clouding over. His brows drew together, and his lips tightened to a thin line. Abruptly, he rolled off of me, quickly putting as much distance between us as possible.

I propped myself up on my elbows, hurt and confusion flooding my chest. "Sean?" I asked softly. "What's wrong?"

He rounded on me angrily, his eyes burning. "*What's wrong?*" He asked, half-shouting. "Everything about this is wrong, Claudia!" He ran a hand through his hair in frustration. "You were right: I'm really fucked up. *This* is really fucked up."

"But I -" I began, but he cut across me.

"I'm taking advantage of you, Claudia. And you're letting me." He was furious, and I couldn't tell if his ire was directed at me or at himself.

All of the lust went flooding out of me. My cheeks flamed as I drew my ripped shirt together, covering myself.

"And you're letting me."

I blinked hard against the stinging at the corners of my eyes. "I'm sorry," I whispered.

Sean's fists clenched. "You're sorry," he said, his voice hollow. He wasn't looking at me any longer. "Maybe it's better if you aren't in here with me."

No. Would he really leave me at Bradley's mercy?

"Please," I begged. "Don't."

He pushed himself up off the bed, moving carefully. "Don't worry," he said, but his voice was cold and detached rather than comforting. "I'm going to stay on the couch."

I didn't dare speak lest he change his mind. So I watched in silence as he left the room, locking the door behind him.

I suddenly felt cold, utterly alone. I hugged my knees to my chest as I fought to swallow back the hard lump in my throat. I refused to cry over Sean.

Chapter 8

The next day, I was thoroughly bored. I was too wound up to focus on my book, too distracted by memories of my erotic encounters with Sean. Never before in my life had I experienced anything like it. Well, it wasn't exactly like I had had a plethora of sexual partners, but I was fairly certain that this kind of sexual chemistry wasn't easy to come by.

I knew that I should feel guilty, even disgusted, by what I had let him do to me. But when I searched my soul, all I found was a sense of feminine satisfaction. And disappointment that he had pulled away from me, leaving me wanting. Not to mention hurt. He had seemed so angry with me, as though it was all my fault that he had ended up atop me, fucking my mouth with his tongue.

Despite my resentment, I shivered at the memory.

But what occupied my thoughts most was my visceral reaction to the way he had dominated me, my answering pleasure when he had bitten my nipple and slapped my breast. I wasn't completely ignorant of varying proclivities; I knew that some people achieved sexual gratification from pain. Never in my wildest dreams had I thought that I would be one of them.

The rational, analytical part of my brain told me that I probably liked it because it finally gave me some sense of release from my usually guarded, carefully-controlled manner. And if I was honest with myself, the constant effort of keeping my walls up weighed on me more heavily than I had ever realized.

I wanted more, more of the dark submission that Sean brought out in me. Even though the thought of being so vulnerable with anyone still terrified me, I had come to the realization that my captivity had forced me to renew human contact for the first time in years. I knew that I wasn't ready to share my past, my pain, with Sean, but surely I could keep my secrets while only opening up to him sexually?

I wondered idly if I truly was falling prey to Stockholm Syndrome. While it was a distinct possibility, a deeper part of me knew that the connection I shared with Sean was more than that.

I hoped.

By midday, I found myself pacing around the room, trying to release some of my pent-up energy. I hadn't been this inactive in all my life, and it was starting to grate on me. And, looking around the small room, I realized that it was sadly lacking in potential activities. Sure, there were plenty of books to keep me company, but I was too distracted to read.

Then my eyes fell on the chest of drawers, the only other piece of furniture in the room. My gaze was drawn to the bottom drawer, the one that Sean kept locked.

I wonder what he's hiding in there...

My curiosity piqued, I knelt down and tugged at the brass handle. The drawer didn't budge. Yep. Definitely locked.

I debated for a moment. It really wasn't right to invade his privacy in this way...

Boredom and burning curiosity won out over respecting Sean's secrets. He had already pried a few of my secrets out of me; it was only fair that he do some sharing of his own. Even if he didn't realize that he was doing so.

Pulling two pins from my hair, I made quick work of the simple lock, smirking to myself as it clicked open. I hesitated a moment longer before opening the drawer, wavering in my decision.

What the hell, I decided.

With a decisive tug, the drawer slid open. My jaw dropped as my mind struggled to process what was inside. I had never seen anything like this in my life.

The drawer was full to the brim with sex toys. And not just any sex toys: decidedly kinky implements for causing pleasure or pain. As I stared, wide-eyed, something disconcerting stirred in my belly. Okay, I had enjoyed Sean pushing me around, even him slapping my breast. But this was on a whole different level. There were several clearly electronic devices that I couldn't put a name to or even begin to come up with a use for. A length of rope was coiled meticulously in one corner. I reached out and ran my fingers over it, surprised to feel my sex stir to life at the roughness of it against my skin. How would it feel against the delicate skin on the inside of my wrists, the contours of it pressing into my flesh as it went taut around them…?

I shook myself, blinking away the torrid fantasy that had begun to form in my mind. My fingers explored further, tracing the outline of a fur-lined paddle. My eyes were drawn to something long and thin tucked in at the back of the drawer. I reached for it, pulling it out so that I could inspect it more closely.

A soft, leather-coated handle tapered to a thin line. I brushed my fingertips over the material, marveling at how it was braided, creating a delicate, crisscrossing pattern up the length of the crop. The square of leather at the tip was supple and buttery-soft. Curious, I tapped it across my palm a few times.

"Claudia, did you want -"

I jumped at the sound of Sean's voice, dread forming in the pit of my stomach as my head whipped around to face him. I had been so entranced that I hadn't heard him approaching. Something quaked inside of me as I took in his livid expression.

"Sean," I gasped his name stupidly, dropping the crop as though it had burned me.

"What the fuck do you think you're doing?" He closed the distance between us in three long strides.

I never had a hope of escaping him. His hand shot out, grabbing my wrist as he yanked me to my feet. He gripped my upper arms hard, shaking me slightly.

"That's private," his voice was a growl. "How did you open that drawer, Claudia?" He demanded harshly, the threat in his eyes daring me to lie.

"I..." I hesitated, disoriented by the sudden turn of events.

He shook me again, his fingers digging into me with almost bruising force. "How?!"

"My hairpins," I admitted quickly. "I picked the lock."

Impossibly, the fury in his eyes blazed hotter. "You lied to me," he accused. "That's how you escaped. Isn't it?"

"Y-yes," I gasped, more frightened of him than I had ever been. "Sean, I'm sorry. I didn't mean -"

He barked a cold, humorless laugh. "You what? You didn't mean to pick the lock? You did it by accident?"

"Look," I said breathlessly. "I don't mind. It's okay." I wanted to let him know that I wasn't judging him for what I had found. In fact, it was just the opposite: I was perversely intrigued.

"It's *okay?*" He said angrily. He shoved me suddenly, and I fell back onto the bed. I was disoriented for a moment, and he took advantage. His hands were on my hips, lifting me up. Within moments, I found myself staring down at the floor, draped face-down over his lap.

"Is this *okay?*" He asked, his voice gruff. But there was more than just anger in it this time. There was definitely a low, lustful tone to it. His fingers tangled in my brunette waves, tugging my head back sharply so that my back arched, forcing my ass up. I gasped as my scalp tingled where he pulled my hair, the little pinging sparks shooting down my spine to my sex.

"This is who I am, Claudia. This is what I want to do to you." Through the lust in his voice, I could detect a note of pain. "I tried to save you from this."

Save me?

Sean thought that his desires were wrong. At least, he thought they were wrong when it came to me. And truthfully, the idea that he wanted to tie me down and hurt me when I couldn't escape him was very wrong indeed. But there was one very significant factor that he hadn't grasped: I wanted him to. I certainly wasn't ready to face everything that I had found in that drawer, but I desperately wanted for him to touch me. And if that touch came with a little pain, then so be it. I had even enjoyed the small flares of pain he had given me the night before.

"It's okay, Sean," I said again, my voice steady. "I want this too."

His hand gripped my flagrantly positioned bottom, squeezing my cheeks hard. "Is this what you want, Claudia?" He asked softly, a dangerous edge to his voice. "To be punished?"

Punished? Did I want that? I wasn't sure that I felt comfortable with the idea of being reprimanded.

But my pussy was on fire for him, and there was a growing wetness between my thighs. I was quivering in his grip, practically panting.

"Yes," I assented before my brain could take back control.

"You might regret saying that," Sean said huskily. With that as my only warning, he gripped the hem of my dress and flipped it up over my ass. Without a moment's pause, he grasped the elastic at the top of my white cotton panties and yanked them down to my thighs. My cheeks burned as he exposed me, and I couldn't help instinctively struggling against him. I squirmed in his lap, but the friction only caused my rapidly-hardening clit to rub against his hard thigh, teasing me. His fist tightened in my hair, tugging at it sharply.

"What have I told you about staying still?" He demanded, his voice hard.

I stopped moving instantly, all of my muscles taut with the effort of restraining myself.

His hand caressed my ass, his rough palms sensually rubbing against my skin. I couldn't help moaning at the sensation as my core throbbed, silently begging him to move his touch lower. "Now, Claudia," he said, his voice suddenly brusque and even. "I want you to remember that you asked for this, that you wanted to be punished. You know that what you did was wrong, and you want me to discipline you. Don't you?"

Discipline? I bit my lip, unwilling to admit that I had indeed asked for this. What was wrong with me? How could my body be burning with lust at the thought of him treating me like a child? But I wasn't a child. I was a woman, a woman whose needs had become suddenly, acutely evident. And the flames licking at my flesh told me that I certainly did want this.

But he wasn't pleased at my hesitance. *"Don't you?"* He said more insistently, his fingers digging into my ass cheeks for emphasis.

I couldn't lie; this was exactly what I had just foolishly agreed to. I nodded jerkily.

His grip on my cheeks tightened, and I whimpered as his short fingernails pressed half-moons into my sensitive flesh. "I didn't hear you," he said softly.

"Yes," I forced the word out, my voice unnaturally high and thin.

His hand was stroking me again, rewarding me. "Good girl," he praised. Something within me glowed at the words.

What was happening to me? I hardly recognized the wanton woman draped across this god-like man as myself. But all thoughts, all doubts, were driven from my mind at the first resounding blow.

Sharp, hot pain seared my flesh where his palm had landed hard on my ass. My shocked cry mingled with the loud crack as it echoed around the small room. But he didn't give me time to absorb the sensation. His hand came down on me again, harder this time. The stinging intensity took my breath away. I tried to move away from him, to avoid the next hit, but he held me firmly in place with his grip on my hair. A low, warning growl stilled my efforts instantly.

I shuddered, fear, pain, and pleasure intertwining in a heady cocktail that overwhelmed my senses, taking me to a place where no thoughts existed. There was only the sting on my flesh, the pulsing of my pussy, and his utter control. When the third blow landed, something halfway between a whimper and a sensual moan clawed its way up my throat, coming from somewhere deep and primal within me.

His fingernails traced a vertical trail across my burning flesh, starting at the tops of my thighs and stopping at the upper curve of my ass. My eyes rolled back in my head as pleasure shot through me, the sudden gentle touch on my abused flesh making my head swim. Then he lightly touched his forefinger to the little patch of skin where the crack of my ass met the base of my spine, tracing a small, circular pattern.

I cried out in shocked delight as he awoke a secret bundle of nerves that I had never before known existed. My clit pulsed almost painfully in response, desperate to be touched.

"Do you like this, Claudia?" He asked, a smirk in his voice as he continued torturing me sweetly, never breaking contact with that delicious erogenous zone.

I hesitated, pursing my lips. Wasn't it enough that he had made me verbally agree to this? Hadn't he embarrassed me enough, stripped away enough of my dignity?

"I don't know," I lied after a moment.

Then his fingers were at my inner thigh, swirling in the juices that coated it.

"You might lie to me, Claudia, but your body doesn't."

I closed my eyes and was unable to hold back a low whine. God, I needed him to touch me. My sex was on fire; surely the heat of it would burn me up if he didn't grant me some release. If only he would touch me where I needed it most...

A strangled moan escaped me as his forefingers drove into me in one swift movement, sliding easily through my slick folds until he was in me to the hilt. He paused for a moment, letting me adjust to the sudden intrusion. Then he slowly pressed his fingers apart, stretching me, filling me. My inner walls contracted around him as pleasure overwhelmed me. But he stopped his movements immediately, holding me there on the edge. I couldn't take any more.

"Please," I begged, letting go of the last shred of my pride. "Sean," his name was a desperate moan.

I was dimly aware of the low, satisfied groan that escaped him. "How can I deny you when you say my name so sweetly?" He asked huskily.

But I hardly registered his words. As he spoke, his fingers curled within me, stroking that sensitive spot inside of me. At the same time, his thumb came down on my clit, pressing hard against it.

I screamed as the most powerful orgasm of my life hit me, shattering me. My body thrashed across Sean's lap, but his fingers inside me pinned me in place as they continued to stroke me. Stars burst behind my closed eyelids, popping in my brain like fireworks as I came completely undone. White-hot bliss soared through me, searing my veins. My sex contracted around Sean's fingers, greedy for more. It was only when he had wrung the final delicious tremors from me that he finally slid out.

I lay there limply, trembling and gasping for breath. He turned me gently, hooking a strong arm around my back and pulling my torso up to press against his hard chest. I took a deep breath, drawing in his rich, masculine scent. His fingers touched my hair, stroking it tenderly back from my forehead before cupping my cheek in his large hand.

He was smiling down at me gently. I grinned back at him like a fool, reveling in the perfect moment. That had been the singular most amazing thing I had ever experienced in my entire life. And Sean had given it to me.

"Are you okay?" He asked gently.

Okay? I was more than okay. Amazing, actually.

But my brain took that moment to start re-forming after being blown apart by my orgasm. All of the delicious endorphins that had flooded my system dissipated as my rationality returned with cruel insistence.

What had I just allowed Sean to do to me? I had let him break me down, destroy my defenses. Hell, I had volunteered for it. I had allowed myself to be completely vulnerable to him. And I had loved every second of it. My head was spinning; I was so confused about what I felt towards him, about what I felt about myself. Who was I becoming? I didn't recognize this needy woman who sat compliantly in his lap.

Sean had been right before: this was so fucked up.

"I'm fine," I said quietly.

But he could sense my unease, and his expression suddenly shifted, his eyes clouding over and his face going blankly indifferent. Still, he didn't push me away from him, and I was grateful for that. As confused as I was, I didn't think I could handle the sting of rejection after what had just transpired between us. I was already on the verge of being an emotional wreck, and I was sure that that would push me over the edge.

The sound of the front door unlocking jolted me out of my tangled thoughts.

"Sean!" Bradley called out. "We have a visitor."

Relief washed through me as I realized that Bradley hadn't been in the apartment to hear my shameful wantonness.

Sean grasped my hips, quickly pulling me off of him before getting to his feet. He grabbed my wrist, jerking me upright. "Come on," he hissed. "And play along with what I say."

I glared at him indignantly to hide the hurt at his suddenly cold treatment. Without a word, I pulled up my panties and smoothed my dress down, making sure that I was covered before I allowed Sean to lead me out into the living room.

There was an older man standing beside Bradley. He had a thick head of grey hair, but his face was only lightly lined with wrinkles. His square jaw and defined cheekbones gave him a roguishly handsome air, making it difficult to pinpoint his exact age. I guessed he was in his mid to late forties.

Out of the corner of my eye, I saw Sean tense up at the sight of him. "Ronan." He said the man's name in a clipped tone, inclining his head only slightly.

But rather than returning the greeting, Ronan's keen eyes focused on me, the obvious disdain in them making me bristle. "Is this the reason you haven't been at work?" He demanded of Sean. "You've been too busy fucking your whore?"

Sean's expression turned livid, and he half-bared his teeth at the older man as he spoke. "She's not a whore," he ground out. "She's my girlfriend."

I opened my mouth to snap that I was neither of those things, but Sean shot me a warning look that told me I had better keep quiet if I knew what was good for me. I pursed my lips together, holding back the furious tirade that wanted to spill forth. I had no idea who this Ronan was, and there was clearly no love lost between him and Sean. He might prove more dangerous than Bradley if he found out why I was truly here.

Ronan looked at Sean levelly. "Then she's a whore. What other kind of woman would put up with your sick perversions?"

I felt my face flame red.

Whore. Was that what I was for letting Sean treat me the way he had? For enjoying it?

"What do you want, Ronan?" Sean asked, his voice carefully controlled.

"I want to know why the fuck you haven't been at work. And no more of this 'sick day' bullshit that Bradley keeps feeding me. I can see that you're fine."

Sean hesitated for a moment, reluctant to tell the man the truth.

Ronan's eyes narrowed. "Don't think you can lie to me, boy-o," he said threateningly. I registered that he had an Irish accent. It might have been appealing if the man himself weren't so repugnant.

"I was shot, okay?" Sean said finally.

The older man scowled. "When? And by whom?"

Sean eyed me, his expression anxious, as though he didn't want to answer in front of me. But why would that matter? If he didn't plan on letting me go, who was I going to tell?

"Tell me, boy!" Ronan barked.

Sean's attention snapped back to him, and the words flooded out of him, as though he couldn't resist the man's direct order. "Ten days ago," he said in a rush. "It was Santiago. The deal went south, and he pulled a gun."

I had guessed right; Sean had been committing a crime when he got shot. The reminder that he was a criminal made my gut twist. Somehow, my brain seemed to have conveniently forgotten that fact. But he hadn't revealed much, and I still didn't have a very clear picture of what had actually happened.

Ronan spat. "That little shit," he muttered. Then his attention turned back to Sean. "Seeing as you're not in jail right now, I take it you at least had the sense not to go to a hospital."

Bradley interjected quickly. "No, sir," he said. "She's a doctor." He jerked his head at me, seemingly unwilling to say my name. I hated how he referred to me in the third person right in front of my face. The jackass.

Ronan eyed me again, his gaze coming to rest on my bruised cheek. "I would think a doctor would have enough sense not to be with a man who beats her," he said rudely. He cocked his head at Sean. "Seems the apple didn't fall too far from the tree after all, did it, you little fucking hypocrite?"

Sean's face turned thunderous, and he took a step towards the man as his fists clenched. "I am nothing like you," he hissed. "I didn't do that."

Ronan squared his shoulders, suddenly seeming to grow taller. That same aura of power that Sean seemed to gather around him now surrounded the older man. "Are you going to try to fight me again, boy-o?" He asked, his voice gravelly, dangerous. "Your mother's not here to save you this time."

Sean's expression twisted into a furious snarl. "Get out, Dad," he growled.

Dad? This horrible man was Sean's father? I stared at him, taking in his chiseled features that were so like Sean's. And his eyes: that same deep, gorgeous green. It was horribly disconcerting to see Sean's eyes looking out of that malevolent face. I suddenly understood the curious lilt to Sean's accent that I loved so much; it had been infused with his father's Irish brogue.

The two men stared at one another for a long moment, years' worth of mutual hatred roiling between them.

"Listen," Bradley interjected in an effort to break the tension. "Everything's fine now, Ronan," he assured the older man. "Sean will be better soon, and then he can come back to work." He shot me a hard look. "Can't he, doc?"

"Yes, he should be fine," I said as coolly as I could manage.

Ronan's glare suddenly rounded on me, and I had to fight the urge to take a step back. "You had better not be lying, whore," he said threateningly.

I swallowed hard, forcing myself to hold his gaze.

"Fine," he snapped after a moment. He turned to Sean. "You have one week before I come back here and personally haul your ass in. Got that, boy?"

Sean nodded, a single, short jerk of the head. It seemed that was enough to satisfy Ronan. Barely. After sparing one last contemptuous glance at me, he let himself out of the apartment.

Bradley breathed out a relieved sigh before turning a scowl on Sean. "What were you thinking, antagonizing your old man like that? And for *her?* Do you realize what that could cost you? What it could cost me?" He shook his head angrily. "You really need to get your shit sorted out, man. I should have killed the bitch after she stitched you up."

"That's enough, Bradley," Sean snapped, still seething after facing off against his father.

Bradley looked at him disgustedly before stalking into his room, slamming the door behind him.

Sean was still standing stiffly, tension in every line of his body.

"Sean?" I said his name tentatively as I approached him. He didn't acknowledge me. He seemed lost in his own head; his eyes were stormy, full of fury and pain and grief. My hand reached out to him as though of its own accord, my fingers gently closing around his curled fist. He was trembling. His eyes didn't shift to me, but after a moment his hand relaxed, and his fingers entwined with mine. I tugged at him gently, leading him back to the bedroom. He followed, walking mechanically at my side. I pulled him down on the bed beside me and sat with him in silence for long minutes, tracing my thumb in little circles over the back of his hand.

After a while, he blinked. His gaze fell on our interlocked hands as though surprised to find me touching him. Then his eyes found mine. They were so lost.

"Claudia?" He said my name beseechingly. My heart twisted at the sound of it.

Chapter 9

I reached out for him, helplessly drawn to this beautiful, damaged man. I traced the line of his strong, square jaw, the roughness of his stubble lightly scraping at my fingertips. His eyes darkened, and he flinched away from me.

"Don't," he ordered softly.

"It's okay," I whispered soothingly, wanting nothing more than to ease the pain that marred his handsome features. I extended my hand towards him again, but his fingers instantly closed around my wrist, keeping me at bay.

"Don't touch me, Claudia," he said, almost angrily.

"Why?" I asked quietly, frustrated and hurt.

"*Why?*" He repeated, his expression tightening. His eyes speared me in place, and I was shocked to find something akin to anguish in their depths. "Because if you touch me, I won't be able to stop myself." His voice was low and rough, and his fingers gripped my wrist harder as his muscles went taut from some unseen strain.

The feeling of being caught by him, held in his strong grip, re-awoke the lust that seemed to constantly simmer within me when I was near him. I drew in a shaky breath. "What if I don't want you to stop yourself?" I breathed.

My stomach did a little flip as the full power of Sean's anger was unleashed upon me, the flames in his eyes burning me. The sensation of being caught up in it was terrifying. And darkly thrilling.

"Don't say that," he ground out. "I refuse to force you to take part in my... *sick perversions*." He repeated his father's words, hurling them out like a curse.

"*Force me?*" I hissed, my anger rising to meet his. "Do I seem like a woman who allows people to force her into things?"

Maybe seduced into things, I admitted to myself. *But never forced.*

Sean stared at me for a moment, incredulity bleeding into his furious glare. And there was a hint of wonder there too. "Fuck," he muttered, and I watched as he gave in to the lust that he had been working so hard to hold at bay. His muscles went from tense with restraint to gracefully supple, moving with the swift, hypnotic fluidity of a predator.

His hands were at the hem of my dress, ripping it out from under me and up over my head. He did it with such swiftness that my mind only processed what was happening when the cool air hit my naked skin. He swallowed my shocked gasp as he brought his lips down on mine. There was nothing slow or hesitant about his kiss this time. He sucked my lower lip into his mouth, tracing the line of it with his tongue before biting down hard. I moaned into him at the sharp pain of it, glorying in the way that it made my clit pulse in response. He pushed me back down onto the bed, never taking his hot mouth from mine.

My hands were roving over his hard body, finally exploring him as I had longed to do since I had first laid eyes on him. His arms were corded with the effort of holding his weight off of me, and I traced the contours of them, shuddering pleasurably as I fully realized his strength. I felt so small beneath him, utterly at his mercy. I craved more of him, and my hands snaked under his t-shirt as his tongue plundered my mouth.

My fingernails raked over the curves of his abs, pushing up his shirt for easier access.

Knowing what I wanted, Sean pulled it up over his head, flinging it away from him. Now that he had pulled back from me, I could finally look my fill, drink in all of him rather than stealing furtive glances from across the bed. He was glorious in his perfection, and a part of me was distantly amazed that he could possibly want me.

But that thought was driven from my head by the sight of the gauze wrapped around his arm. He leaned back into me, but I pressed my palm against his hard stomach, stopping him short.

"Your stitches…" I warned breathlessly, not wanting him to tear them open again.

But his eyes were dark, determined. "Fuck the stitches," he growled. "I want you, Claudia."

I shuddered, thrilling at his words. I wanted him too. More fiercely than I had ever wanted anything. In that moment, I didn't care about what this meant, about who I was becoming. All I cared about was having him inside of me, taking me to that place where nothing existed but his touch upon me, granting me the mental and physical release that I craved.

I fumbled at his jeans, hastily unzipping them. I couldn't wait for him to take them off. Instead, I reached inside his boxers, my hand touching his impressive erection for the first time. I grasped the hard length of it in my fist, stroking it from the base to the tip, exploring him as I pulled it free of his jeans. I marveled at the sight of it, momentarily entranced. My forefinger traced the line of his bulging vein, circled the purplish head of it before sliding across the bead of wetness at the tip.

Sean hissed in a sharp breath. "I won't allow you to tease me," he said, his voice low and gruff. "I control this fuck."

His hands were on my thighs, gripping them with almost bruising force as he jerked them roughly apart, opening me for him. He tore at my panties, pulling them down my thighs so that I was bare for him. His fingers slid into my soft curls and found the wetness at my heated core. My wrists were suddenly caught up in his strong grip as he let out a low growl. He pressed them into the mattress on either side of my head, and his eyes burned down into mine.

I let out a small whimper at the overwhelming intensity of his dominant gaze, but it turned into a shocked, delighted cry as he abruptly drove into me in one long, swift thrust. My arms jerked against his grip as I writhed beneath him, trying to adjust to the sudden large intrusion that stretched me so ruthlessly after years of emptiness. But he held me fast, his steely grip and his hard cock pinning me in place. He stayed utterly still for a moment, his face contorted with the effort of holding himself back. My pussy swelled, relaxing to accommodate him. I was ready for him now, desperate for the stimulation of him driving in and out of me. I tried to press my hips up into him, to move him inside of me.

He stared down at me forbiddingly, the ferocity of his expression instantly stilling my efforts. "What did I just tell you?" He asked harshly. "Who controls this fuck, Claudia?"

I quelled under him, my body trembling as I felt myself submit to him completely, ceding to his will. "You do," I whispered.

A twisted, triumphant smile spread across his face. He pulled his hips back, almost drawing out of me completely before driving into me to the hilt. The force of it made me gasp as he branded my body with the heat of him. "Your pussy is mine now, Claudia," he said roughly, driving home his possessive words with another harsh thrust. "Isn't it?" Another demanding thrust. "Tell me," he growled.

"Yes," I said breathlessly, almost delirious from the pleasure he was giving me. "I'm yours, Sean."

With a satisfied grunt, he began to take me in earnest, sliding in and out of me rapidly, driving all the way home with every powerful stroke. I moaned beneath him as ecstasy rippled through my core with every possessive thrust. My legs wrapped around his waist, inviting him further in. His cock hit my g-spot, and his hips ground against my clit as he moved within me.

"Sean!" I cried out his name as my orgasm hit me, my pussy contracting around him as I came. Bliss emanated out from my core, racing through my body from my belly to my fingertips, making my flesh tingle and burn as though flames were dancing across every inch of my skin.

But he continued to pump into me, his teeth gritted as he held himself back.

"Another," he ordered, his voice floating down to me through my bliss-induced haze.

I couldn't deny him. The power of his command and the continued stimulation of my sex drove me over the edge once again. This time, he came with me, throwing back his head and letting out a howl of satisfaction as he reached his own completion. His hot seed pumped into me, searing my insides as it lashed at me. I moaned in satisfaction at the sensation. Nothing had ever felt more right.

He collapsed atop me, breathing hard. But he didn't pull out. He stared down into my eyes as he stroked my hair, as though he was just as entranced by me as I was by him. His lips brushed against mine, gentle and sweet this time.

We stayed like that for a long time, our mouths gently moving against one another as he softened inside of me. My head was still swimming as I basked in my post-orgasmic glow, momentarily holding all of my self-doubt at bay.

But as Sean slid out of me, my mind began to whir back to unmerciful life. My first thought was concern at the fact that I had just had unprotected sex. Thank god I took a birth control shot to regulate my periods. But did Sean have any STDs? I knew that he was a playboy. Who knew how many women he had done this with?

That thought made me go cold. Was I just another woman in a long string of conquests? A convenient distraction while he was holed up in his apartment healing from his bullet wound?

I glanced at his bandages as he rolled off of me, propping himself up on one elbow. There was a small red stain blooming against the white gauze.

"You're hurt," I said softly.

He shot me a lazy grin. "It was worth it."

I couldn't help blushing, but I forced my voice to its usual controlled tone. "Let me patch you up."

He chuckled at me. "Already bossing me around again," he said, amused. "You bounce back quickly."

If only, I thought. If I truly was my normal self, I wouldn't feel so stripped bare in his presence, so confused about who I was now.

But I said nothing. I climbed out of bed, pulling up my panties and tugging my dress over my head to rid myself of the sense of vulnerability that suddenly struck me as I became acutely aware of my nakedness. Out of the corner of my eye, I saw him frowning slightly, and he tucked himself back into his jeans.

I could feel his gaze on me as I replaced the three stitches that had broken open, but I determinedly refused to look at him. When I finished, I sat down heavily on the bed beside him, staring blankly at the wall.

His thumb and forefinger gripped my chin, forcing me to turn and face him.

"What's going on in that head of yours?" He asked softly, anxiety evident in the lines around his eyes and mouth.

"I…" I began shakily, not wanting to share my fears, my self-doubt with him. He had already claimed so much of my identity, breaking down my walls to grasp at my soul. Could I bring myself to give him more?

"Are you really going to keep me here forever?" I asked finally, dreading his answer.

He smiled slightly, but his eyes were pained. "Right now, forever with you doesn't seem like such a bad fate."

Tears pooled in my eyes. "Please," I said, my voice ragged. "I can't stay trapped here for the rest of my life. I can't bear it."

I can't bear being around you any longer. But I couldn't bring myself to say the words aloud, to worsen the pain and hurt that I saw in his eyes.

His hand dropped from my face and his expression closed, his face schooled to blankness. "I'm sorry, Claudia," was all he said. He was no longer looking at me.

I stood quickly, desperate to put distance between us. A part of me hated the thought of leaving Sean, but my sane self was screaming at me that staying near him was more dangerous than staring down the barrel of Bradley's gun.

"I'm going to take a shower," I said softly, suddenly needing to wash away the evidence of our fierce, passionate coupling. Without waiting for an answer, I fled from him and into the refuge of the bathroom. It was only when the sound of the shower would mask the noise that I allowed myself to go to pieces. I slid down into the tub, hugging my knees to my chest as I cried.

I had been drawn to Sean from the first moment I had seen him, attracted to his beauty and his undeniably charming cocky demeanor. But it was the pain that I had glimpsed within him that had made me unable to resist him. When I had looked into his eyes after his confrontation with his father, so lost and alone… I knew that feeling, knew the unbearable weight of concealing such pain.

And then when we touched, he ignited such a fire within me, one that made me forget my internal anguish, granting me release from the burden of the agony that had scarred my soul… I couldn't resist the allure, couldn't resist *him.*

But in releasing me, he had broken me, and now my pain was exposed and raw. I was finally forced to face what I had held at bay for so many years. And it *hurt.*

He wasn't going to let me get away; he was going to trap me in my agony forever, exposing it every time he touched me. The high that I experienced when he seduced me only sent me crashing lower than ever before when I came down from it. I was becoming drawn to the ecstasy like a drug, going down a path of self-destruction through succumbing to addiction.

I had to escape, no matter what it took. I would never stop trying. I didn't care if Bradley decided to kill me; even that would provide me the release I so desperately needed.

Drawing several shaky breaths, I forced myself to stand. The water was going cold, and I needed to clean myself up. I almost fell apart all over again at the reminder of my coupling with Sean as I washed myself, the soreness within me summoning up the all-too-sharp memories. I swallowed back the urge.

As I reluctantly left the privacy of the bathroom, Bradley's furious voice boomed from Sean's room.

"I'm done playing nurse," he said coldly. "If you're well enough to fuck her, you're well enough to get your own goddamn food."

I stopped in my tracks, my gut twisting with shame. He had heard us. Of course he had heard. He had borne witness to my wanton cries, my utter submission to my captor.

"Why can't you see that she's manipulating you?" He continued angrily. "You're going soft. She's only fucking you to win you over. She's using you, man."

"Shut up, Bradley!" Sean's enraged roar made me take an involuntary step back. The power in it was terrifying. "Just get out. I can take care of myself. I don't need you anymore."

There was a moment of stunned silence. Then Bradley strode out of the room, storming towards me. He spat on the floor as he glared at me contemptuously. "This is all your fault, whore," he flung out the venomous accusation.

I wanted to return his baleful look, but the words struck too close to home. I dropped my eyes, shrinking away.

"I should have killed you when I had the chance," he said, his voice lowered so that Sean couldn't hear.

I jumped as his fist connected hard with the wall beside my head, my shocked gaze drawn to his. "Let that be a warning to you. Sean won't protect you forever. I'll make him see sense."

I couldn't suppress the tremor that ran through me, and I swallowed hard. We stared at one another, and for a moment, I thought he really was going to hit me. His face contorted with fury, he turned from me, flinging open the front door and then slamming it behind him.

Breathing a sigh of relief, I slowly made my way to Sean's room. He was lying on his back, staring up at the ceiling. His fists were clenched, and his face was tight with anger. I stopped in the doorway, unsure of what to say.

"It's not true," I finally said quietly. "I'm not using you."

He grimaced, still not looking at me. "I know," he said hollowly, but there was a thread of doubt in his tone. I couldn't help being hurt at the sound of it. Even the slightest hint of his suspicion cut me to the core.

"I've been thinking," he continued quietly. "I know that you want to leave. But you know that I can't let you go." His gaze finally flicked to me. "It must be miserable for you to be cooped up in here. It hasn't been so easy for me either." He hesitated, his eyes searching my face. "I want to take you outside. Then at least you won't feel so... trapped. I don't want you to be unhappy, Claudia." That touch of anguish, of shame, was back in his expression.

I'll be unhappy as long as I'm with you, I thought. But I didn't say it aloud. Going outside meant people, maybe a chance to escape.

"Okay," I breathed. "Thank you."

He smiled at me gently, that sweet smile that tugged at my heart.

Drawing on years of practice, I forced my walls all the way back up. I refused to let my feelings for him hold me back. I was getting away from him tomorrow. Resolved, I returned his smile.

• •

I lifted my face to the sun and breathed in deeply, relishing the scent of grass, damp earth, and the hint of asphalt. Sean had brought me to Central Park, and I couldn't help feeling a touch grateful towards him for bringing me somewhere with some greenery. And plenty of people.

I knew that I could scream for help, start making a scene. We even passed a police officer, but something held me back. As much as I wanted to get away, I couldn't bring myself to betray Sean, couldn't bear to cause him more pain. The last thing I wanted was for him to end up in jail. The idea of him hating me for doing that to him was unbearable. I would just have to find another way.

My eyes were drawn to the children who were happily playing in the park, beaming as they enjoyed a day out with their parents. I missed my work, missed making children smile every day. There was a steady stream of them headed towards the carousel, several of them practically skipping as they approached it.

The carousel. This was it. My way out.

I took Sean's hand in mine, and he looked down at our intertwined fingers in surprise. Giving him a gentle tug, I pulled him in the direction of the ride. "Come on," I said, smiling. "Let's go on the carousel."

He stared at me. "Seriously?" He asked. "Aren't you a little old for that?" But he began following my lead.

"Come on, old man," I teased. "What are you, scared?"

He chuckled at me. "I know you're trying to manipulate me, woman," he said, amused. "But I'll bite."

"Thanks," I beamed. My smile wasn't forced this time. My stomach fluttered in anticipation; I was almost free.

I tried to keep from bouncing on the balls of my feet as Sean paid the four dollar admission fee. He glanced over at me.

"You're really excited, aren't you?" He asked, smiling. It seemed my joy was infectious. If he only knew what was really making me happy, he wouldn't be so pleased.

I carefully tucked my dress beneath me before straddling a beautifully-crafted palomino horse. Sean mounted the whinnying white stallion beside me.

"Ready?" He grinned over at me.

"Yep," I said happily. But my gut twisted as guilt suddenly struck me. I forced it down.

The ride started, the carousel beginning to spin. Adrenaline began pumping through my veins as I waited to act. I let us run the circuit once, twice before making my move, hoping that Sean would be disoriented from the motion. Then I dismounted swiftly, jumping from the edge of the ride. I stumbled, almost falling as the world spun around me for a moment. But I had to move.

"Claudia!" I heard Sean call out to me as I began to run. I knew that I was making a scene. I felt the eyes of the crowd on me, but I didn't care.

"Claudia!" His voice was closer this time, and I redoubled my pace. I was going to have to find a policeman, after all.

But his long legs carried him faster than I could run, and he closed the distance between us within less than a minute. I swallowed back a scream of frustration as his hand closed around my upper arm.

"Claudia!" He said my name angrily. "What the fuck do you think you're doing?"

"Getting away from you!" I fought to keep from shouting hysterically. Too many people were watching us already, and I still couldn't bring myself to betray him.

"I can't let you leave me, Claudia," he said harshly. "You know that. Stop fighting me."

I twisted in his grip, and his fingers dug into my flesh. "Never," I hissed. "I will never stop fighting you, Sean. I will never stop trying to get away from you."

Angry, frustrated, desperate tears were streaming down my cheeks. Sean was staring at me, wide-eyed. "If you care about me at all..." I choked on the words. "If you feel anything like what I... Please," I begged. "I need my life back. I need *myself* back. I don't know who I am when I'm with you. I don't *like* who I am when I'm with you."

His hand dropped from my arm, his eyes clouded over with such an intense cocktail of emotions that I couldn't separate one from the other.

"Go," he said softly.

I sucked in a breath, incredulous.

His muscles tensed. "Go," he said more harshly. "Before I change my mind."

I obeyed his command, turning on my heel and walking away from him as quickly as possible. I didn't dare start running again lest it awaken the predator within him, goading him into pursuit.

I breathed deeply, but the scent of freedom didn't smell nearly as sweet as I had thought it would.

Chapter 10

I got a taxi to take me all the way back to Yonkers, paying the cab driver when I reached my house. Bradley still had my purse. And my phone too. I supposed I would have to buy a new one, and I would have to cancel my credit cards. Not to mention that I had no idea how I was going to get my car back.

I enumerated the mundane things that I needed to take care of in order to fill my head with something other than thoughts of Sean.

But he was impossible to banish from my mind. I lay awake for hours that night, unable to take comfort in the feeling of being back in my own bed. It felt cold and empty without Sean's reassuring warmth beside me.

I had never cried so much in my life, not since my parents had died. I cried in anguish, in anger, in hatred. Sean had broken me, and I couldn't forgive him for that. How could I have been so foolish as to give in to him? How could I have actually wanted him to take me, wanted him to *beat* me? Thinking back on it now, the memories didn't quite feel real. The thought of me submitting so completely, so meekly giving myself over to a man was so jarringly different from my normal self that I could hardly believe what I had let him do to me. The disparity between my two selves was made excruciatingly evident now that I was back in my own life. I had always loved the protection of my solitude. But not anymore. Now I felt empty, unfulfilled. And it was all *his* fault.

It was nearly three in the morning when sleep finally pulled me under. But my dreams were haunted by him: his fierce gaze, his cocky smile, his erotic touch. I felt far from rested when I awoke the next morning at seven AM.

I was going back to work today. Surely returning to my normal routine would help me rebuild my life, would allow me to gather up the pieces of myself and force them back together. Mechanically, I took a shower and got dressed, feeling oddly confined by my slacks and high-collared shirt. I pinned my hair back in its usual tidy bun, but it felt tight against my scalp.

This is who you are, I told myself firmly. *You are Dr. Claudia Ellers, not some little woman who lets a man dress her up as it pleases him.*

I was distracted from my thoughts when my doorbell rang. That must be the rental car service; I had ordered one the night before.

But when I pulled open the door, I found a sharply-dressed man wearing a pair of aviator sunglasses. He was tall, about six-foot-two. His strong jaw was clean-shaven and his dark blonde hair was carefully styled. He certainly didn't look like someone who worked for the rental car company. Peering around him, I saw only one black sedan parked in the street, with no U-Rent van in sight.

"Claudia Ellers?" The man asked, his voice a deep timbre.

"Yes," I replied hesitantly, utterly confused.

He reached into his pocket and pulled out a black leather wallet. He flipped it open to reveal a card with an official-looking stamp emblazoned upon it.

"I'm Agent Clayton Vaughn, FBI," he said in a brusque, business-like voice. "Can I come in?"

I blinked at him, taken aback. *FBI?* Could he possibly know about my abduction? I bit my lip, not wanting to tell him about Sean. But how could I refuse him without raising suspicion? I stepped back to admit him.

"Come in, Agent Vaughn," I said courteously. I led him over the foyer and into my living room, gesturing towards an armchair. "Please, have a seat," I invited as I positioned myself on the couch across from him, my back ramrod straight. "What can I help you with?" I asked as casually as I could manage once he had settled himself down.

"I'm here to ask you about Sean Reynolds," he said bluntly.

My heart sank. How could he possibly know?

"Oh?" I said, trying to keep my voice cool and steady.

He took off his sunglasses, and his light blue eyes regarded me seriously. "You were seen in Central Park with him yesterday," he said. "You seemed to have some kind of altercation. What were you fighting about?"

"It was nothing," I said quickly. "He's my boyfriend, and we just had a disagreement," I lied.

Agent Vaughn's brows drew together. "Your boyfriend?" He asked, clearly skeptical. "How does a well-respected doctor from Yonkers end up with a drug dealer for the Westies?"

My heart stopped. "What?" I asked faintly, my mind refusing to process what he had just said.

He looked at me sternly. "Are you telling me that you seriously didn't know about his criminal activities?" He said disbelievingly. "You were seen leaving the apartment that he shares with Bradley Smith. We've had them under surveillance for a week. And you were never seen entering the premises in that time. Do you honestly expect me to believe that you spent more than seven days in his home without suspecting anything?"

"Sean…" I choked on the words. "Sean is one of the Westics? He's in the Irish mob?"

It couldn't be true; this couldn't be happening.

But Agent Vaughn didn't let up. "I have to admit that I'm surprised at you, Dr. Ellers," he said reprovingly. "We know that your parents died as a result of mob violence. What are you doing with a man like Sean Reynolds?"

My head was spinning, and I couldn't seem to draw breath. My heart was shattering. My parents had been gunned down in the street for being in the wrong place at the wrong time. And Sean was a part of that world? How could I have let him touch me? How could I have ever felt anything for him other than disgust?

I hugged my arms around my stomach, suddenly feeling sick as the world blurred around me.

The sofa shifted beside me, and a large hand firmly stroked up and down my back. "Breathe," a deep voice ordered. I gasped, forcing air into my lungs before my panic could take me completely. The room began to materialize around me again as my breathing slowly returned to some semblance of a normal rhythm.

I glanced up to find Agent Vaughn looking at me pityingly. I hated that look.

"I'm sorry to have been the one to break the news to you," he said gently. "But I had to be sure."

I nodded numbly, my mind barely processing his words.

"Now that you know," he continued on. "Would you be willing to give us a statement about his activities? You may not have noticed anything suspicious, but there might have been some signs that you didn't pick up on." He looked at me earnestly. "You could be a great help to our investigation, Dr. Ellers."

I didn't answer; I was unable to formulate any words.

"After what happened to your parents, I would think that you would want to help us," he pressed.

The man was mercenary. It was too much. Everything was happening faster than I could process. And my pain was back, as keen and cutting as it had been on the night that I had found out that my parents were dead. Only now there was another layer of agony as I learned what Sean truly was.

"I would like it if you left now," I told Agent Vaughn coldly. I couldn't handle this, not when I was so desperately trying to put my life back together. I was tired of hurting, tired of hating myself. This stopped today.

He regarded me for a moment, his eyes searching my face. Finally, he stood. I walked him to the door, my movements stiff and jerky. He paused at the threshold, reaching into his pocket and pulling out a business card.

"In case you change your mind," he said. I took it from him automatically, just wanting him to go away.

My doorbell rang again, giving me the excuse that I needed to break eye contact. I pulled the door open gratefully, and Agent Vaughn silently stepped around the rental car deliveryman. I didn't watch him leave.

I signed the papers for the car blindly, hardly feeling the man pressing the keys into my hand. I almost fell apart all over again, but I wanted nothing more than to put off the moment when I would have to face this fresh agony. Maybe I would never have to, if I just made my walls strong enough. Resolutely, I pulled them back up as I walked out to my temporary car, ready to return to work and my real life.

Work passed by in a haze of cut knees and little coughs. My co-workers murmured condolences for my dead foster mom, and I forced myself to thank them for believing Bradley's lie that he had used to trap me. Every comment, every pitying look, was like a hammer blow to the walls around my heart, threatening to break through my resolve by reminding me of my captors. So I focused on what I loved most about my job: helping kids. But even my smiles at my little patients felt forced, and I couldn't quite grasp the joy that I usually did. I was expending too much effort trying to make myself numb.

I stayed in the office late, trying to catch up on the cases that I had missed. And using work as an excuse to put off the moment when I would find myself alone again. But eventually my eyes became bleary, and I could no longer force them to focus on the words in my files. I let out an involuntary yawn. It seemed that staying longer would be fruitless; it was time to go home.

My car was the only one left in the lot, and I walked to it slowly on leaden legs. I was so absorbed by my exhaustion that I didn't hear the man coming until he was on me.

My back slammed against the SUV, jarring me. I parted my lips to let out a shocked scream, but his hand was over my mouth, muffling my cry. He was wearing a black ski-mask, and all I could see were his cold aqua eyes.

"Are you Claudia Ellers?" He asked in a low, gravelly voice.

I didn't answer. How did he know my name?

There was a clicking sound and a flash of silver as he flicked out a switchblade.

"I won't ask you again," he said menacingly.

My eyes were wide and terrified as they focused on the knife. I nodded jerkily, too scared to lie to him.

Never taking his hand from my mouth, he slowly brought the knife up to my face. I tried to finch away, but he held me firmly as he pressed the flat of the blade against my cheek.

"I have a message for Sean Reynolds from the Latin Kings," he said coldly.

I whimpered as fear overwhelmed me. This man was going to hurt me, and I didn't understand why.

"Shhh," he said, leaning into me. "I'm not going to kill you, *chica*. I'm just going to cut you up a little."

He applied the lightest pressure, and I felt the blade's cruel edge make a long, shallow cut in my skin. I sobbed, but it didn't hurt much. Yet.

There was a savage growl and a large hand closed around the man's wrist, jerking the knife away from me. He tightened his grip, and my attacker cried out as the blade dropped from his hand, clattering to the asphalt. He was pulled from me, thrown to the ground. I heard his skull crack against the pavement.

My savior bent down, scooping up the knife before advancing on the man. Dropping to his knees beside him, he raised the blade high before driving it down into my attacker's shoulder. The man screamed, a high, piercing sound. But my savior wasn't satisfied. He twisted the knife cruelly, tearing at the man's flesh. Another scream rent through the silence of the night.

"Sean!" I cried, horrified by his actions. "Sean, stop!"

But he didn't seem to hear me. He reached out and ripped the mask over the man's head, revealing his identity. Even through his tanned skin, his face was pale and taut with pain.

"If I ever see your face again, you're a dead man," Sean snarled, fury rolling off of him in waves. "Understand?" He twisted the knife again for emphasis.

"Yes!" The tortured man cried out. "Yes! Please…"

"Sean!" I screamed his name this time. "Stop!"

His head swiveled to me, and his eyes honed in on the thin red line that marred my cheek. His face twisted into something savage and terrible. He wrenched the knife from the man's flesh and stood. Then he brought his foot down hard on my attacker's injured shoulder.

The man's broken cry made my stomach turn.

"Let him go, Sean!" I demanded shrilly, disgusted by his violence.

He turned to me again, his enraged, maddened eyes burning into mine. But I held his gaze, and slowly, his expression melted into one of concern.

He lifted his foot off of the bleeding man, who pushed himself upright and fled into the darkness, cradling his injured arm. But Sean didn't watch him go; he only had eyes for me now.

"Claudia," he said my name like a prayer, striding towards me.

I brought my hands up quickly, my palms facing out as though warding off a rabid animal. "Don't come near me," I said shakily.

He paused, confusion flooding his features. "Claudia, I-"

"Leave me alone, Sean!" I shrieked. "I know what you are!"

His brows drew together, suddenly angry. "You don't know anything, Claudia," he ground out, his hands clenching to fists.

"I know that I hate you!" I hurled the words at him. "I never want to see you again!"

His eyes went wide, stunned and hurt. But they quickly filled with ire once again

"Fine!" He snapped. "Next time I'll just let them torture you. Is that what you want?"

"It's your fault that I was attacked in the first place!" I shouted. "You're like poison, Sean. And I'm going to purge you from my life if it's the last thing I do." I clenched my jaw and lifted my chin defiantly.

His expression turned blank. "If that's what you want," he said coldly. "I won't be saving your life again. You're on your own now, just like you like it. Alone, isolated. Go back to your life of solitude that you love so much." He said the words harshly, and they tore at me as though he was driving the switchblade into my gut repeatedly.

I swallowed hard, but I refused to let the hurt show on my face. I stared at him, keeping my expression schooled to a hard mask.

Jerking his hand through his hair, he turned from me with a curse, striding away from me. I watched him until the darkness swallowed him up, fighting down the feeling of abandonment that was clawing at my heart.

Fumbling with the keys, I sought refuge in my car, locking the doors as soon as I was inside. I tried desperately to make my mind go blank, but the images of Sean torturing the man played in my mind over and over again.

That was his life; that was who he truly was. The cocky, sweet, sometimes vulnerable man who I thought I had been falling for was nothing but a hardened, heartless criminal. I shuddered at the memory of that horrible, twisted look of vindictive satisfaction on his face as he had made the man scream.

I came to a decision. I needed to get to a phone. Gripping the steering wheel hard to still my shaking hands, I drove home as fast as I could. I flung myself from the car and ran for my front door, scared that there might be more sadistic men waiting for me, lurking in the dark.

My chest was heaving as I locked the door behind me, adrenaline still pumping through my veins. Without allowing myself a chance to think twice about my decision, I grabbed up my landline phone, pulling the business card from my pocket as I did so. My fingers were trembling as I dialed the number, and I prayed that it wasn't too late for him to pick up his phone.

It only rang twice.

"Agent Vaughn," came his deep voice from the other end of the line.

"This is Claudia Ellers," I said in a rush. "I'm ready to talk to you about Bradley Smith and..." I hesitated for the briefest of moments, then forced out: "And Sean Reynolds."

It seemed that I was willing to betray him, after all.

The End

Traitor

Impossible #2

By Julia Sykes

Chapter 1

I sat ramrod straight in the cold metal chair, my fingers twisting together anxiously as I waited in the grey cinder-block room. A large mirror took up half of the wall to my left, and I could practically feel the eyes of Agent Clayton Vaughn watching me, staring through the glass from the other side. I took a deep, shaky breath to calm myself, telling myself for the umpteen-millionth time that I was doing the right thing. But Sean's face, haunted by the pain of his past, kept appearing in my mind's eye. I tried to shove it away, concentrating on the memory of his rictus snarl as he had ruthlessly twisted the knife in my attacker's chest, mercilessly mutilating his flesh.

To protect you, a small voice whispered in my mind.

But I shook it off. Sean was nothing but a criminal, a monster of a man to whom violence was second nature, deeply ingrained in his soul. Had his demanding, dominant touch on my body been a reflection of that ruthlessness that I had refused to fully contemplate beyond the satiation of my own lusts?

"You're on your own now, just like you like it. Alone, isolated. Go back to your life of solitude that you love so much." His words echoed in my mind, tearing at me like a knife to my gut. I had become so dependent on him in such a short time; the idea of retreating behind my walls again was more painful than I cared to admit to myself.

But not as painful as the realization that Sean was involved in the same criminal activity that had claimed my parent's lives. I hardened my heart, steeling my resolve.

Agent Vaughn joined me in the room, the door clicking shut behind him. He moved to a small video recorder in the corner and pressed a button, causing a red light to appear beside the lens. He was filming me.

When he sat in the chair across from me, his expression was kind, his light blue eyes regarding me softly.

"Don't worry, Dr. Ellers," he assured me. "This is a debriefing, not an interrogation. I just need you to answer my questions as thoroughly and as honestly as you can."

I glanced at the camera nervously, but I swallowed, nodding my understanding. Still, I couldn't fully force down the feeling of unease in the pit of my stomach.

"I need you to start at the beginning," he said directly. "How did you meet Bradley Smith and Sean Reynolds?"

I closed my eyes, unwilling to face the fresh pain of reliving the memories of terror. But I had to do this. If I could do anything to take a blow at the mobsters who plagued this city, then I would.

"It was thirteen days ago," I began quietly. "I left work for the night, and he… Bradley," I forced myself to say his hated name, "he was waiting for me in my car. He held a gun on me and forced me to drive to his apartment."

Agent Vaughn's brows rose in surprise. He hadn't been expecting that. "So you were abducted?" He asked.

"Yes," my voice was tremulous as the feelings of fear that had flooded my senses that night came crashing back down on me. I paused for a moment, overwhelmed.

"You're in a safe place now, Dr. Ellers," Agent Vaughn assured me. "Tell me what happened next."

I forced myself to stay in the present, to remain in the grey-walled room where I was surrounded by FBI agents.

"Sean had been shot," I continued finally. "He was bleeding out, and Bradley told me that he would kill me if I didn't save him."

But looking back, I knew that I would gladly do it again, even without being threatened. As much as Sean had hurt me, I couldn't bear the thought of him dead.

"So I did," I said. "But then…" I faltered. "Bradley was going to kill me anyway. Sean stopped him."

That memory pained me. It was when I had first begun to think of him as my savior, the beginning of his deception, of his manipulation of my mind.

"Why?" Agent Vaughn asked. "Why did he do that?"

Why did he?

But in my heart I knew the answer.

"Because Sean isn't a killer," I said softly.

Agent Vaughn's expression hardened. "He may not be a killer, but he has committed plenty of other offenses," he informed me harshly. "I know that you might feel indebted to him for keeping you alive, but I need you to see past that. Can you do that for me, Dr. Ellers?"

I knew that he was right. I had let Sean's protective act lure me in from the start, blinding me to his true nature. Hell, I had even let myself gloss over the fact that I knew he had been involved in some sort of crime when he got shot. God, I had been so stupid.

"He told me that I couldn't leave," I said, my voice growing stronger as it was tinged with anger at the memory of Sean's harsh refusals to let me go. "They kept me there for ten days," I skimmed over the details of what I had been doing during that time, unwilling to admit how stupid I had been to think that I was falling for Sean. "Then he took me to Central Park, wanted me to get outside."

Agent Vaughn was puzzled. "Why would he do that? Didn't he suspect that you would run?"

"I..." I couldn't hold back my blush, the shame that I knew filled my eyes. "I earned his trust. And then..." I took a deep breath, remembering the anguish in Sean's features as he had ordered me to leave him. "Then he let me go."

"How did you earn his trust?" He asked, pressing me. My face flamed crimson, giving me away. He speared me with a look. "Did you form some kind of relationship with him?"

Some kind of relationship. I knew what he was asking.

"Look," I said desperately. "I didn't know... I didn't know what he was. He protected me from Bradley. I thought he cared about me." I buried my face in my hands, pressing my palms against my eyes to hold back the tears.

"It's okay, Dr. Ellers," he said gently. "I understand. It would be very difficult in your situation not to feel that way."

My fingers twined in my hair, pulling at it. "I should have known better," I said in a broken voice. "I'm a doctor. I even suspected... But I ignored it. Why would I do that?" This time I couldn't hold back a sob.

I had allowed Sean into my heart, making myself vulnerable to him. How could I have done that when he was the last person in the world that I should have trusted?

"You were trapped with him for a prolonged period," Agent Vaughn tried to allay my distress. "And he showed you kindness when Bradley threatened you. He stood up to his friend on your behalf. It makes sense that that would mean something to you. You can't blame yourself. This wasn't your fault."

Wasn't it? Sure, Sean had made passes at me, and I had rebuffed him for days. But I was the one who had pulled him in for that first scorching kiss.

"I'm taking advantage of you, Claudia," Sean had said. *"And you're letting me."*

I just stared down at the table numbly, disgusted with myself. Agent Vaughn allowed me a moment of peace before pressing on. "I need to know, Dr. Ellers. Did either Bradley or Sean say anything about the crime they were committing when Sean was shot?"

I searched my mind. They had never revealed much in front of me, except for that one time. "Sean's father came to the apartment," I said quickly, remembering. "They told him about the shooting. Sean didn't say much but he did mention something about a deal going wrong."

"His father knew about the deal then? Ronan Reynolds?" He asked.

"It seemed like he did," I said, feeling a surge of vindictive pleasure at drawing the repugnant man into this, satisfaction filling me as I thought of getting back at him after how he had hurt Sean.

"Did he mention a name at all?" Agent Vaughn snatched me away from my tangled thoughts.

"Yes," I said, struggling to recall. "Santiago, I think."

He gave me a small smile. "That's good."

Something strange stirred in my gut. Would they be able to catch the man who had shot Sean based on my information? I found that, despite everything, a part of me wanted the man to pay for hurting him.

"Will you..." I began hesitantly. "Will you be able to find him?"

"We already know who he is," Agent Vaughn said. "He's one of ours. Santiago has been in deep cover with the Latin Kings for over a year now. But it's good that they trusted you enough to talk in front of you."

I was confused. Surely federal agents, even undercover federal agents, couldn't just go off shooting people?

"Oh," I said, somewhat dumbly. "Can he do that? Just shoot people when he wants to?" I was surprised to find that I was getting angry at this faceless man who had almost ended Sean's life with the full support of the law.

Agent Vaughn frowned at me. "The Westies – Sean and Bradley – shot first. It was self-defense."

My stomach dropped. So Sean really was a ruthless mobster who would go to any lengths to protect his precious drugs. I had just told Agent Vaughn that Sean wasn't a killer, but apparently it meant nothing to him to shoot another man. I again recalled his horrible snarl as he had tortured my assailant with his own switchblade. That was the real Sean Reynolds.

"Is there any other information you can give us?" Agent Vaughn cut through my dark thoughts. "Do you remember them saying anything else about their activities?"

I searched my mind, and all I found were memories of terror, pain, confusion, and lust. No, there was nothing else. All I had done was spend time skirting around Bradley and bantering with Sean. And fucking him. God, how could I have…?

"Dr. Ellers?" Agent Vaughn prompted me.

"No," I breathed. "Nothing." Then Sean's furious, twisted visage flitted across my brain again.

"Well…" I said hesitantly. "Sean did stab one of the Latin Kings last night."

Agent Vaughn's eyes widened slightly. "Oh? And how do you know that? I thought you said that he let you go the day before yesterday."

"He… He must have followed me," I said tremulously. "I was coming out of work, and… And a man attacked me." I gestured to the small cut across my cheek. "He knew my name. He said that he had a message for Sean from the Latin Kings. He…" I swallowed. "He was going to hurt me. But Sean was there. He stopped him."

Agent Vaughn eyed me levelly. "So Sean killed the man?" He asked.

"No!" I said quickly, hardly able to contemplate the thought of Sean murdering someone, despite all of the mounting evidence that he was fully capable of doing so. "No. But he did hurt him. Badly."

"Well, I'm glad that you're alright," Agent Vaughn said. "And I'm sure that having him save your life again must have made it that much harder for you to call me."

My resolve hardened. "That's *why* I called you," I said, unable to keep the disgust from my tone. "What he did to that man… It was terrible. That's when I knew… When I knew that he wasn't who I thought he was." I took a deep breath. "Sean is a dangerous man, and he shouldn't be out on the streets."

Agent Vaughn nodded in approval. "I couldn't agree more," he said. "I'll get some of our forensics team over to that parking lot to see if we can salvage some DNA evidence. Then we can start building a case against Sean Reynolds."

I swallowed hard at the thought of Sean in handcuffs. It seemed all wrong. And the orange jumpsuit. He might be sexy as hell, but it would clash horribly with his hair. Okay, so maybe I was getting jittery at what I was doing, my thoughts turning flighty in an effort to avoid the feeling of guilt that was growing in my gut.

"That's good," I said, but my voice sounded hollow in my own ears.

Agent Vaughn's eyes searched mine. "You're doing the right thing, Dr. Ellers," he assured me.

"I know," I said softly. My mind turned to Bradley. "And what about Bradley?" I asked, my voice hard. "Will he go to jail too?" I definitely had no qualms about putting that jackass behind bars.

"With your testimony, we have a good chance of putting him away for kidnapping and attempted murder." He paused. "But I won't lie to you; it will be hard to get a conviction without any physical evidence. We'll see if there are any surveillance cameras that caught your abduction, but I can't make any guarantees."

"Oh," I said faintly. The idea of Sean going to jail while Bradley stayed free made me feel sick. Sean didn't deserve that. Not when what his friend had done to me had been far more heinous. Not to mention if he found out that I was responsible for testifying against Sean but didn't put him away as well I would be in danger. Without Sean to keep him in check, who knew what Bradley would do to me? He had already classed me as "enemy" in his mind, removing his perceptions of my humanity. And the fact that Sean had defended me against him had only earned me his hatred, as though it was my fault that his best friend had turned against him. Bradley's loyalty to Sean ran so deep that it had perverted any sense of morality that he might have possessed. If my testimony sent Sean to prison, Bradley was sure to come after me. I shuddered. I couldn't think about that.

Agent Vaughn regarded me seriously. "There is a way that you could ensure that we had enough evidence against him to put him away for life," he said slowly, carefully. "In fact, with your help we might be able to take down the whole organization, get all of them off the streets."

"How?" I breathed. I wanted to do anything that I could to help bring that about.

"You resume your relationship with Sean Reynolds. You watch and wait, and report anything about their activities back to us. We haven't been able to plant anyone inside the Westies for years. This could be the opportunity we've been waiting for."

I gasped. "You... You want me to go back to him?" I could hardly comprehend what he was asking of me. "After

everything he put me through? You want me to resume my...
relationship with him?"

Did he really know what he was asking? For me to
whore myself out in order to take down the Westies? For me to
make myself vulnerable to Sean all over again? I didn't think
that I could survive that. Not with my soul intact. Nor my self-
respect.

He eyed me levelly. "I would never ask you to do
anything that you were uncomfortable with. You wouldn't have
to take the relationship to a level that you weren't comfortable
with. But if you could even resume a friendship with him, earn
his trust. You have no idea what that could mean for us. His
father is likely a linchpin in the organization. If we can get
enough evidence against him, the whole thing might come
crumbling down."

My eyes were wide, and I shook my head vehemently. "I
couldn't do that," I said, my voice high and thin. How could I be
anywhere near Sean and have a hope of resisting him? If I had
been stupid enough to fuck him when he was holding me captive,
how could I possibly imagine that I could resist his power over
me now?

Because you know what he is. Yes, I was disgusted by
him now that I knew his true nature. I would never be able to let
him touch me again considering what I now knew. Would I?

"This could be your chance to avenge your parents,"
Agent Vaughn said, relentless. "I know that that means
something to you, Dr. Ellers."

My heart twisted. Could I finally get closure after all this
time? Finally heal the scars on my soul that had pained me for
fourteen years?

"You can join the human race again," Sean had said. Now that he had taught me what it was like to feel, to connect again, I didn't know if I could face going back to my life of cold isolation. Yes, being so exposed hurt like a bitch, but it had also been incredibly freeing to be completely emotionally honest with another human being for the first time in years. God, Sean had fucked me in more ways than one.

"And," Agent Vaughn continued, "I would reopen your parent's case. I know that the cops never found their killer. I would personally help you hunt down the person responsible for their deaths."

My heart leapt. To know who was responsible, to finally make him pay for what he had done, for destroying my life… Could I turn away from that opportunity?

Why was Agent Vaughn doing this to me? Wasn't it enough that I had to wrestle with the turmoil of betraying Sean?

No. I couldn't do it; I wouldn't survive it. I knew that if I allowed myself near Sean, I would find myself in his grip once again. And I couldn't risk exposing myself to that.

I dropped my eyes, tearing myself from Agent Vaughn's intense blue gaze.

"I'm sorry," I said quietly. "I just can't do it."

There was a moment's pause. "Okay, Dr. Ellers," he said. "I understand. We'll need your statement against Bradley Smith, and then we'll see what evidence we can gather. At least we'll get two of these scumbags off the street."

Scumbags.

I thought of Sean's sweet green eyes. The word seemed so… wrong.

Chapter 2

I was barely keeping it together as I turned the key to get into my house. As soon as I found refuge inside, I would allow myself to fall apart. But not before. I had been holding it in ever since I had left Agent Vaughn, refusing to let the FBI see how torn up I was about my decision. I knew that they would find blood in the parking lot outside of my office; the man had been bleeding profusely. Despite what he had wanted to do to me, I still hoped that he had gotten some medical help. If he had survived, then Sean wasn't a killer. I couldn't bear the thought of him being a killer. Still, with that blood evidence, he might go to jail for attempted murder. How long they would put him away for that?

No. I didn't care. I didn't. Sean was dangerous, ruthless. He lived in a world steeped in violence, and he clearly embraced it. No matter how tender he had been towards me, no matter how many times he had protected me, I had seen his true nature. How long would it be before his heart hardened completely? Before he attacked innocent people for the sake of his stupid drugs?

Innocent people like my parents.

I locked the door behind me and leaned up against it for support, closing my eyes and pinching the bridge of my nose to stop the spinning in my head.

"You weren't at work today. Where were you, bitch?"

My heart skipped a beat, and my eyes flew open. No. He couldn't be here. Not in my safe haven.

"Bradley." My voice was several octaves higher than usual as I forced his name through my constricted throat. "What are you doing here? How did you get in?"

"You left your keys in your purse. Your address is listed online. It wasn't exactly hard to find you."

Fuck. Why hadn't I thought to change the locks? *Stupid stupid stupid!*

"Are you here to kill me?" I asked tremulously.

"Unfortunately, no," he said. "Don't think I haven't thought about it. But you've really fucked with Sean's head, and I'm not going to risk you causing further damage to our relationship."

Some of the tightness in my chest loosened. It seemed that Sean was saving my life again, even if he wasn't here. And I knew that he had honored my wishes to leave me alone; otherwise Bradley wouldn't be standing in my foyer.

He abandoned me. My heart squeezed at the thought. But that was what I wanted, what I had ordered him to do. It had been my choice.

"So where were you today?" He continued harshly. "If you went to the cops, I might just change my mind about killing you. It won't be by my hand, but someone else will gladly do it. If you can't testify, then you have nothing on me. And nothing on Sean."

"No!" I said quickly. "I took a personal day. I was attacked last night, in case Sean didn't tell you." I gestured to the small cut on my cheek to back up my story. "Is it so ludicrous that I didn't feel like going to work today?"

"Then where were you?" He asked, skeptical.

"With my foster brother," I lied. "I needed to be with family."

He eyed me suspiciously. "And why wouldn't you go to the cops?"

"Because…" I hesitated. "Because I couldn't do that to Sean, okay?" I turned a glare on him. "I might want you to rot in jail for what you did to me, but I couldn't do that without turning him in too."

There. A kernel of truth would make my story more believable.

His hands clenched to fists. "You expect me to believe that you actually care about him? You were just using him. You fucked him so that you could manipulate him into letting you go." I wasn't sure if his fury was entirely directed at me or his friend for betraying his trust. Sean had put Bradley at risk when he decided to let me go. And after Bradley had risked everything for his friend by abducting me in the first place, I could understand why he would feel such hatred towards me for turning Sean against him. But understanding it didn't make his presence in my home any less terrifying. I had to remain calm if I was going to talk my way out of this.

"No," I said staunchly. "Believe what you want, but if I had gone to the cops, wouldn't I have a security detail on me right now? Wouldn't I be dialing 911?"

I wondered briefly why I hadn't been given a security detail. I was going to have to take that up with Agent Vaughn.

Bradley regarded me for a moment. "Fine," he barked. "But don't even think about changing your mind. You'll be dead if the cops come for us. And then we'll be freed anyway. They have no evidence against us without you. So understand that your life is over if you even think about turning us in."

I swallowed hard and nodded vigorously. "I understand," I said quickly. It seemed I was going to have to demand a security detail before the FBI went after Bradley and Sean. I hesitated. "But leave my keys here. I never want to see your face again. If I do, I will go to the police, regardless of the consequences."

He fixed me with a hard stare, but I raised my chin and met his glare defiantly.

"You always were too mouthy for your own good, you stupid bitch," he said. But he reached in his pocket and dropped my keys on the floor.

I heaved a small sigh of relief. Regardless, I would get my locks changed first thing in the morning. But at least this way he couldn't sneak back in tonight if he changed his mind.

I opened the door. "You said what you came here to say. Now get out of my house," I demanded. I knew that I was playing with fire, but I needed him to get away from me.

He glared at me, but mercifully he stalked out, all of his muscles tensed with suppressed violence. I slammed the door behind him, sliding the lock home. I walked into my living room on leaden legs, falling back onto my couch in a heap. Adrenaline pumped through me, making me feel light-headed.

What if Bradley found out that I had gone to the FBI? I knew that he hadn't been lying; if he and Sean were arrested, someone else in their organization would come for me. What were my options? Have the FBI protect me indefinitely? Go into witness protection? I didn't want that. I didn't want to have to abandon my life and start over.

There was nothing for it: if I wanted to protect myself, I was going to have to take down the Westies. No matter what it took. Could I make myself vulnerable to Sean once again in order to make that happen? Did I value my life enough to put myself in that position?

Yes. I would just have to resist him. I could have a relationship with him without having a *relationship* with him. It was my only choice. Not to mention that I would finally be able to avenge my parents, possibly discover who was responsible for their murders and put him away for life. The determination to take action restored my sense of control that had abandoned me on the night that I had been abducted. My captors had robbed me of my free will, and Sean had slowly chipped away at the little vestiges of self-control that I had left. He hadn't done it out of malice, but that didn't change the fact that he had shaped me into a woman that I barely recognized. I used to be self-assured. I didn't need anyone or anything in my life other than my work. Within a matter of days, Sean had me begging for him to touch me, leaving me feeling so much more than just physically vulnerable.

Bradley didn't know that he had just sealed his own fate. I hadn't failed to notice how he had been so quick to defer to Ronan, how he had accused Sean of putting his position at risk by challenging his father. Bradley's ambition to rise in the mob, to protect his compatriots, would be the very thing that would bring them all down. I was suffused with a grim sense of satisfaction at the idea. The only way he would be able to protect himself from retribution from his buddies in prison would be a lifetime of solitary confinement.

I reached into my purse and pulled out the cell phone that Agent Vaughn had given me so that they could track me through GPS at any time. I dialed.

"Vaughn," he answered simply.

I took a deep breath. "This is Dr. Ellers," I said. "I want to do it. I want to take down the Westies."

- -

My stomach was in knots the following evening as I slowly walked down the damp-ridden corridor that led to Sean's apartment. I paused when I reached his door. Could I bring myself to enter this dreaded place again? When it had taken everything within me to escape from it? What if he wouldn't let me leave?

I had to take the chance. I didn't have another choice. I would never be able to rebuild my life, my sense of self, until I had taken action against the Westies. Long years of allowing my foster brother Marcus to intimidate me had left me more determined than ever that I would never again allow fear of any man to rule my life. Hardening my resolve, I knocked sharply on the door.

My chest tightened when Bradley opened it. His face twisted into a snarl.

"What are you doing here?" He demanded angrily.

"I…" I began faintly. I gathered up my courage, forcing my voice to harden. "I came to see Sean."

Bradley spat. "Get the fuck out."

"No," I said resolutely. "Not until I see him."

"Claudia?" His deep voice, with that delicious lilt when he said my name, sent a shiver down my spine. His gorgeous green eyes were wide and disbelieving as he appeared behind Bradley's shoulder. My heart fluttered in my chest when his gaze met mine.

"Get the fuck out of the way, Bradley," he demanded. His friend didn't move. Sean's hand closed around his shoulder and shoved him aside.

Bradley growled. "Are you fucking serious, Sean?" He asked angrily. "Why would she come back here after working so hard to mindfuck you into letting her go? If you care about saving either of our skins, you'll kick her ass out."

Sean tore his eyes from mine, pinning his friend with a level stare. "This is none of your business, Bradley," he said, his voice tense.

"Fuck you both," Bradley said sharply. "You've lost your goddamn mind, Sean. Let me know when you're ready to stop thinking with your dick." He shoved past me, bumping my shoulder hard as he stalked out of the apartment. Sean's mouth was a hard line as he glared after his friend.

But his attention quickly returned to me, his eyes drawn to mine as though by a magnet. My breath caught in my throat. Had I really forgotten how stunning he was in my short time away from him? I had been so fixated on the image of his face twisted in fury that I was struck by his perfection all over again as he looked down at me in wonder. I found myself staring up at the man who had tugged at my heartstrings. He was so much more complex than I had allowed myself to recall. His cocky arrogance was charming, but underneath that façade was a man who was deeply passionate about everything, be it discussing a book, defending my life, or setting my body on fire.

"Hi," I breathed, stupidly.

His lips quirked up at the corners. "Hi yourself," he said. He reached out and took my hand as though he couldn't help himself. I wanted to jerk away, but one touch of his skin against mine and I knew that I was lost. I couldn't resist the allure of that delicious feeling of sparks dancing over my flesh. Nor could I fight the pull of the unadulterated joy that lit up his handsome features. No matter what Sean was, he cared about me deeply. And I couldn't deny the answering joy that arose in myself at the sight of him. When I was away from him, I felt torn, conflicted, raw. I had been desperate to escape him because the intensity of my unbridled emotions that he elicited terrified me. But when I was caught up in him like this, the tangled thoughts that tortured me so mercilessly quieted. It was disturbing how *right* it felt to be back in his presence.

He pulled my hand, drawing my body up against his. His arms wrapped around me, holding me tightly to him. I stood stiffly for a moment, trying desperately to fight his magnetism. But his scent surrounded me, enfolding me. Before I knew what was happening, my arms were around him as well, and I buried my face in his chest, breathing him in.

Safe.

"I thought I would never see you again," he said, his voice low and rough.

"Me too," I said softly.

He ran his hand through my hair, grasping a fistful of it at my nape. He pulled back gently, forcing me to face him. But I couldn't meet his eyes. I knew that I would break if I did.

He tugged more sharply on my hair. "Look at me, Claudia."

I couldn't resist his direct order. My breath caught in my throat as our eyes met, and I froze under his steady gaze. He held me in place, his strong arm around my back, and he began to slowly, tentatively, lean into me.

My breathing turned shallow, and my pulse raced through my veins. I was trapped, a bird held captive by the eyes of a snake. He was going to devour me. I felt a stirring in my loins at the prospect, and my lips parted for him.

No! My rational mind screamed at me. *Don't do this, Claudia.* In a moment of clarity, I knew that I would never be able to escape him if I allowed his mouth to take mine. His erotic touch would obliterate all thoughts of resisting him, and I had to maintain my distance if I was going to betray him.

God, what I was doing to him was so wrong. But being in his arms felt so right. I didn't want him to stop touching me, but I didn't want to lead him on when I was pulling him towards his own destruction. His kiss would destroy *me*.

"Don't," I said, but my voice was husky and lacked conviction. His lips twisted up at the corners in that beautifully cruel, knowing smile, and he continued his agonizingly slow approach.

"Please," I begged, desperation lacing my tone. "Sean, don't."

He paused, his brow furrowing. "Why?"

"I'm not…" I swallowed. "I just can't. Please."

His face was suddenly schooled into a blank mask, and he released me abruptly. There was a pang in my heart at the loss of the heat of him. But I fought to match his unconcerned expression. I couldn't show any further weakness. Otherwise I wouldn't survive this.

"Can we talk?" I asked softly.

"Sure," he said calmly, as though it was of no consequence to him. He stepped back, silently inviting me in. I skirted past him, careful not to touch him as I entered. My eyes were instantly drawn to his bedroom, and memories of our time together flashed across my mind: our quiet companionship, my confessions about my past, the discovery of the electric connection between us that I was helpless to resist.

"Right now, forever with you doesn't seem like such a bad fate."

He had said that after our wild, passionate sex. And I had craved to believe it. But it was more than I could handle; the thought of being trapped in his grip was too... tempting. And I knew that if I hadn't escaped, I would have lost the will to leave him.

Yet here I was, falling into his arms all over again. I had to keep my distance; I couldn't succumb to him again.

I tore my eyes from the bedroom and settled myself down on the couch. Sean joined me, but mercifully he sat as far away as possible, giving me space to breathe.

"What are you doing here, Claudia?" He asked, his voice detached.

"I..." I braced myself for the lie, but deep down I knew that it was the truth. "I couldn't stay away."

His expression hardened. "You told me that you never wanted to see me again. You told me that you hated me." His eyes blazed with anger, but there was a hint of pain there as well.

I dropped my eyes. "I'm sorry," I said quietly. "I was scared." My gaze flicked up to his. "*You* scare me. What I feel for you scares me. I haven't felt... I haven't felt anything for anyone in years."

His face twisted in anguish. "I don't want you to be afraid of me, Claudia. I would never hurt you. I would never let anything happen to you."

"I know," I said, my voice breaking. Again I recognized the truth. "But now I know what you are. You're... you're involved with bad people. Why else would that man have attacked me? He said he was a member of the Latin Kings, Sean. He wanted to hurt me to get to you. How could I not be scared?"

His eyes were filled with pain, with regret. "I never wanted you to know," he said. "You don't understand."

"Then explain it to me," I pressed gently.

"I can't," he said, aggrieved. "I can't tell you any more. It will only put you in more danger."

"Please," I said. "I want to know. I want to understand."

"Just know that I can't help what I am. I never asked for this." His voice was strained. "And now it's too late for me." He speared me with a sincere gaze. "I'm sorry. I can't tell you any more than that."

I took a deep breath, knowing that I wouldn't get anything further out of him. And although I knew that my task was to find out more about his organization through pulling information out of him, a part of me didn't want to know. If I heard it from his own lips, I wasn't sure if I would be able to hold back. I would confess the full pain my past, breaking down and telling about my parents. Then I would beg him to stop, to change. To take the risk for me.

But I knew that I couldn't do that. I had to stick to my plan, regardless of my feelings for him. I would never be whole otherwise.

Is that what you were before you met Sean? Whole? Yes, before my abduction I had my life together and my emotions carefully in check, but I had been hollow inside. The joy within me had died along with my parents. And the callousness of my foster mom and cruelty of my foster brother had taught me that existing in a state of cool, controlled detachment was far less painful than being hurt repeatedly by the people closest to you.

Being close to Sean hadn't healed me, no matter how sweet our moments of intimacy were. I wasn't whole; I was a mess. I had to regain my sense of control over myself if I was going to survive life after Sean Reynolds, and that entailed bringing him to justice along with the rest of the Westies.

You're doing the right thing, I assured myself again.

It was time for me to set the parameters of our relationship. I couldn't resume anything physical with Sean, I knew that much. But I couldn't stay away from him either, not if I was going to keep my promise to the FBI. Not if I was going to avenge my parents.

"Okay," I agreed, deciding that now was not the time to press him for more information about his involvement with the Irish Mob. "That's okay. You'll tell me when you're ready."

"Claudia, I can't -" He began, but I cut him off, holding up my hand.

"I want to know you better, Sean," I said. "I… I want to keep seeing you."

His eyes lit up, and he reached out for me. But I quickly pulled away from him.

"But not in that way," I said quietly. "I can't handle that. Not right now. I'm so confused about how I feel about you. Can we start at the beginning again? Take things slow?"

He moved away from me reluctantly. "Alright," he conceded softly. "I can understand that. We'll go as slow as you want. I won't scare you off again," he promised. "I won't lose you again."

Oh, Sean, you've already lost me, I thought, my gut twisting.

"Thank you," I said instead.

"But if we're going to be seeing each other, I'll need to protect you. I can't risk anyone coming after you again."

No. I couldn't have him following me. Then he would find out that I was working with the FBI, and everything would be ruined.

"No, Sean," I said firmly. "I need some space. I still want to see you; I can't stay away. But I'm not ready for that. I can't be with you all the time."

His face fell. "But you won't be safe," he insisted. "Please, Claudia -"

"This isn't up for debate," I said. "I'll carry mace. I'll take self-defense classes. I can protect myself."

He frowned, anger flooding his features. "Why are you so goddamn stubborn?" He demanded. "You're taking your life into your own hands. I won't allow you to do that."

I shot him a cold look. "You *won't allow* me?" It was my turn to be angry. "I'm not negotiating on this, Sean. I need my independence. I refuse to be completely dependent on you. Don't you understand that that makes me feel trapped? I might as well be your prisoner again if you do this to me."

He looked as though I had slapped him. Then his face darkened. "Fine," he said after a moment. "If that's how you want it to be."

I breathed out a small sigh of relief.

He stood abruptly, stalking across the room to a table set by the front door. He opened the drawer set into it sharply and pulled out a revolver. It was Bradley's gun.

"What are you doing?" I asked, my voice high and thin. I knew that he wouldn't hurt me, but was he going to threaten me, to try to force me to stay here again? I trembled, panicking at the thought.

His expression softened. "Don't worry, Claudia," he said, his tone soothing. He proffered the gun to me, and I recoiled. "Take it," he ordered.

"No!" I protested, alarmed. I hated guns. After what had happened to my parents and how Bradley had threatened to end my life, the idea of touching one made my stomach turn.

Sean's face hardened, his expression forbidding. "This isn't up for negotiation," he said, echoing my words. "If you won't let me protect you, then I'm not leaving you without a weapon. Do you really think mace will be enough if someone pulls a gun on you? I don't care if you become a master kick-boxer, there's no way you can stop a bullet."

I stared at the revolver, wide-eyed. "I can't," I insisted, my voice tremulous.

He glared at me, that aura of dominance, of power, surrounding him. "You can and you will. Either you carry this or I'm going to shadow your every move. Do you understand?"

"Fine!" I snapped, realizing that I had no choice in this. But my fingers shook as I took it from him.

He smiled down at me, satisfied with his victory. "Good girl," he said.

A shiver ran down my spine as I thought of the last time he had praised me like that, after he had punished me, breaking down all my defenses, setting me free from the constant weight of keeping up my walls…

I leapt up from my seat. I needed to get out of here, to escape from the erotic memories that surrounded me in this place. "I have to go," I said, trying to keep the panic from my voice.

He frowned. "Why?"

"I just do," I said, tucking the gun into my purse.

"Okay," he said reluctantly. "When will I see you again?"

"I'm not sure," I said. How long until I succumbed to his draw again? "Soon," I admitted.

He stood, taking a step towards me. I backed away quickly. "I'll call you," I promised.

"You don't have my number," he said.

"Oh, um, yeah." I pulled out my phone and handed it to him.

He quickly added himself to my contacts, a small smirk on his face. When he passed it back to me, the smirk stayed in place as he intentionally brushed his fingers against mine. That familiar heat shot straight from my fingertips to my sex. I jerked my hand away, disconcerted.

"Bye," I said quickly, turning away from him. I half-ran to the door. As I shut it behind me, I could have sworn I heard him chuckling.

The cocky, sexy bastard.

Chapter 3

After work the next day, I found myself pulling into the parking garage at the office building where the FBI's office was discretely located. This one wasn't publically listed, so I was more protected from the Westies finding out what I was up to. Even though Sean had promised not to tail me, that didn't mean that Bradley wasn't going to.

Agent Vaughn met me in the elevator, and he swiped a key card that allowed us access to the correct floor. We rode up in silence; I wanted to put off the moment that I would have to talk to him about what had transpired between Sean and me. About how I had almost let him kiss me.

"Just know that I can't help what I am. I never asked for this."

Sean's words echoed in my head. I had been turning them over carefully in my mind as I wrestled with what I planned to do to him. If what he said was true, then the fact that I was using him was just that much more wrong. There had to be a way that I could take a blow at the Westies and spare Sean. After seeing him again, I was more convinced than ever that he was a good person. He certainly didn't deserve to be punished as Bradley did. Sean had a moral compass, whereas Bradley was a loose cannon. He was willing to hurt innocent people in order to get what he wanted. He was the one who needed to be locked up, not Sean. Maybe I could negotiate a deal for Sean in exchange for my information?

What information?

I hadn't learned anything from Sean, and it seemed that he was determined to remain tight-lipped around me.

Agent Vaughn took me to that grey-walled room again, and I shuddered as I entered. Despite his assurances that he was only debriefing me, it sure as hell felt like an interrogation when he turned on that camera.

He noticed how stiffly I was sitting in the metal chair.

"Take a deep breath, Dr. Ellers," he said gently. "You're safe here."

I did as he bade me, but I still couldn't stop my hands from twisting in my lap.

"We know that you went to see Sean," he said. "We still have his apartment under surveillance. What happened?"

"I… We…" I swallowed hard. "Nothing much," I hedged. What was I going to say? That I was still hopelessly attracted to him? That he refused to tell me anything about the Westies?

Agent Vaughn's brow creased. "You were there for twenty minutes," he said. "You must have talked about something. Unless…"

He trailed off. *Unless you were fucking him.*

"No!" I said quickly. "Okay, we talked. But he wouldn't tell me anything. He didn't even mention the Westies. But he did say that he didn't want to be a part of that world. It sounded like he had been forced into it."

Agent Vaughn frowned. "You do realize that he could just be saying that because he doesn't want you to know the truth?" He asked harshly.

I frowned right back at him. "I don't think so," I said staunchly.

"You don't want to think so," he said ruthlessly.

I glared at him. "Sean is a good person," I insisted. "I know it."

"Does a good person deal drugs? Does a good person torture someone with a switchblade? We found the blood in the parking lot. There was a lot of it. You're letting your feelings cloud your judgment, Dr. Ellers."

I bit my lip as I remembered the man's terrible screams. Why was Agent Vaughn making me doubt myself like this? Why was he making me doubt Sean?

He pierced me with a hard stare. After a moment, I hung my head.

"Maybe you're right," I said quietly.

"I know that it's hard to swallow," Agent Vaughn's voice was gentler this time. "But I need you to stay focused. Can you do that for me, Dr. Ellers?"

I nodded glumly.

"Was there anything else? Anything at all?" He pressed.

"He wanted to follow me in order to keep me safe," I admitted. "But I knew that I couldn't let him do that if I didn't want him to find out about me meeting with you. I made him promise to stay away. So he gave me a gun."

Agent Vaughn regarded me for a moment. "That's not a bad idea, actually," he said. "You need to be able to protect yourself."

I shook my head. "I could never use it. I only took it to make him back down."

His expression hardened. "Taking another life is hard to deal with. I know that." His jaw tightened; he really did understand that. I wondered briefly who he had killed and why. "But if it comes down to you or them, I want you to choose yourself. Promise me," he demanded.

I balked. I didn't think I could ever do that, no matter the circumstances. But I nodded, agreeing just so that he would drop the subject.

"Did anything else happen?" Agent Vaughn moved on.

I thought for a moment. I wasn't about to tell him about my lingering attraction to Sean. And Sean hadn't revealed anything else to me anyway.

"I don't think that Sean will ever tell me anything about the Westies," I said hollowly. "He doesn't want me to know."

Agent Vaughn appeared unconcerned. "Don't worry about that," he assured me. "He might slip up. And you can learn things just from watching him, even if he doesn't say anything." He fixed me with a piercing stare. "I need to know that you are with us on this, Dr. Ellers."

I said nothing for a long moment.

"Listen," he said, cajoling, "If Sean really has been forced into this, then this is the only way we'll find out. I might be able to lessen his sentence if it turns out that he had no other choice."

I peeked up at him. Could I trust him to keep his word? I had already condemned Sean by confessing about his assault on the rival gang member. Maybe if I could prove that he truly didn't have a way out, they would be more lenient on him?

"Would you really do that?" I asked hoarsely. "You'll help Sean?"

I held my breath. Everything hung on his answer. I wasn't at all sure that I could do this if I knew that I was condemning Sean with every word he spoke to me. If there was some chance that I could lessen the sentence that he faced, then I might not hate myself so much for deceiving him.

Agent Vaughn looked at me levelly. "If he really has been coerced, then I promise that I'll do everything I can to help him."

Some of the tension in my chest eased. "Okay," I said. "Then I'll do this."

"Thank you, Dr. Ellers," he said sincerely. "You have no idea how much this means to us, how important you are." He paused for a moment, then pressed me again. "Is that all that happened?"

I thought over what Sean and I had talked about. We had agreed to end our sexual relationship. But that was none of Agent Vaughn's business.

"Yes," I confirmed, nodding decisively.

"We saw Bradley Smith leaving the building shortly after you arrived. Did he say anything to you?"

Bradley.

"He was his usual dickish self," I said, a thread of anger tingeing my voice. "He and Sean had a bit of an altercation over my being there, but Sean forced him to back off."

Agent Vaughn cocked his head, considering. "So you're driving a wedge between them. That might not be for the best. You could learn just as much from Bradley as you could from Sean. Do you think it would be possible to turn him around?"

"No," I said definitively. "Not in a million years. He hates me. And the feeling is mutual," I added. "In fact, he came to my house the night before last and threatened to kill me if I went to the cops. So, no. We aren't going to buddy up any time soon."

"Shit," Agent Vaughn cursed under his breath. "We should have put a security detail on you."

I looked at him coldly. "Yes, you should have. But I managed to talk him out of it. It seems that he won't risk pissing Sean off by hurting me." I sighed. "Besides, if you had arrested him, then this whole thing would have been blown and I wouldn't have to opportunity to spy on the Westies."

He regarded me seriously. "You're a brave woman, Dr. Ellers," he said.

"No," I countered. "I'm just getting used to being threatened. And frankly, I'm finding it more annoying than terrifying by now."

Agent Vaughn surprised me by chuckling. I had never imagined that he was capable of laughter; he always seemed so serious. "Then heaven help the Westies," he smiled. "If anyone can do this, it's you," he assured me.

His faith in me bolstered my resolve. Not only would I take them down, but I would exonerate Sean in the process. I *was* doing the right thing. And for the first time, it didn't feel like I was lying to myself.

"Now," he continued, his expression sobering. "I believe I promised you that I would help you track down your parents' killer."

Hope welled within me. To finally know, after so many years...

"Yes," I said eagerly.

He smiled broadly, revealing his perfect white teeth. I couldn't deny that the effect was momentarily stunning. He had all-American good looks, with his strong, clean-shaven jaw, bright blue eyes, and perfectly styled dark blonde hair. I decided that I liked it when he smiled. This man was far more approachable that the mercenary FBI agent who had questioned me relentlessly.

"Come on," he said. "We're done in here. Let's go somewhere more informal to talk. Do you like Chinese food?"

I returned his smile easily. "Yeah, sounds good."

A few minutes later, we were sitting in his office, waiting for his co-worker to go on a food run to the nearby Chinese restaurant. Since I rarely cooked, I was no stranger to frozen dinners, and I only got take-out as a special treat. Chicken lo-mein was one of my favorites.

"I pulled your parents' case file," Agent Vaughn said, sliding a manila folder across his desk. I hesitated, unwilling to open it. I wasn't sure if I could face it.

"Don't worry," he said gently. "I've removed the crime scene photos."

I stared at the folder for a moment, then I shook my head. The cold, clinical reports that I would find inside were too terrible to face. "I can't," I said tremulously. "Just tell me what it says."

"Okay," he said, a strange note in his voice warning me to brace myself. "They were both shot in the heart at close range. They died instantly."

I flinched at hearing the horrible reality of it. I hadn't spoken to anyone about my parents since the night they had died. Not even Sean. All I had told him and Bradley was that they were dead, but I had lied and said that it had been a car crash that claimed their lives.

I had lost everything on the night that they were so violently ripped from me. My parents had been loving, doting. I was their only child, and perhaps I was a bit spoiled. My father had a good job, and I had never wanted for anything. I was naïve back then. It had never occurred to me what a charmed life I led until it was abruptly gone. I was plucked out of my comfortable existence when I was assigned to live in the Ames household. I didn't know anyone at my new school, and Marcus had been sure to scare off anyone who thought about befriending me. At thirteen, I hadn't known anything about the world or about the changes I would go through as I grew into a woman. My foster mom, Darla, hadn't been any help there.

Whoever it was who had murdered my parents hadn't just taken them from me; their killer had robbed me of the happy life that should have been mine.

"They didn't suffer," Agent Vaughn assured me.

I blinked back the tears that were stinging the corners of my eyes. Was that supposed to be a comfort to me? Not that I wanted them to have suffered, but they shouldn't be dead in the first place. And what about my suffering? What about the long years that I had spent with my foster family, with Marcus hurting me...?

No. I couldn't think about that. That was all behind me. I didn't care anymore. They couldn't hurt me anymore. No one could. I had made sure of that.

No one except for Sean, a small voice whispered to me. Yes, I was vulnerable to him; I couldn't seem to help myself. But this was one thing that I could never trust him with. I would never tell him about my parents. That would give me away. Besides, I couldn't risk him drawing me in any further. Not if I was going to be able to spy on him without breaking down completely.

When I didn't say anything, Agent Vaughn continued on. "They were found near New York Methodist Hospital."

"Yes," I said quietly. I knew that much. My father had been thinking about transferring there. They had offered him the Chief of Surgery position.

"We're not sure why they didn't get a cab," he said. "Maybe they were trying to find one. In any case, they ended up three blocks over. An anonymous source reported gunshots, and when the police got there, they were found in the alley."

My throat was constricted. Although his voice was gentle, the way that he was describing their deaths so matter-of-factly was jarring. Images of them lying broken and bloody in a dirty alleyway, their eyes staring at nothing, flashed through my mind. I was suddenly very cold, and I hugged my arms to my chest, shivering.

Agent Vaughn was at my side in an instant, his hand on my shoulder. He crouched down beside me, and his eyes met mine. I dreaded seeing the pity in them, but I was shocked to find nothing but compassion.

"I'm sorry," he said softly. "I know that this must be hard to hear."

I felt something warm and wet on my cheeks. I was crying. I hated crying, and it seemed that I had spilled enough tears to fill a river in the last few weeks. Why did it still hurt this badly to hear about their deaths? Surely some of the pain should have dulled in fourteen years?

But I had never faced the pain, had never dealt with it. I had locked it away, buried it deep within me. And now it rose up, just as harsh and cutting as it had been on the night that I was told that they had been murdered. I felt like a child again, bewildered and utterly lost.

Heaving in several deep breaths to choke back the sobs, I wiped the tears from my face. "I'm sorry," I told Agent Vaughn. "I'm fine."

His expression was concerned. "It's okay to be upset, Dr. Ellers," he assured me. "I can't imagine how hard that must have been for you. You lost your only family that night. I know that you were in the foster system, and that you overcame the incredibly difficult circumstances to graduate top of your class at Columbia and then went on to earn your MD." He looked at me seriously. "I know that you're a strong woman, Dr. Ellers, but it's okay to grieve. It's natural."

This time I couldn't hold back a sob. No one had ever spoken to me like this; no one had ever told me that it was okay to be sad. They had just looked at me with pity, and I hated that. I had been determined not to show any weakness just to wipe that look from their faces. My heart had hardened, and I tried my best never to think about what had happened to my parents. I tried not to think about them at all. Remembering how happy my life had been with them was too painful.

I buried my face in my hands and let myself go. Agent Vaughn stroked his hand up and down my arm, comforting me. I cried until my chest was aching from the wracking sobs, and he let me.

A knock at the door jerked me out of it. Agent Vaughn was still looking at me kindly. "It's okay," he said. "I don't have to get that."

"No," I said, my voice ragged. "I… I think I'm done."

He gave my arm a gentle squeeze before breaking contact. He pushed a box of tissues towards me and went to answer the door.

I was suddenly ravenous as the delicious smell of Chinese food wafted toward me. It occurred to me that I had hardly eaten anything in days. I had been too preoccupied.

Agent Vaughn settled himself in his chair across the desk from me once again, and I was slightly relieved at his renewed distance. Now that I was pulling myself back together, I couldn't help but feel embarrassed by my complete melt-down. And I was amazed that I had actually allowed him to touch me, to comfort me as I cried. I hadn't allowed that kind of physical contact with anyone other than Sean in years. But while Sean's touch was decidedly discomfiting given my intense, uncontrollable reactions to him, I felt nothing but a steady warmth from Agent Vaughn. It was… nice.

But it was out of my system now; it definitely was not going to happen again. I had faced my grief, I had dealt with it. Time to move on.

"Are you okay?" He asked as he handed me my chicken lo-mein.

"Yeah," I said, forcing my voice to come out steady. "I'm fine."

He studied me for a moment. "I know that this is going to be hard for you, Dr. Ellers," he said seriously. "We have a psychologist who you can see if you would like -"

"No," I said quickly. The last thing that I wanted was someone picking my brain. I was having a hard enough time holding myself together without someone actively pulling me apart, forcing me to dredge up my painful past. "That won't be necessary. I'm fine."

He was frowning at me slightly. "Okay," he conceded. "But if you change your mind, the offer is always open. And if not, you can always talk to me if you want to."

I thought of the feeling of his hand against my arm, the feeling of relief at finally being given permission to grieve. As much as I hated the idea of crying in front of other people, I found that I felt better, lighter somehow, after completely letting myself go.

"Thanks, Agent Vaughn" I said quietly, meeting his clear blue eyes.

"You can call me Clayton, you know." He gave me a small smile.

"Okay," I said. "Clayton, then. And you can call me Claudia." It struck me that I hadn't given anyone permission to call me by my first name since I had gotten my MD. Well, no one other than Sean. And I hadn't exactly given him my permission so much as he had insisted upon it.

Agent Vaughn – Clayton – beamed at me, and I found myself returning his smile, the sight of it pushing back the grief that weighed on my mind.

Chapter 4

As I walked up to my front porch that night, the motion-sensor floodlights that I had installed flared to life. My heart skipped a beat as they illuminated the form of a man sitting on the steps leading up to my door. But even though his face was buried in his hands, I recognized him instantly. When the lights hit him, his head jerked up, and his eyes met mine. They were wild, full of pain. And there was a bruise darkening on his jaw.

"Sean," I said, startled. "What are you doing here?"

I hadn't told him where I lived. It really was too damn easy to find my house. I needed to un-list my address. But this was one man that I wasn't afraid to find waiting for me on my stoop.

He straightened quickly, that cocky light returning to his eyes as he looked me up and down, a lazy, lopsided smile spreading across his face. Heat flared between my legs at the sight of it. Even at a distance, his effect on me was intense.

"I'm here to see you, of course," he said, pleasure evident in his voice. His eyes roved over me again, and his grin widened as he took in my professional slacks and neat bun. "Look at you all prim and proper." There was that playful light in his gaze again, as though he found me cute. I told myself that I hated it, but it sent a shiver dancing across my flesh. God damn this cocky, infuriating, sinfully sexy man. He had barely uttered two sentences and already I was melting for him.

I forced myself to frown at him. "These are the clothes that I prefer to wear when I'm not being forced to play dress-up," I said snidely.

His face darkened momentarily, but he quickly masked it. "You're beautiful either way," he said, his voice turning low and husky as he closed the distance between us. My mind told me to back away from him, but my body ignored it. His hand closed around the nape of my neck, pulling me up into him. I didn't resist as his lips came down on mine. His tongue swept into my mouth, delving into my depths with no preamble, kissing me voraciously. My body pressed against him as though of its own accord, melting into him as he consumed me. I was losing myself, succumbing to his power over me.

Don't do this, Claudia, a small voice demanded inside of me. But I wasn't listening. The feeling of Sean taking me felt too... *good.*

God damn it, Claudia, what the fuck are you doing? The voice was stronger this time, more insistent. It was right; I couldn't allow him to manipulate me like this. I knew that I would break under his onslaught, and who knew what I might reveal to him if I allowed him to strip me bare once again?

I pressed my hands against his chest, trying to push him away. But I might as well have been shoving against a brick wall. With a low growl, he gripped my wrists and jerked them away, pinning them behind me and pressing them into the small of my back. He secured them there with one of his large hands, and his other returned to my nape, forcing me to stay where he wanted me.

I couldn't help it; I moaned up into him as lust overwhelmed me. He continued to fuck my mouth with his tongue, claiming me, demonstrating my utter helplessness to his control over my body. And I reveled in the heady release. It was as though I had been starved of his touch, and now I gorged myself on the sweet ecstasy of it.

But soon, too soon, he tore his mouth from mine. I gasped for breath, going lightheaded as oxygen flooded back into my lungs. His lips were quirked up in that knowing, satisfied smile, and I trembled in his grip.

His breath was warm against my lips as he spoke. "We should probably go inside," he said.

At a loss for words, I just nodded dumbly. My mind was flooded with images of him fucking me roughly, granting me that sweet release as the lust wiped all thoughts from my busy mind. I unconsciously licked my lips as he reluctantly pulled away from me. I was grateful when he kept his hand on me, not holding mine, but still gripping my wrist possessively.

I fumbled for my keys, missing the lock a few times as I tried to open it with shaky hands. Sean's hand tightened around my wrist and he chuckled at me.

Forcing away the tingles that shot down my spine, I glared up at him. But he just cocked an eyebrow and smiled at me, amused. I pushed the door open with an indignant huff, and he pulled me across the threshold. Automatically, I flipped the light on.

He pressed my back up against my door, pushing it closed with my body. But as he leaned down for me again, the light fell on the dark shadow on his jaw. I reached up for him and gently touched my fingers to his face. Although I knew that the pressure was too light to cause him pain, he flinched away from me.

"What happened?" I asked quietly.

His eyes clouded over, and he released me abruptly.

"Nothing," he said shortly.

I reached out and grabbed his arm, keeping him close to me. "You can talk to me," I breathed. Lines appeared around his eyes, and his lips pressed together. I remembered how he had been holding his head in his hands when I had first found him at my door, his shoulders slumped. "Why are you really here, Sean?" I asked quietly.

His muscles were corded beneath my touch. He was pulling up his walls, and the sight pained me. It was awful to watch him compartmentalizing the pain, taking on the weight of it. I knew what that felt like. It was only recently that Sean had made me realize what a terrible burden it was.

And I was more than a little hurt that he wouldn't trust me enough to open up to me after all that I had revealed to him about myself. It occurred to me that he had broken me down, and while I had glimpsed his internal anguish, he had never really shared with me.

"Please," I said. "You can trust me." A thread of the hurt that tightened my chest must have colored my tone, because his eyes softened.

"I know," he said quietly.

But as I heard those two simple words, guilt twisted my gut. *"You can trust me"?* Had anyone ever been less deserving of trust?

I swallowed back my consternation, telling myself that my intentions were pure; I really did want to ease his pain. This wasn't about digging up more information on the Westies. It was his pain that drew me to him more intensely than his handsome features and cocky demeanor. Although our lust for one another was all but irresistible, this was what truly bound us together.

I tugged on his arm gently, guiding him into my living room. He sat down beside me on the couch, dropping back onto it heavily. His thigh brushed up against mine, our bodies unwilling to break contact. But he wouldn't meet my eye. I gently cupped his uninjured cheek in my hand and guided his face to mine. He didn't resist.

His eyes locked with mine, and I saw turmoil in their green depths.

"Who hurt you?" My voice was gentle, but my question was direct, not allowing him the option of reticence. Uncharacteristically, he was allowing me to take control.

He let out a long breath. "My father," he admitted.

Anger bubbled up within me, and I fought to keep it from showing on my face. "You fought him?" I asked.

Something akin to shame flickered his eyes. "No," he said hollowly. "He's my father."

My body stiffened as fury flooded me, and I couldn't hold back my angry words. "He's a cruel asshole, and he would deserve anything you gave him. I know that he's hurt you, Sean. More than this one time. Why do you let him?"

Now it was his face that drew down in anger. "You don't understand," he said, his voice tight.

"Then explain it to me," I demanded.

He shot me a level look. "You don't fight Ronan Reynolds. You take what he gives you and you keep your mouth shut. That's just the way it is."

"Then 'the way it is' is stupid," I insisted.

Sean's expression hardened. "I won't allow you to say anything against him," he said, his eyes blazing.

"Why are you defending him?" I asked, exasperated and more than a little annoyed that he was telling me what I wasn't *allowed* to do again.

"He's a dangerous man, Claudia," Sean said, struggling to keep an even tone. "You wouldn't talk about him that way if you knew what was good for you."

I threw up my hands. "You can't just expect me to stand idly by when he hurts you."

His face twisted in anger, and I fought the urge to shrink away from him as he called upon his powerful aura. "You can and you will," he said harshly.

We glared at one other as each of us dug in our heels, fuelled by our righteous frustration. But then it struck me that I was antagonizing him after I had begged him to open up to me. I knew that what I was doing wasn't fair to him, and it would only make him more unwilling to talk to me in the future.

I sighed heavily, all the fight going out of me. "Okay," I conceded. "I'm sorry for snapping at you. I just can't…" I cut myself off. "Thank you for telling me."

"You're welcome," he said, but his jaw was still tight. After a moment, he sighed, concern replacing the ire in his eyes as he brushed the line of my cheekbone with his thumb. "If it were just myself that I was worried about, I would have stopped putting up with his shit a long time ago. And he knows that. Ronan is a ruthless man. If I challenged him, it wouldn't be me that he came after. He would hurt the people that I care about. That's why he can't know about you."

I was momentarily dumbstruck. He cared about me deeply enough that he would take a beating from his father in order to keep me safe? This new knowledge only served to confirm my assertion that Sean wasn't a bad person. I was more determined than ever to help him.

My stomach sank. *Help him?* No matter how I colored it, I was condemning him. But it was too late to go back now. Without my continued cooperation, the FBI would move in on Sean and Bradley, and Agent Vaughn wouldn't be able to help me secure a reduced sentence for Sean.

Although he didn't understand that I was going to betray him, I was desperate to communicate to him that I cared about him too. Even if I couldn't say it in so many words, I could demonstrate it in the only other way I knew how. Helplessly drawn to him, compelled by the need to erase his pain, I leaned into him quickly. His eyes widened in surprise, but he responded almost instantly, closing the distance between us. This time it was my tongue that traced the line of his lips, demanding that he open for me.

His hand closed around the front of my throat, gently pushing me away. He was smiling at me cruelly. "I don't think so, little one," he said softly.

Little one. He had never called me that before. And although I knew that I should feel indignant at the diminutive moniker, it sounded sweet in my ears, a term of affection. With his gentle grip on my neck, reminding me of his dominance, the name felt... right. It reinforced how fragile I was in his strong arms, driving home his power over me. It was everything that drew me towards him, that made me lust for him.

I gasped as he squeezed, applying the slightest pressure as he guided me onto my back, pressing me into the couch as his body settled over mine. A low, husky moan escaped me at the eroticism of the act, and I could feel him hardening against my hip. I hungered to have him inside me again, to fill the emptiness within me and drive away my confusion and guilt with every demanding thrust.

He was staring down at me. "Fuck, Claudia," his voice caressed my name. His free hand moved to cup my cheek. "You are so beautiful."

I blushed at his praise, warmth filling my chest. He groaned, and his thumb brushed over my cheek. "Do you have any idea how delicious that color is?"

I shuddered beneath him, my sex tingling at the lust that darkened his tone. My nipples were almost painfully hard as they pressed against the inside of my bra. I let out a low whine and ground my hips up against him, physically demonstrating my intense need. I remembered how he had punished me before for moving against him without his permission, and I found myself longing for his harsh correction.

I watched his expression turn forbidding, and his dominant aura washed over me. I was caught up in it, my mind swept away by the raging torrent.

Then he released me suddenly, drawing away from me and sitting upright. I gasped at the abrupt deprivation of his touch, and the world seemed to crash back down into existence around me. My gut twisted as I was flooded with a sense of rejection. I pushed myself away from him, hugging my arms across my stomach.

"What's wrong?" I asked, unable to keep the tremor from my voice.

He wasn't looking at me. "You don't want this, Claudia," he said, his tone detached.

I blinked, confused. How had my actions indicated that in any way? "What?" I asked faintly.

He turned to me, his eyes hard. "You said that you wanted to take things slow. You aren't ready for this. I'm manipulating you again." He ran a hand through his hair in frustration, mussing it in that way that I loved.

Yes, I had asked if we could take things slowly. But that was when I was determined not to let him touch me, not to let him pull me in. It was too late for that now; I was lost already, inexorably drawn in by his beauty and his pain.

"You're not," I insisted. "*I* kissed *you*, in case you don't recall."

"There's a difference between a kiss and what I want to do to you," he said roughly.

Heat flared between my legs at his words. "Oh," I said quietly. "But what if I want that too?"

He closed his eyes for a moment, and when he opened them again I could detect intense longing tinged with a hint of anguish.

"You don't know what you're saying," he insisted. "You don't know what you're asking for."

I remembered the ferocity of our passionate coupling after I had found the contents of his locked drawer, and I couldn't hold back the small smirk that played across my lips. "I think I have a pretty good idea."

"No," he said harshly. "You don't. You've had one other sexual partner, and I know that you have no idea what you are asking for when you say that you want me."

I didn't appreciate that he was treating me like an ignorant child, and his reference to my inexperience stung. "You spanked me, and I didn't run, did I?" I demanded.

His expression tightened. "No, you didn't," he conceded. "But if you knew..." He hesitated. "What I want to do to you is wrong, Claudia. I know that it's sick, but I can't help myself."

"Don't you say that, Sean," I said angrily. "Don't you dare. Okay, so maybe I'm inexperienced. That doesn't mean that I'm completely naïve. Maybe your desires aren't everyone's cup of tea, but you are by no means alone in your tastes. And I'm assuming that you know that based on the fact that you seem to know what you're doing. There must have been plenty of other willing women..." I trailed off, jealousy filling my gut at the thought of Sean with other partners.

His expression was tormented. "But you're different, Claudia," he insisted. "The way that we met, the way that I trapped you with me... You couldn't escape me, and I took advantage of you. I can't forgive myself for that."

My expression hardened. "Well, you're going to have to," I ordered. "Because it took both of us to do what we did. What we're doing. I want this. I want *you*. And you beating yourself up about it isn't going to change that."

He opened his mouth to protest, but I held up a hand, stopping him.

"You said that you can't help yourself," my voice was quieter this time. "Well, I can't either. I need this just as much as you do. So if your desires are sick, then mine are too. And I'm okay with that."

I reached for him, and he flinched away from me.

"God damn it, Sean," I said angrily. "You may control my body when you want to, but my mind is my own."

Well, mostly, I admitted to myself. I couldn't deny that his sway over me affected my decision-making processes. But I didn't care about that right now. All I wanted was to be with him, to experience more of that dark submission under his dominant touch. I wanted the passion, the release. I wanted to connect with him in that most intimate way, where none of our problems, none of our pain, existed.

"I demand your respect," I said staunchly.

He regarded me seriously. "Of course I respect you, Claudia. You're the strongest woman I've ever known." One corner of his mouth pulled up in a small smile. "Sometimes I forget how fiery you are," he said, his easy amusement returning. Lust clouded his eyes again. "It's one of the reasons I find you so irresistible."

I swallowed as he entered my personal space. "And for some reason I feel the same, despite how damn cocky you are."

He grinned at me. "It's all part of my charm," he said. "You love it, really."

"You wish," I retorted. I meant for my voice to be flippant, but instead it came out low and breathy.

I could feel his lips still curved up into a smile as they met mine. A sense of triumph flooded me as his mouth came down on me. I might submit to him, but it seemed that I had my own sort of power over him.

His hands were suddenly gripping my waist, jerking me up with him so that we were standing. I twined my arms around the back of his neck, holding him to me so that he couldn't break the kiss. His hands fumbled at the buttons of my blouse in an effort to expose me for him. But he wasn't satisfied with his progress. His low growl rumbled through me as his hands fisted in my shirt. With a jerk of his powerful arms, he ripped it open, the buttons flying free, making small popping noises as they bounced against the hardwood floor.

I gasped in delight, not caring that he had just destroyed one of my favorite blouses. I was too caught up in the eroticism of the moment, too caught up in his power over me. My hands were gripping the hem of his t-shirt, my nails raking against his muscles as I shoved it up his torso. He quickly pulled the shirt over his head, and I couldn't help trailing my fingers over his taut abs, enjoying the way that they rippled under my touch.

His hands were at my back, expertly unsnapping my bra with one hand. I shrugged out of it and pressed myself into his chest, moaning as my hardened nipples brushed up against him.

He unzipped my slacks, his fingers hooking beneath the top of my panties before he shoved both down my thighs, baring me to him completely. I returned the favor, feverishly tugging at his jeans and boxers until his cock sprang free. I grasped the length of it, marveling at the hard girth as I remembered how it had stretched me mercilessly. He caught my wrist and jerked my hand away with a warning snarl.

"I didn't give you permission to touch me," he said forbiddingly. "What have I told you about teasing me, Claudia?"

He was glaring down at me, and I swallowed hard even as my pussy pulsed at his harsh words. I knew that he was going to punish me again, and I longed for it, for the light pain that would push me over the edge as I was forced to submit to him completely, thrusting me into blissful oblivion.

"On your hands and knees," he ordered.

My eyes widened. "What?" I asked breathlessly, my independent streak getting the better of me.

His hand fisted in my hair, and he pulled sharply, forcing me down. I fell to my knees, thankful for the thick rug that cushioned the impact. Still, I knew that I would have bruises tomorrow. But I didn't care. He shoved me forward roughly, and I caught myself on my hands before I collided with the floor. He applied pressure at the back of my neck, ruthlessly forcing me down until my face was pressed against the carpet. He kept me pinned there, and I became acutely aware of the fact that my ass was raised for him, flagrantly exposed. Cool air caressed my sex, making it pulse almost painfully as need built within me. My thighs were wet with my desire.

His hand came down on me hard, and pain bloomed hot and sharp on my ass. I gave a small cry, and I wasn't sure if it was from the pain or from the way that my inner walls clenched, longing to have him inside of me.

"You will learn not to question me, Claudia," he said, his voice rough with unconcealed lust. His fingers swirled in the wetness on my inner thigh, trailing their way upward before pausing just beside my clit. I whined in need, but I resolutely forced down the instinct to rock toward him; I remembered his order not to move against him without permission. I trembled with the effort of resisting.

He traced the line of my swollen folds. "You see? You're learning. Good girl," he rumbled.

I shuddered beneath him as my clit throbbed painfully, desperate for him to touch me there. There was a ripping noise behind me, and I was relieved to realize that he was slipping on a condom. He was going to take me.

Please, I silently begged. *Please...*

A sharp cry was ripped from me as he entered me with one powerful thrust, driving in to the hilt. Then he drew almost completely out of me.

"Don't move," he ordered through gritted teeth.

He began to rock against me, entering me in swift, shallow thrusts, only the head of his cock penetrating me. I let out a low whine as he teased me, desperately trying to resist the urge to drive my hips back against him. Slowly, agonizingly, he eased further into me each time as he rocked forward. I was panting by the time he almost reached my g-spot, my fingers curling into the rug beneath me as I bit my lower lip to hold my resolve. I wanted to obey, I wanted to...

But he stopped his progress, keeping me on the edge. All of my muscles were taut with the effort of keeping still. His low chuckle floated down to me. The bastard was enjoying torturing me, making me wait as he tested me.

I couldn't take it anymore; I shoved back into him in one sharp motion, nearly climaxing as his dick hit me where I craved it most.

He let out a low growl, and I felt his cock twitch within me as he almost lost his iron control. His hands were around my shoulders, jerking my body upright so that my back pressed up against his hard chest. One arm closed around my waist, trapping my arms at my sides as he pinned me in place. His other wrapped around my neck, catching my throat between his forearm and bicep.

A tremor ran through me as I realized how breakable I was in his grip. But the slight pang of fear only heightened my arousal, and my inner muscles contracted around him.

"Fuck, Claudia," he groaned, tightening his hold around my throat incrementally. I could still draw in ragged breaths, but he was pressing against my arteries, restricting the blood flow to my brain. He moved within me, thrusting into me with jarring force.

His movements were possessive and punishing. I was growing lightheaded from the lack of oxygenated blood reaching my brain. My focus honed in on the feel of him inside of me, our sweat-slicked bodies sliding against one another as he took me completely. I moaned in wild abandon, reveling in it.

He hardened impossibly further, his need for release mounting even as I was pushed towards the precipice. As he jerked inside of me, his fingers found my clit, pinching hard. At the same time, his grip on my throat eased, and blood rushed to my head. The high was incredible. I was shoved over the edge, falling into a bliss-filled haze. Sean was the only real thing in the world as I flew out into the abyss, pleasure consuming me. I didn't recognize the strangled cry that echoed around the room as my own.

His cock pulsed inside of me as he reached his own orgasm, his low grunt reverberating throughout my entire body. My pussy fluttered around him as I floated in ecstasy.

He didn't release me from his grip as we tumbled to the floor. He held me tightly against him as he curled around me, his cock still inside of me. I trembled as the little aftershocks tingled through me, making me shudder against him.

My body was limp, completely spent as I huddled in his arms. I remained floating in warm darkness, relishing the sensation of his hand gently stroking up and down the curve of my waist as he softened within me.

I sighed happily, completely sated and utterly content.

Chapter 5

I let out a small moan when Sean pulled out of me, the friction against my hyper-sensitive nerve endings making me tremble. I didn't want to move yet, and I was glad when he remained curled against me. But my mind was whirring back to life, the bliss-filled haze beginning to lift.

What had I just done?

You had amazing, mind-blowing sex, that's what, a smug, satisfied part of me responded.

But at what cost? Hadn't I been resolutely telling myself that I had to keep my hands off of Sean if I had any hope of spying on him without breaking down? My gut twisted.

"You can trust me."

Regardless of my intense attraction to him, of my undeniable feelings for him, the cold, hard truth was that I was deceiving him. It was possible that I might be condemning him to years in prison by carrying out my task. How could I sleep with him when I knew that?

It was made worse by the fact that I had forced him to open up to me. Had I done that because I wanted to know more about his father so that I could report it back to the FBI?

No. No, I truly had wanted to comfort him. When I asked him about how he had been hurt, I hadn't known that it was his father's doing. Anger bubbled up within me again at the thought of him hurting Sean.

Sean had said that he hadn't chosen his life for himself. It was becoming pretty clear to me that his father had something to do with that. Clayton had promised me that he would protect Sean if he truly hadn't had a choice in becoming what he was.

I was just going to have to find out more about Ronan Reynolds. The only way that I could protect Sean and avenge my parents was to ensure his downfall.

See? A kind part of me said. *You're helping him escape this life.*

Maybe if I succeeded in taking down the Westies and managed to get Sean off the hook, then we could be together...?

Yeah, right. As though he would ever be able to look at me again once he discovered that I had betrayed him. It would be made all the worse by the fact that I knew that he was a very guarded, private person, just like I was. And I was going to actively tear down his barriers in order to extract information from him. How could he ever forgive me for that?

He couldn't.

Despite Sean's heat against me, I shivered. He rubbed a hand up and down my arm as goose bumps covered my flesh.

"Are you cold, little one?" He asked, kissing my shoulder tenderly.

A pang shot through my heart at the endearing term. I rolled away from him quickly, no longer able to bear his touch. I didn't deserve it.

"What's up?" Sean asked as I pushed myself to my feet.

"Ummm... Bathroom," I muttered by way of explanation.

He propped himself up on one elbow, his deep green eyes studying me. I couldn't hold up under his scrutiny. Dropping my gaze, I turned on my heel and tried my best to appear calm as I walked towards my bedroom. Once I rounded the corner and was out of sight, I took the stairs two at a time, flinging myself through my room before locking the bathroom door behind me. It seemed that I was beginning to associate bathrooms with refuge from Sean.

I closed my eyes and took several deep, calming breaths. I was in my own house, for god's sake; I shouldn't have to hide here.

Gathering my resolve, I forced myself to face the mirror. Every time I caught my reflection these days, I was always shocked to find just how normal I looked. How could I appear so unchanged when I felt like a completely different person than I had been two weeks ago? I felt as though I should have aged at least five years.

But other than my over-bright eyes and my slightly flushed cheeks, nothing was out of the ordinary. Well, almost nothing. I noticed that my hair was in disarray. Tendrils that had been pulled from my bun fell wildly around my face. I definitely looked like I had just been well-fucked.

I frowned at myself, at the evidence of what I had just done. Angrily, I began jerking pins from my hair before running a brush through it. The sight of it down just reminded me of my time as Sean's captive, and I was tempted to put it back up again. But that was stupid. Pursing my lips, I stalked away from my reflection and out of the bathroom. I stopped short as soon as I opened the door.

Sean was sprawled out across my four-poster bed in all his masculine glory, completely naked. My tongue darted out to wet my lips at the sight of him, and I noticed his cock twitch in response. I flushed, forcing my gaze to his face.

"What are you doing in here?" I asked, my voice high and thin.

He grinned at me, obviously amused at my discomfiture. "Well, I wasn't going to sleep on the floor," he said matter-of-factly.

The presumptuous ass! I huffed indignantly. "I didn't say that we were having a slumber party," I said snappily.

His smile turned predatory. "I don't think boys are usually invited to slumber parties. Especially not boys who want to do the things that I want to do to you." He had the audacity to wink at me as he patted the bed beside him. "Now come over here and get in with me. I don't want you catching a chill." His eyes flicked to my hardened nipples.

I threw up my hands and marched to my dresser. I saw him frowning at me out of the corner of my eye.

"What are you doing?" He asked.

"I won't be chilly if I put on extra layers," I said coolly. Yes, I definitely needed to hide my body from him. The way he was studying it was making me decidedly uncomfortable.

He was out of the bed and across the room before I could fully open the top drawer. I gasped as his arm closed around my waist, jerking me away from the dresser and back into his body. His cock was hardening against my ass.

"I didn't say you could cover yourself," he said, a warning in his voice.

I squirmed in his grip, trying to push his arm away. He didn't budge. "I don't need your permission," I snapped.

He tutted at me, and suddenly the world spun around me as his grip shifted. I found myself in his arms, cradled against his chest. He closed the short distance to the bed in three long strides before dumping me onto it unceremoniously.

Even though the impact was soft, all of the air was momentarily knocked out of me. But as I stared up at him, I wasn't sure if I would have been able to draw breath anyway. His eyes were blazing, his expression forbidding.

"I think you'll find that you do need my permission," he said coldly.

Now I was getting angry. "No," I insisted. "I don't." I moved to push myself up, but his hand was between my breasts, shoving against my sternum and pressing me down into the bed.

He pinned me with a hard stare. "Don't you?" He asked. "You wanted to get dressed a moment ago. Are you wearing clothes now?"

I glared at him and clawed at his hand that held me down. He frowned at me, quickly gathering up my wrists and pinning them above my head with his free hand. He was hovering over me now, his face inches from mine. I tugged against his grip, but he held me fast. Despite my frustration – or perhaps because of it – I felt my sex stir back to life.

"Answer me," he demanded. "Are you wearing clothes now?"

I held my baleful look. "No," I ground out. "Obviously I can't get to them with you holding me down like this."

He released me abruptly, a smirk breaking out on his face as he eased up. "There," he said, amusement evident in his voice. "I'm not restraining you anymore. What do you think your chances are of getting to your dresser before I stop you? And even if you did manage, how do you plan on preventing me from ripping the clothes right back off of you?"

He was toying with me, the light in his eyes practically daring me to try to get around him. He made me feel so helpless. I was sharply reminded of how he had trapped me in his bedroom, how my life had no longer been my own. What was even more disturbing was the way that my body reacted lustfully to his treatment even as my mind shuddered at the sensation of utter powerlessness.

I folded my arms over my chest, but the gesture was more protective than defiant. "You've already destroyed enough of my articles of clothing for one day," I said coldly. I reached for the covers and jerked them up over my body before turning away from him, curling up on my side. "Goodnight, Sean. You can let yourself out."

There was a moment of stunned silence, and then he cursed softly. "Shit, Claudia, I'm sorry. I just... I guess I got caught up." His hand touched my shoulder lightly, hesitantly. "I didn't mean to upset you," he said quietly. "I'm sorry if I crossed a line."

Fuck. Yes, he had upset me. But I was more upset with myself for liking his treatment than I was upset with him for threatening me. I sighed heavily and rolled onto my back so that I could face him again.

"It's okay, Sean," I said. I was the one who had cajoled him into dominating my body even though he had tried to resist; I had been the one to provoke this side of him. But he wouldn't meet my eye, and all of his muscles were tense. I reached out and grasped his hand in mine. He flinched at my touch, but he didn't pull away. I tugged on him gently. "Sit with me?" I asked.

He hesitated for a moment, but then his knees folded and he sat carefully on the edge of the bed. I didn't release my hold on him.

"I'm not upset," I said gently. Now his eyes met mine, disbelief filling them. "I mean, I was. But I'm not anymore."

He studied my face carefully. "Are you trying to fuck with my head, Claudia?" He asked.

"No!" I said quickly.

His brows drew together. "Well you sure are doing a hell of a good impression of it."

"Listen," I said, squeezing his hand. "I'm sorry. I know that I asked for you to treat me that way." He winced, but I carried on. "But I want you to. I like it. It's just... My reactions confuse me sometimes. The way I am when I'm with you doesn't match up with how I think of myself at all."

I really shouldn't be confessing this to him. I should be maintaining my distance – emotionally, at the very least. But damn it if I was going to let him leave me when he seemed so hurt. Especially when I was the one at fault.

"I'm a very independent person," I continued on. "I get angry with myself for enjoying what you're doing to me when it goes against everything that I am. I don't recognize myself when I'm with you," I admitted quietly.

His expression tightened. I had clearly said something wrong. "That day in the park. The day you left me. You said that you didn't like who you are when you're with me." His eyes burned into mine, a hint of fear glinting out through the anger that filled them. "Is that true?"

I dropped my gaze. "I thought so," I said, my voice barely audible. "But meeting you, being with you… It's changed me, Sean. And that scares me."

His finger hooked under my chin, forcing my face up so that my eyes met his. His expression was indecipherable as he regarded me. "I feel the same way," he confessed. "I don't know how to be around you, Claudia. Hell, I shouldn't be around you at all, not after what I did to you. But I can't stay away. I don't know what I would have done if you hadn't shown up at my apartment. Probably would have come to you on my knees, begging for forgiveness."

I couldn't hold back a small smile. "For some reason, I'm having trouble picturing you begging for anything. And certainly not on your knees. Besides," I added, more soberly, "I couldn't stay away even if I wanted to."

He stared down at me in wonder. "So what do we do now?" He asked quietly. "I hate the thought that I'm pushing you too hard, that I'm scaring you. You say that you want the same things I do, but I don't think that you understand what all that entails."

I opened my mouth to protest, but he held a finger to my lips, stopping me short. "I hadn't really wanted to have this conversation; I never thought that things would get this far. But we need to talk about what we're doing, about what I'm pulling you into."

"You're not pulling me into -" I began, but his hand covered my mouth.

"Let me speak, please." He worded it as a request, but his tone was authoritative. My nipples pebbled in response to him silencing me, and I was grateful that the blanket covered my lustful reaction to his treatment.

I nodded, letting him know that I would let him say what he needed to. He removed his hand, but his fingertips lingered on my lips, tracing them lightly before pulling away. I resisted the strong urge to draw one on them into my mouth and suck on it.

He took a deep breath. "Do you know what BDSM is, Claudia?" He asked finally.

"Um, sort of," I confessed. I knew that it meant kinky, like tying up your partner, spanking them. The thought of Sean doing that to me made my clit pulse.

"The meaning of BDSM is threefold," he said, his tone turning lecturing. "Bondage and Discipline; Domination and Submission, and Sadism and Masochism." His eyes searched mine briefly, looking for signs of fear. But all I felt was rapt curiosity. "The first two aspects very much define my interests. The last one not so much. I don't want to harm you, Claudia. I want you to know that." There were lines of anxiety around his eyes.

"I know," I breathed. Even though he had put me through the wringer emotionally, I knew that Sean would always protect me from harm. He had proven that time and again.

He gave me a short nod, satisfied. "I am a Dominant, or a Dom. You are a natural submissive, or sub."

I couldn't hold back a frown. "I don't know if I like the sound of that," I admitted.

He reached out and cupped my face. "Just because you are sexually submissive doesn't mean that you are outside of the bedroom. I love your fiery spirit; I've never been a fan of doormats. But I see the constant strain that you inflict upon yourself, your determination to remain strong no matter how much you're hurting. Submission can free you from that."

I quivered inwardly, disconcerted that he had seen past my façade in a way that no one had before. It seemed that despite the short time that we had been together, he knew me better than anyone. He hadn't allowed me to hold back around him, had chipped away at my walls. And I knew that he recognized my internal anguish as a reflection of his own. Despite coming from different worlds, we were more alike than I had ever realized.

He ran his fingers through my hair, and I couldn't help leaning into his touch. "You know that I respect you, Claudia," he said seriously. "And your instinctive reaction to my dominance of your body doesn't change that. I want you. All of you. It scares me how badly I crave to take you in every way imaginable. I'm afraid that I'll push you too far and scare you away."

"You do scare me sometimes," I admitted quietly. "But I'm more afraid of what my desire for you means about myself. I'm not afraid that you'll hurt me."

Not physically, anyway.

He smiled at me gently. "You don't know how relieved I am to hear that. But just in case, you should have safe words so that if you ever get too uncomfortable, we can stop what we're doing immediately."

I liked the sound of that. The idea was comforting. "Okay," I breathed.

"I want you to use 'yellow' if you need a break. We can stop and talk about your concerns. Say 'red' if you can't handle any more, and everything will stop."

I gave him a small smile. "That sounds good. Thank you."

A part of me was distantly amazed at this calm, matter-of-fact conversation that we were having as I agreed to surrender my body to him completely. But mostly I was relieved. I felt freed, like I didn't have to expend energy on resisting him any longer. I could let go of the guilt and confusion that I felt at what I allowed him to do to me.

But I knew that the emotional turmoil over deceiving him would only multiply tenfold as I allowed him to be intimate with me. Our raw, honest confessions affected me deeply. It was the most I had ever opened up to anyone, and I had a feeling that it was the same for him. I was treading into dangerous territory, walking the tightrope of letting my walls down while still hiding my deception from him. But I couldn't resist him. I knew that it was disgustingly selfish, but I wanted to enjoy all of him for as long as I could before the day came when he realized that I had betrayed him, before I lost him forever. If I could only impress upon him now how much I cared through connecting with him physically, then maybe one day he would be able to see that. Maybe he would be able to forgive me.

I forced down my consternation, struggling to keep my conflicting emotions from showing on my face.

"Come on," I said, smiling gently. "I guess we can have that slumber party after all." I scooted over, inviting him to join me.

He grinned and tucked himself under the covers, drawing me towards him until I was draped across his chest. I inhaled his intoxicating scent and snuggled closer, needing him to hold me, to ease my troubled mind.

But even his warmth wasn't enough to soothe me, and I laid awake for long hours after he fell asleep, my mind a tangle of emotions. I had told myself that I was doing the right thing, but I no longer knew the difference between right and wrong. I only knew that I needed him, and I would cling to him for as long as I could. No matter what the cost.

Chapter 6

I awoke to Sean nuzzling my hair. His body was pressed up against my back, his arms wrapped around me. And his hard cock was poking insistently at my ass. Startled, I tried to jerk away from him. But he just held me tighter, groaning as my movements caused me to rub against him.

Fruitlessly, I tried to pull away from him again, and his grip became so tight that it constricted my lungs.

"Stay," his voice rumbled in my ear.

I shivered in his arms, stilling instantly. I wanted nothing more than to stay there, enfolded by his delicious heat, but my eyes were drawn to the clock on my bedside table.

Crap.

It was seven-fifteen. I had overslept.

"I can't," I said regretfully. "I have to go to work."

He propped himself up on his elbow, checking the time.

"Shit," he cursed softly. "I am going to be so late. Ronan is going to kill me."

I frowned, tensing in his arms. "Call in sick," I said quickly, concerned that his father would exact retribution for Sean's tardiness.

"I can't do that," he insisted, rolling out of bed. I glanced over at him. His hair was mussed from sleep. It reminded me of how he looked after he fucked me, and my sex clenched. I had never been a fan of morning sex, but it seemed that Sean was an exception. But my fear for him was stronger than my lust.

"I'll write you a doctor's note," I said firmly.

Sean sighed heavily. "Trust me, that will only make things worse. I don't want you drawing attention to yourself, and you'll only attract his ire if you try to make excuses for me."

I frowned at him. "Promise me that you won't take any crap from him, then," I ordered. Despite his age, his father was clearly a physically powerful man, but I knew that Sean would be able to take him on if he wanted to.

Sean just shook his head, his lips pursing into a thin line. "I thought I explained this to you yesterday. That just isn't possible. Especially if he suspects that you're the reason that I'm late. It will just piss him off more if I try to defend myself. And I don't want him to blame you. I need you to stay under his radar."

My frown deepened. "He called me a whore, Sean," I said, my voice hard. "I'm pretty sure he remembers me."

His hands clenched to fists, and his expression tightened. "I don't know what else to tell you," he said, irritation bleeding into his tone. "This is the best way. I'm sorry if that pisses you off."

The tension in his muscles made me relent. I didn't want him to leave when he was angry with me. I reached out my hand to cover his fist.

"Okay," I said softly. A blush colored my cheeks as a thought crossed my mind. His eyes softened, and he curled his index finger under my chin, lifting my face.

"What was that thought?" He asked.

"I, uh…" My cheeks heated further. "Do you at least want to take a shower here? With me?"

He let out a soft groan. "You're torturing me, Claudia. That's not a good idea. If we do that, I don't think I could bring myself to leave you."

"Then don't," I whispered.

He drew his hand away from me regretfully, but he was smiling softly. "Temptress," he said huskily. "My balls are going to be aching all day." His grin took on a cruel edge. "You'll pay for that later."

I shivered as images of what he might do to me flicked through my mind, and heat stirred in my belly.

"Now who's torturing whom?" I asked shakily.

"Payback's a bitch," he said cheerily. "I can't let you upset the balance of power here. What kind of Dom would I be if I let you walk all over me?"

Dom. Sub. The reminder of our conversation the night before only further stoked my lust.

"You had better go before I wrap myself around you and force you to stay," I warned.

He laughed. "I'm pretty sure I could fight you off, little one." But that dark flame was flickering in his eyes again. "But I'm not sure if I would want to."

He glanced at the clock again. "I have to go," he said, standing up quickly and putting distance between us.

"Alright," I sighed. "I'll call you a cab."

When I climbed out of bed, the covers fell away, exposing my naked body to him. His eyes darkened further, and he tensed.

"Fuck," he said huskily. "Cover yourself up. Please." His tone was clipped.

I was secretly pleased to see how difficult it was for him to restrain himself, and even more gratified to see his hard cock standing erect for me. He noticed the direction of my gaze.

"Now, Claudia," he barked.

I jumped slightly, tearing my eyes from him. "Sorry," I mumbled as I darted to retrieve my towel from the bathroom. I quickly wrapped it around myself, and I heard Sean heave in a shaky breath. Still, I couldn't help swaying my hips slightly as I walked from the room. He let out a low, warning growl behind me, and I allowed myself a satisfied smirk since my back was to him. I wouldn't have dared if he could see my expression.

Once I had ordered a cab for him, I retrieved his clothes from where they were scattered across the living room floor. My gaze fell on my destroyed blouse, and I smiled at the memory of him tearing it from me.

I tossed his jeans, t-shirt, and boxers to him once I returned to my bedroom, carefully avoiding looking at him until he was fully clothed. Even then, the sight of his muscular torso filling out his shirt made me weak in the knees.

He crossed the room and gathered me up in his arms, hooking an arm around my lower back and pinning me to him. His other hand gripped my jaw, forcing my face up to his, locking me in place as he plundered my mouth.

Sean was right: he had to go. I pushed against his chest, trying to pull away from him. He held me for a few more seconds, unwilling to allow me to dictate when the kiss ended.

"Okay, get out of here before I lose my resolve and jump you," I said when he finally released me, my tone low and lustful.

He gave me a sardonic smile. "As you command, ma'am."

He was mocking me, and god damn it if it didn't make my clit pulse. My expression must have betrayed my reaction, because he smirked at me with satisfaction.

"Will I see you again tonight?" He asked.

I struggled to keep the guilt from showing on my face. I was meeting with Clayton tonight to report on what I had learned from Sean. "I can't. I have to work late to catch up on my cases," I lied.

He frowned, but nodded. "Tomorrow then?"

I smiled up at him, unable to conceal my joy at the thought of seeing him again. "Of course," I said. "I'll text you when I'm off work."

He planted one last swift kiss on my forehead before leaving me. I stood there for a moment, regretting the loss of the heat of him. Then I shook myself. I was going to have to rush if I wanted to make it to work on time.

The soreness between my legs as I washed myself in the shower was a bittersweet reminder of our passionate coupling the night before. I relished the memory even as my gut twisted at the thought of my betrayal.

Keep to your task. If you do this, Ronan will never be able to hurt him again.

But the thought did little to assuage the feeling of guilt that made my heart weigh heavy in my chest.
■■

"Sean's father has coerced him into being a member of the Westies. I know it," I told Clayton firmly as I tried to ignore the camera in the debriefing room. I sincerely hoped that no one other than the FBI would ever see these tapes. If they were used as evidence in court and Sean learned that I had revealed his weakness when it came to his father, I knew that he would never forgive me.

As though he will ever forgive you for spying on him, I thought dejectedly.

Clayton eyed me, his professional Agent Vaughn persona back in place now that we were discussing official business. "Did he tell you that?" He asked skeptically. I decided that I preferred Clayton to Agent Vaughn.

"No," I replied. "But I can just tell."

I wished that Agent Vaughn would take my word for it, that he wouldn't press me to reveal why I made this assumption. But I had no such luck.

"I can't work with 'I can just tell.' That doesn't constitute hard evidence," he said reprovingly. "I need you to be honest with me, Dr. Ellers."

So we were back to Dr. Ellers again. It got my hackles up. I glared at him.

"He showed up at my house last night," I admitted, my tone clipped. "His jaw was bruised, and he admitted that his father had hit him."

"A fight doesn't constitute coercion," he said.

"It wasn't a fight," I insisted, irritation coloring my tone. "Sean didn't fight back. He just said 'You don't fight Ronan Reynolds,' and he wouldn't say anything else. He got angry with me when I spoke out against his father. He seemed to think that I would be putting myself in danger if anyone found out that I had." I speared Agent Vaughn with a hard look. "Does that sound like Sean has a say in the matter? He's intimidated by Ronan," I bit my lip as I made the admission. Sean certainly wouldn't appreciate my sharing that. But I had to. To protect him.

Agent Vaughn considered me carefully. "That does sound suspicious," he conceded. "But we'll need more proof than that, I'm afraid."

My hands clenched to fists beneath the table. What more did he want?

"And what about when he came to confront Sean when they were still holding me captive?" I demanded.

Agent Vaughn cocked his head at me. "What happened then?"

"After he left, Bradley seemed scared of the consequences for Sean standing up to Ronan to defend me. He asked Sean if he realized what his actions could cost both of them. I'm telling you, Ronan Reynolds has some power over them."

"So you think Bradley is being coerced too?" Agent Vaughn asked, his brows drawing together.

"No," I said firmly. "He's a ruthless asshole. There's no way he's innocent."

"You can't have it both ways, Dr. Ellers," he said. "Either Sean and Bradley have been intimidated into working for the Westies, or they are both just wary of him because he's a higher-up."

I frowned at him, crossing my arms over my chest. "You're wrong," I said staunchly. "It's not that black-and-white."

"Then gather more evidence to the contrary," he told me. "That's the only way forward here."

I scowled at him, and his expression softened. "I'm not trying to antagonize you. I'm just being realistic about what we need if you want to exonerate Sean. Do you understand that?"

I held my glare for a moment, but I gave him a jerky nod. If the FBI needed more evidence, then I would get it for them.

"One thing is becoming clear, though: Ronan Reynolds is a linchpin in the organization, as we had suspected. I know that Sean is trying to distance you from him, but any further information you can gather on him will be a great help. I know that your relationship with Bradley is... tense."

I snorted derisively, but he continued on over me. "But if you could spend any time around him at all, you might learn more. If he truly is a willing member of the Westies, then he might be keener to put you in the line of fire when it comes to Ronan than Sean is." He fixed me with a hard look. "I know that what I am asking of you is dangerous, and I understand if you're not comfortable with this. We can put that security detail on you if it will make you feel safer."

I took a shaky breath. Given Sean's warnings about his father, I couldn't deny that the idea of exposing myself to him scared me shitless. But if this was what it took to avenge my parents, to save Sean, then I would do it. "No," I said after a moment. "A security detail could be detected, and then I would be a target. I don't want to have to go into witness protection and abandon my life if they find out about me. Besides, if you do have to take action against someone if I am threatened, then my cover will be blown. Sean will protect me, and..." I hesitated. "And I do have a gun," I said quietly.

Clayton nodded at me approvingly. "I'm glad to hear that you are considering using it if you have to."

I swallowed hard, suppressing a shudder. Just the thought of it made me queasy.

"Is there anything else you can tell me?" Agent Vaughn asked.

I'm fucking Sean again. I lasted all of two days before succumbing to him.

But I shook my head. That was none of the FBI's business. I couldn't bear the thought of them thinking that I was whoring myself out for information.

It's not like that, I assured myself. *I care about Sean.* Every word that I had said to him the night before was true. Well, except for the part where I told him he could trust me.

Agent Vaughn stood and shut off the video camera. He shot me a wide smile. Clayton was back, and I was relieved to see him.

"Sorry about giving you the third degree," he apologized. "It's my job."

I was slightly mollified that he acknowledged that he was a bit of a coldhearted bastard when he questioned me. "I understand," I said.

"Come on," he urged me. He looked me up and down, but there was nothing sexual about it. "You look like you could use some food. Chinese again?"

I returned his smile. "Sure. Thanks. I can give you some cash for it." I was uncomfortable with the idea of him paying for me.

He held up a hand. "Don't worry about it. It's on Uncle Sam. It's the least he can do to repay you for your courage."

A few minutes later, I found myself in the privacy of his office. I braced myself for the discussion about my parents' deaths, determined not to break down into a blubbering mess this time.

"So," Clayton began, "I wanted to give you the game-plan. I've managed to track down an inmate, a former member of the Latin Kings, who might talk to us. He was incarcerated around the time that your parents died. The area where they were killed was disputed territory between his gang and the Westies, so he might know something about it. He's had a hard time of it in prison; he's been getting hassled for snitching on some of his friends. I'm willing to offer him protection and a reduced sentence in exchange for information."

Hope welled within me. "You can do that?" I asked.

He nodded grimly. "As much as I hate the idea of releasing the bastard, I'm willing to do it for you. I promised that I would help you, and I'm going to do everything in my power to do so."

I was amazed that he was going to such lengths to make good on his promise. "Thank you," I said quietly.

He gave me a small smile. "It's not a problem. We'll watch him closely when he gets out, and if the bastard so much as passes one of the Latin Kings on the street, we'll haul his ass back in. He'll probably high-tail it out of New York pretty quickly though. He betrayed too many of his friends to survive long once we let him out."

He regarded me seriously. "I don't want to pry into your personal affairs, and I understand if you don't want to talk about it, but are you alright? Emotionally, I mean. You know that you can talk to me if you're having a hard time. Nothing you say will leave this office. I swear."

I was touched by his sincerity, again stunned by his kindness. He really did want nothing more than to help me, than to comfort me. No one had ever offered that to me before. I bit my lip. "I can't lie," I said. "It hasn't been easy. Nothing has been easy since my parents died," I found myself admitting quietly.

"I'm sorry for what happened to you, Claudia."

"It's not your fault," I said, trying to brush it off.

His bright blue eyes captured mine, and I was relieved not to detect a trace of pity. "I know that," he said solemnly. "But that doesn't mean that I'm not going to do everything in my power to help make it right. As far as that is possible. I know that you lost your only family that night, that you were put into foster care."

I flinched.

"Were they unkind to you?" He asked gently.

"'Unkind' doesn't begin to cover it," I said, anger tingeing my voice.

"Have you ever talked to anyone about it?" He pressed. "Have you seen a counselor? I know that I've offered before, but we have someone that you could see if you wanted to."

My expression turned stony. "I don't want to talk about it," I said sharply.

He held up his hands, placating. "Okay," he backed off. "I don't want to upset you. It's just... You've taken on a lot, and I can see the strain it's putting you through. I want you to know that I'm here for you."

He could see right through me, just like Sean. I really must be cracking if my emotional burdens were becoming so obvious. I shifted uncomfortably in my seat. I wanted to change the subject. I plastered on a weak smile.

"It's not fair, you know," I said lightly. "You seem to know everything about me, but I don't know anything about you." I needed to deflect him.

He frowned slightly, but he rolled with the change of topic. "I guess it's only fair that I share, then. Although I warn you that you'll probably be bored; my life story isn't all that exciting."

This time my smile was genuine. "I highly doubt that. You work for the FBI. Isn't your life all crime-fighting? Sounds pretty interesting to me." I looked at him expectantly, and he chuckled.

"Alright," he conceded. "What do you want to know?"

"How did you decide to join the FBI? And why did you decide to join the War on Drugs in particular?"

He grinned back at me, revealing his perfect white teeth. "Do you want the long version or the short version?"

"The long one, please." We might as well chat over dinner. I didn't want any more uncomfortable silences that might be filled with further questions about my past.

"Remember that you asked for it," he warned. "I grew up in a small town outside of Des Moines called Indianola. My dad was a cop there, my granddad was a cop. I guess I was destined for law enforcement."

"I get that," I said. "I decided to become a doctor because my dad was a surgeon."

He nodded. "Exactly. It was pretty much expected of me. Don't get me wrong; I wasn't resentful or anything. But as much as I love my hometown, I wanted to break the cycle and move to a bigger city. I did try to resist my fate for a while, and I got a little rebellious in college. I had been playing football since I was a kid, and I got accepted to the University of Iowa on a full athletic scholarship."

I eyed him, realizing that his musculature was obvious under his suit. And he definitely had captain-of-the-football-team good looks. I smiled at him slyly. "Why am I not surprised that you were a football player?"

"Is it that obvious?" He asked.

"Definitely," I nodded. "I bet you dated cheerleaders and the whole nine yards," I teased.

He chuckled. "Guilty as charged. I guess I'm a walking stereotype. Please don't think less of me."

I tried not to smile too broadly. "Not at all," I said, but I couldn't keep amusement from coloring my tone. "So how did you get back into crime-fighting then?"

This time he laughed aloud. "You make me sound like a superhero or something. I'm not Spiderman."

I studied him pointedly. "Nope," I said definitively. "Not nerdy enough to be Spiderman."

"Stop it. You'll make me blush," he joked. Then he continued on. "Well, I wanted to go pro, but I screwed up my knee in my junior year of college, and that was it for me." He looked slightly regretful.

"I'm sorry," I said. "That sucks."

He shrugged. "I wouldn't be where I am today if that hadn't happened. And I'm pretty happy with my life." He grinned at me. "Besides, it doesn't hurt that I get to help out beautiful damsels in distress."

I huffed indignantly. "You do realize that you sound like a chauvinistic ass, right?"

He laughed again. "It's not hard to get a rise out of you, is it?"

I couldn't help laughing along with him. "I guess not," I admitted. "I should probably work on that." A part of me couldn't help registering that he had called me beautiful. No one but Sean had ever called me that. But I detected nothing but a playful light in Clayton's eyes, so I shrugged it off, deciding that it didn't necessarily mean that he was interested.

"What's the rest of your story, Morning Glory?" I pressed.

"'Morning Glory'? What are you, from the fifties? If so, you have exceptional skin for someone so old. What's your secret?"

"Morning Glory" had been something that my mother had always said to me. I hadn't used the saying in years, and I was vaguely surprised to realize that it had popped out of my mouth. It just felt natural.

"Uh-uh," I said. "I won't rise to your bait again."

"Damn. You're a quick study," he said, amused.

"I do try," I smiled easily. "So," I prodded. "Tell me more. I promise I am positively enthralled."

He rolled his eyes at me. "Who's baiting whom now?" He asked. Then he sighed dramatically. "Okay, so after college, I accepted my fate as a crime-fighter," his lips quirked up at the corners as he echoed me. "But just to be a little different, I decided to go with the FBI rather than becoming a cop."

"So why choose to track down drug dealers?" I asked. "Any particular reason, or were you just assigned to your division?"

His expression turned somber, and I regretted asking the question. I didn't like that I had wiped the smile from his face. "Sorry," I said quickly. "That was personal."

"No," he said. "You've shared a lot with me, and it's only fair that I do the same." He hesitated for a moment before plowing on. "I had a girlfriend in college. She was a fun, sweet girl, but she got really into smoking pot. She became a different person, losing all interest in socializing. She just retracted into herself and didn't want to do anything other than sit in her apartment and smoke. But instead of talking to her about it, I just broke things off with her." His brows drew together and guilt filled his eyes. "She started to get into heavier drugs. I knew about it, but I didn't say anything. I figured it was a phase and she would be fine." His handsome features twisted in anguish. "Then one day I found out that she had taken too much acid."

I couldn't keep the sympathy from showing on my face. "She died?" I asked quietly.

"No," he said. "She lost her mind. She'll be in an institution for the rest of her life. And I did nothing to prevent it."

I gasped, horrified. "That's terrible," I said. Instinctively, I reached out my hand and covered his, squeezing gently. "But you can't blame yourself for that."

He met my gaze, his expression pained. "Can't I?" He asked softly. "If I had just talked to her instead of blowing her off… I abandoned her. And now she's worse than dead."

"She made her choices," I said, my voice firm. "What happened to her is awful, but it's not your fault. Do you really think that you could have stopped her?"

He pursed his lips. "Maybe not," he admitted.

I traced small circles on the back of his hand. He looked down, his brows lifting as though he was surprised that I was touching him.

"I don't usually talk about her," he said softly.

I smiled at him gently. "I don't usually talk about my parents." I studied him intently. "You can talk to me."

He turned his hand so that our palms were pressed together, and his fingers closed around mine. "Thank you," he said, his voice rough with emotion. He returned my smile weakly. "Come on. We should probably eat. You look like you need it."

I allowed him to change the subject, recognizing that he had shared enough for one day, just as I had felt earlier. We seemed to understand one another, and I marveled at the fact that I was connecting with someone other than Sean. Maybe being around Sean had been good for me; maybe Clayton could help me heal if I opened up to him. And perhaps I could help him to heal as well. The thought made me feel... good.

Was it possible that I was making a friend for the first time in fourteen years?

Chapter 7

"Are you off work yet?" I texted Sean the next evening.

It had taken me a little while to find his number in my phone. I had to scroll all the way through my contacts – it was a short list, so it didn't take too long – to find him. The cocky bastard had listed himself as "Sexy." I rolled my eyes, but I didn't change it to "Sean." It was funny, to be honest. And appropriate. I would let it slide.

It was almost six o'clock, and I hoped that he was still busy. Maybe I could catch Bradley at home alone. The thought made my stomach quiver, but I had promised Clayton that I would try to interact with him. I just prayed that he wouldn't lash out at me. I was counting on his fear of Sean's retribution to protect me.

Sean replied instantly. "Yep. Just .have to swing by my place to shower before coming over. Unless you want me to take you up on that joint shower? ;) "

I laughed out loud. "Really? A winky-face emoticon? What are you, a fifteen-year-old girl?"

"Watch yourself, little one. You're in enough trouble for teasing me as it is. What about that shower?"

As much as I was tempted to take him up on his offer, I needed to get into his apartment before he did. And without him finding out about it before I did so. If I went up now, then I had a chance at catching Bradley but not talking to him for too long before Sean got home. I was already in his parking garage. I guessed I had maybe ten or fifteen minutes before he arrived. Enough time to talk to Bradley without him killing me before Sean came home. I hoped.

"Tomorrow morning. I promise," I responded.

"Looking forward to it ;) ."

I snorted. It seemed that Sean had a silly side. It just further endeared me to him.

My mood soured instantly as my mind returned to my task. Taking a deep breath, I forced my body to get out of my car. I remembered the code to get into the building; it was burned into my brain from when Bradley had forced me to enter it on the night that he had abducted me.

A chunk of ice threatened to form in my chest at the memory of my terror, but I shoved it back, strengthening my resolve. Still, dread filled my gut as I knocked tentatively on their apartment door.

"Damn it, Sean, did you forget your keys again? Where is your brain these days?" I had a moment to register Bradley's irritated tone before the door swung open.

His mouth immediately pressed into a grim line and he folded his arms across his chest. I noticed his bulging muscles and fought back the urge to swallow hard.

"Um, hi," I said, my voice shaky. "I'm here to see Sean."

He glared at me. "He's not here, whore." I tried not to flinch at the insulting term.

I had to press on. "Uh, could I at least wait inside until he comes home?"

"You have got to be kidding me. If you think I'm letting you cross my threshold, you're even more of a fucking idiot than I thought you were."

I fixed him with a hard stare. "Do you want Sean to come home to find me waiting in the hallway? Do you think he would take that well?"

Bradley ground his teeth together, and a muscle ticked in his jaw. But after a moment, he stepped aside. "Fine. Just this once. But I swear to god if you ever come here again, I'll hurt you. Sean can use your house as your fuck pad. If I hear you with him one more time I am going to personally haul your ass out of here and chuck you out on the street stark naked. You got me?"

This time I did swallow, physically forcing back the fear that was rising in my throat, and I nodded jerkily.

He shifted his body so that I had barely enough room to skirt around him. Somehow, I managed to squeeze through the small gap without brushing up against him. Who knew what he would do to me if I touched him? I was relieved to recall that his gun was safely stashed in my purse. I hoped to god that he hadn't yet realized that Sean had given it to me. I turned to face him once I had gotten a few feet into the apartment, careful to keep some distance between the two of us.

"So," I said awkwardly. "You work with Sean, right? How come you're home and he's not?" I decided to break the ice with an innocent question.

But his brows drew together and he glared at me with disdain. Maybe it hadn't been so innocent. "Because I haven't been flaking off work to fuck some whore."

I flinched.

As if any woman would ever sleep with you willingly, I wanted to hurl at him. But I bit my tongue, forcing myself to remain civil.

"Does Sean's father work there too? He mentioned something to me about going into the family business."

Bradley's eyes narrowed, regarding me with suspicion. "Why are you asking me about Ronan?" He demanded.

"Ah, just trying to make small talk," I said quickly. "I was just curious. I want to know more about Sean."

"Then ask him yourself," he snapped.

"It seems to be a bit of a sore subject." I knew that I was playing with fire by pressing him like this, but I needed him to tell me more. "When I met Ronan, he, um… He didn't seem to like me too much. I was wondering if I did anything to offend him? I don't want to be the cause of bad blood between Sean and his dad."

"It's a little late to prevent that. But yes, you're making things worse. Sean would be better off without you in his life. Is that what you wanted to hear?" He snarled.

I couldn't help scowling at him. "I'm not leaving Sean," I said staunchly. "So what can I do to make things better?"

He threw up his hands. "What do you want me to tell you? Bake him some fucking cookies and it will make things all rosy? Ronan is a hard man, and if he chooses to hate you, then he's going to hate you. In fact, I've never known him to like anyone. If you're smart, you'll leave it alone."

"Why is he such an ass to Sean?" I demanded. "I know that Ronan hit him."

Bradley's hands clenched to fists. "He told you that?" He said angrily. "He must be losing his fucking mind." He studied my face, his eyes assessing me carefully. I tried my best to school my expression to blankness.

"Why are you really asking questions?" He asked, his voice dangerous. "Has someone put you up to this?"

"No!" I said quickly, panic shooting through my gut. I had pushed things too far. Talking to Bradley had been a bad idea.

He started to advance on me, and I backed away quickly. I was stopped short when my thighs hit the back of the couch, and he got right up in my face, invading my personal space. I leaned back from him, my hands gripping the couch, and I bit back a frightened whimper. I couldn't deny that he was intimidating as hell, and he hadn't hesitated to hurt me before. Had I pushed him over the edge? Was he going to make good on his threat to hit me?

"I don't believe you," he growled. "You're scared shitless. You know I'm on to you."

I shook my head vehemently. "Of course I'm scared. You're threatening me when I just asked you some simple questions about Sean's family. You're seriously over-reacting."

His hand wrapped around my throat, not squeezing, but silently threatening. "I don't believe you," he said softly.

I heard a lock turn and the door opened. "Sean!" I cried, relief washing over me.

Bradley dropped his hand a backed away quickly, but Sean's eyes burned with a furious light, and he advanced on his friend. "What have I told you about threatening her?" He snarled.

Bradley held his hands in front of him. "She was asking questions," he said in a defensive tone.

"And she deserves to be strangled for that?" He demanded, all of his muscles tense as he fought to restrain himself.

"I wasn't hurting her," Bradley insisted. "Bitch was a little too curious for her own good. I don't trust her, Sean. She's got you so screwed up. Does she have a magical cunt or something?"

Bradley had just fucked up big time, and that knowledge registered in his eyes in the split-second that it took Sean to launch himself at him. Sean's fist connected squarely with his friend's jaw, and he went sprawling to the floor.

"Son of a bitch!" Bradley ground out even as Sean drew back his foot to kick him in the stomach. But Bradley anticipated the move, and he grabbed at Sean's ankle. He went crashing to the ground, and Bradley rolled on top of him.

"Sean!" I cried out, terrified for him. He might be larger than his friend, but Bradley's scowl was murderous. He punched Sean viciously in the gut, and he curled up into himself, clutching at his stomach as he gasped for air. Bradley's furious gaze returned to me, and he pushed himself up to his feet. I quickly moved to dart around the couch, trying to put the piece of furniture between myself and him. But he was faster than I was, and his hand tangled in my hair, jerking me painfully back into him. I couldn't hold back a terrified scream.

I heard him grunt behind me, and he released me instantly. I spun to find him clutching at his lower back; Sean had punched him in the kidney. He turned to Sean and drew back his fist, but I caught his arm, desperately trying to deflect his blow. He thrust his elbow back sharply, catching me in the stomach. Agony ripped through me as all of the air rushed out of me. I fell, gasping and clutching at my middle as my insides ripped apart.

Sean snarled and I watched through watering eyes as he tackled Bradley. He landed on top of him and immediately brought his fist down across his face. Bradley's head snapped to the side, and I saw blood spray from his mouth. Sean drew his arm back to hit him again, but I couldn't bear to see any more, couldn't stand to see this violent side of him.

"Stop," I gasped weakly. Sean glanced over at me. "Please."

Sean stood immediately and came to crouch at my side. Bradley stayed down, groaning.

Sean gently ran his fingers over my cheeks, wiping away the tears that I didn't know I had spilled. "Are you alright, little one?" He asked gently.

"I..." I took inventory of my body. The back of my scalp tingled where Bradley had yanked at my hair, and my stomach muscles were still spasming painfully. "I think so," I lied.

He eyed me skeptically. Then his arms were around me, and he drew me up against his chest, cradling me in his arms as he lifted me up.

"I can walk," I protested. He just shot me a forbidding look, fury still burning in his eyes. I quivered in his grip and pursed my lips together.

"You asshole," Bradley groaned, turning his head to Sean and touching his face tenderly. "I think you knocked one of my teeth loose."

Sean stared at him coldly. "I told you that I wouldn't tolerate you abusing her. You're lucky that she stopped me from doing worse."

Bradley's expression twisted into something horrible as he bared his teeth at his friend. They were stained red with his blood, and I shuddered at the sight. I hated that Sean had done that to him, even as I was grateful that he had protected me.

"You think you're protecting her?" Bradley said threateningly. "What do you think Ronan will say when I tell him about this? When I tell him that the bitch was asking questions about him? You've just made everything worse for her," he sneered.

Sean's arms tensed around me. "So now you're tattling on me?" He hissed. "Some friend you are."

Bradley turned his head and spat out blood. "Consider our friendship over until you come to your senses and cut that whore loose. She's really fucked you up, man. I'm not standing up for you anymore."

A trace of pain flickered through the ire that filled Sean's eyes.

"Fine," he snapped. "If that's how you want it. I don't even know who you are anymore. My friend wouldn't attack an innocent woman; he wouldn't threaten to kill her after she saved my life."

Bradley growled in frustration. "Everything I did that night was to protect you. Even now I'm only thinking of what's best for you, despite the fact that you're pissing all over me. She's dangerous, Sean. You're making a mistake trusting her. If I have to talk to Ronan in order for him to convince you to give her up, then that's what I'll do."

"You fucking traitor," Sean ground out. "Goodbye, Bradley."

Sean turned on his heel, shifting me in his grip to slam the door behind him. He refused to release me, holding me as we rode down in the elevator and entered the parking lot. He carried me towards the passenger side of my car.

"I can drive," I protested.

He pinned me with a hard look. "I didn't ask whether or not you could drive. I'm taking you home. This isn't up for discussion."

His muscles were tense, but he was gentle with me as he placed me in the passenger seat and drew the seat belt across my chest. He shut the driver's side door a little harder than was necessary when he got in, and he didn't look over at me as he cranked up the car and threw it into reverse, backing out of the parking garage.

We were silent for long minutes, a horrible tension building in the confined space. Sean was seething. Was it from his anger at Bradley, or was he mad at me?

"I'm sorry," I said softly.

He glanced over me, and the fury that I saw in his expression made me press my body deeper into my seat as I instinctively tried to draw away from him.

"You're sorry," he echoed me, his voice tight. "What the fuck were you thinking, Claudia?" He burst out, half-shouting.

I shrank back from him further. "I… I just wanted to surprise you," I lied, my voice small and tremulous.

His knuckles turned white as he gripped the steering wheel hard. "I told you that I wasn't home," he growled. "You knew that you would be alone with Bradley. Why would you put yourself at risk like that?" He demanded.

"I didn't think he would hurt me," I desperately defended my actions. "He…" I wasn't sure if I should admit that Bradley had threatened me at my house, but it seemed that I didn't have a choice. "I came home a few nights ago, and he was waiting for me. He wanted to make sure that I hadn't gone to the cops. I was afraid of him, but he said that he wouldn't hurt me because he didn't want to make you angry. I thought I was safe from him."

Sean let out a furious snarl. "Son of a bitch! And when were you planning on telling me about this?"

"I wasn't," I said, trying to make my tone stronger. "I've caused so much trouble between the two of you. I might hate Bradley for what he did to me, but I can't stand to see that I'm destroying your relationship with your best friend."

That had a grain of truth to it.

"It's his actions that are destroying our relationship," he said harshly. "It's not your fault. And given his hatred of you, it was beyond stupid to show up to my apartment tonight when you knew that I wasn't there." He speared me with a hard, intimidating glare. "Swear to me that you will never do that again. If I hadn't arrived when I did…" He trailed off, closing his eyes for a moment and grimacing.

"Okay," I said meekly. "I promise." Regardless of what I had said to Clayton about trying to mend my relationship with Bradley, I knew that I would never dare confront him again.

I hoped that some of the tension between us would ease, but Sean's features remained twisted with suppressed fury.

"And why the fuck were you asking questions about my father?" He demanded. "Haven't I warned you about him?" He cursed softly and ran his hand through his hair. "There's no way he won't take notice of you now. If Bradley really does go to him… Do you have any idea of the position that you've put yourself in? That you've put me in?"

"I'm sorry," I said again, at a loss for words.

"'Sorry' doesn't cut it," he said angrily. "Why were you asking questions about him when I specifically warned you not to?"

"I just… I just wanted to make things better. I'm not comfortable with the idea of him hating me, especially if it's causing him to turn against you. I was asking Bradley what I had done wrong."

"You allowed me to care about you, that's what you did wrong," he snapped. "I told you not to fuck with my father, and you deliberately disobeyed me. And look at where it got you. Bradley hurt you."

I opened my mouth to protest, but I snapped it closed when he shot me a cutting look.

"And don't you dare tell me that you're alright," he growled. "He hit you, Claudia. What were you thinking trying to get between him and me? Do you have any idea what he could have done to you?"

This time my voice was stronger, anger coloring my tone. "If you think that I was just going to stand there and let you take a beating, then you don't know me at all. I hate the sight of violence, Sean. It goes against everything that I am; I have dedicated my life to saving people from pain. And to see him hurting you... I couldn't bear that."

He grimaced. "You'll have to learn to. I won't allow you to put yourself in the line of fire ever again. Do you know what it would do to me if you were harmed?" He glared at me, his expression dark. "I am going to tan your hide until you learn not to defy me in this."

That got my hackles up. "Yellow," I said sharply, using my safe word.

His brows rose in surprise, his mouth falling open slightly.

"Let's get one thing straight," I said angrily. "You can discipline me when it comes to our sexual relationship, but know that I will never tolerate you punishing me for something that I've done outside the bedroom. This is my life, Sean. I make my own choices, and I refuse to allow you to dictate what I can and can't do. That's called abuse." I knew that that last part was harsh, but I needed to drive my point home.

His mouth hardened into a grim line. "Fine," he barked out. Then he took a deep breath, and his expression softened. "Of course I understand that, Claudia. I was way out of line. It's just... Please. You have to listen to me on this. I can't protect you if you're recklessly placing yourself in danger. Can't you understand that? You're small, weak, and you don't stand a chance against my enemies."

"I am *not* weak," I said staunchly.

He raised a cool brow at me, eyeing me up and down. I let out a sigh. "Okay," I conceded. "Maybe I'm not the strongest person ever. But I can work on that."

He considered for a moment. "I'll teach you some moves for self-defense when we get to your house," he said. "As much as I hate the idea, I might not always be there when you need me, and you have to be able to defend yourself. Just swear to me that you won't goad people into attack."

I folded my arms across my chest. "I'm not stupid," I insisted.

"You certainly are doing a good impression of it," he said harshly.

I frowned at him.

"Sorry," he muttered. "I'm out of line again." To my surprise, he shot me a small smile. "Do you have any idea how infuriating you are?"

"Right back at you." I tried for a hard tone, but I reacted instantly to his renewed levity. It was so much better than his ire.

He chuckled. "Fair enough. I guess we're a good match, then."

I was momentarily stunned by his words. It was almost as though he was defining us as a couple. Was that what we were now? I hardly dared hope. I reached out and covered his hand with mine.

"I suppose we are," I said with a smile.

Chapter 8

"Okay," Sean said. We were standing in my living room as he instructed me on how to defend myself. "Your best move is to hold your hand out in front of you, your palm facing your attacker. I want you to warn him to stop before he is on you. At least *try* to prevent a physical altercation. If he advances on you anyway, I want you to slam your palm into his nose. This will break it, and if you're lucky will shove the bone back into his brain. That will put him down completely."

I gasped. "But that would kill him," I protested, alarmed. "I couldn't do that!"

His mouth thinned into a grim line. "We've been over this, Claudia. If it comes down to you or him, you're going to choose yourself. Do you understand me?"

I swallowed against the bile rising in my throat at the thought of taking a human life, but I nodded reluctantly, not wanting to argue.

"If you can't put him down completely, then follow up by kicking him in the balls. That should drop him and give you time to get away."

"Okay," I agreed. I definitely didn't have a problem with that one.

"His other main weakness will be his eyes. Go for them if he's in close range. The best way is to use your keys. Make a fist and press them between your fingers and then strike. If you don't have your keys on you, I want you to use your index and middle fingers. Don't claw at him; hold them out straight and jab hard."

My stomach churned. I didn't think that I would ever be capable of causing such damage to another human being. The thought of seeing a man's eyes, bloodied and gouged by my own hand… I wrapped my arms around my middle, hugging myself.

Sean's expression softened, and he enfolded me in his arms, running a reassuring hand up and down my back. "I hate that I'm putting you in this position, Claudia," he admitted, his voice strained. "But the fact is that it's too late to turn back now, and you have to be able to defend yourself if I'm not around." He pulled back and cupped my cheek in one of his large hands. "I'm so sorry," he said softly. His eyes were filled with shame and regret.

"It's not your fault," I said gently. "Bradley is the one who brought me into this world. All you've done is protect me from it. I would be dead by now if it weren't for you."

His expression tightened at the mention of Bradley. "I hate him for that." He couldn't keep the rage from his voice.

I reached up and traced my finger along his jawline. The rough sensation of his stubble against my fingertips sent heat shooting through me. I stared up into his eyes, which were burning with a furious light. "Please don't say that," I said softly. "I know that you can mend what is broken between you. Just give him time. I can understand why he thinks I'm a threat, and while I'm not thrilled with the fact that he attacked me, I know he'll come to realize that I'm not trying to hurt you."

Bullshit, I said harshly to myself. Well, a part of it was true: I didn't want to hurt Sean. But that didn't change the fact that I was inevitably going to.

He grasped my hand gently and turned his face into my wrist, breathing in my scent deeply. "You're so *good,* Claudia," he said, a hint of wonder lacing his tone. "And so innocent. Some might even go so far as to say naïve."

I opened my mouth to retort that I was not naïve, but he pressed his fingers against my lips, silencing me.

"I'm not trying to offend you, Claudia," he insisted softly. "I've never met anyone as brave and as goodhearted as you. Despite everything you've been through, you still care deeply for humanity. You are so remarkable, and I can't believe that you can't seem to see that."

I was stunned into shocked silence. How could he think so highly of me? He didn't think me cold; he saw right through my walls, peering into my soul. How was it that he could see goodness there when I felt like such a traitor? The knowledge of my deceit and his ignorance of it made my heart twinge painfully.

"Thank you," I whispered, my lips brushing against his calloused fingertips. The roughness of them against my soft skin made my flesh tingle.

He took a deep, shaky breath and reluctantly pulled away from me. "Come on," he said. "I need to teach you how to throw a punch." His fingers curled around mine, forcing me to make a fist. "You'll want to hit him in the nose or the mouth; that's where the most nerve endings are. If you can follow it up with a blow to the solar plexus, it should put him down." He gave me a lopsided smile and ran his free hand up my arm, lightly squeezing my bicep. "You're so small in my grip," he said, his voice husky. "I like that, Claudia, but you're going to need to practice this so that you can get stronger."

I swallowed hard. "I doubt I could ever take you on," I admitted, a bit breathlessly.

His smile took on a slightly cruel edge, and his fingers moved upward to caress my throat, tracing the line of my carotid artery, threatening. My eyes widened and my breathing hitched. "No," he said silkily. "I don't think you could." He cocked his head at me. "But I don't think you would dare try." His eyes were dancing, and I knew that he was challenging me to rise to his bait. And damn it if I wasn't tempted to. I longed for his raw power to wash over me, for him to force my body to submit to his far greater strength.

Throwing caution to the wind, I pulled back my free hand and aimed for his nose, just as he had instructed me. He caught my fist easily, then shifted his grip to my wrist. He grinned down at me evilly before wrenching my arm behind my back. I gave a sharp cry as he pulled it upward behind me, sending a slight pain shooting up my arm. I was forced to twist away from him, turning to relieve some of the pressure. But he didn't relent, and the pressure drove me to my knees. His other hand came down on the back of my neck, shoving me down until he had my face pinned against the floor. My free hand scrabbled against the carpet, trying fruitlessly to push myself up. He held me patiently, implacable, until I went limp beneath him. He chuckled above me.

"Well isn't this familiar?" He asked, amused. It was the same position he had held me in the last time he had taken me, and my sex swelled at the memory. I bit back a moan, trying to cling to my willpower. I was enjoying the fight, enjoying pushing the limits of his tolerance for my resistance.

"Very original." I tried for a disparaging tone, but it came out as more of a gasp.

"You want to try something new then, do you?" His voice was low and dangerous, and I couldn't help quivering beneath him. "I want you to remember that you asked for it."

Suddenly, his hold on my neck and wrist eased, and his fingers twined in my hair at the back of my head. He pulled relentlessly, and I quickly pressed my hands against the floor to push myself upright before the strands parted company with my scalp. When I was on my feet, I reached up to rake my nails against him arm, trying to make him release me. But he grabbed my wrists, pinning them at the small of my back. He held them in one hand while his other returned to my hair, tugging back sharply in reprimand. Staying stationed behind me, he shoved me, never releasing his grip on me. I was forced inexorably forward, helpless to prevent him from directing my body where he wanted it to go.

"Where are we going?" I asked.

He gave another sharp tug on my hair, sending tingles down my spine. "Quiet," he said gruffly. "I don't believe I gave you permission to speak."

My mouth fell open, but no sound came out. My breathing was turning fast and shallow as he guided me out of the living room and up the stairs. I fought not to stumble up them as my legs went weak beneath me, my entire body turning to jelly as submission crept into the edges of my mind. Remembering our game, I tried to shove it back, but I knew that I would only be able to hold it at bay for so long.

When we reached the center of my bedroom, he turned me so that I was facing the door. His lips were at my ear, his hot breath rippling across my neck as he spoke. "I'm going to let you go now, and you're going to strip for me, Claudia," he told me. "You are not to move from this spot, and you are not to look behind you under any circumstances."

"And if I do?" I asked.

There was a sharp, bruising pain as he pinched my ass hard, and I let out a surprised yelp. "There will be consequences," he said matter-of-factly. "And if you're tempted to test me, know that you are in enough trouble as it is. I'm warning you not to goad me. You might not like the results. Do you understand?" He asked softly.

"Y-yes," I forced out, and he laughed at my stuttering. He released his hold on me, and his hand snaked under the back of my shirt. His index finger slowly traced the line of my spine from my nape to my tailbone. He stroked the little patch of skin just above my ass, and I let out a strangled cry as he stimulated the little bundle of nerves there that he had introduced me to when he had first spanked me.

But he drew away all too soon, and I whined at the loss.

"Now strip, Claudia," he ordered. Cool air closed behind me as he moved away.

With trembling fingers, I gripped the hem of my sweater, drawing it up over my head. Then I fumbled at the button of my slacks. It took a few tries before I was successful and was able to shove them down my legs, stepping out of my shoes at the same time. I straightened, wearing nothing but my bra and panties. I had purchased a barely-there, lacy black set just for Sean. I heard him growl behind me.

"As much as I appreciate the view, you had better take those off. I want you completely bare for me."

I tried to still my shaking fingers as I unclasped my bra and pushed my panties down my legs. I shivered, goose bumps covering my skin and my nipples hardening. I was unsure if it was from the cool air or from my arousal. There was a growing wetness between my legs as Sean watched me, his eyes practically burning into my back as he stared at me, making me wait.

I heard a drawer sliding open.

"What are you doing?" I asked, my voice high and thin as I began to twist my head back to see what he was up to.

"Eyes forward, sub," he ordered harshly. "And I thought I told you to stay quiet."

Sub. He had never called me that before, and my pussy clenched at the term. My head snapped back, my eyes gazing resolutely forward. I heard him rummage for a moment, followed by the sound of the drawer closing. My muscles were so tense from the effort of holding my stance that they were practically quivering.

He stepped so softly on the thick carpet that I barely had time to register his approach before his hand closed around the back of my neck again. He was gentler this time as he guided me towards the bed, but I didn't dare fight him any longer. His hand was on my back, between my shoulder blades. He gave me a hard shove, and I barely had time to catch myself on my hands before I fell onto my front on the bed, facing diagonally so that one of my bedposts was right in front of me. He was instantly behind me, his weight shifting the mattress. His arm snaked under my belly and jerked me upward, forcing me onto my knees. I tried to straighten, but his hand was back between my shoulder blades, holding me down.

I smirked. "This is familiar again," I taunted, referring to the similar position that he had trapped me in downstairs. I could hardly believe that I dared to say it.

His hand came down hard on my ass, and I gave a sharp cry as the intense sting turned to a deeper, throbbing burn. At the same time, my clit pulsed, and I could feel myself growing wetter.

"Oh don't worry," he said smoothly. "You're soon going to see just how different this is. I'm going to push you tonight, Claudia. We're going to see just how much you can handle."

He slapped me again, and I groaned both from the erotic pain and from his threatening words.

"And what did I tell you about speaking out of turn?" He demanded. He raked his fingernails across the burning area where he had abused my ass. "You will learn obedience, Claudia. And I will enjoy teaching you." His voice was rough and lustful.

He bent over me, and I relished the hardness of his body against my back, the pressure shoving me down and pressing my breasts almost painfully against the mattress. I mewled and closed my eyes as my taut nipples rubbed against the sheets, craving more stimulation.

My eyes snapped open as something soft encircled my wrist, tightening around it. I looked up as Sean pulled my arm forward with his grip on the material that bound me. I realized that it was my pantyhose as he looped it around the bedpost. I tried to jerk my other wrist out of his reach, but he caught it easily, stretching it out before me as he deftly secured the silky material around it. He ran his fingertips up my arms, tracing them across my pebbled flesh. When he reached my shoulders, one hand moved to tenderly stroke my hair while the other gripped my chin, turning my head slightly so that I was forced to meet his gaze where he hovered above me.

"Are you alright, little one?" He asked softly, his eyes kind.

Was I alright? I took inventory of my body. My ass burned where he had struck me, but I had to admit that the sensation was delicious, spreading heat to my sex, making my core throb. The bindings on my wrists were secure but painless, and being restrained was undeniably erotic.

I was far, far better than okay. I nodded at him weakly, and he grinned down at me. His smile held a slightly predatory edge.

"Has anyone ever taken your ass, sub?" He asked, his voice suddenly brusque and business-like. My jaw would have dropped if he hadn't been holding it closed with his grip on my chin. Still, I managed to drop my eyes, blushing furiously.

He held my face more firmly, a warning. "You will look at me when you answer me," he reprimanded.

I forced my gaze to meet his, and I trembled as I was captured by the dark flame of his eyes. "No," I admitted, my voice barely audible.

His grin twisted into something satisfied and slightly cruel. He released my jaw to trail his fingers over my cheek. "Then I'll be honored to be the first."

Oh, god. Was he really going to do that to me?

"Will it hurt?" I asked tremulously, knowing that I shouldn't speak out of turn but unable to resist voicing my concern.

His thumb tenderly stroked my cheekbone. "Yes," he admitted, and my stomach clenched. "But I will be gentle with you, and I think you'll grow to like it." He speared me with a hard look. "That pain can turn to pleasure. Do you understand what I'm talking about?"

I thought of how I received pleasure when he punished me, and although I was terrified of what he was going to do to me, I nodded. I trusted him, and I was willing to take the plunge.

His weight lifted from me abruptly.

"Where are you going?" I asked nervously, worried that he was going to leave me.

He said nothing, but it wasn't long before he was behind me once again.

"Open your mouth," he ordered, holding his hands behind his back. I was worried about what he was concealing from me.

"What?" I asked breathlessly.

He looked down at me forbiddingly, and his fingers closed around my face, putting pressure on both sides of my jaw. I cried out at the twinge of pain and my lips parted. He shoved something black into my open mouth, and I realized that it was my panties. I tried to push them out with my tongue, shocked, but he pressed something else between my teeth, tying it firmly behind my head. He had used another pair of my pantyhose as a makeshift gag, and they pushed the panties further into my mouth. I could taste my wetness on them. I thought that I would be revolted by it, but I was only further turned on by his show of utter dominance.

His hand wrapped around my throat, squeezing gently. "I warned you not to speak without permission; I told you that there would be consequences for disobedience. This is your punishment."

I moaned as his words washed through me, stoking my desire to a fever-pitch. The sound was smothered by the gag, and it only turned me on more. His grip tightened incrementally.

"You won't be able to use your safe words, so I want you to snap instead if you become distressed. Can you do that for me now?"

I snapped my fingers obediently, and his grip loosened, his fingers stroking the side of my throat. "Good girl," he praised. Sparks danced across my skin, making me shiver as his words of praise washed over me. I could feel the submissiveness that I had been trying to resist insistently closing in, rolling across my mind like fog blown inland across the water. It seeped into my thoughts, saturating and smothering them. That incredible nothingness was overcoming me, and I welcomed it with open arms. There was nothing but the torturous pressure of the mattress beneath my breasts and the tautness of my restraints, reinforcing my utter helplessness. And there was Sean, his scent infusing the air around me, mingling with my own arousal. It was a heady cocktail, and I breathed deeply, drawing it in until I was drowning in it. I went limp, completely ceding to his will. My body was his to do with as he pleased, and there was nothing I could do about it. I didn't *want* to do anything about it.

There was a rustling sound behind me, and out of the corner of my eye I saw Sean stripping off his clothes. I tried to crane my neck back so that I could take in more of him, so that I could admire his perfect body that I couldn't seem to get enough of.

"If you keep looking back like that I'm going to have to blindfold you," he said coolly.

A part of me wanted that, was intrigued by the idea of being deprived of my sight as he touched me. But I was already overwhelmed by the new experiences that he was introducing me to; I wasn't sure if I could handle another. So I meekly laid my cheek back against the mattress. I could no longer summon up the willpower to resist him anyway.

"Another time, then," he said, the thread of excitement in his tone betraying his anticipation for the night when he would get to do that to me.

His fingers were suddenly at my desire-slicked lips, swirling in the wetness there. I groaned at the silky sensation of his feather-light touch. He gathered up some of the wetness before his fingers trailed slowly backwards, leaving hot, tingling lines in their wake as he made steady progress away from my sex. When he reached the area between my pussy and my ass, he pressed harder, and I gasped as the sensation sent fire shooting through my core and up my spine, the heat searing into my nipples. I moaned and couldn't help shifting my torso, desperate to relieve some of the building pressure in my painfully hardened buds. But it did little to slake my need, which was only building as his fingers continued on their forbidden path. He was moving agonizingly slowly, bringing my flesh sparking to life as I began to pant in anticipation of his touching my most taboo area, the hint of fear that was pulsing through me only intensifying my arousal. By the time he reached the edge of my dark entrance, I was distantly surprised to find that I was desperate for him to touch me there. He hovered there for a moment, and I couldn't stop my back from arching, offering myself up to him in silent encouragement.

His laugh was a low, satisfied rumble deep in his chest. My sharp, shocked cry was lost in the gag as he brushed against me, tracing against me in a circular motion. Nerve endings that I had never known existed jumped to sudden, shocking life, and pleasure ripped through me at the utterly foreign sensation. He pressed against me gently.

"Relax for me, little one," he ordered, the endearment sweetening the command.

All of my muscles were tense, the building ecstasy pulling my body taut like a drawn bowstring, straining for release. It took great effort to comply, to force my muscles to loosen for him.

When he was satisfied, he increased the pressure until he breeched my opening. My fingers twisted in the sheets as he continued to drive slowly, inexorably into me. There was no pain as he gently stretched me, introducing me to pleasure that I had never imagined would be stirred from stimulating this area. He paused for a moment when he was fully seated within me, letting me grow accustomed to the strange but delicious sensation. Then he quickly pulled almost all the way out before driving back into me abruptly, jarringly.

A strangled cry erupted from me, and the way that the gag muffled the sound made my pussy clench. My clit was throbbing with every rapid beat of my heart as it grew painfully hard.

He pulled back again, and there was more pressure at my entrance, a second finger insisting to penetrate me. He pressed his way in, widening me, and I knew that he was preparing me for his cock. The thought of it taking me there now made my mouth water. He began pumping in and out of me in a regular, steady rhythm.

"This is the ultimate submission, Claudia: allowing me to take your ass," he informed me, his voice seeming far away. "I'm going to claim you, Claudia, as no man has ever done. As no man will ever do."

Something akin to a sob escaped me at his possessive words. I wanted nothing more than for them to be true.

No, I thought through the haze in my mind. *No one else.*

Without warning, his cock plunged into my pussy. His fingers remained within me, and the fullness was incredible. He pumped into me a few times, his assault on my sex alternating with that on my ass.

I felt a moment of loss as he completely withdrew from me abruptly, but he was immediately touching me again, the tip of his hard cock, slick with my own juices, pressing at me this time. I gasped at the size of it. There was no way he would fit; I was far too small.

He gripped my hips hard to prevent me from moving away from him and gave a low, warning growl. "This will hurt a little," he said. "Relax for me."

I tried to obey, forcing my body to invite him in as it had done before.

Holding me firmly in place with his hands on my hips, he resumed his ruthless progress. I felt him penetrate me, slowly forcing me to stretch for him as the intrusion became wider. It awoke a distinctly uncomfortable burning sensation, and I pressed my face into the mattress to smother my pained cry. I pulled against my restraints, my body instinctively struggling to escape him. But there was no escape. Not from him.

There was a small popping sensation as his engorged head fully entered me, and the stretching mercifully eased. He paused there, allowing me to adjust to his size. His fingers dug into my soft flesh with the strain of holding himself back.

"Fuck, Claudia, you're so tight," he forced out through gritted teeth.

He reached beneath me, his fingers finding my clit. I moaned at the contact that mercifully eased some of the pain that had tormented the neglected area. He rubbed in a circular motion, and the burning sensation in my ass began to morph into a delicious, hot tingling. His length continued to enter me, and my body went utterly still as I focused completely on accommodating him. He didn't pause when he was in me fully, instead drawing back slightly before pumping back in. He continued to rock against me steadily, drawing out of me a bit further with each thrust. And all the while, he continued touching my clit, alternating teasing around it before gently brushing over it, keeping me torturously on the edge of my orgasm.

He was pulling almost all the way out of me now, taking me harder and faster. My hips began to move against him, meeting his thrusts.

"You're mine now, Claudia," he growled as he drove into me harshly. "Mine!"

"Yes!" I wanted to say, but it came out as an unintelligible groan. Even if I hadn't been gagged, I wouldn't have been able to speak; I seemed to have lost control of my tongue. The only movement that I could manage was rocking my body back against him, and even that was pure instinct rather than an action that I controlled.

His words pushed me over the edge, and my inner muscles began to contract around him. Recognizing my building orgasm, Sean sharply pinched my hardened bud between his thumb and forefinger. My mind was hurled into oblivion as pleasure hit me with the force of a speeding Mack Truck.

I was dimly aware of Sean's savage roar behind me as his heat lashed into me, scorching my insides with branding fire as he marked me as his. His final thrusts sent lightning shooting through my body as my nerve endings became hyper-sensitized, the erotic pain of it shoving me further into the darkness.

I wasn't aware of my soft whimper as he withdrew from me, leaving me feeling empty. A part of my mind registered the gag being removed from between my teeth and the sensation of blood rushing back to my fingertips as I was freed from my restraints. His gentle, calloused hands rolled me onto my side, and I instinctively snuggled up against him, my head resting submissively on his abs, just above his hips. My arm wrapped around him, clinging to him. I felt his hand tenderly stroking my hair as his hard breathing made his stomach rise and fall rapidly beneath me. The undulating motion rocked me like I was floating on gentle waves far out at sea.

"You're perfect, Claudia," he murmured down at me, and I wasn't sure if the words were real or imagined. I found that I didn't care if they were or not.

Sighing happily, I fell into sleep with a smile on my face.

Chapter 9

The blaring of my alarm beeping insistently jarred me from my sleep the next morning. I sat up with a start, disoriented; I couldn't remember getting into bed the night before. The sudden movement caused a twinge of pain to bloom across my stomach, and I winced.

There was a warm hand on my back, and I jumped slightly.

"Claudia?"

Sean. Memories from the night before came flooding back to me, and I felt my cheeks flame crimson as I recalled my wantonness.

He cupped my face gently, turning my head so that I was facing him. He traced his thumb over my hot cheeks and he smiled softly. But his eyes were darkened with concern.

"What's wrong?" He asked.

As my mind flashed over the events of the day before, I recalled Bradley's elbow driving into my gut. I didn't want to remind Sean of the altercation.

"It's nothing," I lied quickly, but I stupidly moved my hand to cover my stomach to hide the damage.

He frowned and reached out for me. His hand closed around my wrist, prying my arm away from my body. He hissed in a breath and his eyes flashed as my flesh was revealed to him. I glanced down and held back another wince as I took in the angry purple bruise that marred my pale skin.

"It's alright," I said in a rush. "I mark up easily."

His angry gaze turned against me. "I'm the only one who should be leaving marks on you, Claudia," he said harshly. "And certainly nothing like this."

"Please," I said. "Don't be angry." I was worried that I had reawakened the ire that had been directed at me the day before over my foolishness for confronting Bradley on my own.

His eyes softened instantly, but the lines of his face were still tight. "I'm not mad at you," he told me. "It's Bradley who - "

"Stop, please," I cut him off. "Don't go antagonizing him. It will only make things worse. If he really is thinking about going to your father, then the last thing you want to do is to push him further."

Sean took a deep breath, closed his eyes, and pinched the bridge of his nose. When he opened them again, their green depths were less stormy. "You're right," he conceded. "Even though I want to punish him with every fiber of my being, it's only going to do more harm than good. I won't risk you like that."

"Thank you," I whispered, relieved that he had agreed. The last thing I needed was for Ronan Reynolds to learn that I had been asking questions about him. That might blow my cover.

At the thought of my traitorous actions, my heart twisted. I was growing closer to Sean, more drawn to him with every minute we shared together. It wasn't just the sex, either. Although he gave me mind-blowing, fantasy-surpassing ecstasy, my feelings for him went deeper than that. I loved our light banter, and I admitted to myself that I even found his cockiness endearing in an infuriating sort of way. He was sweet, silly, and sexy as hell. And vulnerable in a way that tugged at my heartstrings, making me long to heal him.

The knowledge that I was inevitably going to lose him was growing harder and harder to bear. I was falling for him hard. I had never done anything so reckless; it was diametrically opposed to the iron control that I had always exercised. But Sean had come along and turned my life upside down, changing me in a way that I feared was irrevocable.

I realized that he was peering into my eyes, studying me carefully.

"What are you thinking?" He asked.

"I…" I hesitated.

I'm thinking that I'm about to destroy my soul. And possibly yours as well.

"I care about you," I heard myself admitting. I regretted the words almost immediately. Why was I tormenting us like this? Why was I digging myself deeper and deeper into this hole that I would never be able to claw my way back out of?

And to make it worse, Sean was completely oblivious to the agonizing fate that I was pulling him toward.

Still, I waited with baited breath for him to respond, anxious for his response. His jaw tightened slightly, his expression unreadable. For a moment, I feared that I had gone too far.

He let out a long breath. "I care about you too, Claudia," he said softly. "More than you know."

"I think I have a good idea," I murmured, trying to keep the pain from my voice as my heart twisted.

We stared at one another for a moment, but then Sean shifted uncomfortably, pulling his eyes from mine.

"I believe I promised you a shower," I said, trying to keep my tone light to ease the awkward tension that began to fill the space between us.

The smile he shot me was slightly regretful. "I got one last night," he said.

I blinked, surprised that his movements hadn't woken me. "Wow. I guess I was really out of it."

He grinned smugly, clearly pleased with himself. "It's not often that I get the pleasure of fucking a woman into a stupor. You completely passed out on me."

I frowned at him at the allusion to the fact that he had done that to other women. It made me recall something important that I had been meaning to bring up with him. "Um," I began. "I've been meaning to ask you something."

His brows rose. "Okay. Shoot."

"I know you've been with a lot of women. Do you... You don't have any STDs, do you?" The words came out in a rush.

"Oh," he said, surprised by my question. "No. Don't worry about that. I just got tested, and I'm totally clean. I always use protection."

I shot him a level look. "Not with me, you haven't." I reminded him.

He ran a hand through his hair, looking somewhat chagrined. "Sorry about that," he said. "The first time… Well, it took me by surprise. I had wanted you so badly for so long… I kind of lost my mind that day." He speared me with an intense stare. "I want all of you, Claudia. It's like some dark compulsion is driving me when I'm with you. It's all I can do to cling on to my control. I'm sorry if I upset you. I promise I'll do better."

I was shocked by his confession. It was far more than the simple "yes" or "no" answer that I had expected. "I'm not upset," I allayed his fears. "I was just concerned. And I'm on birth control, so you don't need to worry about that." I covered his hand with mine. "We're okay, Sean. I didn't think you would put me at risk. I just needed to know for sure."

His smile was back. "Good," he sounded relieved.

I returned it easily. "So about that shower. Are you sure that I can't tempt you to take another one?"

He glanced over at the clock. "I don't think I can," he said regretfully. "I wanted to let you get as much sleep as possible, so I'm afraid I don't have time."

"Okay," I said, trying to keep the disappointment from my tone. "I'll call you a cab."

"No need," he said. "I called and ordered one last night." He looked at the clock again, then grinned predatorily. "I still have ten minutes to ravage you before I have to leave."

I pouted dramatically. "That's not nearly enough time."

He moved in, pressing my body down into the bed with his weight, caging me in with his arms on either side of me. "It's plenty of time to tease you," he said, an evil glint in his eye.

"Then you'll think of me all day. It's not fair that I walk around with my balls constantly aching because of you. I'm going to return the favor."

I gasped. "You wouldn't."

"Watch me."

He crushed his mouth against mine, stifling my protest. I pressed against his hard chest frantically, trying to shove him away. His lips tugged up at the corners as they caressed mine. He didn't even bother restraining me. There was no need; he knew that I would never be able to fight him off, as he had made abundantly clear the night before. The cocky bastard.

Despite my indignation, I melted for him, and my hands shifted to curl around his shoulders, my fingernails lightly pressing into his skin. His tongue breached my mouth, claiming me with deep, demanding strokes. My body arched up into him, my hips grinding against his. I had thought that he would reprimand me for my actions, but he let me continue to stimulate myself against him. He reached down between us to tweak my nipples, pinching them hard before rolling them deftly between his fingers, easing the ache.

My nails bit into him harder as warmth bloomed between my legs. I began grinding faster, needing more friction against my clit.

Abruptly, he shoved off of me, and I cried out at the sudden, shocking loss. He stood and grinned down at me cruelly, drawing the duvet up over my body as a further barrier between us. My eyes were wide and I was panting hard. I couldn't believe that he was truly going to deny me.

I shot him a scowl and moved to touch myself, desperate for release.

His expression shifted into a forbidding mask. "Stop, sub," he barked. "Don't you dare."

My hand stilled instantly, and I quivered under his hard stare.

Oh, shit.

"Now, you're going to be a good girl and wait for me. You are not to touch yourself without my express permission. If I even suspect that you have…"

He trailed off, leaving the threat open ended, making it all the more terrifying.

"Okay," I said quickly.

His glare didn't ease. "Promise me. Tell me you'll be good."

"I promise."

He just raised an expectant eyebrow at me, silently demanding more.

"I promise I'll be good," I said, blushing furiously.

His smile was back, and I glowed at the sight of it. He bent down and planted a swift, sweet kiss on my forehead.

"I'm glad we've reached an accord."

I snorted. "That would imply that there was some sort of compromise involved," I said huffily as I watched him pull on his jeans.

He chuckled at me. "Pedant," he accused.

I couldn't help cottoning on to his levity. "I suppose I am. It's all part of my charm. You love it, really." I echoed his words from the night that I had found him waiting for me on my front stoop.

He laughed again as he slipped his shirt over his head. "You wish," he threw my retort right back at me.

I started to get out from under the covers so that I could give him one last kiss before he left me, but he stopped me short.

"Don't move," he warned. "If I see your body I won't be able to help myself. Then I'll be late for work again."

A car tooted its horn outside my house. The taxi had arrived.

"That's the last thing I want," I said seriously.

"Will I see you later?" He asked, his tone eager.

I bit my lip. "I have to work late," I lied.

I have to go spill your secrets to the FBI.

He gave me an exaggerated puppy-dog look. It was so wrong on him that I couldn't stifle a giggle.

"Alright. I'll call you when I leave the office if you promise never to look at me like that again."

His smile was wide and boyishly genuine. "It's a deal."

The taxi driver honked his horn again.

"Get out of here," I made a shooing motion at him.

"Yes, ma'am," he said mockingly.

I rolled my eyes at him, and he winked at me before turning and striding out of my room.

I tried to cling to my moment of happiness, but it melted away as I glumly contemplated the long day that I had to get through before I could see him again.

■■

I struggled to hide my embarrassment as I held up my shirt so that Agent Vaughn could photograph the bruise on my stomach. They needed to log it as evidence, but I was decidedly uncomfortable baring any part of my body to a man who wasn't Sean. I trusted Clayton implicitly, but my hands still balled to fists in the fabric of my blouse. Thankfully, he was professional and efficient, and it only took a minute for him to snap the shots that he needed.

"Okay," he said, lowering the camera. "All done."

I hastily shoved my shirt down, but when I lifted my gaze back to Clayton's, his eyes were still fixed on my midriff. Had he simply not had the time to glance away, or were his eyes lingering? I shook it off. He had never been anything but sweet to me. When he touched me, it didn't feel intimate. At least not in a sexual way. His warmth was pure comfort, and I was sure that he was only interested in being my friend. I was reading too much into this; I was just caught up in my discomfiture and imagining things.

He smiled at me gently. "I have to debrief you now. I know that you don't like this part, but it's necessary."

I nodded, squaring my shoulders and lifting my chin. "I know," I said. "It's okay. I'm getting used to it."

That was a bold-faced lie. The guilt that weighed heavily on me would never be allayed. But there was nothing for it. Sean had been right: there was no backing out now. My only options were to continue with my task or run. And that would leave Sean vulnerable, at the mercy of his father for the rest of his life. Or it would condemn him to spend most of his life behind bars. I didn't want that for him.

I followed Agent Vaughn into the interrogation room – I couldn't help thinking of it like that. When the camera was on and he was seated across from me, the questioning began.

"Tell me what happened last night," Agent Vaughn ordered. "How did you come to be injured?"

"Bradley hit me," I replied, anger at the memory of him hurting Sean lacing my tone.

"And why did he do that?"

"Because he's a volatile, hateful bastard," I flung out.

Agent Vaughn raised his brows at me, waiting for more.

I sighed. "I went to the apartment that he shares with Sean before Sean came home from work. I did what you asked me to: I tried to question him about Ronan. Although I couched the questions in terms of concern for his dislike of me, I pressed too far. Bradley became suspicious, and he threatened me physically."

I suppressed a shudder as I recalled his grip on my throat, the phantom feeling of his fingers curled around my neck almost tangibly brushing over my skin even though I was ensconced in the safety of the FBI office.

"Sean came home then," I continued, "and Bradley backed off. But he said that he knew that I was dangerous, and that Sean was blind to it. He was right," I said quietly.

Agent Vaughn allowed me a moment of silence, then pressed me to go on. "What happened then?"

"Bradley said some nasty things about me, and Sean attacked him. I tried to help him, and that's when Bradley hit me. Sean took him down, and then I made Sean back off." I closed my eyes and drew a shaky breath. "Bradley was furious. He said that he was going to tell Ronan about me asking questions so that Sean's father would force him to let go of me. Sean took me home then."

I opened my eyes and fixed Agent Vaughn with a hard, determined stare. "Is that the proof you need that Bradley is willingly working for Ronan? Can't you see now that Sean doesn't want any part of it, but he doesn't have a choice?"

Agent Vaughn was regarding me with concern. "It seems that way," he admitted. "I'm sorry that I put you in that position. If I hadn't asked you to get close to Bradley, then this wouldn't have happened."

"It was worth it if I got you the proof that you needed to back off of Sean," I replied coolly.

He studied me seriously. "You do realize that you might be in very serious danger if Bradley goes to Ronan, don't you? Sean might be in danger as well for refusing to let you go. I understand if you want to stop this now. The situation has changed, and we can put you in witness protection if that's what you want. We would understand."

"I'm not running," I declared definitively.

Agent Vaughn nodded. "Alright then," he conceded. "But we're putting a security detail on you."

"No," I said staunchly. "That might tip them off."

"This isn't up for discussion, Dr. Ellers. What you're doing is important, but it's not more important than your life."

We glared at one another for a moment, facing off. Then I dropped my eyes, realizing that I couldn't argue with the power of the FBI.

"Fine," I snapped. "But you better not blow my cover. I'm seeing this through no matter what."

Agent Vaughn's lips quirked up at the corners, and I could see a hint of Clayton shining through as he tried to suppress a smile. "We'll do our best, Dr. Ellers," he promised.

He stood and switched off the video camera, and he fully unleashed the grin that he had been holding back. "You're a little spitfire, aren't you, Claudia?" He asked, amused.

It was my turn to try to hold back my smile. "If you say so."

"I do," he replied, his eyes twinkling.

Now I smiled back, unable to resist his infectious lightheartedness. I followed him to his office, but when I settled myself across from him I was dismayed to notice that his expression had turned somber. My stomach sank.

"Okay. What's the bad news?" I asked, uncertain if I really wanted to know.

Lines of anxiety appeared around his eyes. "I wasn't sure if I was going to tell you this, but you deserve to know." He paused, but I looked at him expectantly, waiting. He sighed heavily. "That member of the Latin Kings that I told you about talked. He pointed me in the direction of a member of the Westies who was incarcerated with him. I agreed to cut him a deal in exchange for the information." The lines around his eyes deepened. "You have to know that I thought the information was legitimate. He was a known dealer in the disputed territory around the time your parents were killed. It was highly possible that he was the culprit or at least had information. But it turned out to be a false lead. He had an alibi for that night, and he refused to say anything else, even though I offered him a deal. If he does know anything about your parents' murder, he's too scared to talk. Turns out it was a dead end. I'm sorry, Claudia," he said sincerely.

It was a blow; I couldn't deny it. I had allowed myself to get my hopes up that the Latin King would lead us in the right direction; it had been a grave mistake to raise my expectations. If it had been as easy as all that, they would have caught my parents' killer years ago. I closed my eyes and took a deep breath.

"I understand," I said hollowly. "Thank you for trying."

"This doesn't mean I'm giving up, Claudia," Clayton said fiercely. "I'll find another lead. We are going to find the man who took them from you. I promise."

I just looked at him sadly, knowing that was a promise he probably wouldn't be able to keep. But I didn't want to voice my doubts, so I just nodded. I wasn't about to give up either.

"Thank you for telling me," I whispered.

"It's not a problem." The look he shot me was intense, and I was caught up in the lovely depths of his bright blue eyes.

"I won't keep anything from you, Claudia. I don't want to cause you any more pain, but I want you to know that I won't lie to you. You can trust me."

"I know," I said with a small smile. "Thanks. That means a lot to me."

He returned my smile, but I shifted uncomfortably in my seat. That had been a pretty big admission for me. I wanted to be friends with Clayton, and I was amazed at the trust that had so quickly been established between us. Still, it was a difficult and foreign concept to come to terms with after my years of isolation.

"I should probably go," I said, thinking of Sean waiting for me to "get off work."

I paused, a horrible thought striking me. If the FBI was going to be tailing me, then they would know just how much time I was spending with Sean. It wouldn't be hard for them to put two and two together and figure out the nature of our *relationship.*

I blushed furiously, knowing that it would be better to make the admission ahead of time than face the embarrassment of Clayton knowing but leaving it like an elephant in the room, weighing heavily on our easy companionship. I didn't want that.

"Um, I need to tell you something," I said in a rush.

"You can tell me anything, Claudia," he said kindly.

"It's just that... I... I'm seeing Sean."

His brow furrowed. "I know that." He was confused, clearly not getting what I was saying. I bit my lip.

"I mean, I'm *seeing* him." My cheeks flamed hotter.

"Oh," Clayton said. The word was simple, but a hint of surprise colored his tone. After my vehement refusal to resume a sexual relationship with Sean, he was clearly taken aback by this revelation. I was mortified, and I needed to make him understand that I wasn't some floozy who was sleeping with a man just to gain information from him.

"But it's not like that," I said quickly. "I care about him; I can't seem to help it." A part of me was distantly amazed that I was divulging such private information, things that I had barely been able to admit to Sean. But now that I had begun, it was as though I had opened the floodgates, and I couldn't seem to stop myself.

"I have feelings for him, but every word that I say to him feels like a betrayal. And I hate myself for it." My eyes were burning as tears threatened.

Clayton stood quickly, and I watched him through blurring vision as he strode towards me. He knelt beside me and wrapped his arms around me, one behind my back and one holding my head against his shoulder. I turned into him, unable to hold back a sob.

"It's okay, Claudia," he said softly. "You're okay. I didn't realize how much we were putting you through. I can't imagine how hard this is on you."

"I keep – telling myself – that I'm doing this for – him," I gasped out. I was starting to hyperventilate. "I want to help. But I'm just going – to hurt him."

"You are helping him," Clayton assured me gently, stroking his hand up and down my back. "You've proven his innocence now. You're going to free him."

"I'm going to destroy him!" I cried out, finally giving voice to the anguish that had been pent up inside of me for days.

Clayton said nothing. What could he possibly say? He couldn't deny the stark, horrible truth. My vision was tunneling as I gasped, but no air was reaching my lungs. My fingers were going numb where they clung to his lapels.

"Breathe, Claudia," he commanded.

I realized that I was going to pass out, and I forced myself to gulp in air, forcing it painfully through the tightness in my throat. Eventually, my sobs quieted, and I cried silently. I felt wetness beneath my cheek, and I realized that my tears were soaking Clayton's expensive suit. I drew back from him with a shaky, half-maddened laugh.

"Sorry," I said.

His grip shifted, and he placed his large hands on either side of my face, his thumbs gently wiping away my tears.

"There's no need to apologize," he assured me steadily. "You shouldn't hold these things in, Claudia. If you do, they'll consume you. I'm glad that you feel that you can talk to me."

"Thank you." I gave him a watery smile, and this time it was genuine. "I seem to be saying that a lot tonight."

"You are more than welcome." He drew away from me slowly, almost reluctantly. It was as though he sensed my need for space as I came back to myself, pulling the pieces of myself back together. It was easier than I had expected. I felt… lighter somehow, the burden of my guilt eased. Impossibly, sharing with Clayton had helped lift it from me ever so slightly.

I wiped the rest of the wetness from my cheeks. "I really should go now," I said, and my voice barely trembled.

"Okay," Clayton said. "But I want you to call me if you need me."

If you need me. I was astonished to acknowledge that a part of me *did* need Clayton. And that scared me. I stood quickly, not looking at him as I shot a brief "Bye" in his direction. I strode confidently through the building, but I knew that my red-rimmed, puffy eyes gave me away, and I avoided the gazes of the FBI agents as I passed their desks.

When I reached the refuge of my car, I took several deep, calming breaths. I couldn't face Sean. Not tonight. I didn't want him to see how broken up I was. He would question me relentlessly, and I wasn't sure that I could withstand the onslaught. I took out my phone and texted him, too much of a coward to call. The sound of his voice would break me.

"I can't see you tonight. Sorry," I typed.

He answered almost immediately. "Why not? :("

I couldn't hold back a quiet laugh at the emoticon. "I'm totally wiped." Well, that wasn't a lie.

"I don't mind. We don't have to have sex. I just want to see you."

I closed my eyes. God, why did he have to be so sweet to me? I longed to feel his arms around me, for him to comfort me. But that just wasn't an option. "I don't believe you ;) "

" :O I'm shocked you would accuse me of perfidy."

Perfidy? Who used words like that? I did. I realized that he was mocking me.

"Okay, I would jump you. You really wound me up this morning, but I'm just too exhausted to do anything about it."

Several seconds passed before he responded. "Alright then :(. But you had better not touch yourself."

"Damn. I hoped you had forgotten. Alright, you win."

"I always do ;) ."

Damn him and his silly emoticons! They were almost as bad as his puppy-dog look. Completely ridiculous and utterly charming.

"Cocky bastard."

"Watch yourself, little one."

"Yes, sir," I mocked, remembering how he had sardonically addressed me as "ma'am" earlier that morning.

"Why, Claudia, I thought you'd never say that. I rather like it. You should say it more often."

I gasped and my clit pulsed. Was he serious? A smirk spread across my face.

"Goodnight, sir."

"That's a capital 'S', but I'll let it slide this time. Goodnight, sub xoxo"

Hugs and kisses now? The man really was ridiculous. And funny. And sweet. And utterly, painfully perfect.

Chapter 10

The black sedan followed me from the FBI offices to my house, but I was more uneasy than reassured by its presence. The possibility of the Westies figuring out that agents were following me put me on edge. It was a relief when I shut my front door behind me, closing my eyes as I leaned up against it.

Then I heard it: the lightest footfall in the hallway before me. My eyes snapped open just in time to see a black-clad man rushing towards me, something silver glinting in his hand. I didn't have time to scream; I only had time to react. My fist shot out, aiming for his nose as Sean had instructed me. I was unwilling to try to drive his bones back into his brain with my palm. He was surprised at the move, and he barely dodged in time. He turned his cheek, and my blow glanced off his ear. The knife flashed as he brought his arm up to defend himself, and pain sliced across my wrist. Before I could draw air to scream, to alert the agents outside that I was under attack, his fist drove into my gut, hitting the tender spot where Bradley had hurt me. I crumpled to the ground, gasping for breath. I wanted to curl up into myself in a protective position, but I forced myself to roll on my back so that I could see my assailant. He advanced on me, his switchblade held before him.

"If it comes down to you or him, you're going to choose yourself."

Without a second thought, my hand dove into my purse, frantically searching for the gun. My fingers found the cool metal, and I grasped it, flicking off the safety and cocking it as I yanked it free. The man dropped to his knees, the weight of his body pressing into my hips. He raised the knife high, and it began to swing in a downward arc. My finger pulled the trigger before I realized what I was doing. The shot rang out, a sharp and deafening sound that rent through the air around me.

My attacker's eyes widened in surprise for a split second before his body collapsed atop me. Adrenaline gave me the strength to push him off, and I was on my knees beside him in an instant. I pressed my hands against the center of his chest, and hot, crimson liquid streamed over them. I had to stop the bleeding; I needed to save him.

But his aqua eyes were staring blankly out of his tanned face. I recognized him as the man who had tried to cut my face that night in the parking lot when Sean had saved me. I shook my head, my mind denying the horror of what I had done. He wasn't dead. He couldn't be dead. I pushed harder against the wound, and more blood welled up, bathing my hands in horrific, sticky heat.

"Help!" I screamed. "Help me!"

I was dimly aware of my door bursting open as two FBI agents came running in. One of them knelt beside the man, pressing two fingers against his neck.

I looked up into the agent's brown eyes. "Help him," I pleaded. "Call an ambulance."

He looked at me sadly. "He's already gone, Dr. Ellers."

Oh god, oh god, oh god. The words were a panicked litany in my head. I didn't even realize that I was saying them aloud. The world was swirling around me as my mind shut down, unable to cope with what the man had just said. Strong arms caught me around the shoulders as my limbs turned to jelly. The agent pulled me away until my back was pressed against the wall. My knees drew up against my chest, and my bloody hands twined in my hair, pulling at it as though I could yank the knowledge of what I had done from my brain. My body was rocking back and forth, and I trembled as my flesh turned frigid. My teeth were chattering as I drew stilted, shaky breaths through them.

"Stay with me, Dr. Ellers," a man's voice commanded from beside me. But I barely heard him; I couldn't tear my eyes from the gory sight before me. There was a high, keening cry echoing around me, and I didn't recognize that it was being ripped from my own chest.

The man swore softly. "Call an ambulance," he barked to the other agent.

"Already on its way." Their voices drifted to me as though from very far away.

Why would they call an ambulance? He was dead. Oh, god, he was dead. I had killed him, had snuffed out the life of another human being.

No no no no no no no…

This had to be some sick, twisted dream. I wanted to squeeze my eyes shut, sure that when I opened them I would wake up in my own bed, with Sean pressed up against me. But I couldn't stop looking at the fallen man, at the dark red substance that was slowly pooling around his utterly still form.

Someone else was beside me now. "Claudia," his voice was steady. "Claudia, look away," he commanded.

But I couldn't comply, couldn't tear my eyes away from the sight of the repulsive crime that I had committed. Strong fingers closed around my chin, and my face was forcibly pulled away from the sight. Clayton's gorgeous blue eyes were filled with concern.

"Eyes on me, Claudia," he ordered softly.

"Clayton," his name was a sob, and I threw my arms around him, clinging to him like a lifeline. His arms closed around me as well, one snaking behind my back and the other under my knees. He lifted me up, carrying me away from the scene of my unforgivable crime. I closed my eyes and turned my face into his chest, breathing in his masculine scent that I had never really noticed before. It was rich and slightly salty, like leather that had been exposed to the sea air. I associated it with comfort, with safety. I wanted to drown in it, for it to fill my lungs until I could no longer draw breath, thrusting me into warm, dark oblivion. But I was granted no such mercy.

He set me down after a minute, but his arm remained wrapped around my shoulders. A paramedic appeared before me, and I realized that I was seated on the back of an ambulance. The woman shined a light in my eyes, and I blinked against the searing sensation.

"She doesn't seem to have a concussion," she said. She looked at me. "Are you hurt anywhere?" She asked, her eyes appraising me.

"I'm fine," I said, my voice strangely detached. I didn't feel any corporal pain; all there was was the terrible, clawing agony in my chest, shredding my heart.

But the woman noticed the goose bumps on my frigid skin and my weak, trembling limbs. "I'll need to examine her to determine if she needs to go to the hospital," she told Clayton. He nodded and withdrew his arm from me.

My hands shot out, grabbing at his wrist. "Don't leave me," I pleaded.

He gently rubbed his thumb in small circles across my palm. "You need to go inside the ambulance with Sarah. I'll be right outside," he assured me.

Reluctantly, I released him, knowing that I had no choice in the matter. The medic – Sarah – guided me into the ambulance and shut the doors to give me privacy. She sat me down on the gurney inside.

"I don't want to go to the hospital," I protested.

"You might not have to," she said kindly. "But I need to look you over to make sure of that. I can see that your wrist is bleeding. Can you take off your shirt for me?"

I mechanically did as she asked, removing the blood-soaked garment. My stomach turned as I realized that it wasn't my own blood. I didn't look down as her gloved fingers gently brushed across the place where the knife had bitten into my skin.

"It's not deep," she said. "You were lucky."

Lucky? I felt anything but. I felt like the universe had had it out for me since I was thirteen years old, some higher power intent on torturing me.

"I'm going to have to photograph this," she told me. "Are you okay with that?"

I just nodded numbly. A camera clicked a few times as she recorded the cut on my arm and the bruises on my stomach.

There was a slight, stinging pain as Sarah cleaned my wound before bandaging it, wrapping gauze around my wrist.

"Take some Advil to help alleviate some of the pain in your abdomen. I'm afraid that it's not bad enough for me to give you anything stronger."

"That's okay," I said hollowly. I didn't want to alleviate the pain; I deserved to feel it keenly.

"Alright, you can get dressed," she said, her voice professional. "You don't have to go to the hospital if you don't want to."

I shook my head and pulled my blouse back on, my numb fingers fumbling at the buttons. It took me a few tries, but somehow I managed. When I was covered, Sarah opened the ambulance doors and helped me to sit on the back again; I knew that my legs wouldn't support me right now. Clayton was back at my side instantly.

"Is she alright?" He asked the paramedic.

"She's okay. She has some bruising and a small cut on her wrist, but mostly she's in shock."

Clayton pulled me into him again, but this time my leaden arms hung uselessly at my sides as he held me. I was distantly surprised that I wasn't crying. I felt like I should be, but I couldn't summon up the energy to do so.

"I want to go home," I mumbled against him, even though I knew that I was only just outside my front door. All I wanted was to crawl into bed and hug myself tightly.

"You can go inside in a little while," Clayton said. "They're just cleaning up."

Cleaning up. Cleaning up the gory mess that I had made. A hard shudder wracked through me, and Clayton held me tighter.

"You're okay now, Claudia," he reassured me. "You're okay."

Am I? I bit back the words. If I betrayed just how fucked up I felt inside, then they might not let me go home; they might not leave me alone. They might even make me go see a shrink. So I said nothing, and I concentrated hard on stilling my body's trembling. The sooner I composed myself, the sooner everyone would go away.

I didn't know how long Clayton held me, but eventually I heard someone say "We're clear, Agent Vaughn."

"Can you stand, Claudia?" He asked me, his tone cautious.

"Yes," I said firmly. I was determined to make my legs support me, to prove that I was okay. Still, Clayton kept a supporting arm around my waist as we walked through my front door, and I was grateful for it.

I stopped short when we entered the foyer. There was no trace that a man had been murdered there. All there was was gleaming hardwood and the strong, pungent scent of bleach. The FBI worked fast.

He guided me into my living room and sat me down on my couch before settling beside me, still gripping my waist.

"What's going to happen to me now?" I asked, my voice small. "Am I going to go to jail?"

"Of course not, Claudia," he said, slightly alarmed. "You were defending yourself."

"But I murdered a man," I protested.

He pinned me with a hard look. "You didn't murder anyone," he told me firmly. "You were defending your own life. I made you promise me that you would. Do you remember that?"

I nodded. I had made the same promise to Sean. That didn't mean that it made me feel any better.

Sean.

Suddenly, I didn't want to be alone. I wanted Sean. I wanted his electric touch, his sweet smile, and his warm, reassuring embrace.

I drew away from Clayton. "I'd like to be alone now, please," I lied. I couldn't let Sean know about him.

Clayton's eyes were full of concern. "I don't think that's a good idea."

"Please," I whispered. "I just want to go to sleep."

He studied me carefully. "If that's what you want," he capitulated. "But I'm going to be right outside."

That meant that he would see Sean come in; he would know that I had lied to him. But I didn't care at this point. I was desperate for him to leave so that I could see Sean.

"We're going to install an alarm system first thing tomorrow," he told me as he stood to leave. "The guy must have picked the lock and gotten in." He ran a frustrated hand through his hair, a habit much like Sean's. "We should have been watching your house."

I just stared at him blankly, at a loss for words. He jerked his hand through his hair again and turned away from me, striding out into the night. I waited a few seconds until I knew that he was out of earshot, and then I forced myself to stand and retrieve my purse from the table at the front door. I didn't bother locking up; the FBI agents were watching my house, and I didn't want to have to get up again to let Sean in when he arrived. I forced my fingers to steady and dialed. He picked up after one ring.

"Claudia?" He asked, his voice heavy with sleep.

"Sean," I said his name like a ragged prayer. "Please come over."

"What's wrong, Claudia?" He asked immediately. My mouth opened and closed a few times as I struggled to find words.

"Claudia?" His voice was full of concern.

"Sean, I…" I knew that my voice was high and thin. "I had to… Oh, god…"

"Claudia, talk to me. You're scaring me."

"Just come. Please," I choked out.

"Claudia!" He snapped, his tone panicked and a little angry.

But I ended the call. I couldn't say any more. My stomach was suddenly heaving. I was going to be sick. I ignored the ringing of my phone as I stumbled up the stairs, flinging myself across my bedroom. I barely made it to the toilet in time. I retched violently, my gut clenching painfully as it rebelled against me. I heaved until nothing more was coming up, and then I collapsed on the floor, allowing the coolness of the tiles to sink into my heated skin.

I heard my doorbell ringing insistently, but I didn't move. I knew that Sean would figure out that it was unlocked and come in. I should have pushed myself up off the floor, but I just couldn't find the will to do so. My body felt utterly drained, and my mind had shifted into some kind of merciful blankness as exhaustion washed over me.

"Claudia!" Sean's footsteps were pounding up the stairs. I knew he would find me soon enough, so I just waited, closing my eyes and savoring the utter quiet of my mind.

"Claudia!" His fearful voice echoed in the bathroom. His hands were on me, rolling me onto my back. I groaned softly at the loss of the coolness against my cheek. "Claudia! Fuck!" He shook me hard. "Wake up! Look at me!"

I couldn't deny his direct order, and my eyes fluttered open. His hands were roving over me. "Where are you hurt?" He hastily pulled out his phone. "I'm calling an ambulance."

"Don't," I said, my voice sounding foreign in my own ears. "They've already been here." He looked at me in confusion. "It's not my blood," I explained.

His eyes narrowed, and he kept touching me, unconvinced. "What the fuck is going on, Claudia?" He demanded.

"I…" I needed to say it, needed to get it out. If I held it in any longer, the agony that was ripping at my insides was going to destroy me. "I killed a man," I admitted softly.

Sean's eyes widened. "What?" He breathed.

"I did what you told me to do," I said hollowly. "I chose myself."

His arms were around me, pulling me up against his chest. He tenderly stroked my hair as my trembling resumed. An image flashed across my mind: those aqua eyes, so unique in such a tanned face, staring at nothing. My brain was coming back to life, and I dreaded the moment when reality would come crashing back down on me.

"What happened?" Sean asked, speaking softly as though not to spook me.

"I don't… I can't… Please. I don't want to think…" My chest tightened, cutting off my words. I didn't want to face it; I wasn't ready. I didn't think I ever would be.

Sean drew back from me, his eyes dark with worry. I glanced away, but my gaze fell on my bloodstained hand. A small, distressed sound escaped me, like the whimper of a pained animal. He quickly covered my hand with his, hiding it from view.

"We need to get you cleaned up," he said gently. He moved my body so that my back was supported by the storage cabinets beneath my sink before he stood to turn on the shower. This so wasn't the way I had imagined showering with him.

He returned to me, grasping me by the elbows and lifting me to my feet. My hips were propped back against the counter, preventing me from falling back onto my ass as Sean carefully undressed me. There was nothing sensual about it; no heat flared within me at the act. I just felt cold. I shrugged out of my shirt and stepped out of my shoes and slacks compliantly, my eyes watching him but not really seeing him. Once I was bare, Sean quickly stripped out of his own clothes. I focused on the hard planes of his perfect muscles, idly marveling at his beauty as my mind drifted through nothingness.

Taking my hands, he led me to the edge of the tub. "Careful," he warned as I fought against leaden legs to step over the porcelain barrier. Somehow, I managed not to trip, and Sean soon joined me under the warm spray. As soon as it hit me, the water turned pink. I felt sick again as I watched the blood-tinged liquid spiral down the drain.

Sean's chest was pressed into my back, his arm firmly around my stomach. His body was warm against me, but it wasn't hot enough. I was so cold; ice was crystalizing in my veins, the sharp shards of it slashing at my flesh from the inside. I reached out and cranked up the hot water, turning it higher and higher.

Sean's fingers closed around mine, pulling my hand away from the knob. "You'll scald yourself, Claudia," he chided.

"I'm cold," I muttered.

He said nothing, and I was grateful when he didn't turn down the heat. Instead, he reached for my shampoo, and I closed my eyes as his fingers began massaging it into my hair. He stopped suddenly, his touch leaving me.

"Did you hit your head, Claudia?" He asked.

"No," I said, puzzled. I opened my eyes and realized that the soapy water trailing down over my breasts was stained pink.

I shuddered as I recalled running my bloody hands through my hair. "It's not mine."

His touch returned, and I relished the soothing sensation of his fingers moving in a slow, circular rhythm against my scalp. I closed my eyes again, tuning out the world and focusing solely on the sweetness of his hands upon me. When he had finished with my hair, his soap-slicked palms ran over my skin. If I had been washing myself, I would have been scrubbing furiously, clawing at my flesh until my own blood blotted out that of my attacker.

My mind flinched away from the thought of him, and I returned my attention to Sean's touch. I wasn't sure how much time had passed when he finally spoke.

"Okay, little one," he said gently. "All better."

He turned off the water and took me up in his arms, cradling my body against his. I kept my eyes shut tightly, enjoying the comfort of his strong arms wrapped around me protectively. He carried me out of the bathroom, and he draped a towel around me as he walked. When I felt something soft and familiar beneath me, I knew that he had set me down on my bed. The mattress shifted as he settled down beside me, his arm draped across my stomach. I was grateful for the continued contact.

"Open your eyes, Claudia," he commanded softly.

"I don't want to," I whispered. I just wanted to remain in the darkness where nothing existed but the feel of Sean touching me, his scent enfolding me.

"Do as I say, Claudia," he said more firmly.

I frowned, but I did as he bade me.

"I need you to tell me what happened," he said.

My frown deepened. "I don't want to," I said again.

His brows drew together forbiddingly, but there was still a softness to his eyes that tugged at my heart. "I need to know what happened to you, Claudia. And you need to tell me. If you keep it bottled up inside, it will destroy you. Let me help you."

It was so much like what Clayton had said to me. Had that really only been earlier this evening? It seemed a lifetime ago. My whole world had changed since then. I had been a doctor who wanted nothing more to preserve human life. But in the space of a second, I had become a killer.

"He was waiting for me when I came home," I said, knowing that Sean would press me until I divulged everything. "He had a knife, but I had the gun. I used it."

"Did he hurt you?" Sean asked.

I glanced down at the now-sodden bandage on my arm. It would need changing. "Just a small cut," I said.

When my gaze returned to his, I found myself trapped in the green depths of his beautiful eyes. He was staring at me intently. "I know that must have been hard for you, Claudia. But I'm glad that you killed him. You did the right thing."

"Did I?" I asked faintly.

"Yes," he said firmly. "You didn't have a choice."

"But I did!" I suddenly cried out as anguish gripped me hard. "And I chose me! I killed a man, Sean!" I saw his aqua eyes again, saw the look of shock in them just before the light went out of them. There had been so much blood...

"This is all my fault," Sean said, his voice oddly muffled.

I looked up to find that he had buried his face in his hands. "If I had just stayed away, you wouldn't be in this position. You wouldn't have had to do that." He dropped his hands, revealing his agonized expression. "I'm going to leave you alone, Claudia. I promise I'll be out of your life, and you'll be safe again."

"No!" He couldn't leave me. I couldn't lose him. Especially not now, when I needed him most. "Don't leave me," I begged.

It was too much. The panic hit me hard, my chest constricting. I curled up into myself protectively, as though to ward off physical blows. The bone-deep cold returned, and my vision went red, crimson filming over my eyes like blood blinding me.

I was dimly aware of Sean shaking me, calling my name. But I couldn't answer him, couldn't seem to pull myself from the grip that the clawed monster within me had on my heart.

There was a sharp, stinging sensation on my upper arm. Almost at once, my seizing muscles began to ease, and breath returned to my oxygen-starved lungs. My vision cleared, and Sean's face came swimming into view. And so did the syringe that he was holding in his hand.

"What?" I breathed.

He touched my face lightly, tracing the line of my jaw. "Don't worry," he told me. "It's just a sedative."

I blinked slowly, confused. "Where did you get that?" I asked, the words garbled. My tongue felt oddly heavy in my mouth.

"From a friend," he said. "When you called, I thought that someone was threatening you. I knew that you wouldn't want me to hurt him if I could avoid it. So I brought this."

His voice seemed far away. My vision was going fuzzy at the edges, and my eyelids were growing heavy. I didn't want to sleep; I was afraid of the nightmares that would haunt me when I closed my eyes. I was afraid of being alone in the darkness. I tried to reach out for Sean, but my hand barely twitched. My limbs wouldn't seem to answer my demands to move. The world was turning darker, drowsiness covering me like a warm blanket.

"Don't worry, little one," he said, his voice strained. "I won't leave you."

With that knowledge, I stopped fighting and welcomed the black oblivion.

Chapter 11

My body began to stir to wakefulness, but I resisted it. I was warm and comfortable, content. But bright, insistent light pressed against my closed eyelids. Too much light.

Shit. I must have overslept. I was going to be late for work. My eyes snapped open, and I groaned when I glanced at the clock.

Ten-thirty? Really? I never slept this late.

A hand closed around my shoulder, rolling me onto my back.

"Sean," I gasped. "What are you still doing here? You should have been at work hours ago. And so should I. Why did you let me sleep so late?"

"You needed to rest," he said simply. "I called your work to let them know that you wouldn't be in today. I'm taking the day off too."

"But you can't do that!" I protested. "Your father will be furious."

Sean's expression tightened. "I don't give a damn what my father thinks," he said harshly. "I told you that I wouldn't leave you. And I don't intend to."

"Don't worry, little one. I won't leave you."

"You..." I said haltingly, struggling to recall something. "You drugged me."

"I'm sorry. You were having a panic attack. You weren't breathing. I didn't know what else to do." He raked his fingers through his hair. It was extremely untidy, as though he had been doing that a lot. Now that I really looked at him, I noticed the dark circles under his eyes and the fine red veins that crisscrossed the whites of them like intricate spider webs. It occurred to me that he probably hadn't slept.

What was going on? I had been having a panic attack? Why did Sean look so… strained?

I cast my eyes around the room, searching for clues about what had happened the night before. My gaze fell on the pile of clothes on my bathroom floor. They were stained with large splotches of crimson. I felt the blood drain from my face, and all of my muscles turned rigid as the memories came flooding back.

"Oh, god," I groaned, covering my face with my hands. I had killed a man, extinguished his life in the blink of an eye. And there was nothing I could do to take it back. How could I have done that? How could I live with it? Who was I now?

Hot tears leaked from the corners of my eyes. It was the first time I had cried since it happened. Sean's arms were around me instantly, hugging me tightly against him.

"Shhh, little one. You're safe now. You're okay." He rocked me gently, and I felt him take a shaky breath. "Do you have any idea…?" His voice cracked. "Do you have any idea how scared I was when I found you? I thought… Fuck, Claudia, I don't know what I would do if anything happened to you."

"Something did happen to me," I said tremulously. "What I've done has changed me, Sean. I'm not the same person anymore." I stared up at him, my eyes wide, wild. "I'm a murderer." I thought of my parents, how the long years of hatred towards their faceless killer had hardened my heart. The man I shot must have a family. Even mobsters had families. Did he have a wife, children? Had I deprived them of their father?

Sean gently wiped at the silent tears that wet my cheeks, but more flowed over his fingers in an unrelenting stream. "You did what you had to do," he said firmly. His mouth hardened to a grim line. "Besides, if he had hurt you, I would have killed him myself, and he would be dead anyway."

A moment of silence passed between us as his words sank in. They rang with furious, vindictive truth. "Have you ever killed anyone, Sean?" I asked quietly. I was afraid to hear his answer.

"No."

A strange mixture of emotions swirled within me. First and foremost was relief. I had been right in what I had told Clayton: Sean wasn't a killer. But there was also sadness, and maybe even a hint of jealousy. He couldn't understand what I was going through, how my life was now irrevocably altered. I would carry the weight of the man's stolen soul for the rest of my life. And for all of his talk about killing anyone who hurt me, Sean hadn't brought any weapons with him to confront an attacker. He had been planning on drugging him.

Because of you, an inner voice told me. Sean was trying to reign in his violent urges for me. He knew how much it upset me to see him get hurt, to see him hurting other people. But now he was the pure one and I was the one with blood on my hands. I looked down at them, half-expecting to find rust-red half-moons staining the tips of my fingernails. But there was nothing there.

I drew away from Sean, suddenly feeling unworthy of his touch. And more than a little resentful as a part of me acknowledged that none of this would have happened if I had never met him. That thought made me go cold. Did I really wish that?

No. I didn't think so. After everything that had happened the night before, Sean was the only person I wanted to see. He was the only one who saw the real me, the only one who would understand. But now I realized that he didn't understand, that he never could. He could hold me, he could comfort me, he could whisper reassuring words; but he would never really know the depth of my self-loathing at what I had done.

I needed some time away from him to try to sort myself out, to figure out who I was now.

But I couldn't be alone. I had to go to the FBI for interrogation today. They would ask me questions for their official record. I was going to have to re-live the whole thing. And Sean wouldn't be able to be there to hold my hand through it. I suddenly felt utterly, starkly alone, as though I stood naked atop an isolated mountain while bitter wind lashed at my skin until it was raw and red.

I pushed up off the bed and walked over to my dresser as through in a daze.

"What are you doing?" Sean asked, his voice filled with concern.

"Getting ready for work," I lied hollowly. There was nothing real in my world anymore, nothing right. There was only deceit and the bitter tang of betrayal on my tongue as it dripped traitorous words.

"What? Claudia, you are not going to work. You're staying here with me."

"I'm going, Sean," I informed him, my tone even and unwavering. I couldn't summon up the energy to sound angry at him bossing me around. "I don't want to be in this house right now."

"Then I'll take you somewhere," he insisted.

I said nothing, pulling on my clothes in silence.

"God damn it, Claudia, I don't want you to be alone with this. Don't leave me." It was a command, but there was a thread of pleading laced through it.

It was what I had asked of him the night before, and a new fissure crackled across my ravaged heart as I realized that I would have to deny him. I didn't look at him as I finished buttoning up my blouse. "I'm going now, Sean," I said simply.

Out of the corner of my eye, I saw him shove himself out of bed, a frustrated sound escaping him. "I know what you're doing, Claudia," he said angrily as he began tugging on his own clothes. "You're locking it away, putting your walls back up. You're going to destroy yourself."

It's too late for that. I've already destroyed both of us. You just don't know it yet.

Still avoiding his eyes, I moved for the door, stepping around him. His hand closed around my forearm, squeezing hard. "I won't let you do this. Don't shut me out. Please." On the last word, his demanding tone melted to a desperate whisper.

I glanced up into his pain-filled eyes, and my gut twisted. "I'll see you later, Sean. I promise. I just need to do something normal right now. Can you understand that?"

His grip on me tightened, vice-like. He clearly didn't want to let me go. So I held his gaze steadily, praying that he would let me go before I lost the will to leave him. Finally, he released me, and this time he was the one to look away.

"Alright," he said, his voice detached as he pulled up his own walls. "Let's go then."

He followed me down the stairs and out the front door in silence. I paused on the stoop, turning to him.

"What are you going to do?" I asked, resolutely staring at a spot over his shoulder so that I didn't have to meet his turbulent gaze.

"I'll order a cab. You go on." His tone was hard, cold. I hated the sound of it.

I didn't know what to say, so I just nodded and walked away. My gait was awkward and stilted as I forced my legs to carry me away from him. It was as though iron encased my body and I was struggling to pull away from an incredibly strong magnet. Even once I was in my car and driving away, the sensation didn't dissipate. The strain grew and grew until I felt stretched thin. I did my best to ignore the horrible feeling as I drove to the FBI offices. Every once in a while I glanced in my rearview mirror and caught sight of the black sedan tailing me three cars back. I braced myself for the ordeal of interrogation.

When I got out of my car in the parking garage, Clayton was at my side almost instantly; he had been in the car behind me. Just as he had promised, he had spent the entire night outside my house, watching over me. His hair was a mess, and his eyes were tired and bloodshot. It looked like Sean wasn't the only one who hadn't gotten any sleep. He pushed his hand lightly against the small of my back, providing me with support as he guided me to the elevator. The act was tender, and the heat of his skin permeating my shirt was comforting. I found that I was grateful for the bolstering contact.

"I'm going to have to ask you some difficult questions, Claudia," he informed me, his voice a low rumble. "I'm sorry."

I closed my eyes and pushed back into his touch ever so slightly, allowing it to ground me. "I know. It's okay."

He walked alongside me as he ushered me to the grey-walled room. The red light on the hated video camera came on, and I was left bereft of his touch as he settled down across from me.

"I need you to tell me what happened last night, Claudia."

A part of me noticed that he hadn't called me "Dr. Ellers," and it occurred to me that what I had done might be weighing on him as well. I took a deep breath, readying myself for the plunge into icy, agonizing waters. One by one, I forced the words out, trying my best to keep my voice steady as I recounted what had happened: how I had found the man waiting for me, how we had struggled, how I had shot him.

Clayton interrupted every once in a while, pressing me for more details. Every time he did, it was that much harder for me to go on. But his clear blue eyes helped to tether me to the present, keeping me safe in the small room with him rather than allowing me to be consumed by the gut-wrenching memories of what I had been forced to do.

After a while, I stopped talking; there was nothing more to tell.

"Okay," Clayton said, standing to turn off the camera. His hand was at my elbow, and he guided me to the privacy of his office. He sat me down in my usual chair before crouching in front of me. He rested one hand on my knee, as though unwilling to stop touching me. I was glad about that; I didn't want him to stop.

"You were very brave in there," he said gently. "I know how hard this is for you."

"Do you?" I whispered.

He pierced me with a sad, solemn look. "Yes," he said. "Because I had to do the same thing once. And I'm so sorry that it's happened to you too."

My breath caught in my throat. I recalled the day that he had told me to use the gun if I had to, how I had realized that he must have killed someone.

"Please," I said. "Tell me how it happened." I needed to understand how Clayton was able to live with himself now. I could plainly see that he still carried the guilt around with him, but he seemed to be able to function normally on a day to day basis. Would that ever be possible for me?

He took a deep breath, but he didn't close his eyes. The bright blue orbs stayed locked on me, full of empathy and earnestness and understanding. "It was seven years ago, and I had barely been with the FBI for a year. We were raiding a place, and I had been told that it might be dangerous. But I was eager to help, and I didn't really seriously contemplate the potential fallout. I was one of the first in. The men had weapons, and one of them aimed at me. It was a split-second decision. In fact, it wasn't even a decision; it was instinct. I fired, and he was dead. And there was nothing I could do to take it back. There will never be anything I can do to take it back."

"I know," I breathed. "How do you deal with it? I don't feel like *me* anymore. How do I get that back?"

His expression was sad. "You don't," he said bluntly, and I flinched. He reached out to cup my face in his palm. "I'm not saying this to hurt you, Claudia, but I won't lie to you. You will never be the same. But that doesn't mean that you can't be okay. The weight of what you've done will follow you; you wouldn't be human – you wouldn't be *you* – if it didn't. What you have to let go of is the blame. What happened wasn't your fault, Claudia. You have to accept that." He was so close to me that I could feel his warm breath fanning over my face.

"Tell me you won't blame yourself. Promise me."

The sense of his words pierced me to the core, reaching some deep part of my mind that recognized the truth, chipping away at the self-loathing that had filled my entire being.

"I promise."

His hand moved from my knee to lightly touch the other side of my face. I was barely breathing, caught up in his hold and the intensity of his glowing eyes.

"Do you have any idea how remarkable you are?" He asked, his tone colored with something akin to reverence. My lips parted at his words. I was completely thunderstruck.

He didn't wait for me to answer. He closed the short distance between us and cautiously, tenderly pressed his lips to mine.

Chapter 12

Clayton's kiss was warm and tender and comforting. It was sweet and slow, tentative even. Nothing at all like Sean's dominant, demanding mouth that branded me with its scorching heat.

Sean.

What the fuck was I doing? I pressed my hands against Clayton's chest for leverage and jerked away from him. And unlike Sean, who would have held me to him until he was good and ready to let me go, Clayton released me instantly.

His eyes were wide, as though he was as stunned by his own actions as I was.

"Claudia," he said, sounding slightly horrified. "I'm so sorry. That was way out of line. I -"

But whatever he was going to say was cut off abruptly by a sharp knock on the office door. Clayton stood and quickly backed away from me. I just sat there dumbly, my overloaded brain tripping over itself, as he put several feet of space between us.

"Yes," he said loudly, inviting the person to enter.

"Agent Vaughn?" A man with thick-rimmed glasses poked his head through the open door. "Ballistics just came back on Garcia. We rushed it like you asked. When we ran it through the database, there were, ah…" He paused, glancing over at me significantly. "A few hits."

Clayton took the file that the man proffered and flicked it open. His eyes widened and his mouth fell open slightly. He looked up at the man. "You're sure?" He asked.

He nodded. "I double-checked it myself." He shot another glance in my direction, looking somewhat nervous and apologetic at the same time. "I'll just leave you alone, then." He turned quickly, as though he couldn't get out of there fast enough.

"What is it?" I asked, my hands twisting anxiously in my lap. What else could have possibly happened?

Clayton didn't look at me as he walked around the desk and sat down heavily in his chair.

"Clayton?" My voice wavered as I said his name questioningly.

He sighed and set the file down before him, staring at it for a moment. When he did finally look up at me, his expression was enigmatic.

"The man you shot last night was named Hector Garcia. This is the ballistics report on the slug we pulled from him. They ran it through the database, and it matches bullets found at several other crime scenes."

"Oh?" I asked, a sense of foreboding creeping over me.

"Do you remember the day that Sean got shot? I told you that he and Bradley had fired on one of our undercover agents. The marks on this slug match that one."

I nodded. That only made sense. It was Bradley's gun, and he had used it that day against Santiago.

Clayton paused then. He was watching me warily. "It also matches the bullets that were recovered from your parents' bodies."

My heart stopped in my chest. I couldn't have heard him right. "What?" I asked faintly. My mind was whirring. How could this be true? It just wasn't possible. I refused to believe that I had killed someone with the same gun that had ended my parents' lives. "You're wrong," I insisted.

"Ballistics is not as exact a science as they make it seem on TV, Claudia, but the evidence is here."

What did it mean? Bradley had killed my parents? No, there was no way that that was possible. He wouldn't have been much older than I was when it happened. So where had he gotten the gun? ___ ··

A keen, sharp clarity came over me as I realized what I had to do.

"I have to go," I said, standing quickly.

"Where are you going?" Clayton asked. "Claudia, we should talk about this."

I didn't look back at him as I strode towards the door. "We've done enough *talking.*" I imbued my tone with as much venom as I could muster. Maybe if he thought I was livid with him for kissing me, then he would back off. I knew that my words would hurt him, but right then I didn't care. It worked; he didn't follow me.

I moved as though in a dream, feeling oddly detached from the world around me as I passed through it. It seemed a matter of seconds before I was parking my car in the garage beneath Bradley and Sean's apartment. My breathing was normal and my heartbeat steady as I walked down the short hall. My mind was completely focused on my task. Nothing else existed.

I knocked on the door and waited patiently. It only took a few seconds for Sean to fling it open.

"Claudia!" He reached for me, but I sidestepped his embrace, pushing past him into the apartment.

"Where's Bradley?" I asked, nothing more than mild curiosity in my tone.

Sean eyed me worriedly. "Are you okay? I thought you were going to work."

"I came to see Bradley," I said firmly.

Sean moved towards me, gripping my upper arms before I could step out of his reach this time. "Claudia, what's happened?"

I glared up at him, my anger rising. He was getting in my way. And I was so close…

"Where is he, Sean?" I snapped at him this time.

He frowned at me. "He's not here. And I'm not going to let you stay here long enough for him to come back. Something's going on with you, Claudia, and you're going to tell me what it is. And you can tell me in the car. Come on. I'm taking you home."

He kept his hold on one of my arms and started pulling me towards the door.

"No!" I half-shouted, panicking. I couldn't let him take me away. I had to talk to Bradley, had to find out where he had gotten that gun. I twisted in Sean's grip, but all I earned were bruises as his fingers dug into my flesh harshly. He turned to me, glaring.

"Don't argue with me, Claudia. We're not staying here, and you aren't going to see Bradley."

Hot, desperate fury rose up in me, and I acted before I thought. I raised my fist, and in the space of a second it connected squarely with his mouth. He cursed loudly and clutched at the injury with his free hand, but still he didn't release me.

"I'm not leaving!" I shrieked.

Sean was staring down at me as though I had gone insane. And maybe I had. But I wasn't about to let him stand in the way of me finding the man who had murdered my parents. He lowered his hand from his mouth, and a twinge of guilt pierced my heart when I took in his bleeding lip. I shoved it back, unwilling to let it distract me from getting what I wanted.

His eyes narrowed. "I could tie you up, throw you over my shoulder, and drag you out of here," he said dangerously. "Is that what you want? Because that's what I'll do if I have to."

My own eyes turned to slits, and my lips twisted into something like a snarl. "I will never forgive you if you do that," I warned.

His jaw tightened. "If that's what it takes to keep you safe, then that's what I'll do," he said grimly.

"You don't understand!" I cried out in frustration, knowing that he would make good on his threat. "I have to ask Bradley about his gun. Once I do that, I'll leave with you. I promise. Please, Sean."

His determined expression wavered in the face of my blatant desperation. "What do you want to know about it?" He asked, his voice calmer this time.

"Where did he get it?" I asked quickly. Maybe Sean could tell me. Maybe I was seconds away from finding out who had killed my parents…

"He got it from me."

It was as though Sean had repaid my punch in kind, and I physically reeled back from him. "What?"

"It was my father's. I didn't want it, so I gave it to Bradley. So if you're worried about not getting it back from the police, don't be. It's not really his anyway."

Everything clicked into place in one horrible instant. "Your father killed my parents." I didn't even realize that I had spoken the words aloud.

Sean's brow furrowed. "What are you talking about, Claudia?" He was eyeing me like I truly had lost my mind. "You said your parents died in a car crash."

"No! They didn't!" I was yelling now. Why was he being so slow on the uptake? Why couldn't he see it? I was already down, but the universe just wouldn't stop kicking me. I gathered my anger at whatever malevolent higher power was responsible for my torment and turned it on Sean.

"They were murdered, Sean," I flung out the words. "Your father gunned them down in the street when I was thirteen years old. Oh my god, oh my god…" I jerked against his grip again, suddenly disgusted by his touch. In a way, he was a part of his father, and it was as though an echo of their killer's taint clung to his skin, seeping into me, poisoning me. "Let me go!" I demanded, desperate to get away from him.

But he just gazed at me levelly, suspicion stirring in the green depths of his eyes. "Why do you think my father killed your parents, Claudia?" He asked.

My mouth opened and closed, but no words came out. As desperately as I wanted to get away from him, I didn't want to reveal this. The answer would destroy us. I knew in that moment that I had gone too far; I had said too much.

He shook me hard. "Tell me why, Claudia!"

I swallowed. "The... The bullet that killed the man in my house last night. It came from the same gun that killed my parents." I winced, and I wasn't sure if it was from the increased pressure of Sean's fingers around my arm or from the dawning realization in his eyes.

"And how would you know that?" His expression was furious, pained even, but his voice was low and calm. I pursed my lips, trying to lock the truth within me. My own heart might already be ravaged, but I didn't want to do the same to him. I wasn't ready. It was too soon. I wanted more time with him.

"How, Claudia?" He barked out, shaking me again.

"The FBI told me," I admitted, my voice barely audible.

His hand dropped from me instantly, recoiling. He was looking at me as though seeing me clearly for the first time. "The FBI? Not the NYPD? Bradley was right," he said, sounding as though he hardly believed the words that were coming out of his mouth. "You were just using me."

"No!" I protested, lunging for him. I caught his hand in mine, and it balled into a fist. He glared down at me as though I was something disgusting on the bottom of his shoe. "Please,

Sean. It's not like that. You have to believe me. I was trying to help you."

He laughed hollowly, a cold sound that cut me to the core. "You were helping me by turning me over to the feds? By making me believe that you cared about me?"

"Sean, I *do* care about you!" I clutched at his hand harder, my nails digging into his skin. "Please. Trust me when I say that everything I've done -"

"*Trust you?!* Are you fucking kidding me, Claudia? The fact that you would even think that I would keep buying into your bull just proves how little you think of me." He wrenched away from my grip, and my nails scored his skin as I tried to keep hold of him. He was more furious than I had ever seen him, and I had to fight the urge to shrink away. His eyes studied me steadily, but there was a slightly maniacal glint to them.

"What am I going to do with you now, Claudia?" He mused. "I could just keep you here. That way you can't go blabbing anything else to the FBI."

Now I did back away. Fear coiled in my belly. No. He wouldn't. "Please, Sean," I begged hoarsely. I couldn't bear to be his captive again. I saw the madness in his eyes and realized that I had to get out. His large body was blocking my way to the door, but I made a dash for it anyway.

His arms were around me in an instant, wrenching my own behind my back and securing them there with one hand locked around my wrists. I was pressed up tightly against him, and my body couldn't help but respond. Heat flared between my legs and I couldn't hold back a gasp. His large hand encircled my neck, a true threat for the first time. He squeezed incrementally.

"Do you know how easy it would be, Claudia?" He asked. There was an odd note to his voice, something husky and predatory and utterly terrifying. It made my clit pulse. "I could keep you here forever. You would be mine completely. I wouldn't need any handcuffs or rope to bind you to me. Although I might use them on you if I wanted to. I will fuck you into submission, give you such intense, addictive pleasure that you'll beg me for your next fix like a junkie." A hard-edged, cruel grin spread across his face. I felt him hardening against my hip, and a strange whimper escaped me. I wasn't sure if it was a sound of lust or terror. His smile widened. "You see?" He said, satisfied. "Very easy."

"Please." The word was a moan, and I wasn't at all sure what I was begging for. For him to free me? To touch me? To forgive me?

I watched him with bated breath, all of my muscles taut. Then the furious lust slowly melted from his eyes, giving way to a sadness so profound that it brought tears to my own eyes. He released me, and I liked to think that there was some reluctance in his movements.

"I want you to leave now, Claudia," he said coldly, no longer looking at me. He stepped to the side, clearing my path to the door.

"Sean..." I trailed off, not knowing what to say. My rational mind was screaming at me to run while I had the chance. But the utterly irrational side of me, the part of me that had fallen hopelessly for Sean, was rooted to the spot, unable to leave him when he was hurting so badly.

He let out a low, frustrated growl and advanced on me. My heart leapt as I thought that he was going to draw me up in his arms and kiss me. But he just grabbed me by the shoulders, turning my body and shoving me out the door. It had slammed shut before my back even hit the opposite wall across the hallway. The closed door did little to muffle Sean's furious roar followed by the sound of something smashing to pieces.

I stood there and listened to him destroying his apartment, so many thoughts crowding my mind that none were coherent. They were roiling, each one fighting to be heard until they coalesced into a shrill, utterly bereaved shrieking that resounded in my skull. The horrible sound of it pained me more deeply than any physical wound ever could.

It hurt too much; I couldn't take it anymore. I mentally reached out for my walls, desperate to pull them up, to force this agony away from my heart. But I found nothing. It was as though they had crumbled to dust. And now I was left bare, defenseless. There was nothing inside me but horrible, wrenching pain.

But no. That was wrong. There was something else, something that burned hot and bright and furious: vengeance. I clutched at it, cleaving to the searing heat of it in order to cauterize my internal wounds. I pushed myself from the wall, my back straightening and my chin lifting as I walked away from Sean's apartment. A new sense of purpose imbued my every step; I had a different task now.

I was going to kill Ronan Reynolds.

The End

Avenger

Impossible #3

By Julia Sykes

Chapter 1

I was calm, detached, reflecting the nothingness that I felt inside. It wasn't peaceful, exactly. I was just... empty. The raging inferno that was my desire for vengeance had burned everything away, leaving me unencumbered by feelings of guilt or self-doubt. There was just the stark, cold clarity of my new purpose in life: killing Ronan Reynolds.

I had thought that it was some cruel higher power torturing me, but now I realized that all of the blame for everything bad that had ever happened to me could be laid at Ronan's feet. I could rail against Sean for hiding his involvement with the Westies from me. I could hate Bradley for abducting me. I could rage against my foster family for everything that they had put me through. But the truth was that none of it would have happened if not for what Ronan had done to my parents on that night fourteen years ago, callously snuffing out their lives in the space of a few seconds, and in the process ruining my entire life.

Was he even aware of who I was? Did he know what he had done to me? I realized that it was unlikely that he did. Why would he connect his son's supposed girlfriend with a murder that he had committed so many years ago? In what kind of fucked up world did that even happen?

Okay, so maybe there was some greater force that had thrown Sean and me together, but I didn't set much store in such things. Besides, thinking about it made my head hurt, made the anguish pulse back to life at the edges of my mind. I could ponder it all I wanted, but it would never make sense. It had happened, and that was all that mattered.

And maybe it wasn't some devil torturing me; maybe it was some sort of vengeful angel that had answered my childhood prayers to find my parents' killer. But it hadn't taken me long to give up on prayers. No one was answering them.

And yet here I was, suddenly bequeathed with the knowledge of the identity of their murderer. I wasn't about to pass up the opportunity that some twisted sort of serendipity had brought before me.

"I won't be spying on Sean anymore," I told Clayton over the phone. It had taken me little more than twenty-four hours to sort things out in my mind, to make a plan. And getting rid of the FBI tailing me was my first course of action. Getting them off of Ronan's case was a close second. I had to ensure his safety so that I had a clear path to kill him. So long as I didn't tell Clayton that Bradley's gun used to belong to Ronan, then the FBI would have no idea that he had killed my parents.

"What?" Clayton was clearly taken aback. "Why? Claudia, what happened to you yesterday? We know that you went to Sean's apartment after I told you about the bullets we recovered from your parents' bodies. You weren't there long. What did he say to you? What did you say to him?" Clayton fired questions at me, but I was ready for every one of them.

"I ended the relationship," I explained. "It just hit too close to home, learning that the gun he gave me was the same one that killed my parents. I know that it's random as hell and not his fault, but I just can't be around him anymore. I feel... sick knowing that he's a part of that world."

The truthfulness to my last words made a trace of that sickness stir in my belly, but I tamped it down before the nausea could rise up and overwhelm me. I had to stay focused.

"Claudia," Clayton – no, Agent Vaughn – said my name gently, "I can understand why you feel that way. Really I do. But you do realize that making this choice means that we can't go any further in our investigation against Ronan, don't you? I thought that you wanted to help Sean."

Yep, I was definitely talking to Agent Vaughn, the mercenary FBI agent who would do anything to keep an asset.

"I can't help him," I said coldly. "If it weren't for him, I wouldn't have had to kill a man. I can't forgive him for putting me in that situation."

But now that I am a murderer, I might as well embrace it.

"Please, Claudia, come to my office and we can talk about this. You're being rash. We're so close now. If you could just hold out a little longer -"

"No," I cut him off firmly. "I'm done with all of this. Find a way to do it without me."

Agent Vaughn made a frustrated sound. "There isn't a way to do it without you. You're all we have, Claudia. Can't you see how important you are?"

"Yes," I said coolly. "I can see that my own survival is more important than taking down some mobsters."

There was a pause. "That doesn't sound like you, Claudia. What's going on? What about finding the person who killed your parents?"

Oh, he was a ruthless bastard.

"I've gone this long without knowing. I know how to live this way."

"You're scared," he said accusatorily. "You're scared of what your life will be like if you do know. I can understand how hard something that life-altering might be, but the Claudia Ellers I know isn't a coward."

"And the Clayton Vaughn I thought I knew wasn't such an asshole. Turns out it's easy to misjudge people."

There was a moment of silence.

"I could subpoena you to testify against Ronan, you know," he said matter-of-factly.

So we were threatening now, were we? My eyes narrowed. Two could play at that game.

"I could tell the FBI that you sexually harassed me, you know," I shot right back at him.

His shocked gasp was audible through the phone.

"Fine," he snapped. "You clearly don't know me at all if you thought that I really would subpoena you."

"You clearly don't know me at all if you think I would bend when you use dirty, under-handed tactics. I don't take it well when people tell me what to do, but what I take even worse is when people try to back me into a corner and force me to do it anyway."

"Claudia, listen to me," this time, his voice was contrite. "I'm really sorry about what I did. About kissing you. That was completely unprofessional, and if that's what this is all about, I'll assign you to another handler."

"I don't need anyone to *handle* me," I retorted. "I'm done with this shit. My life has been one catastrophe after another since I agreed to work with you, and I'm sick of it. I'm not doing it anymore."

"Alright, then." Agent Vaughn sounded suddenly exhausted. "I understand. And I'm sorry for trying to manipulate you into staying. That was wrong of me."

My heart tugged for a moment as I recognized Clayton speaking to me. But I had come this far. Going back was no longer an option. And I didn't want to anyway.

"Good," I said. "And I want this security detail gone. I'm returning to my normal life, with everything that entails. No mobsters and no FBI agents."

"I won't agree to that, Claudia," he said, his voice hard again. "They might come after you again."

"Oh? And what good did the FBI do me when they came after me last time? Oh, wait. They didn't. I took care of myself. And that's what I'm going to keep on doing. So unless you're going to pull some Homeland Security bullshit and keep me under surveillance then back off."

"I could easily do that," he said quietly, a dangerous edge to his voice now. "Your refusal to cooperate and your closeness with Sean Reynolds would be all the grounds that I need to argue that you are in collusion with the Westies. I could have eyes on you everywhere you go."

So we were back to threats again, were we? Well, I still had the ace up my sleeve.

"And there's also this thing called sexual assault. You know, when a man touches an unwilling woman? I don't think the FBI would take too kindly to you taking advantage of a distraught asset in the privacy of your office."

There was a moment of heavy silence, and I could practically feel him seething through the phone.

"I don't know why you're doing this, Claudia, but you're going to get yourself killed," he said, his voice tight.

"Well, if you're right, then I won't be able to hear you say 'I told you so' when everything goes to shit. So at least there's that. Tell me that you'll take the security detail off me and leave me the fuck alone," I demanded.

"You don't seem to have given me any other choice," he said angrily.

"Goodbye, then, Agent Vaughn."

I hung up the phone before he could say anything else. A little nagging part of my brain told me that I was being a bitch and should feel guilty for hurting Clayton, but I firmly told it to shut the fuck up. I didn't have any room inside me for guilt anymore. It was a useless, painful, distracting emotion. And it certainly wasn't going to help me kill Ronan.

∎∎

I waited until I was sure that Agent Vaughn had honored my wishes and gotten rid of my FBI tail. Two days had passed, and I hadn't spotted the telltale black sedan in my rearview. I hadn't gone in to work; I had been stalking Ronan. If I kept not showing up like this people were probably going to start asking serious questions, but I didn't really care anymore. Everything in my life was meaningless. Everything but my task.

It had been shockingly easy to acquire a handgun. If I had wanted to buy one legitimately, I would have had to register the weapon with the police, and then it wouldn't have been too hard for them to figure out that I was the one who owned the gun that was going to kill Ronan. But thanks to Craigslist, I had been able to drive across Yonkers and pay cash for the weapon only hours after finding it listed online. And since the FBI was no longer following me, it was a long shot that they would ever link the gun back to me.

Now I was waiting in my car in the parking garage near Ronan's apartment. I had found where he worked the day before, and I followed him home. He parked in this garage, and I was going to wait for him. I had scoped out the security cameras and positioned myself in a blind spot. Although I had only seen Ronan once before, the face of the man who had threatened Sean and called me a stupid whore was burned clearly into my brain. I knew I had the right man.

I glanced at the clock in my dashboard. Only 3:42. It would be a while yet before Ronan went home for the day. But I was willing to wait a few more hours. I had already waited fourteen years.

I reached over to the passenger seat and idly traced the shape of the gun through the supple leather of my purse. The feel of its unmistakable outline was reassuring. I was so close…

Something buzzed against my thigh, and I jumped slightly. It was just my phone. I guess I was more tightly wound than I would have liked to admit to myself.

The caller ID told me that it was Agent Vaughn. I pursed my lips, hesitating. Why would he call me if not to try to convince me to come back into the fold? Whatever he had to say on that count, I didn't want to hear it. On the other hand, it was possible that he had more information on my parents' murder. If he was closer to identifying Ronan as the culprit, then I needed to know. I was ready to act, was only hours away from exacting my revenge, but it would be safer if I knew what he knew. I pressed "Answer."

"What?" I asked without preamble.

"Hello to you too," Agent Vaughn said coldly, affronted.

I said nothing, waiting for him to get to his point so that I could end the call. He sighed.

"I thought that you should know that Bradley Smith was released from holding this morning. We arrested him and Sean Reynolds for shooting Santiago on the grounds that the gun you used against Garcia belonged to one of them. Everything happened very quickly that day, and Santiago has said that he isn't sure who shot at him. Although Bradley didn't say anything, Sean admitted that the gun was his, so we were forced to cut Bradley loose." Up until this point, Agent Vaughn had sounded detached and professional, but now there was a barely-suppressed note of concern and… guilt?

"We didn't tell him that you had been giving us evidence against the Westies," he continued. "But Bradley knew that we had the gun in our possession because you had used it against Garcia. We thought that if we brought him in we would get some charges to stick, but right now we don't have enough to hold him. I'm sorry, Claudia, but he could pose a very serious threat to you now."

I knew that I should feel fear, but all I could focus on was one fact: they had arrested Sean.

"And what about Sean? Is he out too?" I asked. I tried to keep my voice causal and disinterested, but the words were strained as my tongue tripped over his name.

"No."

All of the wind was knocked out of me as though I had been punched in the gut. Sean was in jail? And Bradley and

Ronan were free? How was this possible? I was saved from having to find the air to ask my questions when Agent Vaughn continued on.

"Sean admitted to the gun being his, Claudia. That pretty firmly identifies him as the shooter. He fired on a federal agent, and…" He hesitated, as though he didn't want to tell me the worst. Oh, god, there was something worse? "And we have your taped testimony and the blood evidence from the parking lot outside your office. Without your continued cooperation, we have been forced to charge Sean with the assault and attempted murder of Hector Garcia."

"You *bastard*," I hissed. I couldn't believe that Clayton would go this far. Was he trying to hurt me for backing out on our deal?

"It wasn't my call, Claudia," he insisted, frustration lending his voice a hard edge. "We can't just let criminals walk free when we have hard evidence against them. I don't get to pick and choose who we do and don't arrest. Without having reasonable cause to hold off on pressing the charges, I was forced to act on what we had. He's being remanded without bail, Claudia. He won't be able to protect you from Bradley. Please, let me put a security detail back on you. Let us help -"

I ended the call.

My hands gripped my steering wheel as rage washed over me, my knuckles going white with the intensity of my grip. This couldn't be happening. It just couldn't. Yes, I had been mildly disgusted by Sean when I learned that his father was the man who murdered my parents. I had recoiled from him, sensing his father's taint in his blood. But that wasn't fair. Sean was nothing like Ronan, and it was clear that he had suffered at his hands. He was just as much a victim of his father's callous violence as I was. And now I had betrayed him. I buried my face in my hands, pressing my palms against my closed eyelids as though I could shove the image of Sean's infuriated, anguished expression when he had realized what I had done to him from my brain.

He might hate me – and deservedly so – but I was still hopelessly enamored with him. The sense of loss was keen and cutting as it bloomed in my chest. I tried desperately to maintain my emptiness, but it was no use. With this new knowledge, all of my tangled, agonizing feelings came roaring back, filling up my entire being, torturing me. I jerked my fingers through my hair, and a strangled, frustrated cry escaped me as I voiced my rage and pain. A part of me realized that I was becoming hysterical, coming apart at the seams. I had to fix this. I needed to calm down and formulate a plan. I forced myself to take several deep breaths. It wasn't enough to push back my jagged emotions, but my mind was clearing enough that I could think.

The first thing that I had to take care of was killing Ronan. That way, he couldn't hurt Sean when I secured his release. I was taking care of him tonight, so Sean wouldn't have to be incarcerated for much longer. When Ronan was dead, I would go back to the FBI and somehow convince them of Sean's innocence and Bradley's guilt. I would say that I felt safer with Ronan out of the picture, and I wanted to help again. Would my testimony be enough to sway Agent Vaughn?

It would have to be. I traced the outline of the gun again, centering myself. It would all be over in a few hours.

Chapter 2

I watched as Ronan pulled into the garage, and I got out of my car, closing the door behind me as softly as possible. I crouched beside the front wheel, keeping him in my line of sight while concealing myself as much as possible. When he stepped out of his car, I trained the gun on him. My pulse was racing, and my hand shook as I was struck by a moment of hesitation. Hector Garcia's blank aqua eyes, those eyes that haunted my dreams, flashed across my vision, and my gut twisted. But this wasn't the time for second-guessing myself. I gripped the gun with both hands, steadying it.

A hand clamped over my mouth, and something hard pressed against my ribs. I instantly knew what it was; I had felt this before. Someone was holding a gun on me. Terror shot through me and my pulse sped impossibly faster. My heart hurt with the intensity of its palpitations.

"Don't make a sound," a man's voice whispered in my ear. "Put the gun down slowly."

I hesitated. Ronan was exiting the garage. In a matter of seconds, he would be out of range. Was it worth sacrificing my own life to end his?

"Now," the voice growled.

Hating my captor, I did as he said. I needed to live so that I could get Sean free. If this man allowed me to survive. I carefully set the gun on the ground in front of me as Ronan disappeared from sight.

The hand left my mouth and the gun left my ribs. But my wrists were instantly caught up in a hard grip. There was an ominous clicking noise, and I felt cold metal encircle them. I was familiar with these too: handcuffs. I closed my eyes, tears beginning to leak from the corners. I had missed my chance, and now I was a captive again.

A hand reached around me and quickly grabbed up my gun, clicking the safety back on. My captor grasped my upper arms and pulled me to my feet.

"Claudia Ellers, you are under arrest for the attempted murder of Ronan Reynolds."

"Clayton!" I gasped and jerked in his grip, but he held me firmly.

"You have the right to remain silent. Anything you say can and will be used against you in a court of law."

No no no no no!

My vision was tunneling as I gasped for breath. I sagged back against Clayton as my knees began to give out, but he held me up, supporting my weight. He guided me away from my car, and I stumbled before him as he forced me to move on unsteady legs. I might as well have been walking to the gallows as we approached the telltale black sedan. He opened the passenger door, and I had no choice but to get in. I leaned forward awkwardly, trying to keep my weight off my cuffed hands as he fastened the seatbelt around me. Tears were streaming down my face. Ronan was going to live, and I was going to go to jail. The world really was a fucked up place.

I couldn't look at Clayton as he settled himself in the driver's seat, and I stared resolutely down at my feet. I was flooded with terror, resentment, hatred, even. How could he do this to me?

His fingers gripped my chin, turning my head and forcing me to face him. His gorgeous blue eyes were blazing with a furious light as they regarded me censoriously.

"What the fuck are you thinking, Claudia?" He demanded angrily.

"How did you find me?" I asked shakily.

"You have GPS on the phone we gave you. I knew that something was wrong with you, so I tracked you down. But I never imagined that you would be doing something so goddamn stupid and reckless." He released me, closing his eyes and pinching the bridge of his nose. "Why, Claudia? Why would you go after Ronan on your own? If you had just helped us, you could have put him away for life. But now I'm going to have to arrest you. Fuck!" His eyes snapped open, glaring at me as he half-shouted the last word.

"Clayton, please." My voice was ragged, desperate. "He killed my parents. He ruined my life. And Sean's. Please…"

His brow furrowed. "Why do you think he killed your parents?"

"Sean told me that the gun used to belong to his father," I explained quickly. "And when I confronted him about it, he figured out that I had been spying on him. Now he hates me. And I'm the reason he's in jail." I wanted to hug myself, but my hands just jerked against the cuffs.

Clayton's eyes softened ever so slightly. "I understand how much you must hate Ronan. But this isn't the way, Claudia. If you had just trusted me, Sean wouldn't be in jail and Ronan would have been arrested."

God, I really had fucked up. "I'm sorry," I said quietly. The words were laughably insufficient to rectify the clusterfuck that I had put myself in. That I had put Sean in.

"Sorry doesn't cut it," Clayton said, his voice hard-edged.

"I know," I whispered.

He ran a frustrated hand through his hair. "God damn it!" He turned the key hard in the ignition, over-cranking the engine. The cold, hard reality came down on me: he was going to take me to the FBI. This time, he really was going to interrogate me.

I sat beside him in silence, no longer able to look at him. I couldn't even bring myself to hate him for what he was doing to me. This was all my own doing, and all I felt was self-disgust. I was supposed to be smarter than this. But it seemed that ever since I had met Sean, I had fucked up over and over again as my life crumbled around me. I was self-destructing, spiraling out of control, and I couldn't seem to stop myself.

I stared out the window, hardly seeing the city passing us by as I retreated into myself. But after a while, it registered with me that we had been driving far too long to be headed to the FBI offices.

"Where are we going?" I asked. Clayton's grip on the steering wheel tightened, and he grimaced. He didn't answer me. But it soon became apparent where we were headed: he was taking me home.

What was going on? Hope welled within me at the prospect that he might let me go. Would he really betray the FBI for me? After everything I had done to him? I pursed my lips, holding back further questions. I didn't want to push him lest he change his mind and turn around.

When we parked up outside my house, a full minute passed before Clayton pried his fingers from the steering wheel and turned to face me. I swallowed hard, but I forced myself to meet his eyes. His expression was closed off, enigmatic.

"Let me see the cuffs," he said, his voice gruff. I twisted awkwardly in my seat to give him access to them. I couldn't hold in my sigh of relief when he released me from their cold bite. The feeling of them around my wrists had dredged up memories of the early days of my abduction, of my abuse at Bradley's hands. It made me recall how Sean had stood up for me, revealing his protective side. Had he been as entranced by me as I was by him even then? Maybe. But I knew that he was goodhearted, and he never would have stood for Bradley hurting an innocent. I felt a pang in my heart as the injustice of what was being done to him struck me all over again. He didn't deserve to be locked up; he was a good person. And it was all my fault.

Clayton was opening the passenger door for me. I was surprised when he took me by the hand to help me out of the car. He maintained the contact, gripping me gently by the elbow as he walked me to my front door. I was grateful for the support; I was shaking like a leaf.

I paused when I got to the door, remembering that my house keys were in my purse, which was currently on the floorboard of my car. I hoped to hell that no one would break a window to steal it. I didn't want to have to get new keys, new locks, and change my credit cards again. Sighing, I extricated myself from Clayton's grip and retrieved my spare key that was hidden in an innocent-looking rock beneath my azalea bushes. The beeping of my new alarm system as I entered the house made me jump slightly. I still wasn't used to it. But it was a necessary precaution. No way was anyone breaking in without the cops being notified. I punched in the code and the shrill warning noise stopped. Clayton followed me into my living room, where he situated himself beside me on my couch. I was grateful that he hadn't sat in the armchair across from me. Despite the strained atmosphere around us, I found comfort in his closeness. He had proven time and again to be someone I could rely on, who I could trust with my secrets and my grief. And now that I was in his presence once again, it dawned on me just how out of control I had been without him being there to steady me. I should have gone to him as soon as Sean had thrown me out. Then maybe I wouldn't be in this mess.

My hand reached out for his as though of its own accord, seeking his warmth. I closed my eyes and took a deep breath when we touched. He turned his hand so that our palms were pressed together, and his fingers entwined with mine.

"Thank you," I whispered. When I met his gaze, I found him regarding me seriously, but there was a hint of doubt, of trepidation in his eyes.

"I can't believe I'm doing this," he muttered to himself. "We need to talk, Claudia," he said solemnly. "You need to tell me what you're going through, explain to me why you decided to go after Ronan on your own. It was dangerous and reckless, and I know you're smarter than that. Do you know how much danger you've put yourself in by forcing me to take my security detail off of you? What if it hadn't been me who found you in that garage? What if it had been Bradley? What if you had missed and Ronan saw you? He would kill you, Claudia. Even as it is, it's highly likely that he'll come after you once he finds out why Sean and Bradley were arrested. You have to let me help you. You have to trust me."

"I do trust you," I said quietly. "I know that I fucked up. It's just... I went a little crazy when I found out that Ronan killed my parents. He ruined my life. He's the reason I was in foster care, the reason that I've been alone for fourteen years. And when Sean threw me out... Oh, god, Clayton. I just couldn't handle it. I completely fell apart." I was crying again, and Clayton squeezed my hand reassuringly.

"I can understand that, Claudia. But I wish you had come to me." His brow furrowed, lines of anxiety appearing around his eyes. "This is my fault. If I hadn't kissed you... That was wrong of me, Claudia. I know that's why you stayed away. I just... I can't help caring about you." His voice was strained. "Even though I know how you feel about Sean, I allowed myself to act rashly and selfishly. I'm sorry."

Now it was my turn to squeeze his hand. "It's okay, Clayton. I never should have said those nasty things to you. I didn't mean them. I was just desperate for you to stay away so that I could get at Ronan." I lowered my voice. "And I care about you too. Just not in that way. I'm sorry."

The lines of his face tightened further, but he just nodded. "I know that we haven't known each other very long, but our relationship means a lot to me. I don't want to lose you, Claudia. I hope we can repair what I've damaged between us."

I stared at him earnestly. I wanted nothing more than to wipe the pained expression from his handsome visage. "There's no damage. Clayton, I haven't had a friend since I was thirteen years old. Other than Sean, you're the only person that I've trusted since then. I'm not going to give that up. I'm not going to give *you* up."

He let out a long breath, some of the tension leaving him as he gave me a small smile. "Thank you." He regarded me gratefully for a moment, but then he turned serious once again. "Now please explain to me what you were thinking going after Ronan. I can understand that you want revenge and that you want to protect Sean from his father. But you were so distraught after what happened with Garcia. What changed?"

We were back on the painful topic again. I wanted to shy away from it, but I realized that I needed to share with Clayton. I knew that he would be able to help me sort myself out. I took a shaky breath before diving in.

"After Sean found out that I betrayed him, I just fell apart. It was too much for me to handle. Rage was a much friendlier emotion than what I was going through." I swallowed back the lump in my throat so that I could continue to force out the words that I needed to release. "And then... What I did to Garcia rocked me to my core. I can't help feeling like a murderer, even if it was self-defense. And I figured... I figured if I already was damned I might as well take Ronan out." I hugged an arm around my stomach, trying to physically hold in the grief that was threatening to overwhelm me. "I don't know who I am anymore." My voice cracked, and I looked at Clayton beseechingly. "Nothing used to hurt me, but now everything is so... sharp." I gasped out a soft sob.

His fingers curled under my chin, lifting my face so that I didn't have the option of dropping my eyes. His electric blue stare was so intense that it took my breath away. "What's happened to you has changed you, Claudia," he said seriously. "After everything you've been through, you couldn't possibly be the same person that you were before you were abducted. But I think it goes further back than that. You haven't been *you* since the night Ronan killed your parents. I can understand why you hate him, Claudia; he took everything from you that night. You should be nothing but perfectly happy. You deserve that. And you can have it now, if you just help me."

"I want to help you, Clayton. But I don't think that happiness is possible for me. I don't think I possess the capacity for that anymore."

His thumb lightly traced the line of my jaw. "Of course you do." His voice was low and intense. "You're intelligent, resourceful, brave, and strong-willed to a fault. Even after everything that's happened to you, these are qualities that Ronan was incapable of stamping out. This is who you are: a survivor. And you will survive this, Claudia. Even if I have to dive into the depths of the ocean and drag your ass back to shore, you're going to come out okay. I promise you that."

I stared at him, thunderstruck and at a loss for words. I had treated him like shit, and yet he was doing everything he could to help me. I knew that I had done nothing to deserve his unwavering support.

"Why are you so nice to me?" I asked, truly unable to comprehend the motivations for his kindness.

"I told you, Claudia: I care about you. You're a good person."

"But... But I was going to murder Ronan." A spike of ice stabbed through my gut as I came to a startling realization. "And I still want to. I'm a killer, Clayton. You were going to arrest me, and you should. I deserve it."

He gripped me by the shoulders, holding me firmly as he stared into my eyes. "I don't blame you for wanting to kill him. Hell, the bastard should be dead. You deserve justice, Claudia, but not at the expense of your own freedom. And not at the expense of your soul. I know you; you *are* a good person, Claudia." I opened my mouth to protest, but he spoke right on over me. "You killed Garcia because you didn't have a choice. You've told yourself that you might as well kill Ronan because you're a murderer, but that just isn't true. Despite everything that has happened to you, you are one of the most compassionate people I have ever met. Don't let your hatred of Ronan take that away from you. He's taken so much from you already; don't let him destroy that part of you. You've said that you want to help me. Let's do this the right way. Together."

So many emotions were swirling through me, moving with the swiftness of a raging torrent: anger, self-loathing, wonder, incredulity, gratitude, grief. I was completely overwhelmed, stunned by the lengths that Clayton would go to in order to help me. And I realized that he was right. What I had been forced to do to Garcia had fucked with my head, had made me question everything that I was. And when the loss of Sean came so hard on the heels of that earth-shattering, bloody night, I had spiraled out of control. But now, with Clayton grounding me, I remembered who I was. I was Dr. Claudia Ellers, a woman who hated violence, who couldn't stand to see people in pain. And while killing Ronan Reynolds would end the suffering of many people, it would rip another hole in the foundations of my very self. He wasn't worth that; I refused to give him any more of my life than what he had already stolen from me. Overcome with gratitude and relief at my realization, I threw my arms around Clayton, tucking my face against his neck as I held him to me tightly. For a moment, he stiffened in my hold, but he quickly relaxed, wrapping his arms around me in kind.

"Thank you," I whispered. If Clayton hadn't shown up, if he hadn't forcibly taken me away from that garage that would have been the scene of Ronan's murder and the slaying of the remnants of my own soul, I didn't know who I would be right now. I had thought that I didn't know who I was anymore, but Clayton had reminded me. Ronan was going to face justice - and in a fashion it would be by my hand - but we were going to do this the right way.

I basked in the warm, reassuring heat of Clayton's embrace. A small part of me wondered if I should feel guilty for initiating such intimate contact when I knew how he felt about me, but I selfishly clung onto him. I realized that I could have this is I wanted to. I could have *him*. He was the sensible choice, really. He was solid, stable, safe. And he saw me for who I truly was, even when I couldn't see it myself.

My heart ached at the thought of being with a man who wasn't Sean, but I knew now that there was no way he would ever forgive me, even if my testimony did secure his freedom. He had opened up to me, trusted me. And I had betrayed him.

I breathed in Clayton's salt-kissed leather scent. It was undeniably comforting. Maybe when all of this was over, I should give him a chance. Maybe I could find happiness with Clayton. I would never share with him what I did with Sean, but it occurred to me that perhaps no one was meant to share something that brilliant and all-consuming. It was unstable, volatile, and in the end it had only resulted in our mutual destruction.

I clung to Clayton more tightly.

Chapter 3

Clayton's mouth was hot on mine as his tongue traced the line of my lower lip. I opened for him, and he drew it into his mouth, sucking on it lightly. His body radiated a gentle heat where it pressed against mine. Being kissed by Clayton was… nice. And his gorgeous body was more than nice. I unconsciously ran my fingertips across his rippling abs, my touch tracing upwards until the flat of my palm rested against the hard planes of his bare chest. The light dusting of hair on his tanned skin tickled my flesh. I could feel it brushing against my hand and lower down at my hip, where no clothing separated our bodies. His hard cock pressing against me insistently was a testament to how badly he wanted me.

But did I want him? Clayton was caring, intelligent, and sexy as hell. There was no good reason why I shouldn't be with him.

Well, there was a reason, but it certainly wasn't a good one.

Sean.

But that was over. There was nothing I could do about it now. Sean would never want me, and Clayton was here. Here in my bed with me while Sean was locked away in a prison cell.

Why couldn't my brain just shut up and accept the pleasure that Clayton was offering? Maybe one day I could. But it was too soon. I didn't want Clayton out of my life, but I certainly wasn't ready for him to be in my bed. Turning my head slightly, I broke the kiss.

"Wait," I whispered, pressing both hands against his chest in order to push him off of me.

Strong hands ensnared my wrists, jerking my arms above my head and pinning them there. I gasped and my eyes widened as I stared up at Clayton incredulously. This was jarringly different from his slow, sweet touches a moment before. Instinctively, I tugged against his grip, but he held me fast. His expression was cocky, the twist of his full lips slightly cruel.

"Isn't this what you want, Claudia?" His tone was colored with amusement as he pinned me with a knowing stare, his green eyes cutting to the core of me. There was a strange lilt to my name as his voice caressed it, making me shiver as heat bloomed at my core.

Wait. *Green eyes.*

I blinked hard, and when my eyes opened again my breath caught in my throat.

"Sean!" His name was a strangled whisper. He was looming above me, his gorgeous, deep green gaze burning into me. The lines of his face were drawn into a terrifying expression, something ruthless, merciless. It made my heart race and my clit pulse. A sharp cry escaped me as I was suddenly impaled by his cock. The intensity of his thrust made my body jerk beneath him, but he held me in place. He had done little to prepare me, and the ecstasy that shot through me when he filled me was laced with pain. But he didn't give me time to adjust; he forced my body to accept him, to accommodate him. And I couldn't help but respond with delight. The twinges of pain within my sex and his pitiless, bruising grip on my wrists only served to heighten my pleasure. What had been little more than a pleasant warmth under Clayton's tender ministrations was ignited to a bonfire as bliss soared through me.

As though he could hear what I was thinking, the thought of Clayton made Sean's face twist into a terrible snarl.

"You're *mine, Claudia,*" he growled. The intensity of his thrust as he spoke drew a harsh cry from my throat. "And I'm not letting you go. Not to him. Not to anyone. Do you understand me?"

"Sean," I groaned his name as my head twisted against the pillow. The force of his possessive words, of his ruthless assault on my body and mind, was overwhelming. There was a reason that I couldn't be with him. If only I could remember what...

"Answer me, Claudia," he demanded harshly. Still gripping my wrists in one hand, his other tangled in my hair, pulling sharply so that I was forced to look up into his blazing eyes.

"Yes, Sean," I said breathlessly. "I'm yours. Always."

His hard-edged grin was triumphant, satisfied at his conquest, at his utter possession of me. I was helpless to resist him. I knew in that moment that I would never want anyone as fiercely as I wanted him. No matter the impossible hurdles that separated us, no matter the knowledge that this would never work out in the long run, I allowed myself to surrender to the moment, to relish this time with him that I might never enjoy again. He had ruined me for anyone else. But I didn't care. All I could see was him: his mesmerizing, intense eyes, the strong line of his jaw covered in that sexy stubble that raked across my skin so deliciously. The sensation of his hard body moving against mine in perfect, blissful rhythm was the greatest pleasure I had ever known, ever would know. I groaned in wild abandon as his dominant aura washed over me, his strength and relentless onslaught reinforcing just how powerless I was to resist him. And I didn't want to.

"Sean!" I cried out his name as my orgasm hit me suddenly, ripping through my body as ruthlessly as he held me. Stars burst behind my eyes and my vision wavered as sweetest pleasure wracked my senses. Sean's harsh shout followed mine, and his hot seed lashed at my core as it clenched around him. I relished the heat of it, reveling in the feeling of him marking me as his own.

My eyes snapped open as I jerked awake to find myself alone in my own bed. Perspiration beaded on my brow, and the sheets were twisted around my body. An intense sense of loss filled me as I realized that it had been nothing more than a lucid dream. I lay awake for a long time afterward, and despite my sadness, a small smile spread across my face at the memory of the vividness of it. I concentrated on recalling every detail, not wanting to forget one moment of the dream. Even though it hadn't been real, I had still been able to experience Sean one last time. But dismay soon flooded me again. Had that been the last time? Would I be haunted by such dreams for the rest of my life, preventing me from moving on?

A part of me acknowledged that I would never be able to move on. Even if I was able to find happiness with someone like Clayton, it would never be what I shared with Sean. My heart twisted in my chest, but there was nothing remotely pleasurable about this pain.

∎∎∎

The following afternoon, the feeling of Sean's phantom fingers gripping my wrists lingered, and whenever I looked down at them, I was distantly amazed to find that no bruises marred my pale skin. I sighed heavily, wishing keenly to see his marks upon me.

"Dr. Ellers?" Clayton's deep voice called me back to reality. "Let me get this straight. The gun that Sean Reynolds gave you, the one that killed Hector Garcia, used to belong to Ronan Reynolds?"

Clayton already knew this story, but he was prompting me to make it part of the official record. We were back in that dreaded grey-walled interrogation room, and the red light on the camera was illuminated.

"Yes," I replied firmly. "I had thought that the gun was Bradley's because it was the one he threatened me with when he abducted me. But when I asked Sean about it, he said that he had given it to Bradley after his father had given it to him. Sean didn't want to own a gun." With my last statement, I stared at Agent Vaughn significantly. They might have Sean locked up for assaulting Hector Garcia on my behalf, but I was going to do everything that I could to put it in the official record that deep down, Sean didn't want to be a violent person. I knew that it was too little, too late, but if I could get the FBI the evidence that they needed against Ronan, I might be able to salvage my old deal with Agent Vaughn and get Sean freed. Or at the very least get him a reduced sentence. The problem now was that the charges had been officially filed, and they had to go through the courts. Agent Vaughn informed me that it wasn't within his power to just make that disappear now that the District Attorney's office was involved. Nevertheless, I would do everything in my power to help Sean.

"Thank you, Dr. Ellers. I think we have what we need now." Agent Vaughn stood to turn off the camera, and then Clayton was smiling at me gently.

"Now that I'm cooperating again, do you think that you'll be able to help Sean?" I asked immediately.

Clayton's smile disappeared, and he shifted uncomfortably. "I'll do what I can, Claudia, but I can't make any promises. I'm sorry."

He looked as though he really meant that. I took a deep breath and nodded my understanding.

"Well, do you at least have enough evidence against Ronan now? Can you arrest him?"

Clayton looked even more discomfited. "No, Claudia," he admitted regretfully. "Not right away at least. When we ran ballistics, we linked that gun to several other shootings spanning over the last fifteen years. We are doing what we can to link Ronan to those other crimes to make our case more solid before we bring him in. The last thing that I want is for him to slip through our fingers. If we bring him in with what we have now, he'll know that you're responsible, and then he'll come straight for you. It's a miracle that he hasn't already. I can only guess that Bradley hasn't told him about the link between you and his arrest."

"Bring him in," I insisted. "Then let him come after me. If you can catch him in the act, then your case will be ironclad."

Clayton pinned me with a hard stare and shook his head. "No way, Claudia. It's not the FBI's policy to use innocent people as bait. We won't put you at risk like that."

"But I want to. I volunteer," I protested.

"Let me rephrase that: *I* won't put you at risk like that."

I crossed my arms over my chest defiantly, preparing to argue. His eyes softened in response to my hard stance. "We *will* get Ronan," Clayton promised me. "Thanks to you, we're close. Just a few more days, Claudia. That's all the time you'll have to wait. Then he'll never be able to hurt you – or anyone else – ever again. And the Westies hierarchy will crumble. I just need you to be patient for a little while longer. Can you do that for me?"

I continued to glare at him for a moment, dissatisfied by his answer. I wanted to bring Ronan down *now*. And I wanted Sean to be free. But it seemed that neither of those things was within my direct power to grant.

"Okay," I said finally, nodding. "But I want to know as soon as you bring him in. And I want you to keep me updated on what's going on with Sean."

"Deal. Now let's get you home. It's getting late, and you look like you could use some sleep."

I walked to the elevator with him compliantly, realizing that I really did need to sleep. My brows rose in surprise when Clayton stepped into the elevator with me. "You don't have to walk me to my car," I told him.

"Not only will I be walking you to your car, but I'll be riding in it with you. I'm not leaving your side until we have Ronan."

"But won't there be a security detail tailing me?"

Clayton's jaw tensed. "After their failure with the Garcia situation, I'm not trusting your safety to anyone but me. The security team will be outside your house, but I'll be staying on the couch."

My brows rose further. "I don't remember extending that invitation."

His eyes narrowed. "I'm not giving you an option, Claudia. Now, I could threaten you with telling the FBI about your little rendezvous with Ronan in the parking garage, but you and I both know that I would never follow through with that. So you're just going to have to accept that I'm staying with you. End of story."

As much as I hated being bossed around, I knew that what Clayton was saying made sense. The FBI had failed me when I came home to find Garcia waiting for me. Having someone in the house with me was a good idea. And there was no one who I would trust more being in my home alone with me than Clayton. Sure, he had kissed me and admitted that he had feelings for me, but he was a perfect gentleman. I had no doubt that if he said he was going to stay on the couch, he would stay on the couch. Unlike Sean, who would just come into my room uninvited and sprawl out naked on my bed as though he had every right...

I shoved the memory away. "Okay, Clayton. You win." I paused, then added: "Thanks."

The corners of his full mouth quirked upwards and his bright blue eyes glowed. "You're welcome. And thank you for not fighting me on this."

I smiled slightly and nodded in acknowledgement of his thanks. I was grateful not to fight as well. I was also grateful that Clayton had taken me to retrieve my own car from Ronan's parking garage that morning. It was a miracle that my purse was still on the floorboard.

"So," I said conversationally once we were situated in my car. "Tell me more about your captain of the football team days. Were you Prom King too?"

He knew that I was teasing him, but he grinned. "But of course. It's a given that you'll be Prom King when you're dating the head of the cheerleading squad, who also happens to be the most popular girl in school. She pretty much controlled the entire student body. If she told them to vote for me, then they voted for me. It really had nothing to do with me personally."

"She sounds like Regina George," I said, laughing. For a moment I was concerned that my pop culture reference would be sadly outdated, but Clayton eased my worry by laughing along with me.

"I suppose she was a bit of a 'mean girl,'" he admitted.

"And don't be so modest," I continued. "I'm sure plenty of the girls voted for you without much encouragement."

"Why, Claudia, it's not often that I blush, but it's positively becoming a habit around you. You do know how to flatter a boy." He was grinning, and there was no trace of a blush on his tanned cheeks. I rolled my eyes at him.

"I don't think 'boy' is exactly a suitable term. You're what, twenty-eight?"

"And the flattery continues. I just hit the big 3-0 last month."

I mock-shuddered. "Ew. You're *ancient.* I expect you might kick the bucket any moment now."

"It's a miracle I've lasted this long," he said, smiling.

We continued our comfortable banter during the ride back to my place. It was amazing how he could help me forget all of my worries and make me laugh. It was so easy to be with him. A part of me marveled at the concept that I had a friend.

And even though I knew that Clayton wanted to be more, and that I had contemplated becoming more, having him as a friend was exactly what I needed right now in order to maintain my sanity.

When we arrived at my house, he made me wait in the car until he could come around and open my door for me. Once my feet hit the pavement, he placed his hand on the small of my back, keeping his body close to my own in a protective stance. His touch was familiar, intimate, but I was grateful for the support. I couldn't deny that I felt safer with him by my side.

We were at the steps leading up to my front porch when it happened. Both of our heads whipped around at the sound of my azalea bushes rustling. A masked, black-clad figure emerged from the foliage, and I froze. It was Garcia all over again, but this time I had no means of defending myself; my gun was sitting atop the table just inside my front door.

"I knew you were a whore," the dark figure growled as he raised a gun.

"Claudia, get down!" I wouldn't have been able to move of my own accord, but Clayton shoved me hard. I fell, my knees banging painfully against the steps as I caught myself on my hands. The shot rang out before I had even hit the ground. More deafening *cracks* rent the evening air, and I could see the black-clad figure fleeing.

And then Clayton was dropping to his knees, clutching at his stomach.

"Clayton!" I cried, alarmed. I shoved myself to a kneeling position, not caring if the assailant was still lurking, waiting for a clear shot at me.

He fell back, and I automatically caught him under his shoulders so that his head wouldn't crack against the pavement. But he was too heavy for me to hold him up, so I lowered him down gently. I could see his face now, his handsome features twisted in pain. My eyes darted down to the hand that was still pressed against his stomach. It was covered in blood.

"Are you okay?" He asked, his voice strained.

"Oh my god, Clayton!" I pried his hand away from the wound, and the sight of the gory hole made my stomach twist. I pressed my own hands against it as hard as I could, trying desperately to stem the flow of blood. He cried out at the act. "I'm sorry. I'm sorry. We have to stop the bleeding. We have to get you to a hospital." I was babbling. I could hear the footfalls and shouts of the FBI agents approaching us. "You'll be okay, Clayton. You'll be okay."

I was distracted from the horrific sight of his blood seeping through my fingers when his hand cupped my cheek.

"Claudia." His voice was calm. My eyes were drawn to his. They were filled with that intense, electric light that seemed to shine from within. "Are you hurt?"

There was something hot and wet on my cheeks. I tore my mind from the panic that was engulfing it to take inventory of my body. "No," I answered shakily. "I'm fine."

He smiled softly, and his thumb traced the line of my cheekbone, wiping my tears. "Then it was worth it."

His hand dropped from my cheek and his eyes closed, shuttering the light that shone from them.

Chapter 4

"Clayton!" The panic came crashing back. I moved one hand to his chest, keeping the other pressed hard against his wound. His heart was beating erratically, and his breathing was ragged. "Clayton, stay with me," I demanded of his unconscious form. Oh, god there was so much blood. "Don't you dare die on me. Don't you dare." My voice was furious. I couldn't lose Clayton. I couldn't…

"Shit." I looked up to find who had cursed. A dark-skinned woman was pressing two fingers against Clayton's neck, checking his pulse. "Hang in there, Vaughn. The ambulance is on its way."

An eternity passed before I heard the wail of approaching sirens. I could feel Clayton's life slipping away as his blood poured over my fingers, the beat of his heart beneath my palm becoming more and more unsteady. This couldn't be happening. That bullet was meant for me, not him.

I was aware of paramedics at Clayton's side, but I couldn't tear my eyes from his face. I longed for his striking eyes to open, to see his wide, perfect grin. The idea that I might never see them again was unbearable. I couldn't bring myself to let him go. Someone's hands closed around my shoulders, pulling me away from him so that the paramedics could lift him onto the waiting gurney. I scrambled to my feet, forcing my unsteady legs to support me. I couldn't leave his side. When we reached the ambulance, I moved to climb in after him.

"Ma'am, you can't come in here," one of the paramedics insisted. My hands curled into fists, and I tore my eyes from Clayton to glare at him.

"I'm a doctor. I'm riding with him."

"I don't have time to argue with you. We need to get him to the hospital. You're not coming." With that, he slammed the doors shut, and the sirens blared back to life as the ambulance sped away from me. A frustrated sound escaped me.

Someone's hand gently closed around my upper arm, and I glanced over to the person who held me. It was the dark-skinned woman who had stayed by Clayton's side as we waited for the ambulance.

"Come on," she said. "You can ride with me to the hospital."

I half-ran to her black SUV, and she jogged to catch up with me. I was grateful that she shattered the speed limit as we followed the ambulance.

"I'm Sharon, by the way," she supplied as she expertly wove through traffic. I just nodded in acknowledgement, the rising bile in my throat preventing me from speaking. We reached the hospital in less than ten minutes, but the drive seemed excruciatingly long.

My hands were twisting before me as I strode towards the waiting room. When I reached it, I began pacing back and forth anxiously, wishing keenly to be by Clayton's side in the ER.

"Dr. Ellers, why don't you come and sit by me," Sharon suggested, her voice even in an attempt to calm me. I just shook my head sharply. The adrenaline pumping through my veins demanded that I stay active.

"At least come to the restroom and clean up. I'll come with you," she urged.

Clean up? I glanced down at my hands and saw that they were stained crimson. The sight made my gut twist as my stomach rebelled. I rushed towards the restroom, Sharon following quickly in my wake. I barely made it to the toilet in time. Sharon knelt beside me, rubbing my back as I heaved until nothing more was coming up. Tears were blinding me, and my entire body shook.

I didn't have time to fall apart; I needed to get back to the waiting room in case there was news about Clayton's condition. Sharon helped me to my feet and guided me towards the sink. Mechanically, I washed my hands, scouring my skin with my nails as I scrubbed the blood from them. The water turned pink as it swirled down the drain, and I fought the urge to be sick again. When the water ran clear, I squared my shoulders and rushed back to the waiting room, where I resumed my pacing. Sharon tried to guide me to a chair, but I shook her off. Out of the corner of my eye, I noticed other FBI agents sitting in the waiting room, their expressions strained.

I didn't know how much time had passed when a man in green scrubs appeared at the entrance to the waiting room. His expression was solemn. I wanted to rush towards him, but I froze on the spot. Sharon approached him slowly, dread etched in every line of her face. The doctor spoke to her softly, and her head bowed. He squeezed her shoulder, his eyes full of sympathy. Sharon turned to me, and her face was wet with tears. My chest tightened and I stopped breathing.

"I'm sorry," she whispered. "He..." Her voice broke. "He didn't make it."

Someone caught me beneath my arms as my legs went out from under me. I was lowered into a chair, and I slumped forward, burying my face in my hands. Sobs wracked my entire body as the horrible reality came crashing down on me.

Clayton was dead. My only friend in the world was gone. And I knew who had taken him from me: Bradley.

•••

"I'm so sorry, Dr. Ellers, but the man who shot Clayton escaped. We tried to track him down, but the need to help Clayton was more pressing."

Sharon was regretfully giving me the bad news. It was the middle of the night, and I was exhausted. But I forced my mind to sharpness as I sat in the interrogation room inside the FBI offices. They had told me that I could wait until the next day to come in, but I wanted to put what I knew on the official record while it was still fresh in my mind. I had recounted every detail of the attack, my voice hollow.

"I know who it was," I insisted. "It was Bradley. Bradley Smith. I recognized his voice. You have to arrest him."

Sharon looked at me sadly. "We will do what we can, but just recognizing his voice is too shaky to hold up in court. We'll get a warrant to search his apartment for the weapon that killed Vaughn, but it's likely that he's disposed of it."

"No," I said staunchly. "Don't tell me that it's not enough. He's going to pay for what he did. You know that he abducted me. You know that he assaulted me. And you know that he… He shot Clayton." I couldn't bring myself to say the word *killed*.

Sharon sighed. "We just don't have the hard evidence to prove all of that," she said, her tone laced with frustration. "We'll get the warrant and see what more we can find on him. I swear to you that we're doing everything we can to build a case against him. I just need you to be patient. We'll tighten security on you. You're going to stay at a safe house until we can bring him in."

I scowled at her. "No. I refuse to let him force me into hiding. I'm not giving up my life for him."

Sharon's eyes narrowed. "You could lose your life if you leave yourself exposed like that. Don't let Clayton's sacrifice have been for nothing."

She was as ruthless as Agent Vaughn.

"If I die, then maybe you'll have your goddamn evidence," I said accusatorily.

Sharon crossed her arms over her chest. "Don't be stupid, Dr. Ellers. Go to the safe house."

I shook my head vigorously. "I'm not giving in to Bradley. Maybe this will be motivation enough for the FBI to get their shit together and put him behind bars."

Sharon threw up her arms in exasperation. "Fine!" She said harshly. "I can't force you. But we're keeping a security detail on you, and we're going to monitor your every step."

"I won't let anyone else die for me," I said angrily.

"I'm not negotiating on this. You'll accept the security detail, or I'll authorize it through Homeland Security given your association with the Westies."

It was my turn to narrow my eyes. "I guess I don't have a choice then," I said through clenched teeth.

"No. You don't," she replied coolly.

I stood quickly. "I'm going home."

"We'll be right behind you."

It was the first time I had left my house in three days. And I hated the reason for the end of my isolation. I was at Clayton's funeral. One of his fellow FBI agents was giving the eulogy, but the words just rolled off my mind. This man must have been Clayton's friend, but he was a stranger to me. I realized in that moment that I knew very little about Clayton's life. We had always talked about me. My heart twisted as I realized that I would never have the opportunity to know him better. I regretted all of the minutes I had wasted talking about myself when I could have learned more about him. But I regretted even more that I would never be able to tell him how sorry I was that he had died for me. At times, I felt a hot surge of anger at him for taking the bullet for me. I should be the one being lowered into the ground. Clayton had so much life ahead of him. He was a good person. He could have done so much more. Whereas I was completely fucked up. I was already dead inside; I had been since the day that Sean realized my betrayal. And I had no family to leave behind, no one who would grieve for me. Clayton would have been sad, but he would have gotten over it. He was stable, strong. He would have been able to move on. But I was going to carry the guilt for his death for the rest of life.

I had glimpsed an older couple standing at the front of the crowd that was gathered around the graveside. I recognized the man's angular jaw and the woman's bright blue eyes. They were Clayton's parents. The grief that I had felt at my parents' passing had all but broken me, but I knew that what they were suffering was so much worse. No one should have to bury their child. I was only able to look at them for a moment; I couldn't bear the sight of their devastation. Not when I was the reason that their son was dead.

People were slowly walking away from the grave. The service was over. I wanted to linger. If I left Clayton, then that meant that he really was gone. But then I saw his parents again, his mother leaning heavily on his father as she sobbed into his chest. I had to get out of there before they noticed me. Walking away from them on leaden legs, I blindly followed the winding path out of the graveyard. I had reached the wrought iron gates when someone called me from my reverie.

"Claudia." His voice was soft, but I recognized it immediately. At first I was bewildered at his presence, but my confusion was quickly overcome by a flood of white hot rage. I suddenly realized that I wasn't the only one to blame for Clayton's death. If I had never met Sean, then I never would have known Clayton, and he never would have died in order to protect me.

I ignored him, refusing to look his way as I strode past him. His large hand encircled my wrist, stopping me short. I hated the yearning that rose up within me at his touch.

"Wait," he ordered.

I jerked against his grip. "Let me go," I insisted. But my struggles were fruitless. His fingers gripped my chin, forcing me to look up at him. I glared into his gorgeous green eyes, a mixture of loathing and longing washing over me.

"I'm sorry," he said softly.

"You're *sorry?*" I hissed. "Fuck you, Sean. This is your fault."

"Claudia, please," he said desperately. "I have to talk to you. Please listen to me."

"Get away from me!" I shrieked. I beat my fist against his chest repeatedly, trying to force him away from me. "I hate you! I hate you!" I was sobbing now. He took the blows, refusing to budge. His arms enfolded me, pulling me up against him in a fierce embrace.

"I know," he said brokenly.

And then I was clinging to him, burying my face against his chest as my tears soaked his shirt. I might hate him, but he was all that I had.

Chapter 5

I allowed Sean to guide me to my car and drive me home. My mind was too much of a mess for me to even begin formulating the words to protest. I was devastated at what had happened to Clayton. And I was brimming full of so much anger and hate. It was directed at myself for being alive, at Clayton for having sacrificed himself for me, at Sean for being a part of the violent world that had claimed the life of my only friend. But the more that I focused on my fury, the more it became directed at one person: Bradley. He had fired the shot that had taken Clayton's life, the shot that had stolen him from me. Furthermore, he was the one who had chosen to abduct me, not Sean. It was his fault that Clayton had become involved in my life in the first place. If Bradley hadn't taken me on that night, then I would still be living my controlled, pain-free life. There had been times when I thought that, despite the pain, I was better now for having known Sean and Clayton and learning what it was to really be alive. But I would have traded all of that if it meant that Clayton would still be alive now; I would rather be dead inside than have him dead in the ground.

I had told myself that I died inside again on the day that Sean left me, but that wasn't true. I still hurt. Surely someone with nothing inside should be immune to pain?

Yes, if Bradley had never abducted me, then Clayton would be alive. But a horrible thought struck me: if I hadn't been there to save Sean that night, then *he* would be dead now. And I would never even know it, would never have even known him. Would some part of my soul have felt a distant sense of loss when his soul left the world, even if he was a stranger to me? The cold, logical side of me told me that if we were weighing the two men's worthiness by their deeds, then Clayton most certainly deserved to be the one who was living now. But I had learned the painful lesson that the world wasn't that black-and-white. Sean might lead a life of crime, but he was every bit as good as Clayton was.

My mind spun with these cyclical thoughts as the world passed by the car window in a blur. Sean allowed me to cry silently as he drove. Before I knew it, we were pulling up outside my house. I didn't move when he got out of the car and came around to open my door. He unbuckled my seatbelt for me and took me by the hand, tugging insistently.

"Come on," he said gently. "We need to get you inside. You're not safe out here."

The only movement I could manage was a jerky shake of my head to show my refusal. My whole body was numb, and I knew that my legs wouldn't support me. Sean eyed me warily.

"I'm taking you inside," he informed me. "Don't fight me."

With that, his arms closed around me and he lifted me up, carrying me. He was careful to grip me so that my arms were pinned to my sides. I supposed he was worried that I might try to claw his eyes out if he touched me, and I couldn't deny that the thought crossed my mind. But most of my anger at him had been redirected towards Bradley as I sorted things out in my mind, so I compliantly allowed him to cradle my body against his. As we progressed up the walkway, my eyes fell on the spot where Clayton had lain as his life slipped away between my fingers. There was no evidence that my only friend had bled out there, had given his own life to save mine. I shuddered and turned my face into Sean's chest, trying to block out the bloody memories.

Sean somehow managed to maintain his hold on me while fishing my keys from my purse and unlocking the front door. My security system blared to life, and he positioned me so that I could disarm it. Once it was off and the door was locked behind us, he headed straight for the stairs and into my bedroom. He didn't release me as he settled me down on the bed, instead moving my body so that I was draped across his lap, my head still leaning against his chest as he sat back against the headboard. His fingers gently stroked my hair as he held me, allowing me to cry. My mind was still whirring in double-time, but I was getting a headache from pondering which was the worse fate: Clayton dead at Bradley's hands or Sean dead without my knowledge? The thought of a world without Sean in it was just so profoundly *wrong.*

Growing weary of the questions that had no answers that were swirling in my mind, I forced myself to contemplate my current situation instead. What did it mean that Sean was here with me now? I had thought that he would never want to see me again, but here he was, comforting me. And despite the tumultuous emotions that he stirred within me, I couldn't deny that the feeling of him holding me was impossibly sweeter than I remembered.

But how was it that he was even here? He was supposed to be in prison. Clayton had said that they had remanded him without bail. Had he escaped somehow? No, that couldn't possibly be the case. That graveyard had been flooded with FBI agents, and I still had a security detail following me everywhere. They should have taken Sean into custody on sight.

I shifted in Sean's grip so that I could look up at him. The lines of his handsome face were strained, his eyes full of concern and trepidation.

"How…" My voice was a croak. I forced it to be steady. "How are you here?"

"I told you that I need to talk to you, Claudia. There are things that I need to explain." He took a deep breath and plowed on. "When I found out what you had done, that you had been spying on me for the FBI, it tore me apart. The way that I treated you that day… It was inexcusable. You begged me to let you explain, told me that you were just trying to help me. But I didn't listen." He studied my face carefully as he spoke, his eyes imploring. I listened with bated breath, needing to hear that he forgave me. Was that possible? The way that he was looking at me now made me dare to hope that it was.

"Then they arrested me," he continued. "I kept my silence for a while, but then Agent Vaughn talked to me. He told me everything that you had done for me, how you were trying to keep me out of prison in exchange for your testimony. I realized then that you weren't betraying me; you were trying to free me. And I can't tell you how grateful I am for that. I thought that I was trapped, that I would never find a way out. But you gave that to me, Claudia." His fingers traced the line of my jaw as he stared down at me, his eyes shining with wonder.

Shame flooded me. "But they arrested you, Sean. I was reckless and selfish. I broke my deal with the FBI so that I could kill Ronan, and without my testimony to protect you they put you in jail." It was my turn to look at him beseechingly. "You have to know that I never wanted that. I wasn't thinking straight. I never imagined that they -"

Sean pressed his index finger to my lips, gently silencing me. "It's okay," he reassured me. "Vaughn didn't want to press charges against me. He believed in my innocence. Because of you. He offered me a deal, and I took it. He said that I would walk free if I testified against the Westies. I didn't have to think twice."

I stared at him, thunderstruck. "But... But they're your friends, your family."

As his gaze held mine, his eyes glowed with an intensity that took my breath away. "They've made me what I am, what I hate. And knowing you... You're so pure, Claudia, so *good*. I know that I'll never deserve you, that I can never make amends for everything that I've put you through, but I want to be better because of you. I want to be better *for* you. I know that you can never forgive me, but -"

"Sean," I breathed his name, cutting him off. "There's nothing to forgive. Nothing that's happened to me has been your fault. I can see that now. And *I'm* the one who betrayed *you* by going to the FBI."

"You didn't betray me," he said softly. "You saved me."

His eyes were sparkling as he leaned down into me, and I experienced something that I thought I would never again experience in my life: the sweetness of Sean's lips against mine. He was tentative at first, as though he was uncertain whether or not I would welcome his intimate touch. I responded instantly and voraciously, pressing up into him, eagerly shaping my lips around his. Our mouths molded to one another perfectly as he began to take me more confidently. We poured all of our grief into the kiss, our shared pain fuelling the intensity of it as we clung to each other. I don't know how long we remained locked in one another's embrace, losing ourselves in our passion.

But my busy mind wouldn't stay quiet forever, and a horrible thought occurred to me, jerking me out of our perfect moment. I pulled away reluctantly.

"You have to go," I said, trying to shove back the fresh tears that threatened to spill at the thought of him leaving me. "It's not safe for you here. If your father finds out that you're out of jail and that you're with me, he'll become suspicious. By now I'm sure Bradley has told him that I'm the reason you were both arrested, and he likely told him about Clayton protecting me. I don't know if he realized that Clayton was FBI, but it will be pretty clear that the FBI is tailing me to protect me now that I've been attacked. If Ronan finds out that you're with me and the FBI knows about it, then he'll know that you've turned against him."

Sean's hand curved around the back of my head, holding me against him. The possessive act let me know what he was going to say before the words came out of his mouth. "I don't care what my father thinks. I've told the FBI everything, and they're going to take him down any day now. He won't be able to get to us soon. Until they take him in, I'm staying with you."

I hesitated for a moment before voicing my next question, knowing that it would bring us into more painful territory. "And what about Bradley?" I asked softly. "Will they arrest him on your information too?"

Sean's arms tightened around me as his muscles tensed. His expression was strained, but his voice was even when he spoke. "Bradley is beyond my help now. He abducted you, he abused you, and he's tried to kill you. Even if I were willing to protect him after all that – which I'm not – he's murdered a federal agent. He can't come back from that." Although his tone was calm and rational, there was pain in his eyes.

"I'm sorry," I whispered. As much as I loathed Bradley, I knew how hard this must be on Sean. I was now experiencing firsthand what it was to lose a friend, and I hated that Sean was going to have to go through the same thing, albeit under different circumstances.

"He's made his own choices," Sean said, his voice hard. "And those choices have proven that he's not the person I thought he was."

"How…" I hesitated to delve into this if Sean wasn't ready to share, but I had to know how he could possibly be friends with such a horrible person. "How did you and Bradley meet?"

Sean's brow furrowed, and for a moment I thought that he wasn't going to answer me. "I've known him for as long as I can remember," he finally admitted. "His father and my father were friends. Well, as much as Ronan is capable of sharing friendship with anyone. Bradley's father brought Ronan into the Westies fold when he moved over from London in '82."

"I thought your father was Irish," I interrupted.

"He is. He moved from Dublin to London when he was seventeen to join up with the Clerkenwell crime syndicate. They were just getting powerful, and he saw that there was money to be made. But he was too ambitious for his own good, and the Adams family, the brothers who formed the gang, turned on him. So he came to the States and sought out the Westies. They aren't strictly 'Irish' anymore, but the idea of it appealed to him. And there was more room for upward mobility. A lot of Westies higher-ups were arrested in the early '80s, and there was a power vacuum. Ronan was brutal and efficient and rose quickly." His mouth twisted in distaste.

"But we were talking about Bradley," he redirected the subject away from his father. "We grew up in a tough world, and he always had my back. Even now, in his own twisted way, he thinks that he's looking out for me by going after you. But it wasn't until the night that he took you that I fully realized his true nature. You have to understand." His eyes were full of desperation. "I knew that he was ambitious, that he wanted to be a part of the Westies, but we just pushed drugs. That was all. Then on the day I was shot, the Latin Kings showed up to break up our deal and steal our stash. I was going to let them have it; no way was I putting my life at risk for my father's precious heroin, no matter what the consequences. But Bradley wouldn't let it go, and he pulled the gun. I don't know who shot first, but the next thing I knew I was waking up with you handcuffed to my bed." He shot me a wry smile at the memory. "And then I proceeded to act like a pompous ass."

I couldn't help returning his smile. "I remember all too well. I believe I called you an idiot and a jackass."

"You threw me for a loop. You were this fragile woman, and yet you were bossing me around and putting me in my place. Despite everything we were putting you through, you were fearless." His hand cupped my cheek tenderly and his eyes burned down into mine. "How could I resist falling for you?"

My breath caught in my throat. Sean had turned against the only person who had cared about him for me. "I'm sorry that I came between you when Bradley meant so much to you," I said quietly.

His thumb hooked under my chin and he lifted my face so that I couldn't drop my gaze from his. "He's not the person I thought he was, Claudia. Or maybe I just saw what I wanted to see. No matter what he is, Bradley has never been anything but absolutely loyal to me. But when he took you, when he hurt you... That man isn't my friend. I could never love anyone who harms innocent people. And for him to be capable of that, after everything he knew that my father did, after knowing how he…"

Sean trailed off, and this time he was the one to drop his eyes.

"What did he do to you?" My voice was barely audible. He kept his gaze averted and remained silent, his jaw clenched. "You know that he took my parents from me," I pressed. "Please. Tell me what he did. You can talk to me."

He let out a long breath. "Ronan is a violent man," he admitted softly, still not looking at me. "And not just towards his enemies. He uses fear to control everyone around him. Including his family."

"He beat you?" I gasped. I had guessed as much, but hearing the words come from Sean's lips made the reality of it all the more horrible.

"Sometimes," he said hollowly. "When my mother wasn't around to take it for me." His hands clenched into fists, and the lines of his face were drawn.

Fresh tears were stinging at the corners of my eyes as I came to understand the terrible reality of Sean's childhood. I remembered the night he had told me that his mother was dead. I couldn't hold back my question. "Your mother. Is that how she…?" I couldn't bring myself to force out the word *died*, but my meaning was clear.

"It wasn't by Ronan's hand, but it was as good as." His eyes finally met mine, and they were full of pain so deep that it cut me to the core. I had to force myself to maintain his gaze. "She killed herself. Overdose. I was out of the house, living with Bradley, so she didn't need to protect me anymore. It was her way of escaping him."

"But why didn't she leave?" I asked. "She could have taken you and run years ago."

"You can't run from my father. He wouldn't have stopped hunting until he found us. And when he did, he wouldn't have let us live. My mother only did everything she could to protect me. But I was always too weak to protect her. I thought that she was safe from him once I left. So long as I did what he told me, then he had no reason to turn his anger at me against her. I had no idea that he was still hurting her after I moved out. Or maybe I did, and I just didn't want to see it. When she died, I wanted to kill Ronan. It was Bradley who stopped me. He knew that I was dead if I made a move against my father. Even if I succeeded in killing him, one of his friends would come after me to make an example of me. I didn't care, but Bradley kept me grounded. He saved my life. And ever since then, I've just been… existing. Until I met you."

I was stunned. Through the bits and pieces about his life that he had revealed to me in the short time we had known each other, I had come to realize that we were remarkably alike, despite coming from different worlds. Now that I knew the whole truth, the excruciating depth of his pain, it became apparent why I had felt such a strong pull to him from the very beginning. He was heartbreakingly beautiful, but our souls were bound by something much deeper than physical attraction. We understood each other in a way that others could not fully comprehend. Even Clayton had only been able to sympathize with me rather than empathize. I didn't resent him for his happy childhood, but my past trauma would have always been a barrier between us, a gaping wound at my core that would never be fully healed. But Sean knew, and maybe, just maybe, our deep understanding of just how damaged we were would help us heal each other.

Chapter 6

With these new revelations, I found that I was more drawn to Sean than ever. I turned my body, positioning myself so that I was straddling his lap. My fingers twined in his hair as I pulled him into me, craving to ease his pain through finding our release in each other's arms. His lips were still under mine for the briefest of moments, but the tension in his body quickly melted as we touched. The low growl that rumbled from his chest made me shiver against him as that familiar, delicious heat gathered between my legs. I was reminded of our scorching first kiss, when he reprimanded me for my boldness by dominating my body, bringing out my submissive side for the first time as he pressed me up against the cool tiles of the bathroom wall, his hands pinning my wrists on either side of my head. It was my first taste of that wild abandon, of the hunger that he brought out in me so effortlessly. And although we had shared many kisses since then, my reaction to him now was no less visceral than it had been on that night.

He took control of the kiss with an immediacy that took my breath away. The world spun around me as he forced me down, positioning my body beneath his in a show of dominance. My nipples hardened and I moaned into his mouth, arching up into him as I silently begged him to take me. His tongue swept into my mouth, and I welcomed it. His fist tangled in my hair, angling my head back so that he could take me more deeply. Calloused fingertips lightly traced the curve of my neck, the roughness of his skin contrasting deliciously with his feather-light strokes. Hot lines of pleasure shot to my breasts and then lower, hitting my core. My inner walls contracted as I craved for him to fill me, to slake the growing need that was sweetly tormenting me.

Then the moment was shattered. Shock hit me like a bucket of icy water to the face when he rolled off of me abruptly, and I gasped. He was sitting on the edge of the bed, no longer looking at me. I shoved down the sting of rejection that threatened to overwhelm me. Sean was clearly upset, and it would be selfish of me to break down; I needed to help him with whatever he was going through. Had I pushed him too far in forcing him to re-live the memories of his father's abuse and his mother's suicide?

I moved so that I was sitting beside him. "What's wrong?" I asked, my voice small.

His jaw clenched, and he didn't answer. I sensed that this was one of those moments when I needed to take control. Just as I had once done, he was trying to shove back his consternation, to deny it. He had taught me that I needed to release my dark emotions, and now I needed to convince him to do the same. I lightly pressed my fingers against his cheek, turning his face to mine. The turmoil in his eyes took my breath away.

"Please, Sean. Talk to me."

He was tense again, his fists clenched. "What I want to do to you isn't right, Claudia," he said hollowly.

I frowned at him, and it took effort to keep the irritation from my tone. "We've been over this before," I said. "I want this just as much as you do. I *need* this. I need *you*."

He grimaced. "I understand why you feel that you need it. Your reasons - your need for release from your worries through submission - that makes sense. There's absolutely nothing wrong with that. But my reasons aren't so pure." His expression turned anguished. "I've always needed this, Claudia. But my father... Does this mean that I'm like him? Am I just channeling my violent, cruel needs through what I've rationalized as an acceptable path? I've pushed away my concerns over it in the past, but you're different. I've never felt anything for anyone like what I feel for you. And my need to dominate you is so intense that I completely lose myself to my dark urges. Then I think about how Ronan treated my mother, how he claimed to care for her and yet he beat her mercilessly. He used pain as a means of punishment. How is that different from what I want to do to you? All I want is to protect you, Claudia. And if that means protecting you from myself, then that's what I'll do." His eyes were lost, his bearing utterly defeated. —

I turned his words over in my mind. At one time, I had wondered the same thing. Had his domineering treatment of my body been a reflection of a truly violent nature? But now I knew him better than that. Sean wasn't a cruel person; he was a victim of circumstance, forced into a life that he hated. Now that I fully understood his past, the reasons for his darker needs were clear to me.

"No, Sean," I reassured him quietly. "You're nothing like your father. You've never truly hurt me, and I know that you never would. I believe that with my entire being. And I know that you do too, if you'll just allow yourself to believe. Your urges aren't born of a desire to inflict pain; it's about control. You've never had control over your life. Ronan has terrorized you into following the path that he has chosen for you through threatening to harm the people that you care about. You've sacrificed your capacity to choose, your ability to shape your own destiny, for their sake. I can't imagine anything more selfless or less cruel. You need control as badly as I need release, and I want to give that to you. Please, Sean, let me do that for you. Know that I accept you for everything that you are, and I wouldn't have you change for anything."

His eyes were wide and shining, and a single tear spilled over and trailed down his cheek. I wiped it away gently, as he had done for me so many times. When he spoke, his voice was hoarse with emotion.

"Claudia, I..." He trailed off, and I waited for his next words with bated breath. Was he really going to say what I thought he was going to say? And was I ready to hear it? He swallowed hard, and something shifted in his eyes. "You're amazing. Everything you've done for me, everything you've given to me... I never imagined that I... Thank you."

His hand closed around the back of my neck and he crushed his lips against mine. The roughness with which he took my mouth contrasted sharply with his soft words. I reveled in the dichotomy. He was exactly what I needed: sweet and caring yet harsh in his possessiveness. This sense of being needed, craved, had been a completely foreign concept for me before I had met Sean. And my need for him burned just as brightly. He had awakened me, brought me back to life after my long years of solitude. The process had been painful, but I wouldn't trade him for anything.

His hands were at the hem of my black dress, pulling it up my torso and over my head, and I kicked off my shoes. My own fingers fisted in his t-shirt, tugging at it insistently. He deftly unclasped my bra and freed my breasts before briefly releasing me to tear off his own shirt. My fingertips roved over his perfect body, so muscular and strong. I was completely at the mercy of his raw power, his strength which could so easily overcome even my most determined struggles. But as much as I enjoyed our power-play, I didn't want to struggle today. I wanted to show that I welcomed his dominance of my body, needing to demonstrate how badly I craved it.

He shoved me hard, and the wind was momentarily knocked from my lungs at the impact with the mattress. He straddled my hips, his weight pinning me down where he wanted me. That cocky, lopsided grin that I loved so much was back in place, his turmoil and grief absent from his eyes, burned away by that dark flame that flickered in their green depths. The sight of it made me shudder in delight as I realized that he accepted my words; he had let go of his feelings of uncertainty, of self-loathing. He was embracing the sexual dynamic that gave both of us such unsurpassed pleasure. He was accepting himself.

His expression turned more serious as he reached into his back pocket and pulled out something that glinted silver in the late afternoon sunlight that filtered through my curtains. He watched me carefully, gauging my reaction as I realized what he was holding: handcuffs. My heart skipped a beat and my breath caught in my throat as fear fluttered in my belly. Memories of my cruel captivity at Bradley's hands flitted at the corners of my mind.

"I don't want you to be afraid, Claudia," Sean said soothingly. "Use a safe word if this is too much for you."

I stared at the silvery cuffs, and I couldn't deny that I was afraid. I tore my eyes from the restraints to meet Sean's gaze. The sight of concern warring with lust softened my heart. I remembered the intense pleasure I had experienced when he had tied me up, and I realized that I trusted him implicitly. Besides, I wouldn't let the memories of Bradley's cruelty control my life.

"No," I said definitively, lifting my chin. "I don't want to use a safe word. I trust you." A thought struck me. "But why do you have those?" I shot him a mock-censorious look. "It was rather presumptuous of you to assume that I would have sex with you."

His brow furrowed slightly. Despite my joking tone, he was clearly worried that he had crossed a line. When he spoke, he looked chagrined. "Honestly? I was prepared to restrain you if I had to in order to force you to hear me out."

I knew that I should be angry, or at the very least indignant, but all I felt was amusement. His eyes widened in surprise when a giggle escaped me. "You're a ruthless bastard, Sean Reynolds," I accused.

He shot me a hard-edged grin, and his relief was evident when the tension visibly left his body. "You should watch your language, sub," he warned.

Sub. A delighted shiver ran through me at the word. I had been uncertain about the term at first, thinking it demeaning, but now I knew that it was an expression of Sean's affection for me. He was vocally asserting his claim over my being, and I gave myself willingly, reassured by the knowledge that I likewise owned him in my own way. He was claiming me as his own, but at the same time it was a pledge that he belonged to me as well.

A wide, silly grin spread across my face. He cocked his head at me. "You look far too pleased with yourself," he informed me. "I won't tolerate insults. I'm warning you not to push your luck."

I tried to wipe the smile from my face and look properly intimidated, but there was still a pleased curve to my lips. He *tsked* at me. "It seems a lesson in respect is in order. Arms above your head, sub."

I complied with alacrity, eager for the pleasure that I knew he would bring both of us. A shot of residual fear returned at the sound of the first cuff clicking closed around my wrist, the cool metal encircling it causing unpleasant memories to surface. Sean noticed my distress instantly, and his hand was beneath my jaw, tilting my head back so that I was locked in his gaze. "Stay here with me, Claudia," he ordered softly. "I'm not going to hurt you." It was a promise.

I swallowed hard and nodded, my muscles relaxing as I melted under him. His thumb tenderly traced the line of my lower lip. "That's a good girl." He smiled down at me in gentle approval. My clit pulsed at his words, and the heat that bloomed within me spread from my core to my fingertips, driving away the lingering fear as lust engulfed me. Already my mind was going to that wondrous, blissful blankness as I ceded all control to him.

His attention returned to my restraints, and he looped the cuffs' chain around my bedpost before closing them around my free wrist. I tugged tentatively, testing their hold. The metal was unyielding, threatening to bruise my delicate skin if I offered any form of resistance. My nipples hardened almost painfully, and my panties became damp with my growing wetness.

His hands pressed down on my forearms, holding them against the mattress, as he kissed me deeply. His lips moved from my mouth to the hollow just behind my ear. The warmth of his tongue against my skin there, gentle yet firm, sent sparks dancing over my skin. He pulled back slightly and blew cool air over the inflamed area, and goose bumps pebbled my flesh as the sparks crackled and popped, pinging against my skin. Then his teeth bit sharply into my earlobe, tugging at it. I gasped as the slight, unexpected pain further stoked my need. His lips sucked away the pain, his hot tongue soothing the place where he had bitten me. I writhed beneath him as he awoke yet another erogenous zone that I had never known existed. His low, satisfied chuckle rumbled through me as he skillfully manipulated my body, drawing forth my submission with every touch.

His kisses were feather-light as he moved lower down my neck, between my breasts, leaving a burning trail in his wake. He paused when he reached my sternum. A shocked cry escaped me as his tongue traced the curve of the underside of my breast. The sensation was exquisite, and my eyes rolled back in my head at the decadent pleasure of it.

"Look at me," he commanded. "I want you to watch what I'm doing to you."

My eyes snapped open as I instinctively obeyed his order. I desperately craved for him to continue touching my breasts, but he abandoned them, resuming his trail of kisses as he progressed down my abdomen. By the time he reached the upper edge of my panties, my clit was pulsing madly in time with the beating of my racing heart. It took all of my determination to stop myself from thrusting my hips up toward his hot mouth. I gritted my teeth and held back, confident that he would soon touch me where I wanted it most and finally slake my need. A frustrated whine escaped me as he pulled away. His expressive eyes glowed with cruel satisfaction as he smirked down at me.

I couldn't hold back. "Bastard," I hissed out through clenched teeth. His hand was a blur just before the pain hit. The intensity of the sting on my inner thigh took my breath away, trapping my shocked cry in my chest. Before I could gasp in air, his palm came down on my other thigh, and this time a strangled yelp escaped me. I tried to close my legs to protect myself, but he ruthlessly shoved them apart, positioning his knees between my legs so that I was held open for him. Blows rained down in sharp succession. The pain as he abused this sensitive area was almost unbearable, but after a few moments, I realized that it was doing funny things to my insides. The sting was awakening a delicious warmth that curled upward from my thighs to tease at the edges of my pussy lips.

"Please," I begged, and I wasn't sure if I was asking for the pain to stop or for him to touch me.

He glared down at me forbiddingly as his hand came down on me once more. "What did I tell you about using such language? You will address me with respect."

"Sean!" I gasped. "I'm sorry! Please…"

"I want you to address me as 'Sir'."

My mind went momentarily blank with shock. He couldn't possibly be serious. I bit my lip, uncertain. He raised his hand threateningly, and my resistance cracked.

"I'm sorry, Sir," I whispered.

His grin was twisted and positively evil as he brought down his hand. But this time he didn't strike my thigh. The harsh blow landed directly on my clit. The pain intertwined with sweetest pleasure as he finally touched my aching bud. I screamed as I shattered, my inner walls contracting around nothing as the world went white. As much as I wanted to lose myself to the bliss, I blinked hard against the urge to allow my eyes to roll back in my head. Sean had ordered me to keep my eyes on him, and I wasn't about to disobey him again.

When my vision cleared, he was naked above me, his glorious body fully exposed. His wolfish grin was still in place as his hands fisted in my panties. With a jerk of his powerful arms, the delicate material gave way. I moaned at the eroticism of the act. The aftershocks of my orgasm were still racing through me, but my need flared to life once again as I craved for him to fill me.

His harsh expression told me that he could no longer hold himself back. I watched as the overwhelming possessive need that he had described took over. All vestiges of his careful self-control vanished as he drove into me in one thrust. My sex was still hyper-sensitive from my orgasm, and I let out a strangled cry as pleasure washed over me again. I came immediately, my muscles fluttering around him and heightening his own pleasure. He let out a low growl as he took me roughly, a primal, animalistic urge driving him as he pounded into me. The ripples of my orgasm were fading, but bliss was still coursing through my veins. I was high on pleasure and adrenaline. I could feel him beginning to jerk within me, heralding his own completion. He leaned into me and bit down on my hardened nipple. The pain sent me over the edge a third time, and my entire body began to shake. The motion caused me to jerk against the cuffs, but the slight pain of their unyielding bite only heightened my ecstasy. Sean's howl mingled with my delighted scream as we found our ultimate pleasure at the same time, our bodies in perfect tandem with one another. It seemed to go on and on, completely consuming my body as I shook beneath him. Eventually, Sean collapsed atop me, breathing hard, and my shudders abated, my body too exhausted to manage anything but small shivers as the occasional residual shower of sparks brushed against my skin. Sean kissed my forehead, my eyelids, my cheeks, before finally tenderly brushing his lips against my own. I let myself go completely, sighing up into him happily.

He released me from the cuffs, and he brushed kisses against my tender wrists. He pulled me into him, and I wrapped my arms around him, snuggling into his chest and breathing in his familiar, comforting scent.

For a short, blissful time, he had erased my emotional pain through combining physical pain and pleasure, allowing me the release that I so desperately needed.

Chapter 7

Sean and I followed the FBI's directives and remained holed up in my house for our own protection. We spent the following three days in each other's arms, and I found solace from my grief in his touch. I was still devastated about Clayton, but Sean brought me fleeting moments of happiness when he took me, releasing me from my worries. And I couldn't begin to express how much his presence comforted me. After the agonizing days of dealing with the weight of my grief and guilt in cold isolation, finding succor in my easy companionship with Sean helped me maintain my sanity even in my darkest moments.

Although I accepted his comfort, I couldn't bring myself to talk to him about Clayton, and mercifully he didn't press me on the matter. He didn't understand the depth of my relationship with Clayton, and I didn't want to deal with voicing my tangled emotions over what I had shared with him. I was scared that I would hurt Sean, and the last thing that I wanted was to drive him away. It was selfish, but I couldn't bear to lose him again.

On our fourth night together, I broke my silence.

I heard the crack of the bullet rending the night air, saw Clayton falling. He lay broken on the ground as he bled out beneath my hands. I had to save him, I had to.

"It was worth it."

But I wasn't worth it. He shouldn't be dead. His usually tanned skin was so pale. Unlike on that night, his eyes were open. I watched in horror as the light slipped from them, his face going slack. He was looking at me, but he couldn't see me.

Someone was grabbing my shoulders, trying to pull me away from him. I fought against them, not wanting to leave his side. But tendrils of darkness were twining around Clayton, creeping over him with insidious intent until the shadows hid him from me completely. I screamed in fury at the loss.

"Claudia, wake up," Sean's voice was shaky as he called me back to reality. My cheeks were wet with tears when my eyes fluttered open. I could just make out Sean's face in the early dawn light that was filtering into my bedroom. I flung myself against him, and he tenderly kissed the top of my head as he held me to him, allowing me to sob into his chest. He rocked me gently, murmuring reassuring words that didn't quite penetrate my mind. But the low, rumbling sound of them eventually calmed me, and I gulped in ragged breaths.

When my sobs had quieted to silent tears, Sean addressed me directly. "Claudia, tell me what happened that night. Talk to me."

I shook my head weakly. I couldn't tell him about my relationship with Clayton. If I did, he would leave me. "I can't tell you," I whispered.

"Yes, you can," he said firmly. "You can tell me anything, Claudia. Let me help you."

"If I tell you, I'm afraid... I'm afraid you'll leave me. I'm afraid I'll hurt you."

He hugged me to him more tightly. "I promise that I won't leave you, no matter what you say. I'll never leave you again, Claudia. Even if you do hurt me. I swear."

I trembled against him, uncertain. I needed to tell him, to let everything out. The pain of keeping it bottled up inside was nearly unbearable. Selfishly, I resolved to open up to him. I prayed that he would keep his promise. I had to trust him.

"Clayton was my friend," I said haltingly. "The only friend I've had since my parents died. And he's been taken from me. He gave his own life to save mine, and I can't bear that." I peered up into Sean's eyes.

His hand stroked up and down my back. "I'm so sorry," he said softly. "I didn't know you were so close."

I drew in a shaky breath. I had to tell him everything, had to admit my crimes. "It was more than that. Clayton… He cared about me. He… He kissed me." I dropped my eyes, unwilling to witness the inevitable pain in Sean's expression.

His arms tensed around me. "But I didn't kiss him back," I continued quickly. "I told him that I didn't feel the same. Even though I thought that you would never forgive me for betraying you, I knew that there would never be anyone else for me. He accepted it, but I could tell that he still had feelings for me. I should have sent him away after that, but I selfishly kept him close. I didn't want to lose him as a friend. And then he took that bullet for me… I can't help but wonder if he didn't feel for me that way, he would still be alive. If I had just done the right thing and told him to assign someone else as my handler, then he'd still be here. But I was selfish and now he's dead because of me."

Sean's fingers were under my chin, re-directing my gaze to his. I was shocked to find nothing but compassion there. "I didn't know Clayton as well as you did, but he was a good man. Even if you had been a complete stranger to him, I know that he would have protected you with his life. And if he hadn't been there to save you, then he would have carried the guilt over your death for the rest of his life." He paused. "Not to mention what your death would have done to me. I would have hunted Bradley and my father down and killed them." He traced the line of my jaw. "I don't think that I could live without you, Claudia. Clayton saved both of us, and I'm forever indebted to him for that."

His stark admission made my heart twist, and anger rose up within me. We were far from clear of the danger that lurked around us, and my death was still a very real possibility. "Don't you dare say that, Sean," I said harshly. "If something happens to me, you're going to let me go. If you die for me, I'll never forgive you. Swear to me that you'll never do anything so stupid and reckless." I was glaring at him.

"Claudia, I -"

"I don't want to hear it, Sean. Promise me."

He returned my glare. "Only if you do the same."

I glowered at him. If I lost him, my life would become meaningless again. I wasn't at all sure that I could survive if I was forced to return to my life of solitude.

"Fine," I snapped. "I promise."

"Then I promise as well." I hoped that he wasn't lying too.

We settled back down beside one another, and he continued to hold me. It was too early to awaken, but neither of us found sleep again that morning.
■■

That evening, I opened my door to find Sharon waiting on the other side. Her eyes were tired, but she smiled at me brightly as she offered a Chinese takeout bag. "Chicken lo-mein, as ordered."

"Thanks," I smiled back. Neither Sean nor I was a master chef, so we had been subsisting mostly on sandwiches and delivery food. My lacking culinary skills had never bothered me before, but I suddenly felt the urge to buy a few cookbooks.

"Can I come in?" Sharon asked politely as I took the food from her. "I have some updates for you."

My smile broadened. We hadn't had much news on the FBI's progress since our house arrest had begun. "Please do," I invited.

We settled down in my living room, where Sean had been occupied by reading *A Wrinkle in Time*. It had been one of my favorite books as a child, and I had held on to my battered copy as an adult. It might be a bit juvenile for Sean, but the story was a classic, and he had almost finished it in a matter of hours.

"Mr. Reynolds," Sharon nodded to him in acknowledgement as he set the book down on the coffee table.

"Call me Sean," he offered.

Sharon smiled again. I liked that things were more informal with her and that we were on a first-name basis. After what we had shared on the night of Clayton's death, I felt a bond with the woman.

Once she was seated in the armchair opposite us, her expression turned more business-like.

"Have you arrested Ronan?" I asked before she could speak.

"No," she admitted. "Not yet."

"Why?" I demanded. Surely the FBI had had plenty of time to build a case against him by now.

"I swear we'll bring him in soon," she reassured me. "In fact, it's likely that we'll be able to get him tomorrow. Based on Sean's information, we've arrested several lower-level Westies, and we've offered them deals in exchange for information on Ronan and other higher-ups. Not all of them are talking – they're too scared – but a few have turned on him in order to save themselves. With their information, we've been able to link Ronan with several of the crimes where bullets matching the gun used to kill Garcia were recovered. It has solidified Sean's claim that the gun used to belong to his father."

I nodded, taking in the news. I was pleased that Ronan would be put away soon, but… "What about Bradley?" I asked, unable to keep my fists from clenching as I said his hated name. "Has he been arrested for…" I hesitated. "For Clayton?"

Sharon shook her head, and her lips pursed, betraying her own anger. "We got a search warrant for his apartment, but we didn't recover the weapon that killed Vaughn." She looked at me intently. "He *will* be charged with murder and with your abduction and assault. Between your testimony and Sean's, we'll be able to get a conviction. The fact that your information will result in the downfall of the Westies will strengthen our case against him even without that physical evidence."

"But why haven't you brought him in yet?" I insisted. Every day that Bradley went unpunished was an injustice to Clayton.

"He's too close to Ronan and he's too close to you," she answered gently. "By now, they have to suspect that someone has betrayed them to the FBI, but they have no way of linking it to you. If we go for Bradley too soon, then it will be obvious that you're the one who's been helping us. We have to wait and bring him in at the same time as Ronan. It's for your own safety."

I was still irritated, but her words made sense. "Alright. I can wait one more day, then." I thought back over everything that Bradley had done to me, everything that had happened to me since my abduction. A horrible thought occurred to me. "And what about the Latin Kings?" I asked. "Garcia attacked me twice. Do I still need to be worried about them coming after me?"

This time it was Sean who answered. "I don't think so," he said. "Garcia attacked you because of a vendetta against me. He wanted to make a point. The Irish Mob has been traditionally based in Hell's Kitchen, but ever since my father came to power, he's been pushing his way into Brooklyn. But that's established Latin Kings territory. By targeting me, Ronan's son, they were trying to send a message. That put you in the line of fire as a means of getting to me." He reached over and took me by the hand, squeezing reassuringly. "Once they find out that you and I are responsible for taking down the Westies and removing the threat to their territory, they should back off. We'll have done them a favor."

Sharon nodded in agreement. "And hopefully we won't have to worry about the Latin Kings at all in a few months. We still have Santiago planted in their ranks, and he's been gathering strong intel. If all goes according to plan, the Westies won't be the only gang we wipe out this year."

I smiled. "Thanks so much for the good news, Sharon. I really needed that." I mulled over all of the information I had just received. "If you're arresting Ronan and Bradley tomorrow, can I go back to work?" I asked. Although I was happy to spend time with Sean, I was going a little stir-crazy from being trapped in my house. Besides, returning to normalcy would not only help me continue to heal, but it would also be a final act of defiance against the men who had tormented me; I would prove to them and to myself that I was finally free of them, that they hadn't scared me into hiding for the rest of my life.

Sharon appeared hesitant. "I don't know if that's a good idea. Maybe you should wait a few more days."

"It's a terrible idea," Sean interjected, disapproval lacing his tone.

I straightened my back and lifted my chin, my posture radiating defiance. "I need to do this," I said firmly. "As soon as you make your move against Ronan and Bradley tomorrow morning, I'm going in."

"Claudia -" Sean growled. I shot him a forbidding glance and then looked at Sharon expectantly.

"Well?" I demanded.

Sharon pursed her lips, reluctant, but after a moment she nodded. "Okay," she conceded. "But only once we've moved against them. And you'll keep your security detail."

"Agreed," I said quickly.

Sean's hand tightened around mine. "I'm not going to let you do this," he said angrily. My eyes narrowed.

"You seem to have forgotten how I react when people try to boss me around. I have free will, Sean. I'm doing this. I need you to respect that."

A muscle ticked in his jaw. "Fine," he snapped. "I'll accept it, but I won't respect it."

"Then we've reached an accord," I said smoothly.

"Ah," Sharon interrupted our tense moment, and she shifted uncomfortably in her seat. "How about I let you two eat your dinner before it gets cold." She averted her eyes from Sean's furious visage and focused on me instead. "I'll come and get you tomorrow morning when I get the okay."

"Thanks," I said, pointedly not looking at Sean as I got up to walk Sharon to the door. Despite my brave act in front of Sean, I hid in the foyer like a coward as I called Ava, the woman who worked the front desk at my clinic.

"Dr. Ellers," she greeted me brightly even though I was calling right before close. "It's so good to hear from you. Are you okay? We've been really worried."

"I'm alright now, Ava. Thanks for asking. I've just been going through a lot lately. But I'm ready to come back to work. Can you arrange for me to take some of my usual patients tomorrow?"

"Sure." She sounded genuinely happy. "I'm really glad that you're feeling better."

"Thanks, Ava. I'll see you tomorrow."

When I hung up the phone, I stared at it for several moments, considering. Maybe I had more friends than I thought. I had just never given them a chance. Of course, Ava didn't have an inkling of my real reasons for staying away from the office. Everyone I worked with was under the impression that I was still grieving for my foster mom, clinging to my foster brother for comfort. Exhaustion suddenly struck me as intense emotions swirled through me, so overwhelming in number that they were almost indiscernible from one another. I was elated that Ronan would soon pay for what he had done to my parents, but it would never erase the fact that they had been stolen from me, would never erase the memories of what I had suffered at Darla and Marcus' hands. My shoulders slumped and I buried my head in my hands as my remembered pain washed over me.

I jumped when Sean tentatively touched my shoulder; I hadn't heard him approach. I dropped my hands and craned my head back so that I could look up at him.

"Hey," he said gently. "What happened to all of that fire?"

I just shook my head in defeat. "Everything," I said, my voice heavy.

His arm wrapped around my waist. "Come on, little one. Let's talk about it." He guided me back into the living room and sat me down on the couch. I complied numbly. He kept his arm around me, pulling me up against him as he held me close. "What are you thinking about?" He asked gently.

"My foster family," I admitted, shuddering. There was no point holding back from Sean. He had told me about his past, and it was only fair that I do the same. "Being with them was... difficult."

He regarded me silently as he traced small, circular patterns on my upper arm with his fingertips. His touch was soothing, grounding me in the here and now. I took a deep breath and continued, needing to tell him everything, to purge it from my soul.

"Darla, my foster mom, wasn't so bad, I guess. Her husband had abandoned her, so she didn't get any child support. She didn't want to go to work so she lived off of benefits. The only reason she took me in was so that she could get more. She wasn't cruel, exactly. She just didn't give a shit. Not about me, not about anyone but herself. Not even her own son. All she cared about was her soap operas and her gin. I guess that's why Marcus was so fucked up. I mean, who wouldn't be in that situation? He channeled all of his anger at me; he blamed me for his mom's callousness towards him." I closed my eyes as memories assaulted me. I never talked about this, never allowed myself to think about it. But now that I accessed them, the memories were as sharp as though it had happened yesterday.

Sean cupped my cheek, calling me back to him. His touch was tender, but fury was flickering in his eyes. "Did he hurt you?"

I blinked hard to force back the tears that threatened. I refused to cry over Marcus.

"At first it was just emotional abuse. He called me nasty names and said horrible lies about my parents. He was a year older than I was, and he had a reputation as a bully at school. He intimidated everyone into staying away from me so that I was completely isolated." The words began to spill from my lips, flowing from me in an unrelenting flood. "But as he got older, things became more… physical, and the names he called me became more lewd. I learned to stay out of his way, and I snuck out of the house whenever he was home. Things got a little better towards the end of high school. He would stay out late most nights with his friends, getting drunk or high and doing god knows what else. When I was seventeen, the summer before I went to college, I was so close to being free. But then one night he came into my room. He smelled like whisky and stale cigarettes. And he…" My voice broke and I dropped my eyes, unwilling to see Sean's reaction. "Well, I lied to you when I said that I had only been with one man before you. I left the next day and stayed at a shelter until the semester started."

A heavy silence settled around us, the weight of it unbearable. I peeked up at Sean, and the ferocity of his expression made me shrink away from him. Rage radiated from him like a palpable thing. He hadn't frightened me this badly since my first days of captivity with him.

"Where can I find him?" He ground out through clenched teeth.

My fear ratcheted up a notch. If Sean hurt Marcus, even the FBI wouldn't be able to save him from serving jail time. His criminal history would be enough to condemn him in the eyes of the State. "Please, Sean," I said desperately. "You can't."

The fire in his eyes turned on me, and I flinched. "He's going to die for what he did to you." His voice was harsh, terrifying.

Despite my fear of him, my hands fisted in his shirt as I clung to him. "Don't, Sean. If you do anything, they'll lock you up. I couldn't bear it."

He was still furious. "If you think I'm just going to -"

"Please," I begged, cutting him off. "I can't let them take you from me. I need you, Sean. You swore that you wouldn't leave me."

As I stared up into his eyes beseechingly, thy softened ever so slightly. His muscles were still tense with suppressed violence as he held me, but sanity was returning to his eyes.

"No," he said quietly, a promise in his voice. "I won't leave you."

I pressed my body more tightly against his as I hugged him to me. I never wanted to let him go. We didn't have sex that night; we just held each other. His touch helped to melt away my painful memories, and mine helped soothe his anger.

Despite reliving my dark past that evening, I slept peacefully through the night as Sean held me.

Chapter 8

I awoke the next morning to the sweet sensation of Sean kissing my neck. Something hard pressed against my ass insistently. Despite my sleepiness, the beginnings of lust stirred to life within me as it became apparent how badly he wanted me. I twisted my head further into my pillow, offering him easier access to the curve of my neck. He let out a low, satisfied chuckle as his teeth nipped at the sensitive area where my neck met my shoulder. I groaned softly as heat pooled between my legs. Then my eyes fell on the clock on my bedside table, and this time my groan was regretful.

"I have to get ready for work," I told him.

He blew cool air across my heated skin, and I shivered. "Stay." It wasn't a request.

I rolled over so that I was facing him, and I shot him a level look. "I know your game, and I'm not falling for it. I'm going to work," I declared definitively.

His brows drew together. "It's not safe for you yet. Just wait one more day. Please." His tone was laced with frustration.

"I'm not backing down on this, Sean. It's my first day of freedom, and I'm going to use it to my full advantage. As soon as Sharon gives me the all clear, I'm going." I touched his brow tenderly, trying to smooth the lines of worry. "I need to do this, Sean. Please understand. I hate the feeling of being trapped. It reminds me of when Bradley abducted me."

His expression turned to one of guilt as he recalled my days of captivity. "I can't say that I understand, but I'll do my best to resist the urge to tie you up and keep you here. I couldn't do that to you. Not again."

"Thank you," I said softly, truly grateful that he wasn't going to fight me on this. I didn't want to leave him for the day on bad terms. I gave him a small smile and trailed my fingertips over his hard chest. "We've never had that shower together," I said huskily. "Not properly."

The guilt was wiped from his face, replaced with a predatory smile. "That sounds like an excellent idea." He moved lightning-fast, and I gasped as I found myself in his arms. He lifted me up and carried me into the bathroom.

"This is totally unnecessary," I informed him. "I'm perfectly capable of walking five yards."

His eyes were dancing as he looked down at me. "I know. But that's not the point. I want to hold you." Something darker flickered in his gaze, a challenge. "But by all means, continue to protest. I'd love to demonstrate the consequences of contradicting me."

I pursed my lips to hold back my snappy retort. He was baiting me, and giving him an excuse to put me in a submissive state would give him the leverage he needed to convince me to stay with him. He raised a brow at me, grudgingly impressed that I was able to hold myself back. He sighed heavily.

"I think I'm making you too obedient," he muttered to himself. I smirked at him, and his lips quirked upward at the corners. "Or then again, maybe not."

He set me down carefully on the counter, and I shivered at the contact of the cool porcelain against my heated skin. Sean sensually traced the line of my lower lip with his thumb. "Stay," he ordered. My tongue snaked out, and I swirled it around his finger suggestively. He jerked his hand away, frowning at me.

"What have I told you about teasing me?"

"Sorry, Sir." I smiled at him sweetly, teasing him further.

"You little minx," he accused. "Don't think you can play mind games with me. I won't have you getting cocky."

"You seem perfectly content to be cocky," I pointed out.

He looked at me reprovingly. "I'm your Dom. Besides, I'm sexy as hell. I'm entitled to be cocky."

I rolled my eyes at him. "Your argument seems to be rock-solid. I can't contest either of your points. Well played, Sir."

There was a funny expression on his face, as though he was torn between amusement and disapproval. "You're cute, so I'll let that slide." He tapped his index finger against my nose in reprimand. "But don't make a habit of it."

I wanted to say "Yes, Sir" and give him a sardonic salute, but I suppressed the urge. It wasn't a good idea to push him any further this morning if I wanted to have a hope of escaping him for the day. I settled for a curt nod. He cocked his head at me, studying me for any further signs of defiance. After a moment, he turned from me and started the shower running. When he was satisfied with the temperature, he picked me up again before setting me down on my feet so that I was positioned under the hot spray. Sean was behind me, his chest pressed against my back, his cock growing hard again. My nipples pebbled in response to the knowledge that he wanted me, and I suddenly became hyper-aware of the delicious sensation of the water hitting my breasts, teasing me.

His soapy hands twined in my hair, his fingers massaging my scalp. I moaned in delight and dropped my head back against his shoulder. His touch moved down the column of my throat, tracing lower. The soap made his usually rough touch silky soft as his hands glided over my skin. Suddenly, he gripped my breasts hard, kneading my soft flesh. He pinched my aching nipples, and I writhed against him as I cried out my pleasure. He growled low in my ear as my ass rubbed against the hard length of him. His hands ensnared my wrists, jerking my arms forward. I caught myself on my hands, pressing my palms into the tiled wall for support. The position caused my ass to arch into him like an offering.

"Stay still," he ordered. I bit my lip, resolving to obey. I couldn't challenge him. Not if I was going to get to work.

But all thoughts of leaving were driven from my mind when his touch resumed, his hands rubbing across my abdomen before slipping further down. Skirting around my sex, he moved to my inner thighs, lightly rubbing in a circular motion. I was desperate for him to touch my pulsing clit. My heart skipped a beat as his fingers brushed against my swollen lips, the slickness of the soap mingling with my own wetness. Agonizingly slowly, his fingers moved upwards.

Just a bit higher. Oh god, please...

I was trembling with the effort of staying still, no longer motivated by a desire to escape, but a desire to please him.

I gasped when he finally reached my hardened bud, but his teasing continued as he swirled his finger around it, refusing to touch me directly in the way that I craved. I shuddered pleasurably as the thick head of him nudged at my entrance. He pushed in slowly, matching the pace of his tormenting touch. When he was fully inside me, he paused, and his finger continued to circle my clit, torturing me sweetly.

I whined as I forced back the urge to rock my body against him. "Please, Sir," I groaned, the honorific rolling off my tongue without a thought. There was nothing mocking about it this time.

He allowed me to come in reward. Pulling out almost all the way, he drove back into me harshly. At the same time, he bit down on my neck, and he pinched my clit hard. The sweet pain caused pleasure to overwhelm me, and I screamed out my orgasm as he continued to take me roughly. My knees went weak beneath me with the intensity of it, but he held me upright with a strong arm around my waist.

His continued onslaught was relentless, and his cock hit my g-spot with every powerful thrust. His fingers left my over-sensitized clit to grip my chin, turning my face back towards him so that he could take my mouth as he claimed my pussy. The merciless thrusts of his tongue matched the rhythm of him filling me. He groaned into my mouth as he jerked within me, and another orgasm began cresting. He held back for a few moments longer until my body caught up with his. Just as my inner walls began contracting around him, he let himself go. His lips didn't release mine as we came together, our bodies intertwined as closely as was physically possible.

His kiss turned slower, sweeter, as we both came down from our high. I sighed regretfully when he finally pulled out of me. I wanted him to stay here forever; I knew that I would never get enough of him. He grasped my shoulders gently and turned me towards him before sluicing the lingering soap from my body. Every inch of my skin was still alive from his ministrations, and the sensation of his hands against me was delectable.

Even when all of the soap was gone, his hands continued to rove over my body, as though he couldn't bring himself to stop touching me. I wanted to do the same. Squeezing some body wash into my hands, I returned the favor, relishing the contours of his hard muscles as I rubbed him down. I handled his cock gently, knowing that it would be hyper-sensitive after his orgasm. To my amazement, he began hardening once again, and an answering desire awakened within my own sex in response. I removed my hand reluctantly, recalling my desire to get to work. How long had we been in the shower?

I turned off the water and regretfully stepped away from Sean as I exited the shower. He was behind me in an instant, wrapping a fluffy towel around me and kissing the top of my head sweetly.

I glanced up at him, an apology in my eyes. "I have to get ready for work," I said softly.

He frowned slightly, but he nodded. "If you insist."

I stood on my tiptoes so that I could kiss his cheek, a silent demonstration of gratitude. He followed me into the bedroom and began pulling on his own clothes. I glanced at the clock: 7:48. I would only just have time to blow-dry my hair.

When I re-emerged from the bathroom, hair dry and fully dressed, I found Sean sprawled out on my bed, reading the last few pages of *A Wrinkle in Time*.

He looked up at me and smiled. "This is a really good book, you know. I can't believe I've never read it. It definitely falls in the 'nerd book' category. Seems I didn't have to convert you to nerddom; you've secretly been one all along." He gave me a mock-offended look. "And yet you dared to make fun of me for my reading preferences. That wasn't very nice of you. I'd go so far as to say it was hypocritical." He *tutted* at me.

I grinned at him. "Okay, you got me. I sincerely apologize for being judgmental. I must admit, I'm dying to know what happens in *A Storm of Swords.* I never did get to finish it."

He beamed back at me. "You will. Then we'll start you on the TV show adaptation. Once we get out of here, we'll fully integrate you into the real world. You have years of catching up to do." His smile turned evil. "In fact, I don't know if you'll have the time to do anything else."

The dark flame in his eyes made it clear what he meant by *anything else.*

"Uh-uh," I said staunchly. "Harry Potter can wait. He's not getting any older, but we are."

Sean sighed as though he was very put-upon. "I suppose I could work something into our busy pop culture schedule."

Our banter was interrupted when the doorbell rang. Sean got up and took me by the hand, walking me to the front door. As we descended the stairs, I thought about our conversations over the past few days, and I came to a startling realization: we had been talking as though we were going to be together for a long time. Maybe even forever. That was what I wanted with all my heart. Did Sean feel the same? We had yet to even define the parameters of our relationship, much less discuss a possible future together. I held back my questions, deciding to address them later. I would use my time away from him today to gather up the courage to initiate the conversation.

Sharon was waiting at the front door, but she wasn't smiling this time. Her stance radiated uncertainty; she was clearly still bothered by the idea of me leaving the house today. "We have a team en route to pick up Ronan and Bradley," she informed me. "You can go to work, but you'll be riding in my car."

"Okay," I agreed quickly, pleased that she was still prepared to let me go.

"I'm coming too," Sean said from behind me.

"I'm afraid that's inadvisable," Sharon said firmly. "You're supposedly still in prison, and if anyone so much as glimpsed you it could cause problems. We're about to take your father into custody, but that doesn't mean that there aren't others out there who might be watching Claudia."

Sean's hand closed around my shoulder, pulling me further back into the house. "Well if that's the case, then Claudia isn't going either."

I shot him an exasperated look. "We've been over this, Sean. Sharon and the other agents will be with me the whole time. No one will be able to touch me. But people can't know that you're free."

"She's right," Sharon backed me up. "I promise we'll keep her safe, Sean."

I fully turned to Sean, my eyes pleading. "Please stay here, Sean. I'll only be gone a few hours."

He glared at me for a few moments. "I know that I can't stop you," he said finally. The taut lines of his face told me that he was still angry though. I squeezed his hand and kissed him lightly on the lips.

"Bye," I whispered.

I turned from him quickly, unwilling to see his disapproval. The door slammed shut behind me as I followed Sharon to her car, and I winced. I was going to be in so much trouble when I came home.

■■

I smiled at Tommy as his small leg jerked when I tapped the reflex hammer beneath his knee. "That's perfect," I told him warmly. The day had flown by, and it was already late afternoon. I almost didn't want to go home; I had forgotten how much I loved my job. But now I had a reason to be eager to return to my house: Sean. My smile broadened at the thought of seeing him at the end of the day. And at the potential prospect of seeing him at the end of every day for the rest of my life. I was determined to ask him some very serious questions when I saw him in a few hours.

My happiness was slightly marred by the information that I had received around mid-morning. Sharon had come back to my office to tell me that Ronan and Bradley hadn't been at work. The FBI and NYPD were combining manpower to scour the city for them. Sharon assured me that they would soon find them, but she urged me to return home. I had refused. I was just as safe in the clinic with FBI agents outside as I was at my house with FBI agents outside, I reasoned. No way was I going to spend any more time in hiding. If they still hadn't found Ronan and Bradley by tomorrow, then I would stay home. But for now, I was determined to finish out the work day.

I was listening to the steady beat of Tommy's heart when I was distracted by a knock on the door.

"I have a package for Dr. Ellers," a muffled voice drifted through the thick wood.

I moved to open the door. "You can just take it to the front de-"

The words died in my throat as I recognized the man in the chocolate brown UPS uniform. Bradley was holding a cardboard box in one hand, and his other rested at his hip, emphasizing the familiar bulge of the gun tucked into his waistband. When he spoke, he lowered his voice so that his words wouldn't carry down the hall.

"If you come with me quietly, no one will get hurt." He looked at Tommy significantly, and fear shot through my gut. Surely even Bradley wouldn't hurt an innocent child. I glanced over at my purse where I had stashed my gun. Could I get to it fast enough?

"You have three seconds, doc," Bradley threatened, his eyes narrowing dangerously. "One," he began to count.

"Wait!" I choked out, my voice high and thin. "I'll come with you. Just… Please. Don't hurt him."

I raised my chin and stepped out into the hallway, heading for the lobby. FBI agents were waiting outside. I wasn't sure how Bradley had gotten past them, but they would be on him as soon as we walked out the front door. He caught me by the elbow, redirecting me. My heart sank. We were going out the back.

My pulse raced and my fingers trembled. I struggled to formulate a plan as I walked down the long hallway as though heading for the gallows. I just needed to get outside, to get Bradley away from the kids. Then I could scream, and the FBI would come running. I just prayed that they could make it to me before Bradley had the time to shoot. The odds of that happening weren't good.

As soon as I stepped out into the warmth of the waning sunlight, I opened my mouth to scream. But Bradley was ready for it. I expected to feel a bullet tearing through me, but instead a foul odor filled my nose as he clamped a cloth over my face. Fog instantly began to swirl at the corners of my mind, and I jerked in Bradley's grip. But my efforts were weak as my body began to go limp. I heard his hated voice in my ear.

"As much as I'd love an excuse to hurt you, Ronan doesn't want there to be any defensive wounds."

I heard his words, but they didn't make any sense. Why didn't he just kill me?

But then all thoughts were slipping away as the fog rapidly overwhelmed me. The last thing I saw was an innocuous-looking UPS van before darkness rolled over me.

Chapter 9

The smell of something sharp and pungent jerked me awake. I blinked several times, still disoriented from the effects of the chloroform. The shadowy figure of a man loomed above me, and he tucked the smelling salts that had awoken me into his pocket. I drew in several deep breaths to quell my rising panic as I took in my surroundings. I was seated in a straight backed wooden chair in the middle of what seemed to be a shabby studio apartment. What little furniture there was was threadbare, and the paint was peeling from the walls.

Gathering my courage, I looked up at the man standing before me. I knew who it was before I met his gorgeous green eyes: Ronan Reynolds. Glancing around him, I caught sight of the door and considered running for it. But I knew that I wouldn't get two steps before Ronan took me down. Besides, Bradley was hovering behind him. Even if I somehow managed to dodge Ronan, I wouldn't make it past him a well.

Still, my fight-or-flight instincts were stronger than my rational mind, and I tried to fling my body into forward motion. I was stopped short as my shoulders jerked back painfully. My wrists were bound around the chair behind me.

"I would appreciate it if you didn't struggle. Those restraints aren't rough, but I don't want there to be any marks." Despite his years in America, Ronan's brogue was so thick that it took me a moment to process his words.

I glared up at him. "What are you talking about?" I demanded, drawing on my rising anger in order to push back my fear. "Why am I here? Why haven't you just killed me already?"

Ronan chuckled. Unlike when Sean laughed, it was a cold, horrible sound, devoid of any true joy. I suppressed a shudder as it issued forth from that all-too-familiar face. The resemblance to Sean was jarring.

"So many questions," he said. He cocked his head, considering me. "Bradley didn't tell me how fiery you are. Most people would be pissing themselves right now." He leaned down, closing the distance between us until his face was inches from mine. His eyes bored into me, weighing me up. "Or maybe you're just too stupid to realize just how much you should fear me," he said softly.

I fought the strong urge to drop my gaze. "Oh, I know all about you," I hissed. "You use fear and pain to control people. Well, you're not controlling *me*."

He raised one eyebrow and pulled away so that he was towering over me once again. "We'll see about that," he said softly. "Now," he continued on, his voice turning brusque and business-like. "It seems that the feds have been grabbing quite a few of my men over the last few days. Far too many of my men. That can only mean one thing: we have a snitch. So I had to wonder. What's changed recently? Who might be responsible?" His tone was musing, but his eyes were sharp as he watched me carefully. "You were barely a blip on my radar; you were just some whore my idiot son was fucking. But then Bradley came to me yesterday with some very interesting information. Apparently, you've been quite inquisitive. You were the reason that Bradley and my son were arrested. Of course," his eyes flicked to Bradley, "it was wrong of Bradley to keep this from me for so long. But he's working hard to redeem himself. He just needs to be educated. His first attempts against you were sloppy and foolish. I'll admit that bribing Garcia to go after you on his behalf wasn't a half-bad idea, but personally making an attempt on your life was beyond stupid."

Fury boiled up in me, and I glared at Bradley. "You killed Clayton," I hissed. "He was a federal agent. Did you know that? You're going to rot in jail for the rest of your pathetic life."

Bradley's face darkened to a thunderhead and he took two menacing steps toward me, but Ronan held up a hand, stopping him short. "Don't let her goad you into hurting her," he ordered. "Not yet. She has a choice to make first. We'll see whether or not she submits to my control." His grin was hard-edged and cruel.

My rage overwhelmed me, making me reckless. Suddenly, I *wanted* to make him strike me. If it was his plan not to hurt me, then I would force him to do the opposite. "You murdered my parents, you son of a bitch. And the FBI can prove it. You and Bradley can be prison buddies. You might scare him now, but you're getting old. I wonder how long it'll be before he makes you his bitch?"

He just continued to smile down at me, his eyes devoid of warmth. "I killed your parents?" He asked, sounding no more than mildly interested.

"You gunned them down in the street outside New York Methodist Hospital on October 6, 1998," I hurled the accusation at him, my voice steeped in venom.

Ronan tapped his lips thoughtfully for a moment, his gaze turning inward. Then he shrugged. "I don't recall. As you say, I'm getting old. My memory's not what it used to be." He had the gall to smirk at me.

"You don't *remember?!*" I shrieked. "You ruined my life! And you *don't remember?!*" I jerked against my restraints, my fingernails biting into my palms as my hands curled to tight fists. I wanted nothing more than to beat the shit out of Ronan. In that moment, all compassion, all of my humanitarian urges, left me completely. I wanted him dead. And I wanted to watch him die slowly.

He frowned at me slightly, unaffected by my tirade. "I've told you not to struggle," he reprimanded.

I just twisted harder against the bindings. "And why the fuck would I do anything you tell me to do?" I flung at him defiantly.

"Because if it's going to look like an accident, then there can't be any defensive wounds," Ronan explained as though it was the most obvious thing in the world. "Bradley's methods were misguided and unrefined. This is much more elegant. You're the snitch. If we murder you, then that only incriminates us further. But if you're dead, you can't testify against us in court."

I wanted to tell him that the absence of my testimony didn't matter; Sean would bring him down even if I was gone. But I couldn't tell him that. I had to keep Sean out of this. Ronan and Bradley believed that he was still in jail. They didn't have the slightest inkling of his betrayal. I had to ensure that it stayed that way.

"There are others," I said desperatcly. "Some of the men that they've arrested. They've cut deals in exchange for giving information."

Ronan scoffed. "Criminals will say anything to get a reduced sentence. Besides, I have ways of *persuading* them to maintain their silence." His grin was more a baring of his teeth. "As you say, I'm very good at controlling people. Which brings us back to our dilemma: Am I able to control *you?*"

I wanted to tell him that there was no way in hell that I was going to give into whatever it was that he wanted from me, but then a thought occurred to me. My phone. My phone was still in my pocket. I could feel the hardness of it against my leg. Mercifully, it was on silent, so if it rang Ronan wouldn't know to take it off of me and destroy it. My phone had GPS, and the FBI could use it to track my location. If I could only keep Ronan talking, then maybe they would realize that I was no longer at work. Maybe I could buy them the time they needed to find me.

"Well, that depends on what you want from me," I said coolly.

Ronan reached into his pocket and pulled out a syringe. "I want you to kill yourself," he said simply. "This is enough heroin to make you overdose. If by some slim chance you do survive, it'll be enough to cook your brain. You won't be able to testify against anyone."

I couldn't stop the shudder of revulsion that wracked my body. Nausea rose up within me at his matter-of-fact words. No way was I going to comply. If I had to die, then I would go down fighting. "Fuck you," I snarled.

Ronan smiled at me softly. "But I haven't told you the consequences for disobedience yet," he said. "You can't control people just by telling them to do things. There have to be consequences for defiance. Surely Sean explained that to you?"

"I don't care," I spat. "You can do whatever you want to me. You can hurt me. I'm not going to play your sick game."

"Brave words," Ronan said, but his tone was mocking rather than impressed. "I don't know that you fully understand what you're asking for. I'm quite skilled at torture." I swallowed hard against the bile rising in my throat as all manner of horrible things that he might do to me raced across my mind. "But pain isn't your consequence," he continued. "You see, good people are so easy to manipulate. I learned that from my wife and son. They'll do almost anything to protect the people they care about."

What was he talking about? "I don't have anyone left for you to hurt," I said, unable to fully keep the anguish from my tone. "You murdered my parents, and Bradley killed Clayton. There's no one else."

Ronan's brows rose in disbelief. "Are you sure about that?"

I wracked my brain. No. There was no one else who could possibly be in the line of fire. I didn't have anyone left who I cared about. There was no one except…

"You wouldn't," my voice was a horrified, disbelieving whisper.

Ronan nodded at my dawning understanding. "You're going to kill yourself, or I'm going to kill Sean. It's you or him. That's the choice you have to make."

"But he's your son," I gasped. "You can't do that."

Ronan just shrugged. "He's a useless dumbass who was stupid enough to fraternize with a whore and a snitch. So long as you're alive, he's a threat to me. I could try to keep him in line by threatening to hurt you, but now that you're involved with the FBI, openly doing so is too risky. The choice is yours, doc."

I turned my gaze to Bradley, desperate. "Sean's your best friend. I know how much he means to you. He told me so. In your own twisted way, you've just tried to protect him. You wouldn't let Ronan kill him."

Bradley's expression was hard. "I *am* protecting him," he said angrily. "Ronan's right: so long as you're around, he's a risk to us, a risk to himself. You've poisoned his mind. Once you're gone, he'll see sense again."

I glowered at him. "He'll know that you've done this to me," I spat. "He'll know that you're responsible. He'll never forgive you."

Bradley's expression was pained. "I know," he admitted, his tone anguished. "But I'm willing to lose him as a friend if that's what it takes to save his life."

I marveled at Bradley's sick sense of loyalty. No matter what else he was, he was utterly devoted to Sean.

I stared at the two men, my gaze flicking back and forth between their faces. Bradley's expression was strained, while Ronan's was simply expectant. He was waiting for my answer, waiting for me to submit to his control.

And of course I was going to. There was no choice to make. No matter what happened, Sean had to live. I was struck by a sudden urgency to get on with it. If my prayer had been answered and the FBI was on its way, then I needed to be dead before they got here. Even if by some miracle they rescued me and arrested Ronan, there was no doubt in my mind that Sean would never be safe from his retribution so long as his father was alive.

"Swear to me," my voice was a strangled whisper. "Tell me you won't hurt him."

Ronan's smile was genuine this time, his eyes alight with triumph. "I won't needlessly kill my son. I'm not a monster. If you do this willingly, then I won't hurt him." My shoulders slumped as a sense of relief filled me. Sean was going to live. "You see?" Ronan said, his pleasure evident in his tone. "Good people are so easy to control." He nodded to Bradley. "Untie her," he ordered. "She needs to do this herself. I want the needle at the right angle and her fingerprints on the syringe." As he spoke, he wiped it free of his own fingerprints and held it in a small cloth.

Bradley flicked out a switchblade and cut my bonds. I was going to get one last shot in before I had to die. I fixed Ronan with a level stare. "I want you to know that no matter what happens to me, you're going to jail for the rest of your life. And I want you to know that I'm responsible for that. You will think about me every day for the rest of your miserable existence. I'll live on in your head forever."

Ronan answered me calmly. "I've already explained this, doc. Without you, the feds have nothing. I'm going to forget you ever existed. Just like I forgot your parents." He smiled at me cruelly and extended his hand, proffering the syringe to me. "It's time for you to take your medicine, doctor," he said softly.

I hesitated. I didn't want to die. I had only just discovered what it was to live. Thanks to Sean. My time with him might have been short, but those moments of passion we shared had given me more joy than many people experienced in a lifetime. I could only hope that it had been enough for him too. He was never going to see me again.

My hand trembled as I reached out for the heroin.

Please let it kill me, I thought desperately. I could hardly imagine a worse fate than surviving as a shell of myself. The needle stung slightly as I expertly pierced the vein at the crook of my arm. As I pushed down on the plunger, I stared up into Ronan's beautiful green eyes.

Sean's eyes.

The effects of the drug hit me immediately. My stomach twisted violently, and I fought the urge to be sick. But the sensation of nausea passed within seconds, and a sense of euphoria began to wash over me. I grinned broadly, and Sean's eyes danced in delight. My body felt wonderfully light. There was no pain, no worries, only the bliss that was coursing through my system. My head dropped back as my body began to float.

A loud bang almost pierced my happy bubble, but not quite. Something cold and round was instantly pressed against my cheek, and a hand fisted in my hair, lifting my head. I glanced up to see what was going on, only mildly curious. Bradley was holding a gun to my head. I giggled, finding it bizarrely funny. He couldn't hurt me. Nothing could. Everything was so… *perfect.*

"Let her go, Bradley." I recognized the furious voice instantly. Sean was standing before me, a gun trained directly at his best friend's heart. He was radiating that sense of power that I found so incredibly sexy. Heat flashed over my skin as my body awoke for him.

"Sean," I said his name huskily, longingly. I needed him to take me, wanted him to join me in my blissful world.

"You'll leave now if you know what's good for you, boy-o," Ronan warned from beside me. He also held a gun, and to my horror, he was pointing it at Sean. Something important was swirling at the edges of my mind. There was something that I needed to remember…

"Get out of here, Sean," I ordered, my words slurring slightly. "I have to die."

"We're not leaving you, Claudia," a different voice said. Was I dead already? I blinked hard, trying to focus my wavering vision. I could have sworn the man standing beside Sean was…

"She's right, you know," Ronan interrupted my concentration. "The snitch has to die. It's the only way to protect ourselves. It's the only way to protect you."

Sean barked out a laugh. "As though you've ever cared about my well-being. And she's not the snitch, old man. I am."

Ronan's face twisted into something so terrible to behold that a sliver of fear cut through my happiness. "You betrayed me?" He seethed. "For this *cunt?!* You'll pay dearly for that, boy-o."

His arm swung towards me, the direction of his aim changing. I knew that I should be scared, but I just felt relieved. I was going to die, and Sean was going to be safe.

"NO!" The crack of the bullet leaving the chamber mingled with his furious roar. I watched as Ronan dropped, his body hitting the floor with a heavy thud.

No no no!

He was supposed to kill me. I was supposed to be dead. Sean wasn't safe…

"Step away from her, Bradley," the other man commanded.

The coolness of the gun left my cheek. As soon as his hand released my hair, I slumped forward. I no longer had any control over my own body. I could feel myself falling, but the impact with the floor didn't hurt. Fluffy clouds cushioned me, and I could taste warm rain on my tongue.

"Claudia!" Sean's voice was sharp with alarm. The touch of his calloused hands upon me as he cradled me in his arms was exquisite.

"What's wrong with her?" The other man's voice demanded from above me. He sounded so familiar. But that was impossible. I blinked up at his blurry figure, trying to force him to come into focus.

"She's overdosing," Bradley sneered. "You're too late."

"Fuck!" The man cursed. "Hold on, Claudia. The paramedics are already on their way."

I concentrated on him hard. When his form fully materialized, I knew that I was dying. "Clayton," I smiled. "I'm glad you're here." I was so relieved. Sean was going to live.

"That's right, Claudia. We're here. Stay with us." The beautiful sound of Sean's lilting voice called my attention back to him.

"You're going to be safe now," I told him happily. "I'm dying. He can't hurt you. He promised."

"No!" He said sharply. "You're not dying. You're going to be fine."

"But I have to," I insisted. "I love you, Sean."

And it was the truth. My love for him flooded every fiber of my being, filling my weightless body with a sweet, comforting warmth.

"You stay with me, Claudia. Do you hear me? That's an order."

I savored one last moment with him, falling into his gorgeous eyes before I allowed my own to close.

"No! Goddamn it, Claudia, open your eyes." His voice was shaking. "Look at me!"

I love you, Sean.

I was happy to die.

Chapter 10

The first thing I became aware of was the warmth of his hand on mine. Although I was in the dark, I recognized the electric touch of his fingers instantly. They were lightly tracing the lines that crisscrossed my palm, tickling my skin. I smiled and let out a happy sigh.

"Claudia?" His voice was rough, strained.

"Mmmm?" I responded sleepily. I rolled over in my bed, seeking to shape my body around his. His hand was instantly at my shoulder, pressing me back down.

"Lie still," he ordered. "I'm going to call the nurse."

Nurse? Why would a nurse be at my house? And why wasn't Sean holding me? I usually awoke to him pressed up against me after we spent the night in one another's arms. And last night had been...

Wait. Something was wrong. I hadn't been with Sean last night. I had been in that dingy apartment. I had been... dying. But if Sean was here, then he must be dead too.

No!

My eyes snapped open, and my heart twisted as Sean's breathtaking face came into focus. I clutched at his hand with both of my own, panicking.

"Sean! What are you doing here?"

His eyes widened in surprise. "I wasn't going to leave you, Claudia. Not for one second. I promised you that I wouldn't."

"No," I said staunchly. "You promised that you would go on without me."

His brow furrowed in puzzlement. Then comprehension dawned in his eyes, and he smiled at me gently. "You're not dead, Claudia." His lips abruptly twisted down into a frown. "Despite your best efforts. What the fuck were you thinking letting go like that? If the paramedics hadn't gotten to you in time…" A ghost of remembered horror flickered in his eyes.

I sat bolt upright. "But if I'm alive, you're not safe." My fingernails dug into his skin as terror gripped me. "Ronan. He's going to kill you!"

His hand was back at my shoulder, pushing me down again onto what I could now tell was a hospital bed. His expression was curiously blank when he spoke. "Ronan is never going to hurt anyone ever again. I killed him."

"What?" I breathed, shocked. I searched my mind, trying to piece together disjointed memories. I could perfectly recall everything up to the point when the needle pierced my skin. After that, things got hazy.

"He was going to kill you, Claudia," he said, his voice hard. "And he almost succeeded. I stopped him."

The image of Ronan falling to the floor flashed across my mind. He really was dead. Sean had killed him in order to stop him from shooting me.

"Are you okay?" I asked quietly, studying his face carefully.

Lines of tension appeared at the corners of his eyes. "I'm fine," he replied, his tone clipped.

I eased the ferocity of my grip on him, but I maintained my hold. "He was your father, Sean," I said gently.

Anguish warred with fury in the depths of his eyes. "He was a monster who ruined so many lives. Yours, mine, my mother's. I wasn't going to let him take you from me."

I reached up and touched his face lightly. "But he was still your father. It's okay to be upset."

His handsome features were tight, strained. "He deserved it," he whispered. A single tear trailed its way down his cheek. I caught it with a brush of my fingertips before it could fall. "But yes, he was my father."

"I'm sorry," I said. "I'm sorry that you had to do that because of me."

His expression suddenly turned fierce as he speared me with his intense green gaze. "I would trade him for you a thousand times over and never regret it."

I cupped either side of his face in my hands and gently pulled him towards me, rising to meet him halfway. Our lips met briefly, needing the contact the reassure both of us that the other was real. He pressed his forehead against mine, and his warm breath tickled across my lips as he spoke.

"I love you, Claudia."

A joy so intense swelled within me that I thought my heart would burst from it. This was far better than any drug could ever be.

"I love you too, Sean."

He smiled at me gently. "I know. You told me. Now, do you want to explain to me how loving me goes hand-in-hand with you wanting to die? If you love me like I love you, why would you try to leave me like that?" His voice was laced with pain.

"I'm sorry I almost let go, Sean," I said, my voice small. "I was so strung out at that point. I didn't process that Ronan was dead. He told me that he was going to kill you if I didn't kill myself. He thought that I was the only leak, and he decided that there wouldn't be any credible evidence against him if I was dead. It was supposed to look like an accident so that it could never be definitively linked back to him."

Sean's arms tensed around me. "I wish I could kill him again," he growled. "More slowly this time."

"Don't say that, Sean," I insisted softly. "I know that's not who you are. Don't let him change you. The Sean I know wouldn't hurt anyone."

"The Sean you know isn't a killer," he said hollowly.

I looked at him levelly. "Am I a killer, Sean?" He blinked hard and drew back from me slightly, bewildered.

"No. Of course not. Why would you even ask that?"

"I shot Hector Garcia," I reminded him, my voice tripping over the dead man's name. "You told me that I did what I had to do, that I'm not a murderer. You're not either, Sean. You did what you had to do. And you didn't even choose yourself over him. You chose *me*. You chose to shoulder the burden of another man's soul in order to save my life. It was a selfless act, Sean, not murder."

He stared at me in wonder. "How can you be so good to me, Claudia? After everything I've done? Knowing everything that I am?"

"It's *because* I know everything that you are. Better than you know it yourself. You're always telling me what a good person I am, but you can't see that you are too. I need you to believe that there is goodness inside you, Sean. I need you to see what I see."

"I don't know if I can," he said hoarsely, shaking his head slightly.

I smiled at him gently, stroking away the creases in his furrowed brow. "Then I'll show you. I'll remind you of it every day until you finally give up and agree to see things my way."

The corner of his mouth tugged up in that lopsided smile that made my heart flutter. "So you play the long game, huh? Do you really think that you can manipulate me, little one?"

I cocked my head at him, considering. "I can try." I smiled slyly. "I'll have plenty of time to learn from the best."

"Do you really mean that?" He asked, his eyes shining with hope. "How much time do we have? I want to be with you, Claudia. Will you stay with me after all of this is over?"

Beaming, I flung my arms around his neck, hugging him to me tightly. "Yes, Sean. I want that more than anything. I love you."

He returned my embrace with equal ferocity. "I love you too."

"I don't think I'll ever get tired of hearing that," I declared happily.

"You had better not." There was a hint of true warning laced through his teasing tone.

We held each other for a long time, and I gloried in his warmth, his scent, his touch. I could hardly believe that this was real, that somehow I had survived and Ronan was no longer a threat. Sean and I were finally free from his father. The sense of lightness that spread throughout my being was incredible. What had seemed an insurmountable weight of grief had finally been lifted. The sadness at the loss of my parents and Clayton would always linger, but it would no longer control my life.

Clayton.

Something was hovering at the edges of my mind. I thought back over my memories of the night before. I knew that I was missing something important. Reluctantly, I pulled away from Sean.

"How did you find me?" I asked.

A wide grin split his face. "I have a surprise for you. Let me call the nurse so that the doctor can give you the all-clear." He pressed the call button before I could protest.

"But how did you find me?" I persisted.

He kissed my forehead tenderly. "I promise I'll explain everything. Just be patient for a while longer."

I rolled my eyes at him, exasperated. Why couldn't he just tell me now?

"Watch it, little one. You know that I don't like it when you roll your eyes at me."

The nurse entered the room before I could deliver a retort. She checked me over thoroughly before telling me that my vitals looked good. "You're very lucky that we got you the naloxone when we did," she told me. "It helped counteract the overdose. You should be good to go."

I pulled on my clothes after she left the room, relieved that I was allowed to leave. Even though I was a doctor, the idea of being a patient in a hospital didn't sit well with me. It put me in a position where people could boss me around, and I hated that. A doctor came in briefly and gave me the all-clear. I couldn't wait to get out of there and get home. Then maybe I would get some answers out of Sean.

When we left my room and entered the elevator, he surprised me by taking us up two floors instead of back down to the lobby. "Where are we going?" I asked, curious and a bit peeved that I wasn't going to leave the hospital.

Sean just smiled down at me. "You'll see."

I frowned at him and put a hand on my hip. "I don't really do cryptic, you know," I informed him.

His smile remained in place. "Well, I like surprises. And I'll spring them on you until you learn to like them too."

"Who's playing the long game now?" I muttered, but I was more amused than annoyed. No one had arranged a surprise for me in years, and I honestly couldn't remember if I liked them or not. Maybe I could learn to. It didn't look like Sean was going to give me a choice in the matter anyway.

When we exited the elevator, Sean led me a short way down the corridor before knocking lightly on one of the doors.

"Come in." My heart skipped a beat. That voice... It couldn't be.

Sean pushed the door open, and my knees went weak as shock tore through me. "Clayton?" I breathed as Sean gripped my upper arms, preventing me from falling.

Clayton grinned at me from his hospital bed. "Hi," he said brightly. "You're looking better."

My eyes remained glued to Clayton's blue ones as Sean guided me to the chair beside his bed. I collapsed back onto it as soon as he released me. I looked up at Sean. "Are you sure we're not dead?" I asked him faintly.

"Nope," Clayton answered, drawing my attention back to him. "All three of us are alive and well." He grimaced slightly. "Mostly well. I kind of hurt all over, but other than that, I'm good. The doctors say I'll make a full recovery. You know, if I stop leaving the hospital without authorization. They were pretty pissed when I showed back up with half of their work undone."

My mouth opened and closed like a fish out of water. "How...?" My voice stuck in my throat. I swallowed and tried again. "What the hell is going on? You were *dead*, Clayton! I watched you die."

He frowned, anger flickering in his eyes. "No, you didn't. You watched me lose a shit ton of blood. I didn't die, Claudia. Well, technically my heart stopped for six minutes, but we're not counting that."

How was he so nonchalant about all of this? Didn't he know what he had put me through? I was suddenly furious. "If you weren't clearly already in pain, I would punch you in the face," I informed him hotly. "I was at your funeral, for god's sake! I saw your… Oh, god, your parents! How could you put them through that?" I demanded angrily.

Clayton's easy smile was gone, his expression agonized. "I've contacted them to let them know that I'm okay. I think they'll come around to being pissed at me, but right now they're just so relieved that I'm alive that they're still talking to me." He regarded me intently. "I did something stupid, Claudia. Several years ago, I told the FBI that if I was ever severely wounded they could stage my death so that I could go in deep cover somewhere. Like what Santiago is doing with the Latin Kings."

"You're right," I said seriously. "That was stupid. No gangster is ever going to believe that some corn-fed boy from the Midwest has any street cred."

He smiled self-deprecatingly. "Fair point, Dr. Ellers." His expression sobered quickly. "When I woke up in the hospital and they told me what had happened, I was furious with myself. I should have signed off from the program when I became your handler. You were still in danger, and I was powerless to protect you. I wanted to come to you immediately, but it turns out a bullet to the gut isn't something to take lightly, even if it did miss all of my major organs. Yesterday I was finally strong enough to escape, ah, I mean leave. So I went straight to your house to check on you. Sean told me that you had returned to work but that they hadn't successfully arrested Ronan or Bradley. Incompetent, irresponsible idiots," he muttered.

"Agreed," Sean said coolly.

"Hey," I rushed to Sharon's defense. "If anything, it's my fault. I insisted that they let me go. It was stupid." I glared at Sean. "And don't you dare say 'I told you so'."

He held up his hands in a show of innocence. "I didn't say a word."

"I could hear you thinking it," I accused. He just shrugged, unapologetic. I supposed I deserved that. But I would never admit as much.

"Well, when I found out, I tried to call you to make sure you were okay," Clayton continued. "I got worried when you didn't answer, and I made Sharon go into the clinic to check on you. As soon as she told me you weren't there, I tracked the location of your phone. Sean recognized it as an address where the Westies sometimes deal. We called it in, but we didn't wait for the cavalry to show up. If we had waited, you would probably be dead right now." Something darkened in his eyes as his gaze turned inward.

I reached out and tentatively touched his hand. I marveled at the solid warmth of it beneath my fingertips. Clayton was alive. My friend was alive. And his actions had saved my life once again. Tears filled my eyes and spilled down my cheeks, and for the first time since I could remember, they were tears of joy rather than pain.

"Thank you," I choked out.

"Anytime," he said, smiling as he squeezed my fingers reassuringly. I gave a shaky laugh and wiped at my wet cheeks.

"But don't think I'm not still mad at you for letting me think you were dead."

Clayton gave me a long-suffering look. "Damn. I was hoping saving your life might make up for that. And taking a bullet for you. And keeping you out of jail. But you know, who keeps track of these things, really? It's all water down the drain, apparently."

I slapped him lightly on the arm, confident that he wasn't injured there. "Well, when you put it that way, I guess I don't have a choice in the matter. Fine. I forgive you. But I might not be so magnanimous if you ever pull this on me again."

He was smiling at me, but his eyes were serious. "I won't," he promised. "It was really unfair for me to put people through that. I've got a lot of apologizing to do. I'm pretty sure that dinner's on me for the entire office for the next decade or three. Most people weren't in on the secret. Sharon, in particular, was rather miffed." He grinned affectionately, and I wondered if maybe happiness had been staring him in the face for a long time and he had been blind to it. I made a mental note to keep an eye on the situation.

"Well, I would say that you deserve it, but it seems that I'm in no position to talk," I said lightly. "How long until you're fully recovered?"

"It'll be a few months before I'm fully fit again, but I should be able to leave the hospital in a week or so. Then I can tie up whatever loose ends Sharon leaves and finish de-briefing the two of you." He addressed Sean as well now. "Once we get your preliminary testimony, we'll need you to go into witness protection for a while until we can round everybody up. Then we'll need to prep you to give your testimony at trial. After that, your lives are your own again."

I frowned at the mention of *witness protection*. Hadn't I been staunchly resisting the idea of going into hiding for weeks now? I glanced over at Sean. Maybe hiding out with him wouldn't be so bad. Especially if we weren't confined to the house all the time. Relocating would give us the opportunity to come and go as we pleased. I decided that it was a good idea.

"So where are we going?" I asked Clayton.

"There's this great town I know in Iowa called Indianola."

Clayton's sleepy little hometown. I returned his grin. "Sounds perfect."

Epilogue

A little over two months later, Sean and I found ourselves settling into a happy rhythm in Indianola. Neither of us had jobs – we decided to wait until we found somewhere to settle permanently – but we had plenty to do to pass the time. I was rapidly becoming a pop culture whiz, especially when it came to all things nerddom. I had Sean to blame for that, as he was quite a biased educator. But I didn't mind skipping over the chick flicks and soap operas in favor of the *Game of Thrones* TV series and the *Lord of the Rings* movies. I had devoured the rest of George R. R. Martin's books, and *Harry Potter* followed quickly after that. Sean had seen and read it all before, but his eyes shined with boyish delight as he explored the beloved stories anew when he shared them with me.

But we didn't spend all of our time cooped up in the house. We primarily had Shelley, our next-door-neighbor, to thank for that. She had knocked on our door the day that we moved in, offering us a tray of cookies. I didn't think that people actually did that in real life. She was so friendly, and it was easy to pass the time chatting with her. Before long, she introduced us to several of her friends. We were all around the same age, and I had to admit that it was nice to spend time getting to know people. I was still rusty at remembering how to connect with people, but it was getting easier every day. Now we were on the regular invite list for Shelley's Friday cocktail hour.

I often wondered what we would do when the final trials were wrapped up and the Westies were put away for good. Sean and I agreed that we wanted to stay together for a long time into the future, but we hadn't made any concrete plans about where we would go from here. Most of the Westies had been convicted by now, including Bradley. His trial had been hard on Sean, and

I knew that his betrayal of his best friend still weighed heavily on him. But Bradley would have gone down for his crimes regardless of Sean's testimony; the evidence was heavily stacked against him. With the multiple counts of drug trafficking, kidnapping, assault, and two counts of attempted murder, his sentence had been heavy. He was going to spend the rest of his life in prison. Bradley had cursed at Sean in the courtroom, railing at him for being a traitor. I held Sean's hand through it all, providing what comfort I could. Even though weeks had passed since then, I still caught Sean staring off glumly into space on occasion, and then I would do my best to distract him.

Often these distractions ended with us lying naked in each other's arms, gasping for breath as residual pleasure thrummed through our bodies. In fact, a lot of the time that we spent in the house involved such distractions. A girl can only focus on a book for so long when a gorgeous man keeps shooting her heated glances from across the room.

In the time that we had been here, Sean and I had fallen in love with our life in Indianola. Neither of us had ever known anything but the bustle of city life. Living here was so… peaceful. I had been turning something over in my mind for days now, and I finally plucked up the courage to ask Sean about it.

"Why don't we stay?" I asked, rolling over on the bed so that I was facing him. He caught up a lock of my hair and rubbed it between his fingers absently.

"What?" He asked, clearly lost in his own thoughts.

"Why don't we stay here?" I repeated. "I like Indianola. It has everything we need, and the people are friendly. I could get a job in De Moines and commute."

Hope welled within me as I realized that Sean looked intrigued rather than taken aback. "And what would I do?" He asked.

"Well, you're getting to be a pretty good cook. And you're tidier than most men. You could be my house-husband." I was teasing, but we both froze at the mention of the word "husband." We had talked about a future together, but we hadn't discussed marriage.

Sean moved past the awkward moment smoothly. "So you want me to stay home and do your bidding, then?" He asked, a dangerous, sexy edge to his voice. "I think we both know that that's not the way things work around here. Don't we?"

I bit my lip. "Hmmm. I suppose I could allow you to have a profession. You know, just something small to occupy your time when I'm not around."

He growled and pressed his weight against me, flipping me onto my back and settling his body over mine. His hands were around my wrists, pinning them against the pillow above my head. "Now sub," he said, his voice low and rumbling. "I'm going to be merciful and give you a chance to reconsider your response."

"Well, yes. On second thought, I think that you'd be better off at home. We wouldn't want to put too much strain on you. You're so delicate. I would worry about you." I smiled up at him sweetly.

He grinned back at me, but there was a decidedly dangerous edge to his smile. "I'm pleased to see that I haven't stamped all the disobedience out of you. I do enjoy our lessons."

"I enjoy them too," I agreed. "It seems I know just how to play you to get what I want."

His grip tightened around my wrists with almost bruising force, and he reached between our bodies with one hand to pinch my nipple sharply, twisting it. I cried out at the pain. It was harsher than what I had expected. He rolled my hardened bud deftly between his fingers, soothing the sting to a dull, burning ache that made my sex pulse to life. My breathing turned shallow as I stared up into the twin dark flames of his stunning green eyes.

"Back to basics today, then," he said calmly. "It seems that we have forgotten who is in control."

He took my body roughly, possessing me completely with each harsh touch and demanding word. By the time he was finished with me, I was a quivering mess. He had made his point well and thoroughly. And I had loved every second of it. My body was draped across his as I slowly came down from my high.

"I love it when you make love to me by fucking me," I sighed happily. He chuckled.

"That is an interesting yet accurate way of putting it, little one." He kissed the top of my head affectionately. We lay in silence for long moments, our hands lightly tracing the contours of one another's bodies. It was as though we were addicted to one another. And Sean was a drug that I never wanted to quit.

Eventually, Sean idly picked up our earlier conversation. "I think I'll start my own carpentry business," he said. "If that's okay with you, ma'am," he amended hastily. I smiled, refusing to rise to his bait.

I propped myself up on one elbow so that I could see his face. "I think that's a great idea," I said seriously. "I would love to see some of your work."

He beamed at me. "I'd like that. And yes, I think we should stay in Indianola. The people are great, and we'll have an excuse to see Clayton outside of official FBI business when he comes home to visit his parents. Besides," his eyes twinkled, "it's a great place to raise a family."

My jaw dropped at the astounding words that he delivered so casually. Before I could begin to formulate a response, he sat up abruptly, pulling me up with him. He seated me on the edge of the bed while he got up to retrieve something from his sock drawer.

"What are you doing?" I asked, puzzled. When he turned back to me, he was hiding something in his closed fist. "What's in your hand?" I was getting slightly nervous. What devious plans did he have in store for me now?

He pressed his finger to my lips, silencing me. "It's my turn to ask a question," he said softly. My breath caught in my throat as he dropped to one knee before me. The circle of precious metal that he held between his thumb and forefinger glinted in the light. I was suddenly grateful that I was sitting down, because there was no way that my knees would have supported me in that moment.

"Dr. Claudia Ellers," his delicious, lilting voice caressed my name in that way that made me melt. My attention snapped from the ring in his hand to his eyes. They were burning into mine, and the love and longing that I saw there took my breath away.

"You have given me a life that I never dreamed I would have. Would you do me the honor of sharing it with me?"

I was overwhelmed with emotion, and I couldn't seem to get any words out through the lump in my throat.

"Marry me, Claudia." It wasn't a question.

"Yes!" I gasped out. "Yes!" Tears of joy streamed down my face as I held out my left hand. He slipped the ring onto it, and it fit perfectly. It was a simple gold band adorned with a single diamond. It was simple and classic.

Sean brushed his thumb against the physical sign of our devotion to one another. "I know it's not much," he said, "but it was my mother's."

"It's perfect, Sean. I love it." A wide grin broke out on my face as joy enveloped me. "I love you so much."

He stood quickly and pulled me up into his arms, holding me against his perfect, hard body. "I love you too." He returned my smile. "Are you tired of hearing that yet?"

"Not even remotely." And I knew that I never would tire of it.

Sean bent down and pressed his lips against mine. The kiss was slow and tender at first, but it quickly became more intense as our hunger for one another was once again enflamed. His tongue demanded that I give him my mouth, and I ceded it to him willingly. He was everything that I needed, everything that I had never even known that I wanted. He had come into my life and changed it irrevocably, ruthlessly tearing down my protective walls and building me back up from the inside out. And somehow, I had done the same for him. We had healed each other, had set each other free from the weight of our pasts. Now we were finally in control of our own destinies.

And the first choice that I made with my newfound freedom was to spend the rest of my life in the arms of Sean Reynolds.

The End

Want more of the *Impossible* series and Clayton Vaughn? Here's a teaser for *Savior* (An *Impossible* Novel), now available!

After coming home from work to find her junkie kid brother high out of his mind, Rose Baker is shocked when her sexy one-night-stand Clayton shows up at her door.

A knock at the door made me jump. I pursed my lips, hardly daring to breathe. Maybe if I was quiet whoever it was would decide that no one was home and leave.

The second knock was sharper and more insistent.

"Greg Baker? Open up."

Shit. Someone was here for my brother. What the hell had he gotten himself into? I walked to the door on shaky legs and pressed my eye to the peephole in order to get a look at my enemy. All of the wind was knocked out of me when I saw who was on the other side.

What the fuck? How did he find me? Had he followed me here? And how in the hell did he know about Greg?

"I don't know what you're trying to pull, Clayton, but I want you to leave," I called out angrily so that he could hear me through the door. "Are you stalking me or something? Get out of here now or I'll call the police."

To my great satisfaction, he took a step back, his jaw hanging open in shock. Good. I had scared him.

"Mary?" He asked hesitantly, using the fake name that I had given him the night before.

"Do you know this woman, Clayton?" The feminine voice drew my gaze away from Clayton, and I noticed the short, dark-skinned woman with a mass of curly black hair standing behind him for the first time.

Clayton didn't answer her, but his shocked expression was replaced with one of determination as his jaw tightened. "Open the door, Mary," he said sternly.

"I'm giving you three seconds to get out of here, or I'm calling the police," I threatened.

The woman made an exasperated sound and shouldered her way in front of Clayton. She pulled a wallet out of her pocket, and something glinted gold as she unfolded it so that I could see what was inside. It was an official-looking badge.

"I'm Agent Sharon Silverman with the FBI. And this is Agent Vaughn." Her tone was acerbic as she glared at Clayton.

No way.

"I don't believe you. I don't know what this is, but you both need to leave. Now."

"If you don't open the door, we will use force to enter, ma'am. We have a warrant," the woman said tersely.

I bit my lip, unsure. They said that they were here to talk to Greg. What if they were lying? What if they were here to hurt him?

But what if they were telling the truth? How much deeper shit would he be in if they had to force their way in?

Greg was clearly high out of his mind, and he would be in trouble for sure if they saw him like that. Maybe it was time to get him into rehab. Maybe I could beg Clayton to get him clean rather than throwing him in jail.

It didn't seem like I had a choice.

My fingers trembled as I slid back the lock and opened the door. Even though Clayton had already figured out who I was, his eyes still widened slightly as though he couldn't quite believe that I was standing before him. To be honest, I couldn't believe it either. What were the chances that he would end up here? Had he known who I was? Had he been following me before I had approached him at the bar?

But he had called me Mary, not Rose. He couldn't possibly know who I really was. This was just the most fucked-up coincidence of my life.

The woman – Agent Silverman – pushed against the door insistently, forcing me aside so that they could enter. When she saw Greg, her eyes filled with pity. And a hint of disgust. My hands curled to fists as rage washed over me.

"What do you want?" I snapped.

Agent Silverman spared me a cursory glance before turning her attention back on my brother.

"Mr. Baker," she addressed him loudly. "Can you understand me?"

Greg didn't respond. She pulled out her cell phone and dialed.

"I need a bus here," she said, her tone cursory. "The perp needs medical attention before we can bring him in."

Perp? Bring him in?

Oh no. That wasn't going to happen. I wouldn't let it. I turned to Clayton, desperate. I wasn't above begging.

"Clayton, please. He just needs help. My brother is a good person." He had to listen. He had to believe me.

Clayton looked distinctly uncomfortable. "He's involved with bad people, Mary. I'm sorry, but we're going to have to arrest him." He stepped forward to brush past me. He was going for Greg. They were going to take him from me.

The fury that I so often suppressed came bubbling up. "No!" I shrieked. "I'm not letting you take him!"

Hardly aware of what I was doing, I drew my hand back and cracked it across his cheek. He didn't even flinch. I had a moment to register that his eyes had narrowed angrily, and the next thing I knew my body was pressed up against the wall, my arm twisted behind my back as he trapped me in place.

"Mary Baker," he half-growled in my ear, "you are under arrest for assaulting a federal agent. You have the right to remain silent. Anything you say can and will be used against you in a court of law. You have the right to an attorney. If you cannot afford one, one will be provided for you. Do you understand your rights?"

Cool metal encircled my wrists as the cuffs clicked closed around them. In other circumstances, this would have been pretty hot. But this wasn't kinky role-play. Right now I was pissed off beyond belief, and I jerked against his hold on me. Which of course accomplished nothing.

"Do you understand your rights?" He demanded again.

"Oh, I understand," I hissed. "I understand that you're a heartless jackass. And my name is Rose, asshole."

Want more Rose and Clayton? *Savior* (An *Impossible* Novel) is now available!

Also by Julia Sykes

<u>The *Impossible* Trilogy</u>
Monster
Traitor
Avenger

Impossible: The Original Trilogy

Angel (A Companion Book to *Monster)*

<u>The *Impossible* Novels</u>
Savior (An *Impossible* Novel)
Knight (An *Impossible* Novel) (Coming Soon!)

Dark Grove Plantation (The Complete Collection)

Captured by the Billionaire (The Complete Series)
Kept (A *Captured by the Billionaire* Bonus Book)

Torn: Caught between the Billionaires (The Complete Series)

29241261R00252

Made in the USA
Lexington, KY
18 January 2014